AF373644

To
Catch
a
Sinner

Also by Dylan Allen

Rivers Wilde Series

The Legacy
Book one of the Rivers Wilde Series. An opposites-attract, enemies-to-lovers stand-alone that kicks off this brand-new series.

The Legend
This is a second chance at love story. Remington Wilde has loved one woman in his life and even though timing and family manipulations keep pulling them apart, it's a love worth fighting for.

The Jezebel
Regan Wilde and Stone Rivers were born enemies. But love has other ideas.

The Gathering
A delicious holiday novella with points of view from all six main characters including a scene from Tina and Tyson Wilde's point of view for the first time.

The Daredevil: A Rivers Wilde/1001 Nights Novella
Tyson Wilde laughs in the face of danger and has yet to face a challenge he's not up to. Until Dina Lu walks into his life and threatens to turn it upside down.

The Mastermind: A Rivers Wilde/1001 Nights Novella
He lives under a golden spotlight. She's shackled to a past that must stay hidden. A fire-burning, second-chance romance novella.

The Symbols Series

Then Came You
Set in London, this is a workplace romance that features two people who are trying to outrun their pasts and protect their cynical hearts from more pain. But when their lives collide and their hearts and bodies yearn

for each other, they'll have to decide if they are brave enough to fight
for their love.

Still The One

This second-chance romance features high school sweethearts who were
torn apart by tragedy and treachery. Years later, when they realize that
their feelings haven't changed, they embark on a mission to unravel the
mystery surrounding her father's disappearance. But what they discover
about their past might make a future together impossible.

Best For Last

Lilly and Harry's story is one of star-crossed lovers, self-forgiveness and
bravery in the face of adversity. What starts as a chance encounter at a
sun-drenched, West African beach paradise leads to a fateful reunion in
an idyllic manor house in the English countryside and a love that will
defy all the odds. This enemies-to-lovers romance is nothing short of
epic.

Standalones

The Sun and Her Star

A friends-to-lovers, second-chance story. Angsty, emotional, sexy, and
unforgettable. Graham and Apollo are two people who find each other
just when they need to. What starts as a deep, abiding friendship grows
into the kind of love that can move mountains. This story is a reader
favorite.

Thicker Than Water

A friends-to-lovers and workplace romance that follows the love story
between an undocumented writer and the movie executive who changes
her life. This story is hopeful, honest, and achingly relevant. Go in with
an open mind and prepare to fall in love.

The Sound of Temptation

A second-chance forbidden romance that follows star-crossed lovers, a
talented musician and the artist who becomes his muse. It spans nearly
ten years and is a turbulent, exhilarating, heart-pounding, and deeply
intimate love story you will never forget.

*If you've read my books and haven't already, please leave a review. Nothing fancy,
but a line or two helps so much!*

To Catch a Sinner

Dylan Allen writing as

Lucy Wilson-Tagoe

To Catch a Sinner
By Dylan Allen writing as Lucy Wilson-Tagoe
A Blurred Lines Novel

Copyright 2026 Dylan Allen

ISBN: 979-8-90327-025-5

Published by Blue Box Press, an imprint of Evil Eye Concepts, Incorporated

Dedication

This book is dedicated to my parents—Anthony and Elisabeth. My admiration, love, and respect for you is greater than I could ever say. I am so proud to be your daughter. Thank you for giving me the world.

Author's Note

Dear Reader,

Thank you for picking *To Catch a Sinner*.

When I started writing this book in 2024, I was certain that the Washington, DC Metro area (affectionately called the DMV) was about to undergo a renaissance. In the summer and early fall of that year, the story was my vision board for a future that was close enough to taste.

By the time the year was over, though, I was forced to accept that the closest I'd get to that vision was in the pages of my manuscript.

In my darkest moments, I even considered changing the location…but I couldn't. I have a deep and abiding affection for this region.

The parts of Maryland and Virginia that converge around the District of Columbia are some of the most beautiful stretches of forest and road I've ever encountered.

The monument-rich skyline reminds you of its inextricable important place in the tapestry of this nation's founding.

But most of all, there is no other city that amplifies the culture, art, history, and scholarship of Black people—from all parts of the diaspora—the way that DC does.

This is the *only* city that could hold this story authentically.

I decided to write a fictionalized version of DC. One that my amazing characters (and all of us) deserve.

The Washington, DC in this book is a place where Black women aren't just safe, they are in power, taking up space, and free. And because they're thriving, everyone and everything else is, too.

There are *so* many other things I love about this story—the history, the art, the complex family dynamics, the unique experience of straddling cultures, and a romance that feels inevitable and urgently fragile at the same time.

And for all its drama, suspense, and steam—I found unexpected comfort and hope in this world I created for Kwame and Sin to fall in love and find themselves in.

Their journeys in *To Catch a Sinner* are distinct but carry a truth I believe to be universal: We may have no say in where we're born, but we all have the power to choose how we will live and love.

In a season where they feel more spare than ever, writing stories that end happily is an act of resistance.

And for as long as I live, I will never stop choosing to give love and seek joy.

I hope you find an abundance of both in the pages of this book.

All my best and happy reading,
Lucy

One

Sin

You Don't Send a Saint to Catch a Sinner

"Activity detected."

It takes me a minute to remember that I installed a surveillance camera in the tiny office I've set up in the apartment I share with my boyfriend.

I didn't the set up the cameras because I suspected him of him of anything, but I decided to keep it to myself.

In the nearly two weeks I've been away, he's only been in there once and that was to drop packages from my PO Box on my desk. I feel guilty for not telling him so I decided I wouldn't watch anymore unless I had a reason to.

I check the time on my phone. I've got ten minutes until my appointment, and the last thing I want to do right now is worry about my failing relationship.

Tomorrow would be soon enough.

Today, I'm focusing on the things that make me happy. I put my phone away and cross Constitution and head toward the National Monument.

There's no place prettier than Washington, DC, in the Spring.

This first week of April has been spectacular.

The weather is a nice balance of cool mornings and balmy evenings.

The cherry blossoms are in bloom, but the season is almost over so the tidal basin isn't packed with people.

My braids are fresh and not too tight, my jeans feel good, and my jasmine body oil is turning heads.

If "not looking like what you've been through" was an Olympic sport, I'm pretty sure I'd medal.

The last two weeks have been some of the most trying of my life. I clawed my way back to standing and after two weeks of hard decisions and heartbreak, I've earned a day where all I do is what makes me happy.

I promised myself today would be for things that make me happy.

I walk up the path to the entrance of the National Museum of African History and Culture excited about my behind-the-scenes look at the items that will go on exhibit later this year.

I'm proud of the role I played in making that happen. But it hurts that someone else got credit for the work I did. It will have to be enough that the stolen artifacts I wrote about are on their way back to their rightful owners.

I stand in line with the rest of the ticket holders and marvel at how, nearly ten years after it opened, it's still one of the few Smithsonian's popular enough to require a reservation.

I came down to visit it for the first time and went with my entire family. My father told anyone who would listen that the architect who designed the ten-story building is from Ghana. Just like him.

It's true that the vision for the design came from a Ghanaian man. But the unique corona shape of it was inspired by the pillars used in Yoruba architecture. The nearly four thousand aluminum panels that make up the bronze facade are carved with intricate patterns that are an homage to the ironworks designed and made famous by Black Americans in cities like New Orleans and Charleston.

I too owe my singularity to the melding of several cultures. The kinship I feel for this museum and the history it holds makes every visit feel like stepping on sacred ground.

"Welcome. How can I help you?" A young man stands in greeting as I approach the desk at the center of the gigantic main hall.

"I've got a three o'clock with the Senior Curator of Special Collections."

"Just one moment." The young man at the check-in swipes his mouse around and studies his screen and nods. "Ms. A. Sackey?"

"That's me."

"Here you go." He hands me a printed name badge and then points to his right. "You'll take the elevator to the fifth floor. Use your badge to choose the floor. They're expecting you."

I do as he asks but promise myself I'll take the escalators on my way down. The view from there is magical.

On the fifth floor, I'm greeted by a young woman with gorgeous shoulder length locs. "Welcome Ms. Sackey. I'm going to show you to Mr. Mends' office. You can wait there for him."

She smiles politely but turns away before I can read the name tag stuck to the lapel of her brightly colored maxi dress. I have to hustle to keep up with her. "Do you want some coffee?" She asks and stops outside a double wood paneled door.

"No, thank you." If I drink coffee now, I'll never fall asleep.

She leads me into a large office with a window that faces the National Monument. "Mr. Mends is wrapping up his meeting. And you're a little early."

"Am I?" I instinctively put my hand in my tote to fish out my phone.

"Yes, but it's perfectly okay." She smiles stiffly, and I get the distinct feeling that it's actually *not* okay. "If you change your mind about coffee, you can help yourself from the machine over there." She points to a wet bar in the corner of the room. "There's also water in the fridge."

I wait for her to leave before I look at the time. I scoff. "Just as I thought." I'm not early. It's three minutes until three. In my book, anything less than five minutes early is on time.

Resigned to wait, I unlock my phone and check my notifications.

There's another notification telling me that the recording is finished and ready to watch. It's more than twelve minutes long.

That's odd.

I've got a minute to kill and curious because I don't remember ordering anything this week, I open the app and hit play.

Stephen walks into the frame, talking. I assume he's on the phone until he's joined in the frame by a woman who's back is to the camera.

"What the fuck?" I hiss. They stand in front of my desk, face to face, not talking. She puts a hand on his shoulder, and he laughs at something she said.

The video freezes on that frame. His mouth open, her hand on his shoulder.

I refresh but nothing happens. I check my service and growl. I've only got one bar.

I move to the window and hold my phone up in vain.

"Don't bother. The service in here is terrible."

I jump, so engrossed that I didn't hear the door open. I spin around surprised.

"You scared me," I chide and walk over to meet him in the middle of the room. I drop my phone in my purse and force my attention to the present and smile at the man I'm here to see.

"I'm so sorry to keep you waiting," he says as we approach each other.

"It's okay. I know how busy you are Mr. Senior Curator." I add some flare to my voice.

"Sounds so good, right?" He beams a smile and instead of the handshake I expected, he pulls me into a hug. "It's so good to finally meet you in person."

After a split second of surprise, I return it. "You too." Even though after more than a year of emails, Zoom calls and texts, it doesn't feel like the first time at all. "I'm so glad we could make this happen," I add when we break our embrace.

He wrinkles his nose. "About that. I know I promised you could see the items today, but something has come up in my last meeting that means I can't spare the time after all. I'm so sorry."

Disappointed, I deflate a little but shake it off. I'm a big believer that everything happens for a reason. "It's okay, Leon. I understand. I was surprised when you said you were free. I've been reading all the press about their arrival." The bronzes, carvings, jewelry and other cultural artifacts that we helped reclaim from museums and private collections all over North America have been big news in the art world.

"Yeah, it's been crazy."

"That's what happens when you make history."

He smiles but brushes the praise away. "Hardly. And if history was made, *we* made it together. Have you figured out how that story got scooped by *The Guardian?*"

"Nope."

"But when I read the article, I knew she had used your research because some of those things were direct quotes from me, and I didn't talk to her."

"Well, unfortunately I have no way of proving anything, and my editors didn't have my back."

"God, I'm sorry."

"Just promise me that if she comes to see the exhibit you won't show her the Queen Mother's stool. She doesn't deserve it," I quip trying to make light of something that still hurts.

He doesn't laugh. His expression loses all its humor and he looks away.

"What's wrong?"

He motions for me to take a seat in one of the chairs in front of his desk. He sits in the other and leans forward, hands resting on his knees. "This isn't public knowledge."

"What isn't?" I press.

"This is off the record."

My fifth sense, as I call it, starts vibrating. "Okay."

His pins me with his eyes. "I'm trusting you Sin, but if you say you heard it from me, I'll deny it."

I stifle an impatient growl and nod. "You've got my word. Please tell me what's wrong."

"On its way from Chicago, the truck that was transporting the artifacts for the exhibit was robbed. The Ohemaa's Stool was taken along with most of the ivory and several carvings."

Horrified, I gasp and press a hand to my chest. "When did this happen? And why didn't you tell me?"

He heaves a long-suffering sigh. "We all signed NDAs. The museum doesn't want anyone to know they've lost it."

"I can imagine they don't, but the Interpol database is publicly available. How can they avoid it getting out?"

"They didn't report it."

"Are they trying to find it?" I ask incredulously. "It's scheduled to be returned next year."

He grimaces. "I don't know what is motivating their behavior. I'm new to this role and this team."

I sit up. "Do they have any clue who it is?"

"I don't know what they think, but I think it's The Wizard. Same MO, all the thefts are of West African cultural relics. And they're sophisticated, well-trained people carrying out these heists."

I sigh and shake my head, my mind boggled. "How could they have known the stool was on that truck? It wasn't announced publicly, was it?"

He shakes his head, his nostrils flare like he smells something bad. "They have someone on the inside. Maybe not at the NMAAHC but in the Smithsonian organization," Leon says.

My stomach flutters. "That's what I think, too." It's what I've always thought. "Have you considered making an anonymous report to Interpol?"

He shakes his head and leans away. "No. They'll know it's me. Only three people here know. I'm not trying to lose my job and be sued."

Irritated, I scowl at him. "So why are you telling me?"

"Because *you* didn't sign an NDA. And I think I have a lead on The Wizard. Someone I met told me she works for a man who runs auctions where they sell things that are illegal. She said his name is Oz." He looks at me meaningfully.

My stomach drops as his implication comes clear. I shake my head on dismissal. "No way the criminal mastermind who has been harder to pin down than smoke would give himself such an obvious moniker."

"That's what I thought, too, but I asked her if she'd talk to you."

"Why me?"

"I know your article was more focused on the artifacts return but you were also starting to look into the black market. Do you think *The Times* would let you switch gears and work on it?" His eyes are so hopeful it kills to say no.

I close my eyes briefly and groan. "Oh Leon…I can't."

He presses me. "You can. You're the only person who can. And imagine how explosive it would be if you found the culprit while law enforcement twiddled their thumbs. It would be a huge coup for *The Times*. And you."

I shake my head. "I can't, literally. *The Times* passed on the story. I resigned two weeks ago."

His eyebrows shoot up. "I thought you were locked in over there. Didn't you just get promoted?"

"I didn't get it." Heat rises up my neck at the flash of pity on his face.

"It's fine. I shouldn't have talked about it like it was a done deal," I admit. I blink away the sting of tears.

"Oh man, I'm sorry. Their loss."

It doesn't feel that way but it's nice to hear him say it.

"It's all good. I'm moving back to the DMV. I just accepted an offer from *The Spectator*." I make jazz hands and grin. I feel good about this decision. But saying it aloud for the first time makes it feel scarily real.

His smile brightens. "Wow, that's great. Having a Black woman in the West Wing has been amazing. You reporting on it for the Lifestyle section is perfect. Can't wait to read whatever you write."

I squirm under his praise, and my throat tightens but I return his smile. "Actually, I'll be writing the weekly advice column."

His eyes widen with appreciation. "Dear Diary? My mom reads that religiously."

"Does she? Mine swears she's never heard of it," I quip.

"Well, mine has. She's going to flip when I tell her I know you."

I roll my eyes. "It's not that serious," I say.

"Yes, it is. That's cool as hell." He gives me a sidelong glance. "And very different for you. You done with sleuthing?"

"More like sleuthing is done with me." I chuckle like the words don't break my heart.

"That's a shame. You are great at it." He smiles but it's forced.

Guilt pokes at me but I'm not moved by it. "I wouldn't even know where to begin. The black market's distribution is airtight. Unless you have something solid. Something more than a name that isn't uncommon. I just don't see how I can help."

"You're right. It was long shot." He glances at his watch and stands. "I'm sorry that I put you on the spot like that. Don't hold it against me."

I smile, sad and ready to move on. "I won't. It was nice to see you. I'll be in touch when I'm settled."

While I wait for the elevator, I check my phone's reception. It's still terrible but I press play and rejoice when the video starts to play. I watch, my breath in my throat as the woman he's talking to turns to face him.

The frame freezes with her in profile but it's enough to know who it is.

What the fuck is that bitch doing in my house?

I need Wi-Fi. And privacy.

Leon, the missing stool, and my career heartbreak are forgotten as a sense of urgency to get back to my hotel takes over.

I skip the slow descent on the escalators and take the elevator down to the main hall of the museum.

Normally, I'd take my time on my way out to stop and read the exhibit cards and see what's new in the hall.

Today, though, I weave through the crowd, checking my phone's reception every few seconds, until I run into the solid wall of a man's chest hard enough to send me flying back, my arms flailing for purchase.

My fall is broken by a strong hand around my bicep. I drop my phone, and it lands with a loud clatter.

"I'm sorry. Excuse me," I say to no one in particular while I scan the ground for my phone. I grab it and shout an apology and thanks over my shoulder. I make a beeline for the door, drop my phone back in my bag, and focus on where I'm going.

Two

Kwame

Meant to Be

I've just finished visiting the exhibit hall that my mother endowed when I collide with a woman who's moving faster than she should be in a crowded space.

It all happens so fast. She stumbles backward, windmilling her arms, long braids tumble out of her bun. Someone grabs her elbow to steady her. She scrambles for her phone and stands up in single movement and keeps moving, calling apologies over her shoulder.

A familiar fragrance fills my nose, and I stop and inhale deeply. I haven't smelled it in a long time, but I recognize it right away.

I can picture the small white petals of the flowers my mother grew in her private garden and kept fresh cuttings of on her bedside table.

What was it called?

Like a child hearing the pied piper, I follow the scent and reach the massive glass doors before I come to my senses.

Grief has been a really wild ride. One minute I'm okay, the next I'm panicking because I can't remember the name of my mother's favorite flower.

The truth is it doesn't matter what that flower is called. My mother is gone and nostalgia is an unreliable narrator. Those flowers haven't bloomed in her garden in years. I came to DC to wrap-up my complicated relationship with this city, not to chase ghosts.

I turn down Fourteenth Street to meet the driver I hired for the day and climb in.

"Where to, Boss?" the man calls cheerily over the headrest.

"I'm going back to the hotel."

I sit back and have relaxed just enough to let my eyes drift closed when I realize my phone is ringing on silent in my pocket.

I pick it up and wish I hadn't.

It's my father. I hesitate to answer and miss the call.

A second later, a text appears.

"Sending Paloma instead." In typical fashion, his message is direct and cryptic at the same time.

Not in the mood for his mind games, I call him back instead of typing my reply.

He answers before I even hear it ring. "Hello, Son."

"You're sending Paloma where?"

"To meet you for dinner since I can't make it," he says as if we've talked about this a dozen times.

"Let's just reschedule."

"No, you and Paloma need some time to talk seriously about your future together. I booked the two of you a table at Dogon for seven tonight. I've sent Paloma the reservation details. She'll meet you there."

"We've had this planned for a month. Why can't you make it?"

"Oz happens to be in town, and he's only free tonight."

I grimace at the mention of my cousin. "Since when do you move your schedule to suit him?"

"Don't be petulant, Kwame. There's someone I want him to introduce me to, and tonight is when he's free. Don't act like you wouldn't rather eat with Paloma anyway."

"You couldn't be more mistaken. You should have asked me first. Please let her know I can't make it."

"Why can't you? This has been on your calendar for weeks."

"It's been on yours, too. And yet, here we are."

There's silence on the other end. "Hello?" I say even though I know he's there.

"Fine. I'll have my assistant send her a message."

"Fine." I echo his clipped cadence. "I'll see you tomorrow."

"Yes. Alice says you're staying at The Salamander. Which is absurd when you have a home right across the river. Bring your luggage with you in the morning. You'll stay at The Palms while you're here."

He disconnects the call after issuing his command.

"Dammit, Alice." I drop my head into my hands and close my eyes.

I asked my aunt to play dumb when he asked where I was staying tonight. It's my fault for forgetting how much sway he has over her.

Over everyone, really.

The three months I spent with my parents before my mother died felt like three years. For more than twenty years, I hadn't seen them more than one weekend a year. They had become functional strangers with very little in common.

When my mother and I were alone, we had real conversations. She told me about her life, her family, and gave me advice that I know I'll heed.

But I hated living under the same roof as my father. He was controlling, dismissive, and selfish. I played the role of dutiful son for my mother's sake. But when I left for Los Angeles on the evening of her funeral, I swore I'd never spend another night in that house.

I may have had to come back for her will reading, but it would take an act of God to make me stay a minute longer than I have to.

Three

Sin

Enough

I booked a room at The Salamander because nearly all of them have a view of the Tidal Basin and a balcony. I sit in one of the chairs out there, phone in hand and heart hammering.

I had the cameras installed after someone broke into our apartment, ransacked my office, and stole my laptop.

I had the misfortune of coming home in the middle of the robbery and found myself staring at the barrel of a pistol. The masked man pointing it in my face shoved me to my knees and told me to close my eyes.

I begged him to take whatever he wanted and leave.

He told me to shut up and not look at him. I thought my life was over and all I could do was pray.

When I heard the door close behind him, the rush of relief nearly stopped my heart. But I was too scared to move.

I don't know how long I sat there before I finally found the clarity to call the police.

By the time they arrived, the intruder was long gone and I was a useless witness who couldn't describe anything but the gun he used. They took my statement, gave me a number to call to check on my case, and suggested I consider getting a personal firearm and installing security cameras.

After they left, I called Stephen to tell him what happened. He sent the call to voicemail. An hour later he texted me to let me know he was hopping on a flight for an impromptu basketball game in Houston and promised to call me when he landed.

In the aftermath of it all, I couldn't bring myself to sleep in the apartment, so I checked into a hotel near my office. I called in sick for the next two days and used the time to apply for my federal firearms license and found someone to install the cameras.

The day I was supposed to go back to work, I woke up to an email from the editor in chief informing me that *The Guardian* had published an article that scooped mine. He informed me that they wouldn't run the article I'd just submitted for edits. He also told me that they'd chosen someone else for the editor at large role. A role I'd been a shoo-in for.

It was the straw that broke my heart and my brain all at once. I didn't know what I was going to do, but I knew I couldn't stay in this house, with that man, or at that paper another minute.

I replied to the email with my resignation, told my parents I was coming home for Easter early, and left a note on the fridge for Stephen.

When he finally called a week later, I'd already laid the foundation for my next act. And decided that he wouldn't play a starring role in it.

It had taken another week for me to feel ready to tell him.

He may not be the love of my life, but he wasn't always a terrible boyfriend, and I'd decided he deserved to hear it in person.

But if the video I glimpsed is what I suspect, what he really deserves might land me in handcuffs.

I steel myself and open the app with trembling fingers and press play.

They go from talking, to kissing, to fumbling with zippers in less than sixty seconds.

My stomach lurches as I watch them fuck on my desk.

It's over as quickly as it started but they don't leave. She sits in my chair, puts her feet up on my desk and laughs. I press the volume-up button a half dozen times before I realize the sound is connected to my earbuds.

I walk over to fish in my bag for them.

As soon as I find them though, I change my mind. I've taken enough L's today.

Numb and reeling, I sit outside until the sun has set.

The phrase "To catch a sinner you've got to think like one" was something I used to say all the time. I never imagined I would apply it to the man I shared years of my life with.

But I can't pretend I didn't see him drilling his dick into the woman who just so happened to write an article lifted from my research days after my laptop was stolen.

I didn't even know he knew her.

He must think I'm the world's biggest fool.

Maybe he was right.

But my eyes are wide open now.

As for the woman, she may think she won, but the story she stole isn't even the tip of the iceberg.

I text Leon. "Tell your friend I'll talk to her about this Oz. Let's nail him and everyone around him to the wall."

I put my phone on DND, climb in the shower, and wait for the sadness to come. It doesn't. When I climb out, I'm angry and resolved.

I'm not sure what this next chapter of my life will be but I'm sure that this one is over. It's time to move on.

Four

Kwame

Lady Luck

My phone vibrates with a text from Paloma. "Thirty minutes away, traffic is a nightmare."

I text her back right away. "Hey Lo. Sorry my dad got his wires crossed. I can't make dinner tonight."

An exclamation point appears on my delivered message and then my phone rings.

I groan and answer it.

"I've had this on my calendar for two weeks," she says before I can say hello.

"How? Until a few hours ago he and I had plans for dinner."

"That may be true but his assistant sent *me* the calendar invite two weeks ago and I planned my whole day around it."

"Lo, since when does my dad plan my social schedule? Why didn't you call me?"

"I didn't think I'd have to. I mean, I figured you'd want to see me." She sounds hurt and I could wring my father's neck.

"I would have loved to see you, but this is a quick trip."

"Let's have dinner anyway. I'm thirty minutes away. We're overdue for a catch-up."

"I'm not at the hotel. I made plans with an old coworker," I improvise badly.

"Fine, then I'll eat by myself. I've been dying to try Dogon."

"I already cancelled the reservation." I wince at the lie.

"What the hell, Kwame?" She raises her voice. "Do you know how hard it is to get a table there?"

"Yes. Which is why, when I knew I couldn't make it, I called to make sure they didn't hold it." I'm not proud of how easily these lies are rolling off my tongue. She's one of my oldest friends, but our relationship is complicated and she's unpredictable as hell. "I'm sorry, Lo. Next time."

"I'll hold you to it."

"I know you will."

"See you soon, bye." She sings her exit.

I exhale a deep breath and immediately call down to Dogon to cancel the table. The line rings busy. "Of course."

I should have known my father wouldn't call Lo. I hate that she got caught up in my father's machinations.

It was his micromanagement and need for control that drove me away in the first place. The three months we'd spent playing father and son while we watched my mother die wasn't enough to make me forget all I've ever been to him is a pawn.

I may not be in the mood to eat with Lo but I'm hungry. It's thirty minutes until seven. I could use a drink first.

I slip my shoes on and stab the elevator call button inside my suite, grateful the doors open immediately. I spend the ride down trying to stop my anger from spiraling. Tomorrow, I'll close the door on my life in DC for good and go back to my life in California where no one knows I'm Al Palmer's son.

The bar is packed, but I find a seat and slide into it.

Then, I smell it again.

That fragrance. I look to my right and the seat that had been empty when I arrived is occupied by the woman I ran into today.

Her braids are caught in a high ponytail instead of bun and she's wearing a blue and orange wrap dress instead of jeans, but I know it's her.

I'm about to speak to her when she turns away and answers her phone.

I glance at my watch and settle in to wait for my table.

Five

Sin

Divine Intervention

I order an RG&T from the bartender and then look for a free seat at the busy bar.

My phone buzzes with the unique pattern I've assigned to my younger sister. She's called me three times in fifteen minutes. If I don't answer, she'll escalate and start looking for me.

I turn away so my back is to the person next to me and take a moment to recall my cover story.

"Hey, Mae!" I answer brightly but in a hushed tone. Thank heavens the restaurant is relatively quiet. "Sorry I missed your calls."

"Where are you?" she asks.

The bartender places my drink down and I wave my thanks and fish for my wallet while I talk. "I'm in the United lounge. Just waiting for my flight to board."

There's a beat of quiet from her end. "I didn't realize you were leaving today. Why don't you stay for Easter?"

"I decided last minute. I was going to call you when I got through security and forgot. I'm sorry." I hate lying to her, but she's got a big mouth, and I can't risk my parents finding out I'm still here.

"Yeah, you are," she retorts. "I didn't even get to say a proper good-bye."

"You're having it now."

"You're so mean, Sin."

"I know, but I love you. Is everything okay at home?"

My sister sighs. "Yeah, no, everything is cool. Mama and Daddy went to a special service at church. I came over thinking I'd find you alone. I was hoping we could have dinner. But never mind that."

I bite my lip and wince at the pang of guilt that knots my stomach. I *hate* lying to my sister. "I'll be back, Mae. Soon."

"I know. I can't wait. Oh! I know you have to go, but Stephen texted to say he'd been trying to reach you. Is everything okay?"

Not at all. "Yup. I'll call him when I get to my gate." Time to end this before I say more than I mean to. "It'll be late when I land, so I'll call you tomorrow, okay?"

"Yeah, yeah. Sure. It was great to see you. I love you."

"Love you more, Mae. Bye."

I hang up and drop my head into my hands. Being selfish isn't easy, but I've learned the hard way that it's easier than giving more than you get back.

I needed one night alone to settle my nerves after a week staying with my parents and I don't regret taking it.

The bartender delivers my drink as I hang up. I hand him my credit card. "Can I start a tab?"

He takes it. "Sure, you want to see the menu?"

I hesitate and look back at the hostess stand. "How likely is it that there'll be a cancellation tonight?" I ask.

"Oh, not likely at all."

I pout and give up. "I'll take that menu," I tell him. I'm hungry and the food will taste just the same here as it would at a table.

He takes the card and walks to the register.

I'm starting to relax when a deep voice next to me says, "Excuse me, miss," followed by a hand on my shoulder.

Annoyed and not in the mood for any bullshit tonight, I cast a withering glance at the trespassing appendage. And promptly swallow the "What the hell do you think you're doing?" that's on the tip of my tongue.

Everyone has a weakness and mine happens to be well-formed hands. The one I'm looking at is remarkable—golden brown, nicely veined, neatly trimmed broad nails on long fingers and big enough to cover the entirety of my shoulder.

Well damn.

It's almost enough to make up for being touched by a stranger. Almost.

I slip out of his grasp before I turn to face him.

He's as built, handsome, and well-dressed as his immaculate hand and as confident as his presumptuous approach told me he would be.

Though increasingly rare, men like him are very familiar to me.

I've spent most of my life living in their favorite North American hunting grounds—New York and Washington, DC. They look like a dream but are vessels of mayhem and disappointment. I've just escaped the clutches of one.

I *should* dispatch him with an icy glare, but mustering the energy to be bitchy is more work than I want to do tonight.

I smile up at him. "Yes?"

"I couldn't help overhear you just now. You were trying to get a table, right?" He smiles like he knows it's hypnotic.

"I was." I raise an eyebrow and wait for him to say more.

"I have a table for two and my date just canceled."

I narrowed my eyes. "And?" I prod not sure where this is going.

"I was wondering if you'd like to share my table."

"Oh. Really?" I give him a once-over, warily taking in his immaculately pressed trousers and dress shirt. "What's the catch?"

"There isn't one." He shrugs. "You need a table. I have a spare seat at mine."

The reflexive, "No thanks" that should be on the tip of my tongue isn't.

I booked this hotel for the views and so I could eat at Dogon. I love the chef's restaurant in New York and had been so disappointed when the hostess turned me away. Why *not* eat with him?

I look him square in the eye. God his eyes are dark as midnight. Not even the light's reflection in them reveals his pupils. "No catch? You're just being nice?"

He puts his hands in his pockets and leans back in his seat, smiling. "Crazy concept, right?"

Sometimes it feels like one. I don't reply, but return his smile.

I could do with something nice. He's not asking me on a date, and it's not like we'd be alone. How much damage could he do over dinner in a public restaurant?

I brighten my smile and grab my purse. "Okay, yes. I'd love that. What time is your reservation?"

"In about seven minutes. Are you ready?"

I pick up my drink and step off the stool. "Very."

"Great." He puts a hand against the small of my back and sweeps his other arm out in the direction of the restaurant. "Shall we?"

I nod and step away from his touch as we head back toward the restaurant.

I glance at him from the corner of my eye.

He's facing straight ahead, his jaw set. He's the kind of handsome that's timeless. Smooth, clean-shaven, caramel brown skin, an immaculate goatee, skin that looks like he takes good care of it, and a fresh low fade topped with waves that deserve a round of applause.

His eyes are deep set and narrow, with thick lashes that curl like I wish mine would. He's got broad shoulders, a flat stomach, slim hips, long sturdy legs and is tall enough for me to climb.

Something has got to be wrong with him because if "too good to be true" was a person, it would look *just* like him.

"Kwame. I thought that was you." The hostess's screech drags my eyes away from him and my attention back to the present.

She steps from around her booth and throws her arm around his shoulders. "I saw your name on the list tonight, but I was sure it was an error. I'm so glad I was wrong."

They hug like long-lost friends and I try not to be offended that he doesn't introduce me before we're shown to our table.

It's not a date and we haven't even exchanged names.

We follow the hostess into the heart of the restaurant's sleek, cavernous dining room. The artwork and furniture are a perfect fusion of the Caribbean, African and Black American cultures that inspired the menu. Sleek, plushly covered chairs in dark blue fabric encircle dark wood tables adorned with gold finishes.

It's beautiful.

The waiter places menus in front of us but I don't need to look. I already know what I'm having.

"I'm going to use the bathroom. I'll be right back." I make a quick detour to powder my nose and when I get back he's reading the menu.

"Okay, are you ready to order?" I ask with relish.

He looks up from his menu with a civil smile. "I ordered a few starters for the table, but he'll be right back to add to yours. Feel free to add more." He hands me the menu.

"I was going to order the suya."

"I ordered it."

I grin, excited. "Great. I'll just wait and order my main course when he comes back."

"Your RG&T," the waiter says.

I look up with a smile but shake my head. "Thank you. I didn't order this."

"I did," says Kwame.

"Oh," I raise my eyebrows. "Thank you."

"If you'd rather have something else, he can take your order." His baritone is smooth as bourbon, his gaze is direct, and his smile is easy. I push my troubles away and focus on the boon the universe saw fit to send me.

"No, this is perfect." I smile and pick up the glass.

He lifts his beer glass and tilts it across the black marbled table. "You're welcome. Cheers to…?"

"New beginnings." I lift my glass.

He nods. "And airport lounges." He winks at me before taking a sip.

I wrinkle my nose and wish the floor would swallow me whole. "Oh my god. Don't judge me, please." I snort a deprecating laugh.

"I wasn't."

"I have my reasons," I plead, trying to assuage my guilt and shame at once.

He holds up a hand and gives his head a slight shake. "You don't need to explain."

"I'm not a liar," I add.

"Then you might want to see a neurologist ASAP because this *isn't* an airport lounge."

I laugh despite my flaming embarrassment. "I meant in general."

He chuckles. "I'm giving you a hard time. I did the same thing tonight."

"What do you mean?"

"It wasn't my date who canceled. It was me."

I raise my eyebrows in surprise. "Damn. Why?"

"Because the thought of eating dinner with her made me tired."

I wince but nod in understanding. "Energy vampire?"

He huffs a laugh. "I've never heard that before but it's perfect. I don't always mind, but tonight, I just wanted to relax."

"So you asked a complete stranger to eat dinner with you instead?"

"Yeah. I don't like eating alone. You needed a table. I figured if you turned out to be an asshole, this booth is big enough that I could avoid conversation."

I look around the massive circular booth and nod. It could seat six people comfortably. "That's very well-thought-out for an impromptu invitation."

"I'm quick on my feet. And it wasn't that impromptu."

"It wasn't?" I lean back surprised. "But, that was the first time we saw each other."

He nods. "I saw you earlier."

"You did? Are you sure?" I wrack my brain trying to recall this morning.

"Very. You're hard to miss." He takes a sip of his drink, obscuring his face.

I cock my head to the side. "I can't tell if you mean that as a compliment or a diss."

He puts the drink down and looks away as if he's thinking. "If you need to qualify, it certainly wasn't a diss. But I wasn't trying to flatter you either. It's just…a statement of fact. You're eye-catching. Attention-holding…"

"Keep going," I drawl.

He smiles. "You're striking, sexy, expressive, magnetic."

I've been starved of this kind of attention for so long that I'm about to start purring. If I'm not careful, I'll end up humping his leg.

"Okay, that's enough. You don't have to say anymore."

"I want to say them. I've been thinking them all day."

I blush. "Well, who am I to stop you?"

He smiles wide like he's very pleased and gazes down at me, his eyes soft and focused on mine. "I like your dress. Blue is a good color on you."

I have to stop myself from pressing my hand to my chest. His dark eyes are hooded and liquid mahogany brown. "Thank you. I appreciate a man who pays attention."

"Then you're in the right place because you've got my full attention the way nothing else I've seen today has."

I lift an eyebrow in surprised delight. "Is that so?"

"It is."

"Here we are," our server announces and puts the plates down with a flourish.

My eyes widen as the procession of tray-carrying servers follows suit until our entire table is covered with plates of food.

I stare at it wide-eyed. "Oh my God, did you order everything on the menu?"

"Almost. I wasn't sure what you wanted."

"Wow. That's so…"

"Thoughtful?"

I snort a laugh. "I was going to say indulgent, but yes, it was also thoughtful." I gawk at the food laid out and try not to freak out about what paying for half of this is going to do to my budget. Thank goodness I have points to pay for my room. I'll take a to-go bag and eat my leftovers for lunch this week.

"Here you go." He hands me a huge fork and carving knife. "For the lamb." He points to the platter of sizzling meat in front of me.

"Great choice." I eye the huge bone-in shank and my mouth waters. "I heard this dish is amazing. Thank you." I take the utensils and try to ignore the way the brush of his fingers sends a jolt all the way up my arm and turn to the only neutral thing I can think of. "Kwame. The hostess called it out when we walked in," I add when I can see him trying to remember if he told me.

He huffs a laugh. "Wow. Skipped right over that, didn't we? Yes, I'm Kwame." He grins and sticks his hand out in an exaggerated formal way. "Nice to make your acquaintance."

"Likewise." I take his hand. He's got very nice hands. Soft and dry, but strong, warm, and smooth.

When he lets go, I shove my right hand under my thigh to trap the sensation of the touch. God, when's the last time I felt anything when Stephen and I touched?

When's the last time Stephen and I touched at all? I push that depressing thought away and focus on the very nice evening I'm having.

"What's your name?" he asks.

"Sorry, I forgot. Everyone calls me Sin."

He chuckles and washes down his food with a swig of Stella. "As in a transgression?"

I purse my lips and don't hide my irritation. "No. As in short for my full name, Arsinoé."

"Cool."

"Is Kwame your real name?"

His brows knit together and he crosses his arms over his broad chest. "Of course it is."

His voice loses some of its lightness and I curse my loose tongue. "I'm sorry. It's just that, it's a Ghanaian name, you're obviously *not* Ghanaian. I was—"

"You say that like you've seen my birth certificate." His brows shoot up and his smile disappears.

"I didn't mean—"

"I'm in a Ghanaian restaurant in Washington, DC, wearing an Adinkra pendant, my name is Kwame—I'm practically screaming it."

I can tell I touched a nerve. "I'm sorry that I asked but…It's just that all of those things could be true and you could be from Chicago."

"Well, I'm not." He takes a sip of his drink.

"And *both* of your parents are from Ghana?" Ghanaians are known for being among the darkest skinned people in West Africa and his skin is the color of caramel.

He sighs. "Yes, but my father's parents were both half Scottish."

"Oh, okay…So you're Fante?"

"Why do you say it like that?"

I frown at him. "I didn't say it like anything."

"Let me guess, you're from Ashanti region?" His voice has lost its edge and he's got a teasing glint in your eyes.

"I am. Did my regal bearing give it away?" I grin, glad I didn't offend him enough to spoil the mood.

He snorts. "No, your judgmental 'So you're Fante' did."

I laugh at his impersonation of me. "Why are you people from Cape Coast always *so* defensive?" I ask with a teasing grin.

"Because you people from Kumasi act like we're not all the same people."

I shrug. "We're *not* the same."

"How? We speak different dialects of the same language, eat the same food, have the same naming traditions, customs, systems."

I smirk. "All of that doesn't make up for the one major way we're different."

"What's that?

"While we Ashantis were fighting the colonizers, your people were fucking them." I wink at him.

His jaw drops and my stomach dips for a second. I don't know why I say things like that to people I don't know.

I'm about to apologize when he throws his head back and looks at the ceiling. "Oh my God, it's true." He bursts into a good-natured laugh and reveals two rows of straight white teeth. I wonder if he wore braces or if he was made on a day God felt like showing out.

His features aren't symmetrical enough to call him classically handsome. But his proud, prominent nose, his wide mouth and full lips, the top one with an enviably perfect bow, are the perfect complement to his high cheekbones and exquisite bone structure. I look back at his hands again.

The glint of gold from the signet ring on his right ring finger catches my eye. I can see it's embossed with the same Adinkra symbol as the one hanging around his neck.

How did I miss those details? I blame the cocktail for dulling my senses and thank the universe that he has a sense of humor despite how badly I put my foot in my mouth.

I clear my throat. "Listen, I know how it feels to have your identity questioned because you don't fit the mold. I'm sorry."

He pauses mid-sip, glass still at his lips and slides his eyes to look at me. "You are? Just like that?"

"Yes," I draw the word out. "Why are you looking at me like I just performed a strange but cool circus trick?"

He huffs a laugh and shrugs. "Because I usually have to speak Twi, prove I know how to eat fufu, and produce my passport or birth certificate before most Ghanaians are satisfied that I'm one of them. And this is the first time anyone has ever said sorry for that shit."

"Oh God. That's awful. But you know how hard it is for our elders to say they are sorry. And unfortunately, it trickles down."

"I'm used to it, but I'm always surprised when I have to remind other Ghanaians that the region was colonized and occupied by three different European countries. Cape Coast is full of people who look like me."

"Have you spent a lot of time there?"

"I used to go every year. Usually at Christmas."

"Do your parents live there or here?"

He nods without looking up. "Both. Anyway, enough about me." He cuts into his food and takes a massive bite.

His deflection piques my curiosity, but I let it go.

For now.

His eyebrows shoot up. "Arsinoé isn't very Ghanaian either."

"Touché." I laugh at his clever turnaround. "My parents went to Egypt for their honeymoon. It's where I was conceived so they chose a name from there."

"At least your name has meaning," he says.

"So does yours," I push back.

He scoffs. "'A boy born on Saturday' is probably the *least* meaningful name my parents could have given me."

I shake my head. "That's not true. It's so special to have a name that connects you with your cultural identity. I wish mine had given me my day name. Or anything that didn't require explanation and spelling."

He chuckles. "Look at us. Living proof that the grass is always greener when you're not standing on it."

"True. And honestly, I like my name," I admit.

"Me too. Do you have an older sister named Cleopatra?" He grins and shoves a fork full of rice into his mouth.

I gasp and stare at him.

"What?" he asks around a mouthful of food.

"*No* one, in my whole life has ever known that."

He wrinkles his brow and gives me a skeptical look. "How? When she's the sister of one of the most famous women who ever lived?"

"Exactly," I say throwing my hands up excitedly.

My insides flutter with a sensation I haven't felt in so long I'm not sure it's real. I thought it might be the cocktail making him sexier every time he speaks, but I'm starting to worry that it's just…him. "So, where do you live, Kwame?" I ask casually.

"Los Angeles." He takes another bite of food and I relax.

"Oh cool. I love LA. Is that where you're from?"

"No, I moved there after law school and have been there almost fifteen years."

"Law school, huh? Your parents must have been thrilled. And what brings you to DC?"

"I grew up here. What about you?" He digs into his food again. It's the second deflection when I've asked about family and I wonder what the story is there.

I'm so close to mine, despite how annoying they are, I'm suspicious of people who aren't.

"I grew up in the DMV. I was born in Silver Spring and that's where we lived until my parents moved to Arlington when I was middle school."

He nods. "Where do you live now, Sin?" The way he says my name feels like he's been saying it his whole life.

"New York City." For now.

"And when are you *really* headed back?" he asks with a sly grin.

I roll my eyes but can't fight the conspiratorial smile his words inspire. "My flight is in the morning. Bright and early. So, I'm really glad I met you tonight. It's been fun."

He shrugs and frowns. "I'm still trying to decide how I feel about it."

My burst of surprised laughter feels like pressure being released.

When's the last time a man made me laugh for real? "You know you're having a great time. Stop playing." I wave away his words.

One of his dark eyebrows quirks up. "Getting ahead of yourself aren't you? You seem cool. But, until I know your sign, I can't be sure. I avoid Geminis, Virgos, and Capricorns like the plague." He gives a shiver of disgust and I can't tell if he's serious.

"Are you for real?"

"Yes. Date of birth, please."

"Fine. I don't know anything about horoscopes. But, I was born on February fourteenth. I *think* that makes me—"

"Wha—" He chokes on the sip of drink he was swallowing and the rest of his words are lost to a coughing fit. I'm about to pat his back when his icy glare stops me cold.

Six

Kwame

Perfect

"Are you okay?" She looks alarmed as she watches me try to catch my breath.

My years as a prosecutor have taught me that when a set of facts fit together too neatly, there's something wrong. And all it took was a smile like the sun, a smell like spring, and a laugh like lightening to make me forget.

"Okay, who sent you?"

She narrows her eyes and furrows her brows. "Sent me? What do you mean?"

I scoff and take a sip of my beer, fuming again. "Come on, that was just one coincidence. You shouldn't have thrown in the birthday thing. It gave this whole setup away." I narrow my eyes at her.

"A setup?" Her eyes bug out of her head.

"There's just too many coincidences. How likely is it that we'd run into each other and then happen to be staying at the same hotel?"

She stops wiping her blouse and looks up at me. "What do you mean? I've never seen you before in my life."

I purse my lips, impatience growing. "Right. You expect me to believe that you didn't notice me when we ran into each other at the museum?

Her eyebrows crease. "I've had a lot on my mind today. I'm sorry I didn't fall at your feet and praise your perfect body and interesting face."

"Interesting?" I raise an eyebrow. "What does *that* mean?"

She scoffs and leans across the table toward me. "You accused me of following you?" She manages to express her growing indignation without raising her voice. *Impressive.*

I lean back in my seat. "Maybe not following me, but I'm not exactly easy to miss."

She raises her eyebrows and eyes me askance. "I hate to deflate your ego, but *clearly* you are."

"Ouch," I press a hand to my chest in mock pain.

"The truth hurts, I guess." She picks up her napkin and dips it in her water glass. She dabs furiously at nonexistent stains on her dress.

"You're going to rub a hole in that." I point at her.

She scowls and leans forward, eyes narrowed. "You *spat* on me."

"I didn't mean to. It was all just too much of a coincidence."

"How do I know you're not setting *me* up? You're the one who asked me to dinner."

I watch her the way I do witnesses I'm deposing.

She's either a very good liar or she's telling the truth. "How do *I* know you didn't show up here because you knew I'd be coming down?" It sounds far-fetched as soon as the words are out of my mouth, but my father is the most manipulative person I've ever encountered.

She barks an incredulous laugh. "Do you realize how crazy that sounds? Either you're paranoid or you read too many spy novels."

She picks up her phone, taps the screen a few times and then holds it up. "See?" She points to the place on her phone where her date of birth is entered. Sure enough, it's the same as mine.

"Wow. Okay. That's crazy. Same year and everything."

"I mean, I guess. Something upward of three hundred and fifty thousand people are born every single day. Did you think you were a unicorn or something?" She gives me a playful smile and takes a huge bite of her food.

Growing up with a man who didn't trust anything but his own two eyes taught me to second-guess everything. Believing that nothing is ever what it seems has served me well in my career as a criminal prosecutor. But, I do forget that not everyone walks around with an agenda. On the eve of the rest of my life, it's a timely and welcome reminder. "No, Sin, I don't believe in unicorns, but you're making me think again." I smile at her.

She scowls. "Don't flirt with me when you owe me an apology."

"I'm sorry I accused you of being a stalker," I say.

She bites her lip but it's not enough to hide the smile she's fighting. "God, your smile is beautiful."

She drops her eyes and looks away. "Sweet talkers don't impress me."

"What does?"

"Not having to tell someone how to impress me." She smiles. "Let's eat.'

I honor her request with a nod.

She starts piling food on her plate and ignoring me. I cross my arms and lean back, assessing her.

This evening is certainly unexpected. Something brought us together tonight. My mother's death so soon as after we reconciled was a reminder of how fleeting and miraculous life is. The timing is off. We don't even live in the same city.

When we are forced to go our separate ways tomorrow, we'll probably never see each other again.

But given how our paths have crossed today, I wouldn't bet on that.

"Why aren't you eating?" she asks around a mouthful of food.

"Have you heard of the frequency illusion?"

She nods. "You mean Baader-Meinhof? That's not a real thing."

"We both grew up here. Our parents are from Ghana. We have the same birthday but we've gone our whole lives without meeting. Then we both happen to be in the same city on the same day, staying at the same hotel."

She frowns. "Okay, but I live in New York and you live in LA. So unless one of us is moving, it's not likely."

The thought is depressing somehow. "Unless we *want* to see each other again."

"Why would we do that?"

"It sounds like a good idea to me." I shrug.

She throws her head back and laughs out loud.

I'd thought she was pretty, but damn, the way she laughs with her whole face, mouth open, eyes dancing. "*That*, Kwame, sounds like the first line of a cautionary tale." She digs back into her food with gusto.

I am a firm believer that what's for you will find you, whether you want it or not.

This woman is a whirlwind and I've been in her path all day. Chaos is the last thing I want but I find myself not wanting this to end. "Stay with me tonight."

I blurt it out and then immediately wish I hadn't.

Her smiles disappears and she coughs around the food in her mouth.

"Or not," I retract my offer with a nervous laugh. "Did I misread?"

"Uh, excuse me." She grabs her purse and slides out of her seat before I can even ask if she's coming back.

Seven

Sin

Change of Heart

I stare at myself in the mirror of Dogon's dimly lit bathroom.

The woman I see staring back at me is, admittedly, not an iteration of myself I've seen recently—bright eyes, glowing skin, not a worry line in sight—but I recognize her.

I have a lot of shit to clear up with Stephen but after what I saw, I know our relationship, as we know it, is over. I'm surprised at how little that realization hurts. In fact, the strongest feeling I have right now is relief.

It's time.

I stayed with him because a boring sex life felt like a shallow reason to leave the man I'd spent the last six years with. Our mothers are best friends and had already decided we were getting married. We had a good life. It wasn't perfect but it could be enough.

But I want more than enough.

I deserve to be full.

I deserve to feel good.

Kwame makes me feel good. *And* he lives in California.

I don't know his last name and he doesn't know mine.

It's the perfect set up.

I gaze at myself appraisingly. I look, in my late thirties, like I did in my late twenties. I have nothing to be self-conscious about. I look good as hell.

I've been more turned on during our conversation than I've been in longer than I can remember. I'm not going to overthink it.

I walk back to the table unsure what I'm hoping will happen when I get there. I want to do this but I don't know if I should.

I'm vulnerable.

He's a seasoned professional in the art of seduction. He might turn me out and then have me thinking about him for the rest my life.

My gut is knotted with indecision when I slide

"Are you okay?" Kwame asks. "You look like something is wrong."

I nod. "I had to use the bathroom. Something went down the wrong way."

"Are you sure that's all? You've been smiling all night. And now you look like you want to kill someone"

"This is how I normally look. I had too much to drink before dinner," I say and smile. *Sober me knows better than to smile at men like you.*

"Sorry, what?" He leans away like I shoved him, his brows drawn together in confusion. "Men like me?"

I grimace and wish I could disappear. "Did I say that out loud?"

"Yes. You did," he says with an expectant look.

"You should ignore me."

"Impossible. And now I'm curious. What kind of man do you think I am?"

"Ugh, Kwame. I misspoke." I take a sip of water and look around the room. "This place is nice right?"

"I don't think you misspoke. But if you can't stand behind your thoughts, that's cool."

I take the blatant bait and slap my napkin down. "Okay, you asked for it. You're tall, handsome, Black, you're not broke, you're charming, well-dressed, well-spoken, interesting, thoughtful."

"And those are bad things?"

"Of course not. But obviously you know how attractive those things are to a lot of women and you use them to your advantage."

"Tell me more about myself since you know me so well."

"First, you seemed shocked that I didn't notice you today. You asked me to dinner out of nowhere because rejection, at least from women, isn't something you're used to or expect."

"Is confidence a crime?"

"When it's misplaced."

"Wow. Tell me how you really feel," he says.

"Listen, Kwame, I've been a magnet for men like you my whole life."

"Well, I think you're a magnet period," he says with a cocky grin.

I throw my hands up. "See! I'm telling you off and you're still flirting."

He kills his smile and turns his expression somber. "Sorry, please continue telling me off."

"You know what? Never mind. I've had a lifetime of men who think they're god's gift because they won the genetic lottery. You look good, sound good, but you only care about yourselves. Hell, I've yet to meet one of you who can even make me come."

This time, he manages to catch himself before he spits his drink out again.

"Is that a challenge?"

"No. I've got a vibrator upstairs that's faster and more dependable than any man could hope to be."

"It doesn't buy you dinner first, though."

"You're not buying me dinner. We're going half," I inform him and look around for the server.

"Not in this lifetime."

"Then I hope you're ready to die," I say with a smirk.

He laughs and watches me catch the server's eye and wave him over.

"I'd like to pay for my half of the meal, please." I smile up at him.

"It's already taken care of. Would you like anything else?"

Irritated and bested, I thank him and wait for him to disappear before I look at Kwame again. "Why did you do that?"

He's watching me with his chin resting on his upturned wrist. "I wasn't sure you weren't dining and dashing when you left earlier."

"What?" My jaw drops.

He grins. "Now what were you saying a second ago? Something about upstairs and orgasms?" His voice is so sexy and the way his lips form the word orgasm should be illegal.

"You're hearing things," I snap and cross my legs tight, trying to contain the ache that's spreading from my core.

"And you were making up a story about me with no basis in fact. I'm not sure what happened when you went to the bathroom. But I'm the same person I was when we sat down to eat. We've had a good time, right?"

I snap my eyes back to him and my anger fizzles. "You know what? You're right. This has been a perfect night. You're great, and maybe if we'd met when my life wasn't so complicated, we could have seen where it would go. I've got a big day tomorrow and I think I should just get some sleep."

"You know what? Me too."

"See? Didn't you say you're going back to LA on Sunday? You must have a lot to do."

He sighs and wraps his hands around his glass and stares down into it. "No, actually I don't. I'm in town for the reading of my mother's will. She died three months ago."

It's the last thing I expected him to say and my jaw goes slack before I can school my surprise. "Oh my God. I'm so sorry."

His hesitation to talk about his family makes perfect sense now.

He sighs and lifts apologetic eyes up to mine. "It's okay. I mean, it's not, but I didn't mean to just to blurt it out like that. I sounded so cavalier."

I shake my head and regain my composure. "No, no, it's okay. Don't apologize, and it didn't sound cavalier at all. I mean, grief doesn't look the same on different people."

"Thanks for saying that." His shoulders heave with a heavy sigh. "Actually, she's the reason I stopped to talk to you at the bar. Your perfume—it smells like a flower she always had in the house. I couldn't remember the name and was going to ask you."

He casts me a sideways, bashful glance. I want to give him a hug. "It's Jasmine. I wear an oil made with it. Have for a long time."

"Thank you. I'm going to write it down so I don't forget. It's strange to talk about her in the past tense. I'm still getting used to the fact that she's gone."

His smile is so sad, my heart squeezes. "Were you close?"

"No, but I loved her. I'm glad I got to tell her."

I put a hand on his shoulder and pat him. "Was it sudden?"

"Yes." He stares blankly at his glass, and I wish I'd given him a hug instead.

"She must have been so proud of you. Having a kid who's a lawyer is literally the American dream."

He nods and some of the light comes back to his eyes. "I'm a prosecutor, not quite high-flying enough for them." He snorts a laugh. "We didn't come to America so our son could be a public *servant*." He speaks in an excellent imitation of the postcolonial British accents of our parents' generation.

I burst out laughing. "Oh my God, they're all the same."

He shakes his head in a wry laugh. "Yours, too?"

"They're supportive. Definitely not as strict as some of the other Ghanaian parents I know, but they're also not shy about expressing their disappointment that I chose journalism over medicine."

He smiles wistfully. "It's like you owe them something, right?"

"We do," I say. "They gave up a lot for us."

"Yes." He shrugs. "Who asked them to? They made the choices that were best for them, but I don't think that creates some sort of cosmic debt. I admire your sense of duty, Sin, but I hope you have the same energy for your own dreams, too."

That's not how I was raised to think about family. My dreams are theirs and theirs are mine. But there's a truth in his words that I'm finally in the position to accept—living to make everyone else happy and proud is why I'm so unhappy today. "Thank you for saying that."

"It's true. You've got one life. You deserve to live it."

Who knew words of affirmations could be such a panty dropper? I'm glad I came back. "Are you done eating?" I ask.

He glances at the table, scanning the plates as if to make sure he's licked every single one of them clean. "Yeah. I guess so. Are you ready to go?"

I shake my head.

One eyebrow quirks up. "Do you want to see the dessert menu?" He looks around for our server.

"I already know what I want," I say in a voice laced with innuendo.

His eyes come back to mine and a sexy smile curves his lush mouth. "Oh? And what would that be?"

I drop my eyes and then look up at him through my eyelashes. "*You* live in LA and I," I point at the center of my chest and let my finger drift down before I continue, "as you mentioned, live in New York."

"But tonight, we're here," he finishes my thought and we share a smile.

I sit back. "And *only* tonight. If your proposition is still on the table."

"It is." His smile is so sensual, it could melt the lock off a chastity belt.

My lace panties don't stand a chance. "Then, I'd like to take you up on it."

My heart is racing, my whole body is warm and my skin is tingling.

He's barely touched me and my body is more alive than it's been in years. I have a feeling that he's about to prove my theory about men like him wrong.

I throw my drink back in one gulp and the excess dribbles out of the corner of my mouth. I lift a hand to wipe it away, but quicker than I can get it to my mouth, he's next to me.

"I've been thinking about kissing you since I laid eyes on you." He leans over and licks the droplet away. My giggle turns into a gasp when he shifts to press a lingering, open-mouthed kiss to the spot on my neck right below my ear. His stubble scrapes my cheek and jaw and sends a rush of gooseflesh down my spine.

My head lolls back and his hot, soft tongue strokes a sensual path over my pulse point. "Oh yes." I grasp my seat to keep myself from falling out of it. The sensation is incredible.

"We should go. Right now, before we give the dining room a show." He lets go of my hand, fishes a money clip out of his pocket, and throws a spray of hundred-dollar bills on the table. "Come on."

"Yes." I put my hand in his outstretched one and let him lead me out of the restaurant. We walk through the lobby like we have every right to hold hands and somewhere in my mind I'm aware of how reckless I'm being. But at the forefront of it, I don't care.

What has playing by the rules got me?

We get on the lifts with a crowd of people. He puts himself between me and the crowd and presses his hard body into mine.

I look up into his face and find his eyes trained on my lips. "I want to kiss you right now."

"We're in public." I tip my chin in the direction of the other occupants.

His eyes never leave my face. "I don't see anyone but us."

My pulse kicks into high gear at the gravel in his voice.

So, *this* is chemistry. I smile at him. "I want you to kiss me, too," I admit on a whisper.

He moves so fast, cupping my head in one hand and grasping my hip with the other, that I laugh in delighted surprise. My laugh turns into a soft inhale when his lips touch mine in a soft series of sweeps. My eyes drift closed and I savor the feel of him, the smell of him.

It's spicy, warm, sexy.

He licks the inside of my parted lower lip and pulls away.

I groan in protest and open my eyes to find him gazing down at me. "Damn. My father always said Ghanaian women were the sweetest. He was right."

I grin at him like a fool. "Wait till you taste the rest of me," I mutter.

He growls and places his hand on the wall next to my head. "That's what I'm talking about. I'm going to make you—"

A cleared throat brings me crashing back down to earth and we both turn to face our captive audience.

Everyone is facing front and my face flames in the judgmental silence that fills the car until we get to our floor.

I should be ashamed. My mother would excommunicate me from the family if she knew I was practically fornicating in public. But I'm not ashamed, and my mother isn't here. I just wish everyone was gone.

"Oh my God." I let out the laugh I'd been holding as soon as the doors close behind us. "They'll never forget us, that's for sure. I hope you're not planning on running for office one day," I say through my giggles.

It's been a very long time since I've felt anything like this. I'm not sure I've ever felt it before. That kiss was so brief. But intimate and intense enough that I'm glad we only have tonight. I want to be present and vulnerable and make the most of this because, in all my thirty-eight years, I've never had a night like this and if this is my one chance to taste glory, then I'm going for broke.

I deserve this and my body is primed. We walk in silence, hand in hand to his suite. I have a flutter of apprehension when he presses the keycard to the door handle, but my feet move me forward and my nerves don't have anything on my excitement.

He opens the door to a suite with wall-to-wall windows that face the Tidal Basin. "Wow this amazing. We can see the cherry blossoms from here."

"It's why I stayed here. I love this view." He stands in front of the windows and I admire the way his slacks hug his ass.

"I like this view, too." I kick off my shoes and walk over to stand behind him. He turns to face me. His eyes are molten brown and restless.

"So, you've never kissed a girl from Ghana before?" I ask putting my hands on his waist.

He leans forward, kisses my cheek.

"You're my first," he whispers and his breath caresses my cheek.

He dips his head to kiss me again, but I pull away, coyly, like it's a game and not an act of self-preservation. "What about the rest of me?" I ask.

His gaze lingers on my lips, and he looks like he's about to argue but then, he smiles and nods. "You're right. I've got to prove you wrong."

I snicker and push down the stab of disappointment at how quickly he acquiesced. "Or let me down," I quip. "It's a good thing I remembered to put my vibrator on the charger. I have a feeling you're going to leave me especially frustrated, just like a colonizer."

"You talk so much shit." He steps into me and I take a step back just before he can step on my foot.

"Hey, are you trying to trample me?" I complain.

He grins like a pirate. "Only if you want me to."

My back meets the cool glass of the window and it feels amazing against my heated skin. "All I want is an orgasm."

He presses his body against mine. He's so hard and warm and, god, I could climb him like a wall.

"Take your panties off," he whispers in my ear.

"They won't be in your way."

"Nothing will." He drops to his knees, fists the hem of my dress, and lifts it up. "Fuck, you're perfect."

My body flushes at the satisfaction in his voice. "Tell that to my stretch marks," I say.

He presses his lips to the side of my ass. "You're perfect." He nibbles my skin. "Delicious."

I giggle and have to bite my tongue to stop from telling him that he's perfect, too.

"Do you want my mouth or my hand?" He lifts one leg and slings it over his shoulder and opens me up.

"Both?" I sigh and close my eyes. I'm almost dying from the anticipation.

"I like how greedy you are." He teases the inside of my thigh with his tongue and I writhe my hips. "Look how wet and fat your pussy is." He leans in and licks me through the scrap of fabric covering me.

He pulls the tiny bit of lace to the side and blows on me. I moan from the need throbbing so wildly I'm afraid I'm going to burst. "Hurry," I pant.

He glides one finger into me, strokes me slowly. "I wish you could watch my finger disappear inside of you. I wish you could feel how tight and soft you are."

He palms my clit and he adds two more fingers inside me. "How does that feel?" he croons.

"Amazing," I pant and place a hand on his shoulder for leverage.

"I've got you, Sin." He cups my ass and lifts my other leg over his shoulder, presses me against the window and presses his face between my legs.

The first touch of his tongue makes my body buck. "Jesus." I press a hand to the glass desperate for purchase.

He covers my clit with his mouth and sucks it softly while he pumps his fingers in and out of me.

"Oh my fuck…oh, yes." I yell out my release with a shout and fall forward nearly draping myself in half over his shoulder.

He stands up and carries me like that into the bedroom. "I won't even say I told you so." He grins and puts me down on the edge of the bed.

"You can say it."

"I'm not done proving you wrong." He drops to his knees, spreads my legs and picks up where he left off.

His fingers fill me, his mouth covers me and a second orgasm starts building right away. I fall back, propping myself up on my elbows so I can see the top of his head.

"Oh God, I'm going to come again," I croak, the room's ceiling a blur as I try to ride his hand.

The room fills with the sound of his fingers and mouth fucking me. I'm lost. My body is under his control. I'm so wet my thighs are coated and his hand is soaked.

I come again and so hard that tears trickle down my face. I can't muffle the sound that pours out of me, halfway between a roar and a hallelujah. My back arches off the bed and the pleasure is too much.

"No more." I push at his head and he lifts his mouth from me.

"One more, nice and easy."

He lifts his mouth from me and moves his fingers in and out of me while thumbing my clit, slowly.

"I can't wait to be inside you. I already know it's going to be so fucking good. Your pussy is as luxurious as the rest of you."

The praise sends me over the edge and he keeps stroking me until I come down.

"How do you feel now?"

Every single cell in my body is vibrating. My thighs are slick with me and him, and I'm sweating, trembling, heart racing. I can barely breathe. But I pant out the first word that comes into my head. "Alive."

"Good girl," he croons against my lower stomach, pressing a kiss right beneath my belly button before he moves from between my legs and lays down next to me on the bed.

I thought I was spent, but the heat of him, the faint spicy scent of him makes me throb. I roll over, get to my knees and straddle him.

I grind my hips against him and gasp at the friction between my sensitive, soft center and his rigid bulk. His strong hands grip my hips and he matches my rhythm.

Even with our clothes between us, it's delicious. I cup my breast, squeezing it in time to our simulated fucking.

He sits up and puts his mouth to my free breast and manages to find my nipple through the fabric of my blouse and catches it between his lips.

"Oh my god, what are you doing to me?" I demand and speed up the movement of my hips when I hit a spot that makes my toes curl.

I grip his biceps and my head falls to his shoulder. I put my mouth on his neck and lick his heated skin. His sweat is so salty and clean and I suck the skin I just tasted.

He hisses and tilts his head to give me better access. "Fuck this is so damn hot," he pants and then his rhythm falters. "Shit."

He rolls us so he's on top of me and lifts one leg up onto his shoulder and starts moving frantically between my thighs.

"Shit, Sin. Shit," he pants, his face tight with tortured restraint. A vein bisects his forehead and he bites down on his lower lip.

Then he flings himself off of me and sits on the edge of the bed. I crawl over to watch him take his dick out and stroke himself through his orgasm. He comes all over his trouser leg, trembling and gasping. It's the sexiest thing I've ever seen.

He flops back on the bed, his chest heaving, eyes closed. "I almost came in my pants. I haven't done that since I was sixteen."

He wipes his mouth with the sleeve of his shirt and sniffs his fingers. His eyes open and move to me. "Hey," he murmurs.

"Welcome back to Earth," I murmur, resisting the urge to stroke his face.

"Shit. Woman. You should come with a warning sign that says highly addictive."

"Oh stop," I brush his words away but grin like a loon.

"God, you've got a gorgeous smile." He cocks his head to the side and looks me over. "Gorgeous everything, really."

I'm not used to or comfortable with praise like this. I feel like a thousand lights are shining on me and it's too hot. "You're just trying to get laid," I quip.

"That doesn't make it not true." He winks, reaches over, and squeezes my thigh. He lets to go too soon. "I'm going to get cleaned up.

I'll be right back."

I roll over with an exhausted, sated sigh and stare blankly at the ceiling, wrung out, turned out and greedy for more.

If I couldn't feel my body so acutely, I'd be afraid this was all a dream.

He's perfect. Handsome, thoughtful, curious and maybe…my sexual soul mate. And he's a lawyer from Ghana.

My parents will be thrilled.

I wonder what the job market for journalists is like in LA.

I sit up, horrified. What am I doing? This man just picked me up and made me come like it's what he does for a living.

For all I know, it *is* what he does for a living and I'm over here ready to scribble his name in the margin of my diary.

This is exactly how I ended up with the no-good piece-of-shit man I'm just about to be rid of.

He got me to settle and hold my career back and support his and he didn't even give me orgasms.

What kind of foolery would I find myself in over Kwame?

Sin, girl, you're in danger.

My younger brother's voice is so clear it's like he's in the room with me.

"What have I done?" I crawl off the bed and gather my things, cursing when I can't find my left earring. I drop to all fours near the window, feeling around in the thick area rug.

The shower stops and I freeze. "Shit."

My aunt gave me those earrings. A thud on the other side of the bathroom door makes up my mind for me. "That's what I get for acting like I don't have sense."

My Aunt Agnes, God rest her soul, used to warn me and my sister that good sex was every woman's kryptonite. I've never had sex good enough to understand. Until now. Hell, I didn't even have sex and I'm already imagining what our kids would look like.

My eyes used to be bigger than my stomach.

Figuratively and metaphorically. I've learned the hard way. This is more than I can handle in every sense.

My phone beeps with a text. I slip my shoes on and scribble a note of apology and hurry out of his suite like the hounds of hell are after me.

I nearly weep for joy when the elevator doors close in front of me and I'm certain he's not going to catch up with me.

Eight

Kwame

The Bequest

The crunch of gravel and rumble of the tires drag me from a deep sleep and I wince against the ray of the late afternoon sun pouring through the window. I peer through partially open eyes until my vision comes into focus.

A flare of dread clears the heavy fog of fatigue and I straighten in my seat to stare at the gleaming white and gold gate our car has stopped in front of.

They rise out of the ground like a celestial portal. The bold bullion-gold crest at the center of it, though, is an instant reminder that beyond them is the house that had been my personal hell.

At least I found heaven last night…before she vanished like a thief in the night. I don't know how long she'd been gone when I finally came out of the bathroom, but I'd still been able to smell her on the bed.

I went after her but I had no idea what floor she was on. And it was obvious she didn't want me to find her. So I let it go. It was a better night than I expected and would remain the bright spot of my time in DC.

I know today is what happens when someone dies and has assets to distribute. I understand that my parents come from a matrilineal tribe and I am my mother's natural and legal heir. But it feels wrong to be dividing up her life into pieces when she wasn't done living it.

"It's going to be okay, I'll be right beside you." Next to me, my aunt Alice squeezes my hand. I'd forgotten I wasn't alone.

She's watching me with a frown that forces deep furrows between her brows.

My smile falters. "What's wrong?"

"You tell me." She turns a pointed glance downward and clears her throat.

I follow her gaze to our still linked hands.

I chuckle sheepishly. "You remember."

She strokes my thumb with hers. "Of course I do." Her frown curves up into a smile that is half reproach, half affection. "I may not have given birth to you." She squeezes my hand. "But for as long as you've been able to, you've reached for my hand when you were worried about seeing your dad."

I sigh and relax my hand beneath hers. "I can't pretend I'm happy to be back. This house was never a happy place for me. But I'll be fine."

"I know." She gives my hand a pat and then folds her hands in her lap. "I just wanted to hear you say it."

There's a quick knock on the frosted glass partition in front of us and Alice touches a button above us to open it.

"Do you have the code for the gate or do I need to call up?" Ian, our driver asks when the partition lowers.

There's a couple seconds of silence before I realize Alice is looking at me.

"I don't know the code anymore."

"Of course you do. It's nineteen eighty-seven," she says and then shakes her head. "I can't believe you forgot that when it's the year you were born."

"He never changed it?" I watch the driver punch it in with a skeptical eye.

"Of course not," Alice says, but I don't miss the way her posture relaxes when the gate starts to open. "Your father is a creature of habit. He wanted you to be able to come home whenever you were ready." She pats my leg and casts me a smile.

"Yeah, as long as I agreed to live exactly as he thought I should," I remind her.

Her smile falters.

"Sorry, I know you love him. But you have to understand that he's never even given me that chance."

Alice is my dad's younger sister and has lived with us since I was born. Despite the acrimony between me and her son, Oz, she has always been my soft place to land. But her hero worship of my father clouds her vision and frustrates me.

"Oh, Kwame… Some people just don't know what to do with love. Your mother saw it as a weakness. Your father is scared of it."

"What about me?" I ask before I can think better of it.

"You?" Her hand covers mine and her fingers curl around my knuckles to squeeze the fist I've made. "You're afraid to trust it." She speaks softly but the truth of it echoes through me like a sonic boom.

"It's not your fault," she says before she lets go of my hand.

But it *is* my problem. One I'd like to get over so that I don't end my final days surrounded only by things money can buy. I want to trust it. I want to be trusted.

The car lumbers through the entrance and begins the nearly mile long drive to the main house. I open the window and the breeze rushes in and brushes my skin in warm billows that carry the phantom smells of my youth—fresh cut grass, the bitter green sap mingled with the sweet honey of the blooming cherry blossom trees that line the drive.

Even after it ceased to be the haven it once was, it remained as much a part of me as I am of it.

The green lawns were fertilized by the skin of my knees, my sweat, my tears.

I thought I'd live here one day. Instead, it's a symbol of everything I don't want my life to be—walled off, large and empty.

For most of my life, it was a signal of my father's success and a legacy that I would one day be the steward of. It was sewn into every article of clothing, every piece of luggage, embossed on stationary, the gold flatware, the sheets we slept on at night.

It's a gorgeous spring day and the lavender, germaniums, hyacinth, and roses are putting on a show. But for me, they can't compete with the herbaceous copse of trees that frame the outline of the main house. Native American Beech, White Oak, Red Oak, and the Tulip Poplar that my mother dedicated her time here restoring stand like sentinels on the terrain that only cedes it's rich, rugged run when it comes face to face with the Potomac River.

The house sits fifty yards from its banks and the current becomes audible as we approach the tile-paved circular drive at the front door.

As a boy, the river was my playground. The long-forgotten cabin on the edge of the property that had been my private retreat is the only thing about the house I miss.

The car rolls to a stop under the cream portico that covers the house's main entrance.

The driveway was designed to accommodate thirty cars at a time. On the nights of my father's infamous parties, hundreds of cars streamed through and the army of valets made sure that each guest heard the "Akwaaba" that greeted them as the herald to an evening they would never forget.

Today, six black SUVs are parked ahead of ours and there is no one waiting to greet us.

The driver opens Alice's door first. "I'll be right in," I say, "I just need to make a quick call."

She hesitates for a moment but doesn't push back. "They're starting at one o'clock sharp. I promised your father I'd get you here on time."

"You'll keep your promise. I'll be right in." I turn my attention to my phone until she closes the door. I watch her until she slips inside the front doors.

That's something she wouldn't have done three months ago. This estate operated like a well-oiled machine and my parents didn't have a single security breach or press leaks because of her.

As much as I wish she was still here as the new era of the house's life begins, I'm glad she doesn't work here anymore. She deserves a life dedicated to her own happiness and wishes.

We all do.

I knock on the privacy glass and it comes down again. "You have a minute?" I ask Ian in a playful reproach.

"I thought you were making a call."

"I just said that so we could have a minute."

He meets my eyes in the rearview mirror and the corners crinkle with his familiar smile. "You know your father doesn't like it when we talk to the passengers."

"He's not here. And since when was I a passenger?" He's been driving for my family since I was a kid.

"You became a passenger when you were gone long enough to forget that he's always watching." He nods at the rearview mirror where a green light blinks.

I shake my head and expel a humorless laugh. "What a waste of money and time. I bet he has someone whose sole job it is to watch these. Has he ever caught anyone?"

"I don't know if he's looking to catch anyone so much. More like to make sure he's got receipts if he needs them."

"Yeah, for all the people who are out to get him." We share a smile in the rearview. I glance at my watch. "Better get going, Nice to catch up."

"No problem. Do you want me to go back to the hotel to get your luggage and bring it over?"

"No, I'm not staying here. Could you wait and take me back when I'm done? I have a flight to catch tonight."

His eyes dart to mine in the rearview mirror. "Does your father know that?"

"Not yet."

"What time is your flight?"

"Eight tonight."

He grins. "You're not wasting a second, are you?"

I return his smile. "Nope."

He nods. "I'll wait in the valet lot. Just send me a message when you're ready to leave."

He waits until I've stepped through the threshold before he starts the car and rolls slowly down the drive.

I stand at the front door of the house and wish I still loved it. Wish I could call it home again.

I used to be so proud that my family owned such an important piece of American history. I thought I would raise a family here one day.

Leaving had been like cutting out a piece of my eighteen-year-old heart. Now, I'm sure it was the best thing that happened to me.

The nausea I was sure I'd feel once I got here doesn't come. I search my memories for flashes of that last night but it's like the wind has carried them away. All I hear is the shriek of my mother's laughter and the baritone of my father's voice when he sang Bob Marley at the top of his lungs and me sitting between them watching the river roll by.

I step into the gargantuan foyer of my childhood home and am assailed with memories. It's as opulent as I remember. Gold leaf and marble, crystal and silk adorn nearly every surface of the structure.

My father acts like this house is his magnum opus. But it was my mother's eye for art and knack for myth-building that made The Palms the famed estate it became under their notorious ownership.

As I get further away from the front door, the sound of voices reaches me and some of the trepidation I'd felt all morning comes back.

The last thing I want is to make small talk with the people who abandoned my mother at the end of her life and have come to collect the only thing she was ever worth to them—money.

I grit my teeth and put a rein on my emotions and walk into the lion's den.

My mother's sisters and their partners are already there. I'd been able to avoid speaking with them at her funeral, but there's no avoiding it now. They all hug me and say a variation of words that are meant to make me believe they're sorry they hadn't spent more time with her before she died.

Someone taps lightly on my shoulder and I turn around, rehearsed half smile in place until I see it's Ejos, her personal secretary. Then, it becomes full and real. She'd been here every day in those final months and she had kept a near-constant vigil by my mother's bedside in her final days. My mother told me it was her who convinced her to tell me she was dying. I feel like I owe her so much. "It's nice to see you."

She gives me a tremulous smile in return. "I'm so sorry for our loss. She was my mother too. I miss her so much." She dabs at her large brown eyes. "I hope you will stay in touch. I'll give you my number in Accra."

I nod but lift a brow in surprise. "I thought you'd go back to Port Harcourt now."

"I met someone." She bites her lip to try and hide her smile but her eyes light up and give her away.

"Eiii, I see." I grab her left hand and lift it playfully to my face as if for inspection. "Where's your ring? Don't tell me you're living in sin," I tease, and she lets her smile free.

"You are old-fashioned, brother Kwame." She gives my hand a squeeze before she lets go.

"Didn't my mother teach you better than to tear up the roots of your life for a man who isn't ready to let you plant them in his soil?"

She throws her head back in a delighted laugh. "Oh, my word, you sound like her." She presses a hand to her chest and looks up the ceiling. "God blessed me when she came into my life."

"Thank you for taking such good care of her." I offer her a genuine smile. I'm glad my mother had someone who loved her by her side.

"There he is." My father's voice fills the space left by the hushed voices and I turn around to face him. He strides into the room like he's stepping onto a stage and all eyes are on him.

People are always surprised to discover that he's shorter than average the first time they meet him.

There is nothing small about his presence from his colorful three-piece suits to his ever-present walking stick, to his penchant for speaking in Latin, he is entertaining, even when no one asked him to be.

"Son, as sad as I am to lose your dear mother, I'm so glad it's convinced you to finally come back into the family fold. Thank you for stepping up. I need you."

I want to ask him what family he's talking about, but I promised my mother I would try. "I'll do my best. Once I get back from LA."

"I know you will." His excited smile makes me queasy. "Ah, there's the lawyer, now." He turns and makes for the door, his laser focus on the man who my mother entrusted with her final wishes.

"Excuse me, it's time to start," the lawyer calls out moving to the front of the room and taking a seat before my father can corner him. "Mrs. Palmer left strict instructions for today, and I'd like to stay on schedule."

We sit around the large oval table. Between us, a stack of papers that hold my mother's final words and wishes.

The man lifts a small remote and the lights dim, the curtains draw shut, and a large screen descends from the ceiling.

It flickers to life and a still image of my mother, sitting behind her desk fills it. My throat tightens at the sight of her smiling, healthy, alert.

The room is quiet as she starts talking.

"My dear ones. Thank you for indulging me and being here today. It's strange to record this knowing it will be played when I am gone, but I wanted to make sure everyone can see that I am of sound mind and spirit as I make these bequests."

I glance at my father, curious at whether or not this is a surprise to him. He's watching the screen, unblinking, and for the first time in my life, I feel sorry for him. For all his faults, he loved her and respected her.

"You're all here to learn what I've left you, and I will do that shortly. But if you'll allow me to give you some context first, I'd be grateful. I was married to AP for ten years before his investment in the oil fields off the Gulf of Guinea made him a billionaire overnight. Except it hadn't been overnight. It was the product of years of work, sacrifice, and living on nothing but faith. The investment had been very risky. We put our life savings into it and it took more than a decade to bear fruit. You all know my parents didn't approve of our marriage."

One of her sisters clears her throat and earns a scathing glare from my father.

It's true, though. His story had been one of rags to riches. My mother came from a family of lawyers, doctors, and scholars.

"They cut me off when I got pregnant with Kwame in my second year at Legon. I left school to devote my life to my family and was the unpaid director of operations, marketing, and accounting for my husband's growing environmental engineering firm. After the oil discovery and our permanent move to America, I knew I had to secure my future because there were no safety nets for stay-at-home mothers in this country. I had a post-nuptial agreement drafted that recognized and compensated me for my contributions to any wealth my husband might amass over the course of our marriage. Man that he is, he signed it happily. Today's portfolio review revealed I became a billionaire in my own right a few months ago."

"Wow," someone to my right says.

I had no idea about this. I came here expecting her to bequeath things like property and jewelry and maybe a life insurance policy.

"I've lived a wonderful life. I've lived a tragic life. I've lived a thousand lives. And now, I'm ready to lay down and leave the living to all of you. If you're watching this, I loved you and want my life to be a credit to you. I hope you will live well, give generously, and forgive easily. And to my son, I'm sorry I didn't make it easy for you to come home. I hope by the time I leave this Earth you'll feel like being part of us again. I love you."

The combination of guilt and regret coursing through me is nauseating. I wish she'd said these words a lifetime ago. I wish I'd learned how to forgive sooner.

The screen flickers off, the curtains open, and the lights come back on.

The room is quiet as the lawyer reads the bequests.

She left five million dollars to each of her sisters. Half that amount for each of their children.

Ejos was given ten million dollars and guaranteed her salary for the rest of her life. One of her sisters sucks her teeth loudly at this.

She made gifts to her favorite museums and artists, animal rescues, and universities, hospitals, churches, all around the world.

To my father she left jewelry, personal effects, and her house near the beach in Cape Coast in Ghana.

The rest, more than half of her entire estate, she left to me. It includes her house in Georgetown, her penthouse apartment in Accra, her townhouse in London, her flat in Paris, and a beach house in Carmel. A trust that would start paying me an annual income of around twenty-five million dollars. It would pay me a prorated amount for the current year of seventeen million dollars. Her investment portfolio was where the bulk of her money was held and that, too, was left entirely to me.

"Kwame, your mother left you a key to her safe deposit box. You are to visit within the month."

The man hands me an envelope with my name written on it in my mother's handwriting.

I fold it in half and tuck into my jacket inside pocket and the tips of my fingers brush the earring I found when I was packing this morning and there's a momentary break in the clouds around my heart.

"That concludes the reading. Are there any questions?"

My Aunt Charlotte raises her hand. "You mentioned that we could be reimbursed for our travel here? I came all the way from London." She squeezes her face like it's been a hardship.

"Are you serious, Lotte?" my father hisses.

"It's fine," the lawyer interjects with a polite, patient smile. "Mrs. Palmer recognized the irregularity of asking everyone to gather here in person. She created a budget to cover the costs any of you incurred."

My mother was the youngest of four girls and despite her parents' initial rejection of her and my father, she forgave them when they asked her to. She worked hard to rebuild her relationship with her siblings. Which turned into her being their emergency fund. I never understood how she didn't mind the way they blatantly used her. I can't wait for them to leave and go back to ignoring us.

Like he read my mind, my father stands abruptly and claps his hands and walks over to the lawyer. "Thank you for facilitating. Some-one will see you out." He nods at the door.

When the lawyer is gone, he turns to face the sisters and their families. "My darling wife was overly generous with you. I would advise you to invest your windfalls wisely. Because if your last name is Dickson, that is the very last dime you will ever get from someone with the last name Palmer."

Charlotte steps forward, eyes blazing.

My father rolls his eyes as if he's bored. "She left with me because she knew if she stayed she'd end up just like you. Poor, insignificant, and dependent. I wasn't a perfect husband, but I gave her the world."

She scoffs. "And made her a prisoner. We will be suing the estate *and* letting the press know what kind of man you are. It's time people knew. They think the worst thing you did was support a politician who turned out to be a wanna-be dictator. Wait till I tell them everything I know about you, Aloysius Palmer." She taunts him with his full name.

His jaw twitches with irritation. "You don't know anything about me."

"I know you flaunted your affairs in my sister's face and drove her to an early grave." Charlotte steps up to my father and points her finger in his face.

My stomach drops and for the first time I'm glad my mother isn't here.

His eyes narrow to slits and he swats her finger like it's a tennis ball.

"Heh!" she yelps and cradles her finger like he hurt her. "Is that what you did to my sister, too? You disgraceful man." She hurls the vitriol and her children take a step back from her.

His face turns to stone. "I loved your sister. I won't even countenance your made-up fantasies about me. But if any of you even *think* of talking to the press about me or your sister, I will take that money she gave you and whatever else you have and set it on fire while you watch."

He turns his full attention to Charlotte and she shrinks back. "And then I'll find someone to cut out that lizard tongue of yours."

"I would like to see you try," she hisses back, and I have to admire her bravery. No one stands up to my dad this way.

"No, you wouldn't. Would she, Roger?" He poses the question to her husband with a smile as lethal as a machete

"No, we won't. Shut up, Lotte." Her husband stares at the ground.

"She's not speaking for us," my Aunt Charity pipes up.

Charlotte clutches her throat and stares hard at the balding crown of her husband's head. He doesn't look up from the ground. My aunt's shoulder's sag. "Fine."

"Now, everyone get out. I need to speak to my son alone." My father speaks in a voice that's as cheerful as a flight attendant welcoming passengers aboard. They hurry out of the room without another word.

"Useless people," he mutters and sits in the chair next to me, grimacing. "I don't know how your mother turned out so differently."

"She met you," I say. "At least that's how she tells it."

"I had nothing to do with that woman's greatness. She was born to a struggling engineering student and his functionally illiterate wife and by the time I met her, she was supporting all of them." He smiles to himself. "Look what she did in just one lifetime. She should still be here."

I nod and exhale against the sharp stab of grief. She should be. She was just starting to live when she found out she was dying.

"So, what are you going to do now that you've got money?" My father's question snaps me back to the present.

"What do you mean?"

He leans back in his chair and crosses an ankle over his knee.

"I mean, you don't have to work for anybody. You can afford to buy your way onto any board, even a federal office."

I let disdain show on my face. "Why would I want to do that?"

He mirrors my expression. "Why wouldn't you? Did you *like* needing to ask for time off so you can visit your dying mother? You enjoy working hard to implement someone else's agenda?"

I bristle at the dig. "I'm a prosecutor for the state of California, so yes. I know you've never understood it, but I like the fact that I've earned everything I have myself."

He curls his lip. "I understand being a young man with something to prove. I'll never understand why you felt like you had to do it all on your own."

I open my mouth to remind him that he didn't give me a choice.

He holds a hand up. "That's all in the past now, Son. You've just inherited a lot of money that you didn't earn. Whether you like it or not," he adds with a grim smile. "Don't let your self-righteous bleeding-heart ideals stop you from making the most of it."

"You think buying my way onto the board is how I do that?" I look at him askance.

He sighs. "Enough of this. You didn't want to be the trust fund kid or be accused of nepotism. Fine. You've proven that you can make it on your own. But I didn't work hard so that my son could be a public servant in America."

The flash of memory from my conversation with Sin where I'd mimicked him saying these words makes me laugh.

He slaps the table. "It's not funny."

"I know." I sober. "Listen, I need time to let this all settle. I've got a job and life to get back to in LA." I grab my phone to check the time.

"Read your mother's letter before you decide anything."

"Decide what?" I look up at him and my stomach drops. I know the expression on his face well. It's his "I'm going to enjoy watching this" face.

I have a sick feeling that I'm not going to make my flight after all.

Nine

Kwame

The Request

Three hours later, I stumble into my hotel room at The Salamander. I canceled my flight but drew the line at staying at The Palms.

Finally alone, I read my mother's letter.

My darling Kwame,

There's a saying that "A man never steps in the same river twice. For he is not the same man, and it is not the same river."

I knew, when I asked you to come back to The Palms for the reading, it was asking you to come to a place you only associate with disappointment and pain.

I hope, now that you are here you remember the good things, too.

The money I left you is more than a fortune.

It's my legacy.

It will also be yours.

To whom much is given, much is expected. So I am going to ask you to do three things for me. None of them are easy and all of them will require some sacrifice.

The money is yours whether you heed my wishes or not.

My hope is that in carrying them out, you finally understand what it truly means to be a Palmer.

First, I want you to move back to DC and work for the firm your father founded for a minimum of a year. If it's not what you want, you have my blessing to go back to the life you've chosen in California.

Secondly, if you can't move back to The Palms, I'd like you to make the house I left you your home.

Your father is going to need the support of his son as he grieves my loss. Please be there for him. Even if he doesn't deserve it.

Third, I want you to keep what you find in the safe deposit box to yourself. Your father, especially, must not know. Hand deliver the package to the family without opening it. And if they invite you, stay for dinner. They have a daughter I think you'll like.

I love you. I'm sorry I didn't say it more often and that I didn't try harder to bring you home.

Live a life that lets you sleep well at night. Use your wealth to make a difference.

Love,
Mummy

Three Months Later

Arlington, VA

Ten

Sin

Slippery

"When did you become such a dark horse?" My mother's question is like a clap of thunder that comes right before rain clouds move in and block out the sun.

I didn't see it coming. I'd been nursing a pot of lamb stew and listening to one of the three audiobooks I had on rotation.

"A dark horse?" I keep my voice conversational and my eyes on the pot of simmering stew I'm stirring and savor the last few moments of the peace I brokered with white lies.

"Don't play coy with me." The reproach is accompanied by a smack on the back of my arm.

I scowl at her. In my head, of course.

I may keep secrets from my mother like it's my job but being disrespectful to her face? That's rebelling a little too close to the sun for even me. "I'm not playing coy. I don't know what you mean. I'm just making my mom's favorite stew." I keep my gaze trained on the stove while my mind spins with the half dozen things I've kept from her and which one she's likely to have guessed.

"Your sister told us everything. We are *very* disappointed. To say the least."

I close my eyes briefly and swallow my groan of irritation. I should have known. "I'm sorry, Mom." I apologize despite not knowing which one of my sins I'm taking responsibility for.

"We need you to join us in your father's study. Now." She adds that last part with a wide-eyed look of challenge before she leaves the kitchen without another word. I'm almost forty years old, financially independent, with full agency over my life and I don't want to have this conversation with my parents or anyone. But none of that overrides the fact that I am their daughter and that in this house, their word is law.

I turn the fire off because if I burn this stew, it will add insult to injury.

I pushed a lot of their boundaries in my young adult years but always colored inside the lines. They wanted me to study medicine. I chose to double major in English and History, but I did it at Princeton so they still had plenty to brag about in the letters they sent to family back home.

When I decided to forgo grad school altogether and took a job as a staff writer, I chose the most prestigious newspaper to work for. One that conferred credibility and meant success.

They'd been skeptical about my recent career move and what my return to DC would mean for the rest of my life in New York, and I wasn't ready to have that conversation with them.

I've only been at *The Spectator* for three months and was hoping I'd have more time to figure out how I felt about my new life before I told them everything.

My sister is sitting at the foot of the stairs when I walk past them on my way to the study where my judge and jury are waiting.

She reaches for my hand and draws me to a stop.

I yank my hand away and glare at her. "You're on my shit list, Mae," I whisper, furiously.

"I'm sorry, Sin. I didn't mean to tell her. It just slipped out. I don't know why you told me anyway. You *know* I can't keep a secret. Don't be mad at me, please?" She pleads with those puppy-dog eyes that get her out of everything and I sigh. "Just tell me what they know," I say in a low voice.

Not that it matters. Whether she told them one of my secrets or all, my parents are going to have a lot to say.

She blinks up at me, her eyes sorrowful as if she's the one in trouble. "It was just what you told me that night I found you crying in the bathroom," she whispers.

"I told you a lot of things that night. Be specific," I snap.

Her brows furrow and her eyes move away. "Let's see, you told me you and Stephen broke up." She flinches at my glare.

"I'm sorry, Sin." She grabs my hand again and squeezes it when I try to pull away. "She was grilling me about something two minutes after I woke up. I was confused, and it slipped out. I didn't tell her you said you're never getting back together because you'd rather be alone than settle for less. Also, you're not sorry that you're a cheater because that man made you come six times, and Stephen never could," she says, her eyes growing wider with each word as if she was shocked to hear herself speaking them.

I close my eyes. "I told you all of *that*?" I swear off alcohol in that very moment. It makes me do stupid things.

"Yeah. I don't judge you or—"

"Arsinoé Sackey, we are waiting," my mother's voice booms down the hall.

"I'm so sorry," she repeats, pleading eyes wide.

I roll my eyes.

"Come on, you *know* what she's like when she puts on her inquisitor's hat," she adds.

I pat her shoulder and smother my irritation. "It's not your fault." We called my sister okra-mouth growing up because when it came to secrets, her lips are as slippery as the infamously slimy vegetable.

This is a family where secrets go to die and I knew that once I was back home, it was only a matter of time before they'd know everything.

I knock on the door out of courtesy before I push it open and step into the cozy room. I can't help but check the shelves for books that weren't there a week ago. I love this room. It's where I felt happiest when I was growing up in this house. My father is as voracious a reader as I am and his study was my personal library.

I had what my mother called an "unnatural" curiosity and asked questions until I had an answer that made sense.

My father was the only person who didn't seem annoyed by it. He bought books he thought would feed my thirst for stories and answers. This room was where we spent hours talking about any and everything.

It is also where they bring me when I've earned a talking to.

Growing up, I gave them plenty of occasion for that. But since I turned eighteen and came close enough to disaster to taste it, I've been the model oldest daughter. I've given them reasons to be proud and my siblings inspiration. Until now.

"So, you and Stephen have broken up," my mother says as soon as I sit down.

"Yes." I nod and cross my legs and fold my hands in my lap and keep my face somber and my eyes contrite. "I'm sorry I didn't tell you. I didn't know how to."

"He told us he was ring shopping. He asked your father for permission to ask you to marry him. What happened?" my mother asks.

I look at her. "What do you mean? When did he do that?"

"Just last week. He said he was going to surprise you."

Disgusted and shocked, I suppress the urge to curse. "I wish he had talked to me before he told you that. It would have saved us all a lot of heartache. It's over, and he knows it." I'd rehearsed this answer and I cringe at how lacking in warmth my delivery is.

"But why didn't *you* tell us things were over? Estelle didn't know either."

I flinch at the mention of my ex's mother. "You told her?"

"Of course I did," she says indignant and reproachful at once. "Just because *you* can keep things from people who have a right to know doesn't mean we all have to do the same."

"I'm sorry. I was going to tell you. Just not yet. I mean…until I was sure it was really over."

"Oh, thank God," my mother clutches her lapels and blows a kiss skyward. "So it's not over."

I raise a hand waving in disagreement. "No, no it is. We weren't made to last. He's a great—"

My mother groans loudly and I dart a glance to my father. He shrugs and frowns as if he's helpless to do anything to stop the dramatics she's about to perform.

"Mama. I am sorry. I didn't tell you because I knew you would be upset. He's not great. And he's not faithful."

"Okay. And?"

"What do you mean, *and*?" I look at my father. Accusation turns my voice sharp. "What does she mean?" I demand.

He holds his hands up. "Don't look at me. I love my wife and my peace of mind too much to be stupid."

My mother pets his knee and they share a smile before she turns back to me. "It happens. And at your age, you should be glad that he didn't leave you for her. Try to forgive him."

I look at my mother askance. "I know it doesn't make sense to you, but he wasn't a prize. That man doesn't know how to cook, or clean."

"Why should he? When you do? You sound like an American."

"I *am* American," I remind her.

"Only by passport. We raised you with the values from home."

I sigh. "Mom, I need you to get comfortable with the idea of me not getting married."

"Okay, well if you don't want to marry anyone, then I have plenty of young men who need someone to marry for papers. At least you can help someone even as you break your mother's heart."

"Mom, I am not going to marry someone just for papers. First, it's illegal, and second, it's illegal."

"Hmm, you never know…you could meet your forever man."

I recoil in disgust. "Do you hear yourself?"

"Do you?" she retorts.

"I don't *need* a husband. Why would I sacrifice my autonomy just so I can satisfy an outdated norm that was only ever there to benefit men?"

She looks at my father in exasperation. "Our American daughter says marriage is outdated."

He throws his hands up toward the sky. "Where did I go wrong?"

I sigh in long suffering weariness. "If you wanted a Ghanaian daughter, you should have raised me there."

My parents have lived in this country for almost forty years, but their hearts, minds, and social circles remained on the other side of the world.

At home we watched CNN International, listened to high life, ate rice and stew every day, and every summer we had a house packed with visiting relatives who stayed for months at a time. And we almost always had a cousin living with us while they went to school. My parents both went to boarding school, prized education above everything, and didn't allow us to do anything they deemed "too American." So dating, straightening our hair, calling any adult by their first name, and spending the night anywhere but under their roof were all forbidden.

They ran our house the way their boarding schools had been run. But outside of the doors of their house, we lived what felt like an aggressively American life. Except for the weekends. We spent weekends attending functions and had more aunties and uncles than my American friends could comprehend. We shopped at African and Asian food markets, cooked and ate like they do at home—outside and with our hands.

When I was ten years old, they moved us from the diverse Silver Spring area to one of the whitest neighborhoods in northern Virginia where my father's new job teaching history at Georgetown Prep came with scholarships for his children.

It was a great privilege but isolating in its lack of diversity. It was good in that it prepared me for a life of code switching that has become second nature to me now.

I have three different accents depending on which one of the cultures I straddle is claiming the moment. It wasn't until I got to New York that I realized how wrong I'd been to think of my identity as something fractured. I'm Ghanaian-American and Black and first gen and the child of immigrants. Instead of treating them as competing narratives, I'm learning to hold space for all of those at once.

Their doorbell's ridiculously loud chime snaps us all out of our thoughts. "Oh no. He's here. Thanks to you, I'm not ready. Let me go and get the door." She stands up and sucks her teeth as she walks past me.

"As if I'm the one who demanded we have a meeting right now," I mutter as soon as she's out of earshot.

My father tuts in disapproval. "You make problems bigger for yourself when you try to hide them," my father says in that nonjudgemental tone that makes me wish I was the daughter they wanted.

"Wasn't trying to hide anything. You were already not happy that I was joining *The Spectator.*"

"Sin, at the very best it's a lateral move at a time when you should be leveling up."

I bristle at that. "I'm *pivoting*, Dad. And I'm still making good money."

"Is that the only thing that matters?"

"Dad, it's a job. Getting paid is the only reason any of us have one. I don't want to be defined by it anymore. I'm sorry if it's disappointing to you. I want so badly to make you proud. But I couldn't keep living a lie just so you and Mom have something to brag about at the next wedding or outdooring you attend."

"Oh. Is that what you think we care about?"

"I mean…what else could I think when you both call my step in the right direction a step down? Maybe you're right and I'll regret it, but I want to know what it feels like to taste regret that comes from the back of my *own* throat." My voice cracks and I touch my neck.

"Sin, we sacrificed so you wouldn't have to. We've lived the American dream. We want you to do even better."

"Dad, what if that's not my dream?"

"Who doesn't want stability?"

"I don't think what I want is incompatible with stability."

"Well, first thing you did was end your long-term relationship and leave your long-term job so, maybe."

"Dad, I want to see what I'm really made of. To find my own way. To define what *my* dreams look like." I'm breathing hard when I'm done.

Speaking those words aloud makes my heart race. It took me twenty years to learn that owning my life, my mistakes, my triumphs is what makes me most alive.

My dad gets to his feet and places a hand on my shoulder.

"This is the hottest July I can remember here." He looks out of the huge bay window behind me and wipes the corners of his eyes.

My father is so rarely emotional that I'm completely disarmed by it. "Daddy, are you okay?"

I cover his hand with mine, and he looks down at me with a fond smile that reaches all the way to his eyes. "I was afraid that this weather would be too much for you after a decade living in colder climes. I see I was worried for nothing. You're stronger than I gave you credit for. I'm very proud of you, Sin."

My relief is boundless. I may want to blaze my own trail, but I never want my parents to feel dishonored by anything I do.

"Thank you, Daddy. Can you tell your wife that?"

He barks out a laugh and shakes his head. "Absolutely not. It won't change anything. You'll do what you want, and she'll feel how she feels. You'll butt heads and then find your common ground." He puts an arm around me and steers me to the door. "All we want is for you to live a good life. One that you are proud of. We came here not so you could go to Princeton, but so you'd have the choice. In all things. Now, let's go greet our guest."

"Who is it? She said it would just be us."

"The son of our landlord."

"She has a son?" I ask with a confounded expression.

"Yes. We didn't know until her lawyer called to tell us that she passed away."

"She died? Oh no. Is everything okay?" I pause, worried. They've lived in this house since I was a child and even though they don't own it, I know they see it as their home.

"We hope so. He asked to come by and deliver something on his mother's behalf. Your mother invited him to join us for lunch."

I can hear the deep rumble of a man's voice next to my mom's and I reflexively look in the mirror.

Not that it matters because I'm closed for business when it comes to men, but I'll never hear the end of it if I meet one of my mother's guests looking less than presentable.

I walk out arm in arm with my father, smiling and reassured that the rest of my secrets are safely tucked away.

"Arsinoé, this is Kwame. Kwame, this is our eldest daughter."

In the month since that night at The Salamander, I was certain that my memories were exaggerating how handsome the man I'd met that night had been. I was also certain I'd never see him again.

I was wrong.

About everything.

Fuck.

Eleven

Kwame

No Agenda

It's been the most awkward afternoon of my life.

Despite not saying more than a few stilted words in greeting, Sin and I seemed to come to a mutual decision to pretend we're total strangers.

For my part it was shock that kept me from asking what the hell she was doing there when I first saw her.

I glance at her as stealthily as I can manage, and the fact that she's sitting there takes my breath away.

"Kwame, I don't know if I told you that Arsinoé used to live in New York," my hostess says, and I whip my head in her direction to see if she saw me staring at her daughter.

Her conspiratorial smile tells me she did.

"You mentioned that, yes." I resist the urge to shift in my seat and put my fork down gently. I look at Mae and pretend to be confused. "Are you Arsinoé?"

"No, she is," Mrs. Sackey points at Sin.

"Oh, sorry. Promise I won't forget again." I smile and look at Sin with feigned contemplation. "Let me see, you're a journalist, just relocated from New York, and you have an almost fiancé?" I recite the list of facts her mother shared about her oldest daughter almost as soon as I got here.

Her eyes dart to my face and then away again. "We broke up," Sin says quickly and then takes a big gulp of water.

"Stop saying that," her mother snaps. "You'll make it true."

"Ma, it's already true." She speaks with the weariness of someone who's tired of repeating themselves.

"For now. You were together a long time."

"Too long," she mutters.

Her mother casts her an irritated glance before she smiles at me again. "Kwame, you're single, right? So is Mae." She looks at her other daughter who has been preoccupied with her phone all evening.

"Ma," Mae cries, finally looking up from her phone with horror in her eyes. "Ignore her," she says to me, before she glares at her mother.

"Why should he ignore me?"

"I'm not interested," Mae says. "No offense. You're very, very handsome," she says with a bright smile. "And how do you even know he's single, Ma?"

"Well?" Mrs. Sackey turns her head to me. "Are you?"

"Is this a swap meet or Sunday dinner?" Sin snaps.

"It's complicated."

I take some satisfaction from the way Sin's mouth puckers like she sucked a lemon. But it doesn't last long. She's the complication and this unexpected connection makes it even more so. Her mother introduced me as Kwame Dixon, and I didn't correct her because it was my mother's maiden name and the legal name on all the documents related to the house. Also, I avoided telling people who my father was if I didn't have to.

"Why are you not married? You're almost forty, right?" Her mother's beseeching tone would be funny if she wasn't so serious.

I finish chewing my last bite of chicken and try to think of an answer that's honest without saying too much. "It hasn't been a priority. My career has been my focus the last twenty years."

"Those careers aren't going to love you when life is hard, oh!" She wags a finger at her daughter.

"My friends will, and my siblings will do that," Sin says with a straight face.

Her mother claps her hands together like she's trapping a mosquito. "They are all going to be married with families and won't have time to spend going out or whatever it is you do with your time."

"They aren't all married," Sin says. "In fact, all of the siblings are single."

"They're young. They have time." Her eyes convey a silent "unlike you." "Your best friend has two children already."

"You had Adonis when you were forty," Sin says.

"And look at how I'm paying for it now," she shoots back.

"Thanks," her brother frowns.

"I've decided to have a baby." Her sister's announcement is like someone pressing mute on the conversations in the room. They all stop instantly, and all eyes go to Mae.

I feel like I should leave but the tension in the room is so heavy that I feel riveted in place.

"What do you mean?" Their mother breaks the silence.

"I mean, I'm ready to be a mother."

"How? You don't even have a boyfriend," their mother snaps.

"Mom, come on," Sin interjects.

"Come on what?" She swivels her head to look at her daughter. "How can she have a baby without a man?"

"I am going to do it by myself."

"God forbid." Their mother slaps the table and shoots to her feet and grabs her husband's shoulder. "George, why are you not saying any-thing?"

He looks like he's been caught in a sniper's cross hairs. "Because… there is nothing to say. What can we say?"

Mrs. Sackey looks back at her daughter. "She's our child."

"No, I'm an adult," her sister says.

"This is your fault." The older woman rounds on Sin, hand ex-tended and pointing in accusation.

Sin's eyes widen. "How is this my fault?"

"It's not her fault, Mama. It's nobody's fault," Salomé pushes back.

Mrs. Sackey points a finger between the sisters. "She has set an example and now you're following."

"I'm not following anything."

"Ma, Mae is a grown-up." Sin and her sister speak at the same time.

My head moves back and forth between them like I'm watching a tennis match. "So your sister has shown you how to keep secrets, eh Salomé ? Sin, do you see what happens when you behave the way you do? I've told you."

Sin drops her head into her hands during her mother's tirade and I suspect she's laughing.

"I wasn't keeping it a secret. I just hadn't told you yet because it's early. But I want a baby, and I've found a sperm donor already."

Sin coughs and sprays the table with a mist of water she'd been sipping. We all turn to look at her. She holds up a hand and croaks. "Something went down the wrong way." Her mother reaches over absently and pats her daughter's back with a tenderness that is contrary to her anger a minute ago.

I realize I've been holding my breath waiting for the fight to go from an argument to explosive.

But...no one's saying terrible things to each other. They haven't asked me to leave while they discuss this in private.

I understand now why she's so effortlessly expressive and direct.

The clatter of cutlery hitting the table draws my attention back to the fracas building on the other end of the table.

"You can forget that nonsense. I will find you a nice man."

Mae is on her feet now, and her sister is standing beside her, arms still around her shoulder.

"You are not in charge of my life anymore," Mae says to her mother.

She turns to her husband her eyes blazing. "I told you we should have sent them to boarding school in Ghana." Her mother speaks in Twi.

"As if girls who go to boarding school in Ghana don't get pregnant before they get married," her father responds.

"You aren't helping, George."

"Neither are you. And we have a guest."

"Ma, Daddy, speak English," Sin snaps.

Her mother looks at me. "Why? I'm in my own house. And I don't want the landlord to hear how shameful my wayward daughters are. He won't want to marry Mae if he thinks she's a harlot."

I burst into laughter and all eyes swivel in my direction. "Actually, I do understand," I say.

Mrs. Sackey's mouth gapes like a fish before she presses her lips together.

"Ha!" Sin shouts and then covers her mouth to stifle her victory yell when her mother glares at her.

"I didn't realize. I hope you're not a gossip."

"My mother is dead, and I wouldn't tell my father if I met Jesus himself much less whatever I hear at your dining table."

"So do you not socialize with any Ghanaians? At all?"

I register the disapproval in her question but let it roll off my back.

"No. Somehow, I've got friends from all over. Just none from Ghana."

"Why is that?"

"Maybe because it's exhausting having to answer questions like this," Sin interjects and for a moment, we share a smile.

"It's okay, Sin."

Her mother's head whips in her direction. "Is that what you told him to call you?"

I realize my blunder.

"Yes."

"Why?"

"Because that's what I like to be called," Sin pushes back.

"God, how is this my portion?" Her mother lifts her eyes heavenward, her palms pressed together. I bite my cheek to stifle my laugh at her dramatics.

"You want us to live your way more than you want us to be happy," Mae says with tears in her eyes.

"Of course I don't. I just know what's best for you."

I feel like I'm watching a replay of a conversation with my father and my gut tightens in anticipation of the insults and raised voices that always follow.

Mae shakes her head. "You *think* you do. But I'm an adult. I know what I want."

"Are you sure that's what you want?" It's her father who asks the question, but in my head, I hear my father's voice speaking the words and I want to tell Mae it's a trap and that she shouldn't answer.

"Yes. I don't want to be alone. I want a family." Salomé's honest, clear-eyed response makes my heart kick in my chest.

Sin sighs. "You *have* a family and you're not alone, Mae."

"You were gone for a long time, Sin."

"I know. I wish you'd left, too."

Her sister's eyes fill with tears. "And *I* wish you could accept that this life is what I want."

Sin looks pained and closes her eyes briefly before she answers her sister. "I love you and want you to be happy." She takes a deep breath and stands abruptly. "Okay, enough. We're not going to resolve this tonight." She points to her parents. "You two, *60 Minutes* is about to start." She swivels to face her sister.

"Mae, put the pies in the oven to heat up. We're out of ice cream. I'm going to the store for more."

Her younger brother, Adonis, pulls his headphones down to ring his neck. "What about me?" he asks.

"You can clear the table and help Mae with the dishes until I get back."

"Sorry I asked," he mutters and puts his music back on.

Sin laughs. "I keep telling you not to ask questions unless you're sure you want an answer."

"Whatever," he grumbles but gets up and starts piling plates.

Just like that, the argument that had been brewing, the bombs that had been dropped had all been dealt with for now, and the family was moving on for the evening. I'm not holding my breath, poised for something calamitous to happen next.

I didn't know conflict resolution could be sexy until just now. I just watched a master at work. I didn't expect it from the woman who ran out on me rather than tell me she'd changed her mind.

In the weeks since our encounter I've fantasized about seeing her again, but I was content to live with the fantasy.

I know how hard it is to draw me out, last thing I need is a woman who can't speak her mind.

In the last month, I've been navigating this unexpected diversion in my life and career and it feels like walking down a dark road to an unknown destination.

My mother's letter is a gun at my back.

The last thing I needed was a woman like Sin.

Chaotic.

Impulsive

Unreliable.

Every time I thought of her, I reassured myself that I dodged a bullet when she ran out on me.

And yet, even when I thought she was still in New York, I haven't gone a day in DC without looking for her in every public space I enter.

In the span of an afternoon, my mother's letter has gone from gun at my back to a trail of breadcrumbs.

Maybe she knew me better than I thought.

My vision blurs, and I blink and tears spill from my eyes. What the hell? I don't cry.

I touch my face and then stare in amazement at my damp fingers. *What the fuck is happening?*

"Where's the bathroom?" I ask no one in particular as I head for the hallway before I know where to go.

Her mother calls after me. "Turn left. It's the only door on the right."

I step into the floral wallpapered bathroom, start to unzip my pants then stop to lock the door.

They seem like the kind of people who don't knock first and the thought makes me grin. This is the kind of family I always wish I had but thought I never would.

They're so easy and authentic. For the first time in a long time, I'm grateful to my father for the distance he put between me and the rest of the West African community in DC. They have no agenda other than to welcome their landlord's son. My guard came down without me realizing it. They treat me like they've known me for my whole life when, in fact, they don't know me at all.

I pull out my mother's letter and read it again.

I'd been apprehensive when she extended the invitation for me to join them.

As I wash my hands, I'm glad I came and glad I accepted her invitation to come back.

I step out of the bathroom and find Sin sitting at the foot of the stairs tying her laces. That feeling of being glad swells. When our eyes meet, I smile.

Hers narrow and hold mine with an assessing, stony glare.

I'm not sure why the woman who did a sexual eat and run is pissed at *me*. I smile at her. She scowls and looks down at her watch. "The store closes early on Sunday. Let's go."

Before I can replay, she shouts, "Kwame and I are headed out. Anyone want something?"

"Get me some gum. Orbitz sweet mint, please," her sister says as she walks into the kitchen.

"Text me that. Anything else?" Sin calls out to the room.

"No. Drive safe. Love you." Her mother waves at us and sits down next to her husband and puts her mouth next to his ear to whisper something that makes him grin and wag a finger at her.

"Ready?" She smiles this time, but her eyes are hard and direct.

It's not a question. She doesn't wait for me to reply before she walks out the front door.

"Sure."

At this point in my life, the only person who can tell me what to do is my dad, and even then, only when he has leverage. But I follow Sin out like the general commanded me himself.

"Your family is great," I say when we're outside.

She stops and turns around to face me. "Okay, cut the shit. What the hell are you doing here?"

Twelve

Sin

Pipe Dreams

I've been waiting for this since I laid eyes on him tonight. I thought I would burst.

"Well, what do you really want?" I repeat when he doesn't answer.

"What do you mean?" He holds his hands up in the air.

"I *mean*, what are you doing here?" I enunciate each word.

He squares his shoulders and his jaw. "I came to see your parents. My mother was their landlord. She asked me to personally deliver something to them."

"So where is it?" I demand.

"Where is what?" He blinks at my rapid-fire questioning.

I snap my fingers impatiently. "Whatever you came to deliver. Where is it?"

"I gave it to your mom when I arrived. She said they'd open it later."

I cross my arms over my chest. "So, they're not being evicted?" I press, desperate for that assurance.

"Of course not. I wouldn't have sat down to eat with them if that was the case." He's speaking like he's talking to a hostage taker.

I force myself to relax my guard. He's not dangerous. At least not in any obvious way. I look at him with exaggerated suspicion on my face. "So you *really* had no idea I would be here or who I was when we met in

April?" I press.

"How could I have? Believe me, I was just as surprised to see you as you were to see me." His dark eyes are somber and his gaze is direct. He's right, how could he have known?

"Look at me sounding like you," I quip and he's gracious enough to smile.

"But this is a lot of coincidence. What are the chances?"

He slips his hands into his pockets and rocks back on his heels a little, still smiling. "They're slim. But hey, I'm not complaining. I'm glad to see you. Knew I would somehow."

"No you didn't." I roll my eyes.

He scoffs and reaches into the back pocket of his jeans and pulls out his wallet. "I've been carrying this in my wallet so that *when* it happened, I could return it to you."

He fishes out the small gold earring I lost that night and holds it out to me. My eyes mist and I take it out of his palm and put it on. I reach into my small purse and pull out its partner. "Wow. I'd resigned myself to it being lost forever. Thank you so much."

"Sure. I'm glad I got to give it back. But more than that—we've got some unfinished business." His voice is gruff, and the air between us is instantly charged. I want to close the distance between us.

"Do we?" I ask, my voice just above a whisper. He cocks an eyebrow, leans forward at the waist so his face is close to mine.

"Yes." His dark eyes are so hot my good sense starts to evaporate. Just like it had the night we met. "I want to see that woman whose body purred when I touched her again."

Heat and lust make me clench my thighs. I take a step back and bump into one of the tall boxwood hedges that line the walkway. "I wasn't myself. I didn't think I would see you again, so I just..."

"Let loose?" he finishes for me.

I snap my fingers. "Exactly. That wasn't the real me."

He frowns and raises an eyebrow. "Sure seemed and *tasted* like you."

I flush and thank God he can't tell. "As if you know me."

"Don't I?"

"This may be a good tactic in the courtroom but asking me questions I've already answered isn't going to get you a different answer," I inform him in my best no nonsense voice.

"It's not a tactic. I'm just trying to understand what you mean. Maybe you should speak plainly, Sin," he says with a note of challenge in his voice.

I've never had a problem with confrontation, but I could have done without this one. I clear my throat and choose my words carefully. "I find you very, very attractive, and you seem nice. But I'm not ready to date again yet and even if I were, my focus would still be on getting my career off the ground. Maybe in another life, we could pick up where we left off, but in this timeline, it's a nonstarter. I'm sorry," I add when his expression falls.

He sucks in a breath, and for a split-second, looks like he's about to push back. But then his expression relaxes and he nods with a deprecating smile.

"Hey, if that's what you want, that's what it'll be. I've got a lot going on, too." He gives in so easily I can't help but feel a little offended.

I give him a stiff smile. "Yes, it's what I want. Thank you for understanding." I turn and continue down the path to the driveway. "Come on, let's go. You're driving," I announce.

"No can do," he says when he catches up to me.

"Why not?" I cross my arms and scan the street for his car.

"I've only got two wheels." He jerks a thumb toward the garage. A bicycle that looks like it was built before the turn of the last century is propped up against the door.

I look up at him, perplexed. "What did you say you do?"

"I'm a lawyer."

I look back at him with a puzzled expression. "You need to ask for a raise so you can buy a car." Or a bike that was built this century.

"Why do I need a car when this baby does the job?"

"Rain, snow, late nights, bad drivers," I tick them off my fingers.

"Taxis exist. And this is my preferred mode of transportation and will be until the wheels fall off," he grins.

"Oh, so any day now?" I say as I look pointedly at the rusted wheel spokes.

He snickers. "You're funny."

"I'm not trying to be." I roll my eyes. "I guess we're taking my car." I open my purse to fish for the keys. "But you're still driving." I toss them to him.

He opens passenger door. "Your carriage, Queen." He takes my hand and guides me in and tucks my dangling purse strap in before he closes it.

I have to bite my lip to stop the stupid smile forming. He's probably just doing what his mom raised him to.

"Thank you."

"Yup," he closes the door and runs around the front of the car, and I admire the way his clothes hint at the muscular frame beneath them but still leave something to the imagination. And I love that I don't have to use my imagination. I didn't get to see it all that night, but I felt it all.

He presses the ignition key to start the car and I press my thighs together. The car illuminates and my audiobook starts playing.

"I gasp at the hot rasp of his tongue twirling around my nipple."

"Oh my God," I screech and press the button to pause it. "Sorry." I grin sheepishly and switch to FM.

"What *was* that?" He sounds scandalized, and I laugh.

"It was an audiobook."

"About what? Sucking nipples?" He snorts.

That wipes the smile off my face. I know that I can be irrationally irritable when people give me unsolicited, uninformed opinions on the books I read. "No, it's a romance novel."

He lets out a low whistle. "Wow, I didn't figure you for that type."

I bristle "And what type is *that?*"

"You know, to read fluff." He's making a tight right turn into the grocery store parking but takes a quick glance at me.

"Wait, did I say something wrong?" he asks and pulls into a parking spot.

"Have you ever read a romance novel?" I cross my arms and lean back against my door.

He looks taken aback by the question. "No." He draws the word out and puts the car in park.

"Then what makes you think you know the type of person who reads it?"

"Well, I mean…I don't know. I just…you're a journalist. I figured you'd read history or politics."

"I do…and they've taught me a lot of about the world. But I've been reading romance since I was twelve years old, and those books have taught me more about humanity than any textbook could. Yes, it's something I do for pleasure, but so is eating. So is fucking. That doesn't make them any less impactful. Why should reading be any different?"

"Sin, wait. I—"

"When the world is shit, I can open my book and escape. As a genre, it's got some of the best writers in all of fiction. I don't have to choose. I get to be entertained, educated, enlightened, and embraced. And if you want to have any peace in my presence, you better put some respect on it."

He holds his hands up palms facing me. "Okay, I'm sorry. I spoke out of ignorance."

"Fine," I grumble. I'm glad he apologized quickly, but I'm still miffed. "You're lucky we didn't have this conversation the night we met."

He barks a surprised laugh. "Noted. Sin doesn't play about romance."

"It never lets me down." I wink. "I'll be right back." I smile, open my own door and climb out.

When I get back into the car thirty minutes later, I have an apology on the tip of my tongue.

Instead of the irritated "what took you so long" I anticipated, he smiles and starts the car. "I looked up some books on my Libby app. You'll have to tell me where to start." He hands me his phone.

I shoot him a sidelong glance and take it. I scan the screen and gape at him. "You looked up romance novels?"

He nods and then turns his attention to the rearview image. "I'll pick a few of my favorites," I tell him as I scan the titles.

I buckle in but feel vulnerable as hell as we make our way back to my parents. Taking an interest in the things I care about is a cheat code for earning my devotion. And he has a library card. I try to focus on the task at hand and keep my giddiness at bay.

Oh Lord, why do you have to tempt me so?

"So, do you not like driving?" he asks after a few minutes of comfortable silence.

"I get road rage, especially in Arlington. I prefer being a passenger." I glance over at him.

He's smiling like I just told him a secret. "Now that I know that, next Sunday, I'll bring my tandem extender and you can ride with me."

"Never." I snort, and we share a laugh. I glance out of the window. There isn't a cloud in the sky, and I realize it's a beautiful day and roll it down. I open my music app and then the rest of what he said registers. I snap my head in his direction. "Wait, did you say next time?"

"Oh, your mother said you all have a family meal together every Sunday and invited me to join. I said yes."

I sit up. "You didn't have to say yes. And you don't have to come. If they weren't my family, I wouldn't give up my Sundays."

"That's easy to say when you get to see them so often."

"I do miss sleeping in, going out to a boozy brunch I didn't have to make. Binge-watching Britbox until my favorite Thai delivery arrives." I close my eyes and smile. But the recitation of my former life doesn't spark a sense of nostalgia. It sounds hollow, lonely. And the truth is, on most Sundays, I was working and cleaning up after the slob I used to live with.

"What are your Sundays like that you're so willing to give them up?"

He shrugs. "I usually just do laundry, catch up on work, run, get takeout and early bed. It was nice to be with…family today."

"Even after the melodrama with Mae?"

"They're nice. It's clear you love each other."

The affection in his voice makes me smile. "I complain about them but I do love them and no one has my back like they do. Leaving New York was a lot easier because I was coming home," I admit.

"So…when did you and your almost fiancé break up?"

"April sixteenth."

His eyes narrow. "The day after we met?" he asks and glances toward me.

"Yeah."

"So… I made an impression."

I roll my eyes. "It was already in the works, but meeting you did a lot to clarify things."

He smirks. "I heard multiple orgasms can have that effect in women."

"We both know you turned me out. Stop gloating," I snap.

He holds up a hand. "Okay, sorry. I didn't realize you were still in your feelings about it. I'll leave it alone."

"I'm not in my feelings," I mutter and look out at charming bungalows that line the street leading to my parents' house for a minute. When he doesn't respond, I sigh in resignation. "Okay, I guess I am," I admit. "Honestly, I'm thrown that you're here."

He huffs a laugh. "Yeah, me too."

I shake my head. "No, I mean. The way I was with you that night…" I bite my lip. I hate when people drag things out so, I force myself to spit it out.

"I don't have one-night stands. I didn't think I'd ever see you again. If I'd known there was even a chance I wouldn't have—"

"What? Let me eat you through your panties?" he says in a voice so low and silky it makes me cross my legs to try and create some friction discretely.

"Exactly," I agree.

"Or try to tear my clothes off?"

I nudge his arm in protest. "I did not."

"Oh, the scratches on my chest and hips are evidence that you, in fact, did." He grins.

"Oh my God, I'm so sorry." I giggle and then slap a hand over my mouth in surprise at the weird giddiness in my gut where my embarrassment and regret should be.

"I've never had a one-night stand, either, Sin."

"So why me?" It shouldn't matter, but it does. I have to know.

"I didn't want the night to end. I'd do it again. I have not a single regret that we met."

Heat spreads from my chest up my neck and into my face. I tuck a lock of hair behind my ears. "I'm glad to hear that. Me neither."

"I'm glad." He pulls into my parents' driveway, throws the car into park and turns so he's facing me. "Friends?"

"Yes, absolutely." I'm relieved as I shake his hand and ignore the way my palm tingles even after I let go

He opens the door and then hesitates. "Are we going to tell your family we met before today?"

Horror makes my eyes wide. "No, no, no. You've seen how rabid my mother is about us being single? If she thinks there's a small chance of something between us, she'll start planning. Next thing you know, you'll be bringing a box of Schnapps to my dad and ring shopping." I wrap my hands around my throat and stick my tongue out to mime choking myself.

He snorts a laugh. "Say less. What happened in April stays between us."

"Deal." I stick my hand out for his to shake.

"Deal." He mimics the gesture but crooks his pinky finger.

I smirk. "You want a pinky promise?"

"We're still getting to know each other. I need the reassurance that you'll keep your word." He winks and wiggles his pinky.

"Fine." I roll my eyes but can't fight my smile and wrap my finger around his and tighten it.

The brief brush of skin on skin sends little sparks of awareness up my arm. My heartbeat picks up. I tug my finger to free it, but he tightens his to hold me.

"What are you doing, weirdo?" I ask, trying to keep my voice light.

"Just savoring how good it feels to touch you one last time."

I look up from our hands to find his gaze still trained on our fingers.

I have to swallow before I can speak "One last time?" My voice is hushed.

He looks up at me and the humor that's been dancing on his face since we started talking is gone. His eyes are bright and intent on my face. "You understand why this is the most of you I trust myself to touch?" He uncurls his finger from mine.

I shove my hand into my pocket and trace the tingling skin around the knuckle he'd had in his grasp.

He places a hand on my jaw where it meets my throat and pins me in place with his smoldering dark eyes, making it impossible for me to deny him.

My breath hitches and my heart pounds even harder, and his face drops a fraction and comes closer to mine. My lips tingle and I lean in eager to see if his lips were as soft and warm as I remember.

"Sin," he breathes my name and puts a hand on the side of my neck and tugs me closer. Every single inch of me is leaning, anticipation building by the millisecond.

When he's so close his breaths ruffle my lashes, I close my eyes and sigh, "Yes."

The sound of the front door slamming coincides with the sudden retraction of his hand from my throat. "Shit," we say simultaneously.

I scramble out of the car, my pulse racing. My alarm is tinged with disappointment that I won't get to kiss him. "The line at self-checkout was crazy, but we got everything," I explain as I approach my dad.

"Oh good." My father comes down the short flight of steps. "Your mother is waiting in the kitchen. Kwame, could you join me in the study? I'm about to open the letter from your mom."

"Of course, I'll just take these in and be right there."

"You go ahead." I take the grocery bags from Kwame and hustle to the kitchen before he can protest.

"Took you long enough. The pie is getting cold."

"Sorry, the line was long." I open the freezer and lean my over-heated face inside while my mother starts pulling bowls out.

"Adele!" My father's voice pierces the domestic tranquility like a gun going off.

My mother and I lock eyes, alarm making them wide. "Lord have mercy," she says breaking our stare. She abandons dessert and rushes out of the kitchen with me, propelled by panic, hot on her heels.

"What's wrong?" I ask when I burst into the study a few paces behind her, out of breath.

My father is staring at a piece of paper and tears are running down his face. He hands it to my mother wordlessly.

She takes it, scans the first few lines and then slaps a hand over her mouth.

"Daddy, what's wrong?" I ask shaking his arm when he doesn't reply.

He shakes his head. "Kwame isn't our new landlord."

I turn to Kwame. "Are you kicking them out? Raising the rent?" I move to stand an arm's length away from where he's seated, my panic morphing to outrage.

He takes a step back and raised his hands "No. Of course not. I would never."

"Just tell me why you're not their landlord and who is!" I say struggling to keep my voice from rising.

"We don't have a new landlord. The house is ours," my mother replies.

I freeze mid-rant, the lava of emotion that was boiling in my blood a second ago cools instantly. "Wait. What? She gave them the house?"

"Yes. She did. Oh my God," my mother answers from behind me. She is holding the paper in one hand and my father's arm with the other. "I can't believe it. But it's true."

"Is this for real?" I ask Kwame, stunned but starting to realize the enormity of what is happening.

"Yes. If you keep reading, you'll see that the rent you've paid since you lived here has been deposited in a mutual fund account for the entirety of your lease period. She has made you and your husband the beneficiaries of the account. The debit cards and withdrawal slips should arrive here any day."

My mother screams and collapses in her chair. My father sits on the arm of it and presses a cheek to the top of her head.

I turn to Kwame. "Thank you," I manage to croak.

"Thank my mother. She obviously cared for them a lot."

My heart tugs at the way his eyes soften at the mention of his mother. "She was so nice to my parents. She was like their fairy god-mother and now this?"

"Did you meet her?"

I smile fondly. "Only in passing. She'd stop by every time they made major upgrades to the house. It's been fifteen years at least since I saw her last, but I remember her being so elegant."

"Yeah, she was." His eyes drift away from mine, and he smiles to himself. There's such tenderness in them that I want to wrap my arms around him and absorb some of it.

I want him to smile like that when he thinks about me.

I shake that thought right out of my head. My eyes have always been too big for my stomach. And Kwame is much more than I can chew right now. I'm not biting. No matter how tempting he is.

Thirteen

Kwame

Restless

"This isn't what I asked for. If you can't do the work, stop wasting my time and tell me."

The object of my anger, a first-year associate who thinks his law degree from Yale is a replacement for hard work, stands before me clutching the offending brief to his chest, his eyes stark with fear.

He has nothing to fear from me. The worst I can do is fire him. His father, like mine, is powerful and influential, and he'll never have to go begging for work. But I'm not sorry to see something other than smug overconfidence on his face and I'm in a bad fucking mood. And his work product is actually shit.

"We charged our clients fifteen hundred dollars an hour for your work product and now we have to eat that because that advice," I point to the file in his hands, "isn't worth the paper it's written on."

He flushes. "I'm sorry. I underestimated the research and I talked to Rummer and he said—"

"You could have asked God himself and this would still be wrong." Tobias Rummer hasn't written a motion in twenty years.

"I'm going to fix it."

"You have until close of business today," I warn him.

"I'll get it done."

"I hope so. Now, go away."

"Okay." He scurries out of my office.

He picked the wrong morning to fuck up. Coming to work at this place, in general, pisses me off. But a sleepless night of bone-deep regret and self-loathing has put me in a positively rancid mood.

I swivel my chair to face the large windows in my new corner office.

The hum of the city beneath me, a symphony of impatient car horns and the wail of police sirens and the sight of thousands of tourists flocking to the National Mall, used to invigorate me when I started this job.

Now, the only time I feel excitement in this office is when I'm leaving at the end of the day.

At almost forty, I've achieved what many would consider success. A decade as an assistant attorney general and now, counsel at one of the best criminal litigation practices in the country. I've got the respect of colleagues, and the clients I've taken on have confidence in me already. Keeping wealthy enough to pay my hourly rate from facing the consequences of their actions is not my idea of justice.

I took this job, moved back to the Washington DC area, and forgave my father for his sins in an attempt to honor my mother's dying wish. *Be the son he doesn't deserve but needs.*

It was a lot to ask but I wouldn't deny my mother her last wish. And there remains a part of me that hopes my father and I can have the kind of relationship we ought to.

It only took two weeks for him to remind me why we'd never be close.

He only wanted me on the East Coast so I can be his social proxy.

All he talked about was me running for office so I could funnel money to his projects and investments.

He called it the American dream.

I called it a traitorous grift.

He called me disloyal and announced he was leaving for Accra. He was gone three days later.

In the vacuum left by his absence, I've had the chance to think about my own life and what my legacy would be if stayed here.

Even in his absence, his shadow in this town is long.

My client roster at the firm has ballooned in a matter of months because of my last name and the power it still holds in this town.

I'm as uncomfortable with it now as I was when I left the family fold to make my own way in the world. How did I end up back here?

It's the least you owe your mother.

My phone buzzes and I grin when I see the name "TGlo" flash on the screen.

I lean back in my chair, cross my legs, and relax a little. Titus Glover is my oldest friend and former roommate.

He's always good for perspective on life and women. I answer his video call with a smile on my face only to find myself looking at the ceiling of his office.

"Hey man. What's up?" I ask and switch my camera off.

"There's a position at DC AUSA that I think has your name written all over it."

"What's in it for you?"

"Well damn." His face appears in the screen wearing a sad frown. "Can't I just care about my friend's career?" he protests.

"I *know* you, remember?" I lean back in my chair and relax for the first time all day.

"I swear there's no catch. The process is going to take nine months. You should apply because I know you'd be an asset."

I'm touched. "Thank you. Sorry I'm such a cynic."

"Well…you live in DC. It's kind a survival skill. I can't believe you moved back."

I grimace at his words. I can't believe it either. "When are you coming in for the holiday?"

"A couple days before. Is Lo coming, too?" he asks.

"Not that I know of. Did you invite her?"

"Nah bruh, that's all you." He puts on a mock London accent.

"No it's not. I met someone," I blurt before I can stop myself.

"Oh shit. Does Paloma know?"

No way. Not yet. "Why would I tell her?"

"She's not over you."

I laugh. "You're way off base."

"She hasn't been in a relationship since you guys split. She talks about you all the time. I think she's still in love with you."

I laugh in disbelief. "She was never in love with me. Paloma Persaud only loves money, power, and great clothes."

"Damn. That's harsh," he says.

"It's true. She doesn't date seriously because she wants to run for office one day. It has nothing to do with me. But if she's on your mind so much, why don't you date her?"

"I'm too busy to date anyone. I don't know if you heard, but my executive protection business found an angel investor and we're breaking ground on our new building in a few weeks."

I grin. "I heard. How's it going?"

"Great. This software is going to revolutionize the personal security industry. Thank you for making it happen."

"I didn't do it because I love you. I want my money back," I joke, and we share a good laugh. "But for real, man. I can't wait to invest more. You deserve it."

"I love you man. Thank you. And think about that job. For real."

When we hang up, I go to the federal jobs website and check out the listing.

I promised my mother a year. I wanted to go back to LA when that time was up.

Or at least I did.

I hang up and blow out a breath to try and dispel the anxious energy building in my gut.

I felt energized when I got home that first Sunday night. It was like a second chance. A clean slate.

My mother had put the deed in her maiden name so when they called me Kwame Dixon, I didn't correct them. It didn't matter what name they called me. All they knew was Kwame the lawyer, son of their former landlord, and now Sunday lunch guest. It felt so good. They'll have to know eventually, but until it's necessary or comes up, I'm going to enjoy the perks of my anonymity as long as I can.

Fourteen

Sin

Muscle Memory

Kwame honored my mother's invite and has come to Sunday dinner every single week since that first visit. After his third straight appearance at the house, I asked him to help me with the dishes so I could speak to him alone and reassure him that he didn't have to come.

As soon we got in the kitchen, he'd connected his phone to the bluetooth speaker on the window over the sink. We'd worked in a comfortable, quiet, and perfect sync through a playlist full of D'Angelo, Chaka Khan, and Charlie Wilson. He'd loaded the dishwasher, and while I'd hand washed everything that couldn't go in there, he'd swept the floor. I'd cleaned the counters while he'd dried the pots, knives, and crockery I'd washed. By the time we were done I couldn't remember what I'd wanted to talk to him about.

The next week, he offered to help me as soon we were done eating. Mae was thrilled to be off the hook and my mother extolled his parents for raising such a helpful, respectful son. She dropped hints about him and Mae's simultaneous singledom and didn't seem to notice how uncomfortable it made all of us.

My family was a lot. We argued passionately, laughed loudly, didn't have filters, and didn't take a lot personally. From the little I've gleaned about his family, he's not used to that kind of intimacy. He's never seemed anything but happy to be here. He loves my dad's stories about his boarding school days. He's been reading Adonis' briefs for his moot court class and doesn't seem to mind. The hour of quiet he gives me while I do the dishes is a gift I hadn't even known I needed.

My mother made her famous garden egg stew tonight, and the price for that is the four different pots she uses in the process.

I'm just finishing the last one when Kwame breaks the silence.

"You used to be an investigative journalist?" My hands freeze mid scrub and let the stainless steel pot slide into the sink full of hot soapy water. I turn slowly to face him.

"Why do you ask?" I ask, eyebrow cocked.

"I'm just wondering how you got so good at giving advice. I've yet to disagree with you."

"You read my column?"

"Yeah, even though your name isn't on the byline." He returns my perplexed expression. "Is it a secret that you're the voice behind the page now?"

"No. But the column is the draw. The writers behind it aren't meant to be. The only thing I was allowed to change is the sign-off."

"We're all sinners here. I like that. It's clever. And so is your advice. Do you get to decide what submissions you answer?"

"Thank you, and yes." I flush at his praise and sincere interest. I turn my attention back to the pot while I talk. "Although, I'm starting to get the impression they're sorry they gave me that power," I admit.

"Why? I like that it's not just 'How do I get my husband to pick up his socks?' kind of stuff. I loved your answer to the woman who wrote in about her para-social relationship with a content creator she follows."

My heart flutters at the detail. He really read it. "It's such a common problem. And one of the reasons I like being behind the page."

He nods. "Yeah, I am so glad I don't have a career that requires me to use social media or perform in anyway."

"I think it's a great way to connect but also very easy to blur lines." I hand him the clean pot and he wipes it dry.

"Thank you for reading it. I'm glad you like it," I say honestly touched. No one in my family has read it. At least not to my knowledge.

"It's my pleasure. I went back and read some of your old work when you were in New York and I was surprised by how different this is."

I stiffen at the question and have to remind myself that he's just making an observation. "I know. That's what I wanted." I'm caught off guard by the heaviness in my throat when I say those words. It's true. I took this job, vastly different from what I was doing because I wanted something safe, fun, and anonymous.

"I read your series on the battle to repatriate stolen artifacts. I wonder if my mom knew you were doing that work?"

I cock my head to the side and slide into one of the barstools in front of the island. "I don't know. The story got a lot of attention. When the transit was robbed on its way to DC, I'd started looking into it and even identified someone who I thought was running a black market for West African art and relics."

"In DC?" His eyes widen. He wipes his hands and pumps a drop of lotion into his palm and holds it out for me to use.

My heart skips a beat like he just handed me a flower. That's why his hands are so soft.

"Yup. Not just DC, but it seems to be a hub of activity."

He sits on the stool next to me and his shoulders and thigh brush mine so casually, but I'm acutely aware that this is the closest we've been physically since that first night.

"So why aren't you working on *that* story?"

I roll my neck and groan at the twinge of pain where it meets my left shoulder. "Because I write an advice column now."

"You sound much more excited about your stolen artifacts story," he presses.

I press my fingers into the spot on my shoulder that's tense and rub. "I *loved* investigative journalism. But it didn't love me back."

"What does that mean?" He brushes my fingers away and replaces them with his. The pressure is delicious and I don't bother pretending I want him to stop.

I let my head fall forward and explain. "It means I had a few brushes with great stories that my editors whitewashed and ruined or that turned out to be bad leads. It's competitive, and it can be dangerous when you're telling stories that threaten power. I just want to write, have an impact, and to have time to live my life." It's a jumble of half-truths but it's all I've got.

"You're a prosecutor, right?" I turn the light on him.

He shakes his head. "Not anymore. I took a job with a private law firm when I moved here. My practice area is the same though, antitrust and competition."

"In English for those of us who aren't legal eagles?" I tease.

"I have clients who are trying to merge, acquire other businesses."

"That sounds very different from prosecution. Do you like it?"

"It's weird being on this side of the table. But I'm giving it a chance for the same reason I'm in DC, and the same reason I came to see your parents."

"Wait, your mom asked you to do that, too?"

"Yes. She asked me to give their vision a chance for a year, so I am."

"And when that year is up?"

"I'll see. But right now, it's not looking good for DC."

"You miss LA?" I ask.

"My best friend Titus lives there and I miss being in the same city as him."

"That's nice. My best friends live elsewhere, too," I commiserate.

"Do you still miss NY?" I groan at the question and the extra pressure he puts on *just* the right spot.

His fingers are so nimble. So competent. So certain. Like he has a right to touch me. I don't mind it at all. He never crosses the line and since I can't have sex with him, these massages are the next best thing.

"Thank you," I groan and let my head loll while I ponder his question. "I miss how walkable the city is. Otherwise, I love being back in the DMV. I'd forgotten how picturesque it is. That we get all four seasons here. I think once I find a house I want to call home I'll feel better about it."

"Where do you live now?"

"NoMa."

"What's that?"

"It's the newly gentrified corridor of NE south of Union Station. NPR built their new headquarters there in the twenty-tens and it's gone from a place you'd cross North Capital to avoid to having a Starbucks on the corner and college students walking around at one o'clock in the morning."

"Shit. There goes the neighborhood," he quips

We laugh at the same time. I've never minded the long-distance friendships I've built over the years, but I have to admit it's really nice to have a friend who knows the heart of where you're from.

We settle into a comfortable silence.

"Sin," his voice is low and close.

"Hmm?" I drawl when he doesn't continue.

"Are we still *just* friends?" he asks in a somber, quiet voice.

My heart skips a beat and my eyes fly to his.

The humor that was there earlier is gone and in its place is heat and a question.

I bite my lip, and his eyes move to my mouth.

"I really regret not kissing you more that night." His voice is so husky and inside me something slips loose.

He hooks his hand around the leg of my chair and drags it around until I'm facing away from the counter.

He stands in front of me and cups my face.

It feels so good, I moan. I can't help it.

I close my eyes.

This isn't what I came here for. I should leave.

But I don't want to.

"Do you remember?" His breath brushes my eyes and lean in.

"Every single second," I admit.

"Why did we decide not to do it again?"

"Bad timing," I murmur.

His thumb strokes my throat.

"What about now?"

My heart lurches. I wish I'd met him before the thought of trusting him terrified me.

I want to tell him that I'm not ready.

I start to tell him.

At least I think that's what I was going to say. But all I manage is a "yes" before his mouth touches mine.

It's soft and yet so hot I melt instantly. His mouth is cool and the bitterness of the beer he's been sipping clings to his lips. I want more. I want him. It is all I know.

I sling an arm around his neck, and his arms wrap around my waist and he deepens the kiss. It's urgent and yet savoring.

His tongue teases my lower lip before he and his body feel so solid and sure against mine.

He tastes so good. I *feel* so good…I'm sure I'd float away if he let me go.

One hand slides up my side and cups my breast. "You're perfect, Sin. So damn good and soft," he murmurs against my open, panting mouth. My nipple is hard and painfully taught. His thumb flicks and the pleasure of it burns a decadent trail to the very center of me. If he bent me over right now, he could have me any way he wanted. I reach between us and cup his erection through his jeans and he thrusts into my hand.

"Take it out," he grumbles, and I slide my hand past his waistband

and the heat of him makes me gasp.

The clatter of something hitting the floor in the other room shatters our bubble and we jump apart just before my brother walks into the kitchen carrying the pieces of a mug I recognize immediately.

"What happened?" I ask as he walks over and dumps them into the sink. "You broke her favorite mug? How?" I smack his arm.

He winces and leans away from me. "It was an accident. It's just a mug."

"It's her favorite mug. I bought it for her, and I'm her favorite child," I remind him and walk over to the sink to assess the damage.

Kwame comes to stand by me and my heart starts to thud.

"Let me have a look. I used to fix broken ceramics for fun." He grins at me and reaches into the sink and picks up the fractured handle. Those fingers had just been on my body. God. I like the way he touches me.

I'm practically panting and he's focused on my mom's mug.

He doesn't look like *his* heart is racing. In fact, he doesn't look like anything special just happened.

God. What is it with me and men who don't show their hand? I'm not doing this again.

"I think I can fix this. Do you have Gorilla Glue?"

"Yeah, we do. That would be great." Adonis strides over to the junk drawer and starts rummaging through it.

"This will only take a minute," he says with a nonchalant grin that makes me wonder if I imagined all of that.

I return it best I can and grab my phone. "Take your time." I check the time and feign disappointment. "I've gotta go. I have call I need to take at home. I'll see you next week."

He follows me out of the kitchen. "Sin, wait."

"I can't. I've got a seven a.m. meeting and I am not a morning person."

"It's seven thirty, Sin."

"Ninety minutes until my bedtime." I blow an uncommitted kiss in their direction and stroll out. "See you next week."

Fifteen

Sin

Help

My seven a.m. meeting is almost fifteen minutes late. I *hate* waiting. I dictate a message.

"Hey Leon. I have another meeting at eight-thirty and it's seven-fifteen already. Is she coming?" And hit send.

He replies to my text right away. "She's almost there. Here's her number, fyi."

I'm about to text her when there's a light tap on my shoulder.

I turn to face the woman I'm here to meet.

She looks younger than I expected. She's tall, round faced and doe eyed. Her hair is braided in a single plat that rests on her shoulder. Her pink tracksuit set reminds me of *High School Musical*.

"Are you Violet?" I ask just to be sure.

She nods but doesn't speak. Her posture is rigid, holding herself like she's cold despite the already sweltering morning. Her eyes dart around the restaurant. She looks scared. I can smell trouble a mile away and whatever she's come to ask me stinks of it.

The curiosity I've had about her since Leon texted to say she was finally ready to meet is replaced by worry. "Why don't you sit down?"

I look over my shoulder at the hostess stand. "Can we have another menu, please?"

While they bring the menus and waters for the table, I try to get a read on her. Is she scared or nervous or pretending? I hope Leon isn't wrong about her.

When our coffees arrive, I flip open my moleskin notebook and pick up my pen to signal my readiness to talk. "So, you have a problem with your boyfriend."

She nods. "He broke up with me and kicked me out of the place we were living together."

"That was four months ago. Why have you waited so long to ask for help?"

She looks down at her lap. "He asked me to come back. Not as his girlfriend, but as his employee. He doubled the salary I make on campus and gave me a place to live. I've been saving, and the work was easy. It's been fine. But last week, he did it again. This time he wouldn't let me take anything. Not even my passport. I'm scared. He's dangerous."

Mindful of what I already know about her. "So why did you go back to work for him?"

She shakes her head. "I always knew he was doing something shady. But like, who doesn't have some side hustle, right? The pay was good and he was generous. I wasn't afraid of him. I am now."

I feel for her but I'm not sure I believe her. She's already admitted to being an opportunist who can be swayed to the dark side if the number is right.

"So, if he offered you your job back you wouldn't take it?"

She shakes her head vigorously. "I just want to get my things and leave in peace. But there's a picture of me at reception. I can't even enter the building." She presses her lips to together to stop them from trembling.

"What happened?"

She blows out a breath and composes herself. "Last week I asked him when he'd let me go to one of his auctions. He asked how I knew about them and I told him I'd heard him talking about them on calls. He snapped, warned me to forget everything I'd ever heard him say or he'd make me. He threw me out without letting me get my things together. He has my clothes, my passport, the money I've been saving, all of it."

She's trembling and I can tell that her trauma is real. I put my notebook down. "You're from Trinidad. Have you reached out to the embassy?"

Her eyes widen. "I'm not supposed to be working. And I don't want my parents to know I've gotten myself into trouble. They worked so hard to send me here for school. I just want my things." Her eyes dart around the empty cafe.

"Look, Leon said you're looking for someone who is selling art. Well, he is. And it's not on the level. The apartment where I was living is also his home office. He's got some of the stuff he sells there. I made deliveries for him and have all the addresses in my phone. I will give you all the information I have."

I'm still skeptical but if she's telling the truth, this is a bombshell of a lead.

"You said his name is Oz. Do you know his full name?"

She shakes her head. "I called him The Wizard, too. That's how he introduced himself. But once I answered a call from a woman who asked to speak to Oz. He didn't keep any mail at this place, so I never saw his full name. He was very careful about what he let me know, and I never went into his office without permission."

"I see." I write it down like it's just any other piece of information.

My heart hammering, my pulse racing with excitement at this piece of information, I press my luck.

"Do you know where he's from?"

She shakes her head. "No, sorry. He has a British accent but I'm pretty sure he's Ghanaian or Nigerian. He's very tall. So probably Nigerian," she muses.

"What else?" I ask and press the voice notes button on my phone.

She shakes her head and toys with the end of the long braids that spill over her shoulder. "I knew he was trouble. It was stupid to start sleeping with him and staying there."

I agree but hate to pile on. I give her a sympathetic pat on the hand. "You're doing the right thing. I'm glad you came to me."

"So you'll help me get my things back?"

"I'll do my best. It's been a while since I jimmied a lock but it's like riding a bike."

Violet claps her hands. "Oh! I forgot." She leans over to rifle in her purse and pulls out a small plastic card. "This is my access card."

She puts the key down in front of me. "I have no idea what his schedule is. I'm not even sure he's in town, but this should help."

I smile at the card. Maybe luck is finally on my side. "It will. I need to do some surveillance, figure out the best way to get in and out, and make sure that I don't run into him."

"You can't let that happen. I'd rather not get my stuff back than for him to find out I sent someone to his place."

A knot of dread forms in my gut before I can remind myself that I was good at this part of my job. "I'll be careful."

"Thank you," I reach for the access card and pause before I put it into my purse. "Will he be able to tell it's been used?"

"He doesn't know how to check the logs."

"Okay. I'll see if I can confirm that." I make a note in my journal and close it. "No promises but I'll try." I give her a placid smile meant to manage her expectations.

Inside though, fireworks are going off, and I am itching to leave and get to work.

I decide to walk the half mile to my office to give myself time to think about what to do with the gift that just fell in my lap.

I'm not sure how to do this. Not without significant risk.

And not without the backing of a publication.

I've been content with my column. It's not the life-changing journalism that I used to dream of writing. But it was the life-changing opportunity I needed when I accepted it.

Months in, I can't deny that I'm bored.

I didn't choose this incredibly cut-throat profession to add to the numbers or take up copy space.

I saw the journalist Charlayne Hunter-Gault speak in my final year of high school and knew, immediately, I wanted to do exactly what she did.

It wasn't an easy road, but I loved every challenging inch of it. I wrote stories that needed *my* voice. I centered people who are often side characters that create a foil and serve to reinforce bullshit hierarchy that oppresses more people than it elevates.

It was that passion that led me to this story about the battle to repatriate plundered art, jewelry, and relics to their rightful countries of origin, and it feels like the perfect piece to do that.

The pieces, from monuments to handicrafts, were more than decorative pieces of art and priceless jewelry.

They were the record of a history, a culture, and a people whose very existence they affirmed and immortalized.

What was more universal and human than our connection to our heritage?

What was more fundamental to our cultural identity than the symbols of it? When I asked my editor how we'd feel if the Statue of Liberty was stolen by North Korea, she understood and agreed to give me a budget, and I was off to the races.

I was sure the story would help me clinch the promotion she'd dangled in front of me like a carrot for years.

When it didn't and the story was scooped, I thought I was done.

But now the story has found its way back to me and it's got dimensions I couldn't even have imagined before.

When I was working on this story, I discovered the existence of a person name The Wizard. I took it to the FBI task force assigned to the recovery of stolen cultural artifacts.

They knew of his existence but wouldn't do more than confirm that. They had nothing on this person. They weren't sure if he was even man. Or where he was from.

I can't arrest him myself but if I can unmask him and the ring he runs and write about it, it would force law enforcement's hand.

If I can bring this home, I could write my ticket with it.

If I'm right.

If universe finally bends in my favor.

If.

Sixteen

Kwame

Rug Pull

If I don't leave for the Sackey's now, I'll be late.

I pace outside my front door and grapple with what to do.

I'm not sure I can sit through another meal and pretend I'm good with the way things are. But what if it's too soon.

I call Titus.

"I'm going to tell her how I feel," I announce as soon as he answers his phone.

"Oh boy." I can picture his eye roll and his posture relaxing as if he knows he better get comfortable cause he's going to be here a while. "This is the woman who ran away when you kissed her, friend zoned you, and currently uses you as a therapist?"

I groan and cover my face at his dirty summary of my circumstance "Shit take. She likes to talk. I like to listen. And she *didn't* friend zone me. It was mutual." *Only because I had no choice.*

"Okay, then. What's changed?"

"Time." I respond without having to think about it. "I've spent enough of it with her to know I like her. That I can trust her. I think she feels the same way."

"So why is she holding you at arm's length?"

"She just got out of a situation. She was deep in her 'choose the bear' era when we met. I don't think she's there anymore. If I tell her how I feel, I think she'll admit she feels it, too." Saying it aloud makes me smile, makes my chest feel lighter.

"*I* think you're a hopeless romantic looking for a happy ending."

I tut my dissent. "Should I be looking for a miserable one?"

"No. But does it make sense to chase something that's running from you?"

"Running from me?" I chuckle and stop pacing.

"No, she literally ran from you the night you met."

"Yeah but look how we keep finding each other." I'm glad I called him, having to fight my corner has only made me more sure.

I sit on the step outside my front door and look up at a bough of leaves that frames the wide arch. I see why my mother loved this house.

"You know, I wasn't sure I'd ever feel like DC could be more than a pit stop. She makes me think about standing still. I love her family, too."

He laughs. "Oh boy. Never thought I'd see the day you'd actually want to stop and enjoy the view."

"Well, I guess I found one that's finally made me want to."

"Then tell her how you feel. If you're right, you've got nothing but upside. If you're wrong, worst-case scenario is you'll have your Sundays free again."

The thought makes my stomach sink. Sundays have become the oasis in the desert of my week. Nothing about Sin and me *feels* hard. Timing hasn't been right. But "us"? That's been easy from that first night at The Salamander.

He sighs. "You know I *hate* adding air to your already overly inflated ego…"

"That is pure projection," I say under my breath..

"But you're a very attractive guy. In a purely objective way."

I frown. "This doesn't sound like the buildup to a compliment."

He ignores me. "And you're a good listener. But…" he adds with emphasis.

"Ah, I was right," I mutter.

He continues to speak over me. "*But* you don't share as much because I think you're afraid to lose the people you have so you don't let them get too close. So, despite how nice the surface is, sometimes what's beneath isn't as easy to digest."

"Wow, please don't pull your punches."

"I know why you are the way you are. You grew up with parents who navigated the world by hiding. I mean, maybe they don't like rich people? I know we're used to people wanting to get close *because* of money but maybe she's the opposite. Billionaires aren't the heroes they used to be."

"She doesn't know about my money. Or who my dad is." I think, if I'm honest, that's what's stopped me from making a move for the last few weeks.

"Wait. How can these people be your friends and not know who your family is?"

I blow out a breath. "I left when I was eighteen and I haven't lived as Palmer again until this last year. Why would I just blurt out my father's name and net worth when it's literally never come up? They knew my mother by her maiden name. They think it's my last name, too."

"So, they've never asked whose Rolls that is? Or how you live in one of the biggest houses in Georgetown?"

"They have never been to my place and I ride my bike over."

"So, outright deception then?"

My hackles rise. "No. Of course not. I ride my bike everywhere I go. I live in that house because my mother left it to me. I have that car because *he* bought it for me. They're not *mine*. And you know that."

He sighs. "You're getting defensive because I'm right. You don't want them to know. Why? You think they'll ask you for money?"

"No, come on, T. They're good people. I just…they treat me like I'm normal," I admit.

"They don't know you've got a yacht parked in the Indian Ocean. Or that you're flying around on private planes."

"Again, not mine."

"I hate to break it to you but it is. And that's okay," he adds when I start to pushback. "I have to go in a minute, but I just want to say this. I know this is how your parents operated, and you see where it got them."

"Yeah, with everything and nothing."

"They were extreme, but they had their reasons. Just like you do for not coming clean straight away."

"I don't want things to change."

"You can't control that. But if her knowing you have money changes things, won't you be glad you know what she's really like?"

"You're right." I grab my helmet from the hook beside my door and walk out to get on my bike.

"I always am."

"In your dreams. I'll talk to you later." I hang up and assess the sky for signs of rain. The sky is clear but for a few errant white wisps, and I hop on my trusty old Schwinn and coast down my driveway. I normally love the five-mile ride to the Sackey's in Arlington.

This afternoon, my stomach roils. I should have skipped that smoked salmon and egg sandwich from Tatte after my run this morning. Or maybe it's the thought that this could be my last Sunday performing what's become a bit of a ritual. I normally walk my bike up M Street until I get to Dean and Deluca's where I often stop to pick up something for dessert and then ride rest of the way.

Today, M Street is packed with tourists and locals out in force to take advantage of the beautiful, almost perfect, summer day. The sidewalk is crowded so I hop on my bike and join the vehicle traffic that trudges up M Street at a snail's pace and think about what I'm going to say when I get to their house. I keep reminding myself that it won't be the end of the world if she says no. It'll just feel like it for a while.

Every Sunday, she drops her lush ass into the seat next to mine at her parents' dining room table and the rest of the world disappears. After we share an amazing meal, the two of us break off from the group, find a quiet corner, and catch up. I get a firsthand exclusive on everything she's got rolling around in that incredible mind of hers. She asks for advice about work. She gives pretty good advice herself. Only when I ask for it. My life is full of people who have an opinion on what I should be doing. It's nice to meet someone who sees that I'm capable of managing things pretty well on my own.

We're different in the way the two sides of the same coin are. Every Sunday, I discover something else I have in common with her. Where I am regimented, cautious, and believe in practical, well-reasoned wisdom, Sin is chaotic, audacious, and dangerously clever.

I'm not sure I've met anyone with as much mental horsepower as her.

There's no denying the chemistry between us. It's true that I'm a lifelong admirer of small-breasted, round-hipped, brown-skinned women who play hard to get and are stronger than they look. It's a specific, but bountiful demographic. But my attraction to Sin has moved so far beyond the physical and denying it has turned *me* into a ravening beast.

If we don't fit, I'll move on.

I'll have to stop coming to Sunday dinners for a while. It makes my stomach hurt to contemplate it. But there's no way I could sit next to her wanting her like this and knowing for certain she doesn't want me.

Like I conjured her, headlights land on me as she pulls into the driveway.

I swallow my nerves, slide my helmet off, and prop my bicycle up.

I wave and wait for her to climb out of her car. She looks good enough to eat and is dressed in a pair of tiny denim shorts and oversized black t-shirt. Aside from the generous display of her sexy-ass legs, it should be an unremarkable outfit. But she's got a gold chain belt cinched around her waist that makes it look like high fashion. But then, Sin could elevate a sackcloth.

"Hey you," she walks over grinning and rises up on her toes to give me a hug. She's soft and smells sweet.

It takes all of my strength not to palm her ass and hold her still when she pulls away.

"Why are you staring at me like that?" she asks.

"I like your belt," I say with a nod at it, not answering her question as honestly as I can.

She puts a hand to her waist and narrows her eyes up at me in suspicion. "Are you making fun of me?"

I shake my head in wonder and fall into step with her as she heads for the front door. "Why is it so hard to pay you a compliment?"

She shrugs and digs in her purse. "I don't know," she says without looking up. "I've been like that. Compliments are as comfortable as an itchy ass."

I bark in surprised laughter. "Why do you know what an itchy ass feels like?"

"Oh please." She gives me a side-eye as she slips her key into the lock and wrestles with the notoriously sticky deadbolt. "Don't act like you've never not wiped as well as you should have and—ugh. This door." She shoves it with her shoulder and her hair sways in front of me. I catch the scent of something sweet. I lean in a fraction and take a deep breath just as she's rearing back. Our bodies collide.

She yelps in surprise and whips around to glare at me.

"Why were you standing so close to me?" she snaps.

"I was trying to help," I lie and take a step back but extend my hand. "You want me to try?"

She purses her lips and turns back to face the door. "No, they need to get it fixed and keep putting it off." She presses the buzzer three times. "Maybe if they have to come down and answer it enough times, they'll finally fix this lock."

She crosses her arms, a satisfied smile on her face as she turns to face me and leans against the door.

The door opens with a sudden give that sends her tumbling backward, her arms pinwheeling.

I step forward and place a steadying arm around her waist and use my heel to kick the front door closed.

She straightens, and I sniff the air around her. "What?" She lifts her armpits and sniffs. "Do I smell?"

"No, Just…you smell different."

She whips her head around to look at look at me. "I changed my perfume."

"I can tell."

"You know what I smell like?"

"Yes, you always smell the same."

"I was trying something new."

"Change it back," I suggest.

She jerks a look over her shoulder at me. "Why would I do that? I love the new perfume."

"It's nice. Just doesn't smell like *you*."

She scowls. "No one asked you." She steps away from me, yanks her hat off, and tosses it onto the coatrack.

The sudden loss of heat from her body makes me want to yank her back against me and keep her there all night. I have to get this off my chest or I'll burst.

"Hey, Sin, can we talk before we go—"

"Sin, come and see," her mother shouts from the kitchen. "Hurry up."

"Oh Lord, what now?" She rolls her eyes and rushes off.

I follow her slowly.

Halfway down the hall, the sound of glass breaking rises over their voices and the television. I pick up my pace and enter the kitchen just as Mr. Sackey pushes out of his chair, his hand outstretched, fingers pointing at the television. His eyes are wide with rage. "Look at this fucking stupid piece of goat excrement smiling like he's a good person. Just when I thought I'd never see his face again, here he is."

I've never heard Mr. Sackey curse, so it takes me a second to follow the trajectory of his hand.

The world freezes when I see the headline that's got him so upset. On the screen, a headline screams. "Mr. Palmer is bringing Palm Sunday back. After a two-year hiatus the iconically secret and the most coveted invite in DC is back."

I stare at the pictures of my father that flash on the screen. Him with the famous people he kept like trophies, and try to make sense of what the reporter is saying.

"Idiot," Mrs. Sackey's sharp words make my head turn in her direction. She's on her feet, too. Staring at the television. "Liar and a traitor. Utter disgrace." She snaps her finger between each word.

As it sinks in that they are talking about my father this way, my heart starts to beat so fast I can hear it. "How do you know him?" I ask no one in particular.

"You mean Crooked Mr. Palmer? They *don't* know him. At least not anymore," Adonis says with a long-suffering sigh. He reaches into his pocket to pull out a small case with earbuds inside. He slips one in and glances up at me. "They lost everything because they invested some money with him. They thought he'd cheated them. So they hired a lawyer and sued him."

My thoughts move faster than I can process and my ears ring. "What happened next?"

"Their case was dismissed by the judge. They had to file bankruptcy. They've recovered financially, I think. But they lost a lot, too. They hate him."

My head spins with this new information. "Yeah. I can imagine." I wonder how many more people out there feel this way about my father.

"You better find something else to do 'cause when they get going about him, that's all they'll talk about for the rest of the night." He rolls his eyes and looks back at his phone.

"Who even told him that anybody misses him?" Mr. Sackey shouts in a voice dripping with loathing.

Sin stands and pats her dad's shoulder. "Come on, let's go set the table and eat. Don't let him ruin our Sunday."

My stomach feels like I swallowed a lead ball. I need answers, but I'm afraid to ask. I follow Sin out of the room, but my mind stays firmly rooted in her parents' reaction.

"Do your parents hate The Great Palmer, too?" Sin asks.

"The Great Palmer? Is that what you call him?"

"Are you sure you grew up in the DMV?" She looks look over her shoulder at me with a look of playful disbelief.

My mouth goes dry. "I did. I just…my parents didn't mingle with other Ghanaians much."

"Here." Sin hands me a stack of plates and picks up two fistfuls of silverware, and I follow her to the dining room.

"Al Palmer is a Ghanaian billionaire who lives in the most expensive piece of real estate in northern Virginia. Supposedly, he's the son of a chief in Ghana. But no one's really sure about that. We do know that he made a lot of money in oil and mining for other minerals. And that he did some deals where he ended up holding land people used as collateral when the investments he'd sold them failed."

"I see," is all I can manage. I feel like I've been hit by a hammer. "I've never heard any of this."

"I wish I could say I'd never heard his name because every time he comes up, my parents go ballistic."

I manage a chuckle even though my heart is racing like a locomotive as we walk into the dining room. Cold sweat is forming on my neck.

This is a disaster from every angle.

My father is trying to reinsert himself into DC's political class again just as I'm trying to make a name for myself here.

If that wasn't bad enough, I've finally found a woman I'm crazy about and whose family I've come to think of as my own, and he's managed to taint it.

"Fuck," I hiss.

"What?" Sin looks up from where she's arranging a placement. Her eyes narrow and her brows furrow at whatever she sees on my face. "Are you okay?"

"Yes." I'm not.

It's a miracle my hands aren't shaking when I put down the last of the plates. My entire nervous system is on fire. My chest feels heavy, my heart slams against my ribs, my gut is in a knot. I back away from the table, focused on leaving before I say something I'll regret. I need to think. "I just remembered that I have a meeting early tomorrow morning that I haven't prepared for. I can't stay."

She purses her lips and tilts her head. "Okay. Are you sure that's all? You look like you've seen a ghost."

"Yeah. Just have a lot to do for a meeting tomorrow and totally forgot."

Sin's smile is warm, but her eyes are slightly narrowed, whether with concern or suspicion I can't tell. "Do you want to fix a plate to take home?"

"No. It's all good. I'll see you next week," I call over my shoulder and leave the house through the back door without looking back.

Seventeen

Sin

Missing in Action

Sunday has become my favorite day of the week. I used to spend it sleeping off Saturday's excess and dreading Monday's mania. These days, I'm up with the sun, hit the ground running, literally. Then I spend the rest of the day doing what I call my "body repairs," washing and twisting my hair, facial masks, and the egg and tomato omelette that my mother makes every Sunday morning.

I used to think my self-care ended when I left for my parents' because I went straight into the kitchen to help my mother make our Sunday staple—ground nut soup with pounded rice. Even that chore has started to feel like a sacred ritual that gives me time with my mother, who is the best cook on the planet, learning and catching up while we make the food that nourishes more than just our bodies.

Dinner is a drawn-out affair that ends long after the food is finished.

I usually find my second wind by the time we're done cleaning up. And then Kwame and I go sit outside, feet in the hot tub and talk until my parents start turning off lights and drawing curtains to signal it's time for us to leave.

I go to bed exhausted in the best ways, happy, and ready to take on the week.

This Sunday, though, as we're clearing the table, I'm itching to make my excuses and leave.

Kwame messaged my mother to say he had a cold and would see us next week.

No one seemed to give it a second thought. I felt alone in the surprisingly sharp pang of disappointment I felt when my mother announced his absence.

Never one to dwell on things I can't control, I was sure the feeling would pass.

The old adage "You don't know what you've got until it's gone" kept playing in my head.

By the end of dinner, I'm wondering what I enjoyed about Sundays before Kwame started joining us. No one asks what I'm working on and then actually listens. No one else sits patiently while I try to make sense of something that's bothering me. No one else read my weekly column or shared them in their Instagram stories.

My parched ego and wounded pride soaked up his attention like rain. I've spent the week mentally preparing to dip my toe back into the world I left behind, and I could really use a dose of his praise.

The absence of his physical presence was palpable, too. He's a big man, tall, solid, well-built. He's also very affectionate with me in a way that has never felt misplaced.

His hugs, back rubs, thigh squeezes and lingering looks have been safe. Physical contact from a man who wasn't only interested in getting me in bed.

I should have asked him what was wrong before he left last week.

I hate being pushed to talk before I'm ready, so I let him be.

I took for granted that I'd see him this Sunday.

Regret that is so heavy it's impossible for me to think about anything else.

I abandon the small pile of dirty dishes on the table and pull my phone out of my pocket to call him.

I type his name into my contact list. Nothing comes up.

I search my message history for his name and that comes up blank, too.

How is it possible that I don't have his phone number saved?

I feel like I talk to him all the time. But in reality, I don't. Except for Sundays.

I could ask my mother for it but that would only invite unwanted, overly broad conversations about my private life.

Like I summoned her, my mother sticks her head through the swinging door that leads to the kitchen. "Why are you just sitting there when your sisters are in the kitchen?"

I don't ask why she hasn't asked Adonis the same question. I'm having a bad enough day without adding an argument with my mother to the mix. "I had to answer an email for work."

She trains her disapproving frown on the phone in my hand and raises her eyebrows. "On a Sunday? You write an advice column. It's not life or death. Surely, it can wait."

I'm used to my mother's dismissive attitude toward my work. Kwame's interest and attention have made it even more noticeable. What used to roll off like water on a hot skillet slides right under my skin.

I get to my feet, slip my phone into the back pocket of my jeans, and pick up the pile of plates. "Thanks for the reminder, Mom."

The sarcasm goes right over her head. She smiles at me. "Of course, dear." She reaches out to brush some invisible dust from my arm. "When you girls are done in the kitchen, come join us in the living room. We're watching *60 Minutes* tonight. Did I tell you that Aunty Dorcas's son is a producer on one of the segments? He just got a big promotion, too. I should introduce you one day. He's got good connections. Maybe he can help you with your career." She squeezes my shoulder and then walks away.

A year ago, that passive-aggressive reminder that I haven't lived up to her expectations would have sent me into a spiral of despair about the way my life has turned out.

An explosion of laughter from the living room sets my teeth on edge, and I know I can't be here a minute longer than I have to.

I stick my head into the kitchen where my sister Salomé is already elbow deep in a sink full of dishes.

The counter tops are littered with food that needs to be put away.

It will be at least half an hour before we're done.

I can't wait that long.

"Be right back," I call out to her and hurry away before she can ask me where I'm going.

I tiptoe past the patriarchy party in the living room and slip into the small study where my parent's dark blue leather-bound Encyclopedia Britannica collection has had pride of place in this study since they moved in. Even though everything in them is either outdated or available at the click of a button, my mother dusts and polishes them like they're the holy grail.

I opt for the flashlight on my phone instead of the overhead lights and sit at the built-in desk where my father has sat to pay bills every Saturday morning they've lived in this house. I grab the old-fashioned Rolodex where my mother still keeps a record of every contact and strike gold.

I scribble down Kwame's address and make a note of the zip code as Georgetown.

"Perfect," I whisper. My favorite Vietnamese place is on my way. My mom didn't say what kind of sick, but there's almost nothing a bowl of pho won't cure.

I slink back to the dining room, grab my purse and keys, and slip out of the front door with no one the wiser.

Eighteen

Kwame

Father Figure

"Be there in five." Paloma's text pings just as I'm heading downstairs.

"See you," I reply and then toss my phone onto my bed.

I invited Paloma over today because I couldn't stand the thought of spending Sunday alone. Since then, I've finished half a bottle of Johnnie Walker, and my mood has shifted from self-pity to anger.

I've been avoiding him all week but I'm finally ready to talk to my father. If he pisses me off, I'll have an excuse to hang up in five minutes. He won't want to keep talking once he knows Paloma is here.

I instruct my AI assistant to call my father.

"Hello, Kwame." The voice that answers the phone sounds very pleased with himself and I almost hang up.

Instead, I take a fortifying breath. "Why are you answering my father's phone?"

"Because he asked me to. Hold." The line goes dead silent and I growl.

"Hello, Son," my father says, his voice raspy like he's been sleeping.

It's easy to forget that he's almost eighty most of the time, but tonight he sounds every bit like an old man. "Did I wake you?"

"Nearly, it's very late here."

"Where are you?"

"In London." I glance at my clock. It's one in the morning there.

"What are you doing there?"

"I had a board meeting. I head back to Accra tomorrow.

"Why is Oz there?"

"He had a layover so he stopped to see me."

"So was Palm Sunday *his* idea?" I ask.

"Ah, you've seen the news," he drawls.

"Yes. Why didn't you tell me before you announced it to the world? And why are you bringing it back? It was mom's thing."

"I may not be living there, but I still need to nurture my relationships in the halls of power."

"I thought you were done with American politics."

"It's a new day in DC. We've got a Black woman behind the Resolute Desk, a new crop of politicians in the bordering state houses that my PACs raised a lot of money for. Hell, the governor of Virginia is my neighbor. His daughter and my son might end up married."

I sputter. "Only in an alternate universe where we have no free will," I shoot back.

He ignores me and raises his voice a decibel. "The environment is ripe for new alliances and nothing makes people more willing to kiss the ring than an invite to Palm Sunday. Oz agrees."

His repeated mention of Oz sets my teeth on edge. "You really trust his judgement?"

He sighs. "I do."

"He stole from you."

"Oz, excuse me," he says and there's a full minute of quiet before he speaks again. "Why are you still holding mistakes he made in his youth against him?"

"He was twenty-five years old, and they were crimes, not mistakes."

"He's forty-five now and the head of a very successful consulting firm."

"One that has ties to countries we're not on good terms with."

"Who is *we?*"

"The United States of America."

"Why do you keep talking like you're an American?" he snaps.

I close my eyes and regret making this phone call. "I am."

"Only on paper."

"Dad, I grew up here. I've worked for the government for most of my career."

"You shouldn't be allied to any one nation. They are false borders designed to keep you distracted and poor." He scoffs. "I told your mother it was a mistake to let you take that job."

"Let me?" I sputter, unable to let that dig slide.

"I've given you a long leash, Son. But I didn't get to where I am by not being in control of everything. And everyone."

I'm rigid with indignation. This is why I left home. This is why I didn't see my mother for years. "You don't control me," I say through clenched teeth.

He chuckles. "Everything you have is because *I* want you to have it. One call and you would have been blacklisted from every single government agency in this country you love so much."

"Why didn't you then?"

"Because I love you. And your mother wouldn't let me." He laughs to himself.

"That's the only reason. I could change your life with the snap of my fingers. Don't misunderstand the dynamic just because you've got your own money now."

He can't fathom how little interest I have in money, so I don't bother to remind him. I'll let him think whatever he wants. Since my eighteenth birthday, I haven't done anything *but* what I wanted.

As long as I did well enough to give him something to brag about on the golf course, he let me be. This is how I've managed to survive being the son of one of the most manipulative and calculating men I've ever encountered.

I've learned the futility of arguing with my father about this and change the subject.

"I don't misunderstand anything, Baba. And believe it or not I didn't call you to fight. I wanted to know. Do you know a family named Sackey? They live in Virginia?"

He scoffs. "Of course. Loser husband, sharp-tongued wife, more children than makes sense. They're still in the area?"

He doesn't know she was their landlord. The realization makes me pause. If he didn't know then she didn't want him to.

"Yeah, Mom left them something and asked me to deliver it. I met them."

"Oh, I bet they pulled out their rifles when you said your last name." He cackles.

"They knew her as Dixon. They assumed that was my name, too."

"Why didn't you correct them?"

"It didn't seem important," I say.

He huffs. "Of course not," he mutters.

"That's not what I meant. I just…"

"What did she leave them?" His voice sharpens. I'm glad his mind has found a new focus.

"I don't know. I just delivered the letter. They were sorry to hear of her passing. Seems they liked her, and she liked them."

"She was such a bleeding heart and felt guilty for something that wasn't our fault." He makes it sound like a crime.

"What happened between you and them?" I ask the question that motivated me to make this call.

"It was an investment deal gone bad. They knew the risks, and it wasn't my fault. Or my problem. If he'd been paying attention he would have pulled his money out like I did before things went bad. Then he let his wife lead him around by his dick and talked shit about me to whoever would listen. If I didn't respect your mother's memory so much, I'd find a way to get it back." The venom in his voice isn't surprising. He hates being outfoxed.

"Why? It was what she wanted."

"What did he say? Let him know if he is still talking about me, I can make his pathetic life a living hell." I can hear the sneer on his face.

"Baba, they didn't even mention you. I was just curious. Forget I asked." What a disaster.

"Done. Anything else?" He sounds cheerful again.

"When will you be back in DC?"

"Not until next April. You should come to Ghana for Christmas."

"I'll let you know," I hedge. I'd rather work at the firm for another year than spend a family holiday with him. "Baba, I have to go. Paloma is coming for dinner and she'll be here any minute."

"Wonderful. Glad you're using your free will."

"We're just friends."

"You're a fool to let a woman like her slip through your fingers. But I'll accept someone else."

"What a relief," I mutter.

"As long as she's from the diaspora. Anywhere *but* from Ghana. Our people are judgmental, nosy elitists."

"You know you're talking about yourself."

"Exactly. So you should listen. She can be from *anywhere* else. As long as her father isn't a general in somebody's military or a politician. Clear those bars, and then I'll judge each one case by case."

"Most fathers would say things like find someone who respects you and herself. Who is honest and loyal."

He sucks his teeth. "Most father's aren't me. And they don't have sons like you. I'm telling you to find a woman who understands your position and can help you grow. Not encourage you to shrink. I have to go."

I hang up and look around the mansion I call home now with resentment.

I wish I was in Arlington with a plate of food in front of me and a sweet-smelling, fascinating woman in the seat next to me.

Thanks to my father, I'm about to lose it all.

They don't have to know I'm his son.

Our worlds couldn't be further apart.

I'm going to make sure they stay that way.

My doorbells rings. I take another swig of whiskey and run down to answer it.

Nineteen

Sin

Interrupted

I hurry to my car. A sudden rain shower and wind whips into every piece of exposed skin. I turn on the seat and steering wheel warmer and rub my frozen hands together while I thaw out. I throw that idea out of the window after ten seconds. I am so excited about seeing Kwame I'd be happy to drive wet and hot.

I didn't expect to enjoy living here so much when I arrived last year.

Maybe because I grew up so close to it, but when I left the DMV at the tender age of eighteen, I didn't appreciate any of the things that make it a fantastic place to live. Now that I'm back, I see it for what it is and can't imagine living anywhere else.

When interest rates and the housing market calm down, I'm going to buy a place and Georgetown is the neighborhood that's number one on my list.

I run across the street to Pho Mai, place the order for Kwame's pho, and plug his address into my phone's GPS while I wait.

I frown, surprised when the route calculates that his house is a twenty-five-minute walk away. If it wasn't so cold, and I wasn't delivering hot soup, I'd be up for it.

I crank up my car and follow my GPS. As I amble through traffic on M Street, I let myself imagine a life where I lived in this neighborhood. Where the perks of being home to a major university are amplified by the upscale stylish residential areas that bustle with great restaurants, boutiques, and bookstores, not to mention its proximity to the river.

The redbrick pavements and the uneven colonial-era cement block streets that remain are reminders of their place in America's infancy.

I loved spending my weekends exploring here when I was in high school. My dream of affording something in the area seems further away now than it did then.

I turn onto Volta Pl NW and roll to a stop when all I see on the street are palatial estates owned by hedge fund managers and lobbyists.

I check the address in my contacts against the address in my Maps app. Maybe my mother had the address down wrong. I pull my phone out to call her as I approach the house. I gape at the palatial three-story, dark-red-brick colonial complete with a verandah on the second level.

Certain I'm in the wrong place, I turn to leave when I spy the rusty bike he rides to my parents' every Sunday parked under a small brick porte cochere.

Working the style beat has made me an amateur expert on the hierarchy of property in any major city. There are three tests: proximity to power, wealth, or part of a family with historical significance. In a game of rock, paper, scissors, power crushes family ties, family ties will make up for a lack of wealth, and wealth will buy you proximity to power. And you can tell which hand a person has been dealt by where they live and the size of their yard.

The District of Columbia is a ten-by-ten-mile square with nearly three quarters of a million people living on the thirty percent of that square that's available for residential development. That makes space the most expensive commodity in DC. And whoever owns this house is insanely wealthy and a perfect Venn diagram of wealth, power, and family ties. This house has a history as old as this country.

That's his bike, but this *can't* be Kwame's house.

He told us he just made partner at a boutique law firm in DC. Even then, he couldn't afford a ten-million-dollar home.

Maybe he's renting a room?

From the street, all the lights appear to be off. If he was too sick to come to Sunday dinner, then he's probably asleep. I walk to the front door not sure what I'll do when I get there. As I get closer, I hear the strain of music coming from the back of the house.

It's one of Kwame's favorite songs, "Abiba" by Rex Omar.

He's here and awake. Feeling a little less apprehensive but still on my guard, I follow the sound around the back of the house and come to a wrought iron gate framed by tall boxwoods that double as privacy screen.

I think I hear the murmur of a male voice, but the music is so loud now I can't be sure.

I wrestle with whether or not I should just drop the soup and leave. The excitement I had about coming to see him is a distant memory.

This was a bad idea. The hairs on the back of my neck are standing up. I should leave, but I can't make myself. I need to see whatever is behind this gate.

I turn the corner and step into a brightly lit backyard and experience instant remorse for my curiosity.

The scene spread out in front of me is overwhelming.

Lush greenery frames a large in-ground pool that flows into a connected hot tub. Tall hedges and flowering shrubs create an even greater sense of seclusion, while a few strategically placed magnolia trees offer shade and provide a canvas for the warm, twinkling string lights draped on them and the shrubs along the pool's edge. Elegant lounge chairs and plush outdoor sofas and a large crackling fire pit with massive body-sized pillows arranged around it.

And to the right, an outdoor kitchen with a marble countertop and state-of-the-art grill and a charming alfresco dining area anchored by a large rustic table that is currently the backdrop for the most overwhelming sight of all.

Kwame is standing in front of the table. He's naked from the waist up with his jeans pulled down to the tops of his very hairy thighs. Kneeling between them is a woman dressed in an ironically innocent pink onesie. Her dark hair is caught in a high ponytail that sways with the bobbing motion of her neck. Her moans are loud enough to be heard over the music, you'd think she was the one getting head.

Her back is to me and he's leaning against the counter at the center of the kitchen. His head is bent over his phone and a bottle of malt dangles in his other hand.

I've never imagined myself a voyeur, but of the half-dozen unpleasant emotions running amok inside me, lust is the only one that's not ambiguous.

The muscular frame that the worn t-shirts and jeans he wears on Sundays have only hinted at is a testament to commitment to fitness.

The light layer of hair that covers his chest and thins to a sparse dusting down his abdomen is a surprise, I always imagined him smooth chested, but that was when I thought the wildest thing he did with his time was run marathons.

God, he's sexy.

A bark of sudden laughter draws my eyes back to his face at the same time that he looks up from his phone.

His laughter ends abruptly and the bored amusement goes to wide-eyed, perplexed shock.

I freeze like a burglar when the lights come on.

I should go.

He should cover up and shout for me to leave.

Instead, time slows, the music is muted by the sound of my thundering pulse.

He looks down and I follow his gaze. The woman on her knees seems oblivious to my presence.

His eyes come back to my face and the intensity and hunger in them steals my breath and scrambles the last bit of my brain that was hanging on to sanity.

I've never been so aroused in my life. The way he looks right now is doing outrageous things to my nervous system. My mouth waters and my nipples harden, setting off a chain reaction of pleasure that cascades downward, heating my skin, drenching my pussy, and curling my toes.

His gaze follows the path of my hand down the column of my heated throat and over the swell of my aching breast until my fingers find one of my stiff nipples. I squeeze the stiff peak in search of relief from the tension building.

He raises an eyebrow and a slow smile turns up the corners of his mouth.

"Make me come," he says in a hoarse whisper.

Those three words make the edges of my vision go dark. All I can see is his broad chest heaving, the muscles that wrap around his ribs and ripple with every flex of his abdomen.

There are a hundred steps and a thousand reasons why this is wrong between us. But the weight of his gaze makes them disappear.

When his big hand cups the head between his thighs, I slide mine up and into my hair and would swear that those are the pads of *his* fingers on my scalp.

His hips pump faster and my jaw aches as if it's *my* mouth he's thrusting in and out of.

When his chest bucks and he growls through clenched teeth, the slick of his cum fills my mouth and makes my throat constrict.

The arrogant enjoyment on his face is completely undone by his climax. His jaw goes slack, but his eyes narrow to heavy-lidded slits that stay locked on mine. My name leaves his mouth on a hiss and he shudders before his eyes drift closed. The trap they had me in springs open, and the rest of the world comes rushing in like a river. My lust is doused, and I'm flooded by horror, jealousy, confusion, hurt, and so much shame.

What the hell am I doing?

My eyes fly down to the woman on her knees. Her back is still to me.

I have to leave before she sees me.

Before *I* see *her.*

I take a step back, turn on my heel, and run.

I'm nearly at the side gate when I hear him. "Sin. Wait, please."

Like hell. I make it past the gate and to the side of his house before he catches up with me. He puts a hand on my shoulder and I swear it weighs a hundred pounds. I move my arm and step out his grasp.

It takes every ounce of strength I have to turn around and face him and bite my lip to keep from groaning.

Why is he literally the sexiest man I've ever seen? He slipped a shirt on but hasn't buttoned it.

His jeans are only partially zipped and not buttoned. They're sitting so low on his slim hips that dark tufts of pubic hair are visible.

He's not wearing underwear.

My throat goes dry.

"Kwame? Are you coming back?" The woman's voice carries around the corner and slaps me square in the face and I pull away from him and take a huge step back.

He looks over his shoulder with a scowl. "Shit."

"You should go," I say. "I'm gonna go."

His head whips back around to face me, his eyes wide. "No. Give me a minute. I'll grab my keys and my wallet. We can go somewhere and talk."

I shake why head. "We don't have to."

"Yes. We do." He nods.

"No. I'm sorry I interrupted. I'm really glad you're feeling better. Here. Take it." I thrust the nearly forgotten bag of food at him.

His gaze narrows and his nostrils flare. "Dammit Sin. I know what this looks like, but let me explain."

I roll my eyes. "Why? So you can convince me to believe you instead of my lying eyes?"

He flinches, and his brows furrow, but he's undeterred. "Please. Just give me five minutes."

I'm too tired to argue with him so I nod.

"Thank you. I'll be right back." He gives me a pathetic smile and then hurries away.

My stomach is in knots as I watch him disappear. I can imagine her stretched out waiting for him.

The feeling I couldn't name earlier flares to life so hot and bright that there's no denying what it is.

I'm jealous.

So jealous it *hurts*.

The realization is as uncomfortable as it is confusing.

He's *just* my friend.

I shouldn't be shocked that he's got a girlfriend or a lover or *whatever* she is.

He's handsome, smart, patient, funny, and interesting.

A total catch.

One that I threw back into the ocean.

It was silly of me to think that just because he flirts with me every Sunday that he was carrying a torch for me.

He doesn't owe me a thing.

And yet, I'm standing here dangerously close to tears wanting to say things like "How could you?" and "I thought there was something between us."

Experience has taught me that I almost always regret the things I say when I let my emotions lead.

I turn and head for my car. Words are meaningless and there's too much to unpack from this evening. And I'm not sure I can believe a single word he says.

It's cowardly to leave like this, but I don't owe that man a damn thing.

He told my mother he was home sick when he *clearly* isn't.

He says he's a lawyer, but he lives in a mansion fit for royalty.

My head is spinning with so many questions and warring emotions as I get into my car and drive away.

The Kwame who comes to our house on Sundays rides an old bike and doesn't have a fuck buddy.

I don't know *who* this man is.

I'm not sure I want to.

Twenty

Kwame

Split

I stalk back into the yard and slam the gate closed behind me.

I can't believe this happened.

I grab my half full bottle and drop into one of the cushions around the fire pit.

"Well, that was exciting," Lo drawls and sits down on my cushion.

"No, actually it was a disaster." She's too close for comfort and I bring my body up to sitting and move to the next cushion. "She's probably thinking about never speaking to me again."

"Not probably. Definitely."

I flash her a murderous glare before I turn to face the fire pit, my cold fingers extended toward the flames.

"Kwame's got a crush. I never thought I'd see it." She giggles.

"There's nothing funny about any of this."

"Tell me about it. Peeping Thomasina killed my vibe just when it was finally getting hot, and now I have to figure out how to get it back." She reaches over to run her fingers down my forearm.

"No, Lo." I grab her wrist and place her hand on her lap and let go. "Our friends with bennies situation is past it's sell-by date."

"Jeez, fine," she huffs and falls back in her seat and crosses her arms over chest. "Do…you want me to leave?" she asks in an uncharacteristically quiet voice.

Guilt takes the edge of my annoyance. None of this is her fault. I've given her mixed signals all week. "I'm sorry. No. I wasn't expecting her. I'm rattled." To say the least.

"So, who *is* she?" she asks after a minute of blessed silence. Her voice is casual, but I know Lo. She prides herself on knowing everything about everyone. This is so contrary to that narrative, she's probably reeling. She'll have to stay that way. I'm not ready to talk to her about Sin.

I pick my words carefully. "She's a family friend. From Ghana. Nobody you know."

"Oh." She widens her eyes with feigned awe. "A *normie?*"

I flinch at her use of the word we coined when we were young, dumb, and heartless. Moments like this are a reminder that all Lo's done since is age and get smarter.

"We're not in high school any more, Lo. We're *all* normies now."

"Oh, Kwame." She says my name like I'm an idiot she's humoring.

"What?"

"This populist streak of yours is cute. But you wouldn't last two weeks trying to live like everyone else." She chuckles and shakes her head.

"How do you know what it's like to live like everyone else?"

"I went to public school when my dad was running for state legislature remember?" She sticks her tongue out like she's gagging and shudders.

I curl my lip at her. "You're such a snob. It's not a streak. It's not my fault my dad is rich. I know you don't believe me, but I want a simple life."

"You have no idea what that really means."

Oh, but I do. Two months of Sundays have shown me the life I want. I'm not ready to share that world with Paloma yet. "I'd like to."

She sighs. "You can't look like that, have that brain, all that money, and a father who has power and just…be a worker bee with a partner who you can't bring to the club because she doesn't know which fork to use."

Her alluding to Sin makes my skin feel a size too small. I hate that she even knows she exists. "She's not my partner. We're just friends. But she'd fit in anywhere. She's the most incredible woman I've ever met, and it's me who'd be punching up if she'd have me."

"Wow." She lets out a breathy chuckle. "Good thing I've got a thick skin. My feelings would be hurt listening to you talk about another woman like that."

"First, you'd have to have feelings," I drawl.

"Touché," she sings.

Besides Titus, Paloma is my oldest friend. Our families had been next-door neighbors and her father is a mentor, even though he and my father are politically opposed.

Paloma and I ended up in college together and after three years of being fuck buddies decided to make it official during our senior year.

It didn't last long. We seemed to bring out the worst in each other and the sex was mediocre. We were better as friends, and besides occasional alcohol-fueled hookups, have remained so since.

But when I moved back here things were different.

The previous ten years could have been themed Disasters in Dating. I had given up on the kind of love I thought I wanted. The kind that made any house, no matter the size, feels like home.

When I got back, Lo made it very clear she wanted to pick up where we'd left off.

She was honest about her motivations—an alliance that would give her the money to buy the power she sought.

I could do a lot worse than a gorgeous, intelligent woman I respected and who respected me.

We didn't talk about love. We talked about goals and worldviews. We began a friends-with-benefits situation that included being each other's plus one and blowing off pent-up sexual steam.

But since I started spending time with the Sackeys, Sin is all I want.

"I'm leaving," Lo announces abruptly, breaking the uncomfortable silence that's fallen between us.

I sit up. "You don't have to," I protest, but I'm not sorry she's leaving.

"Oh yes, I do. I'm not going to listen you to talk about another woman all night if you're not going to at least make me come." She grins and sticks out her tongue, but her eyes tell a different story. I should have done this months ago.

"Listen Lo…"

"Spare me." She gets to her feet. "We want different things and have always been better friends than lovers. That's it."

I stand and put an arm on her shoulder. "I'm sorry if I sent mixed signals."

She's quiet for a moment. "I'm sorry if I made things with your mystery woman complicated."

I cast a suspicious glance at her. "You are?" Apologies from her are few and far between.

She presses a hand to her chest. "Of course. I want to make things right. I can talk to her for you."

My gut twists at the prospect of Sin and Lo having a conversation. "Let me see if I can get her to talk to *me* first."

She pats my shoulder. "Give her time."

"I hope you're right." I return my unseeing gaze to the fire and try to decide how best to proceed.

Her phone pings. "Okay, I'm out of here."

"'Night," I reply absently. She brushes a kiss on the top of my head and heads into the house.

What a shit show.

And a wake-up call.

What am I going to do?

I wonder if she's run a reverse address search on the house and what she's thinking and what she'll do once she knows who my father is. If she'll give me a chance to explain that the only Kwame I wanted her to hear, see, or know is the one I get to be on Sundays.

How do I explain that I didn't intend to deceive them?

I told myself that there was no harm in not telling them who I really was.

I only saw them a few hours a week.

No harm, no foul.

Until last Sunday, I believed it.

But over the course of the week that's followed, I found myself facing an existential crisis.

These two worlds don't fit together. The one I want to live in feels like a pipe dream, rusted and full of holes.

Or is it?

For the first few weeks, I was firm in my determination to ignore my attraction to her. Even when her lingering gazes made me think she was feeling it, too. But that wall stayed up and firmly intact.

At least that's what I thought, even when I was prepared to shoot my shot.

Whatever else went wrong tonight, I'm no longer uncertain about where I stand. She wants me. I never thought I'd see the day, but it was clear as a mirror—Sin was *jealous*.

The glimmer of gratification quickly dies when I recall the hurt in her eyes as she left.

I shouldn't have invited Paloma over. Not when I was feeling so fucking sorry for myself and drinking.

Tired and ready to put a period on today, I extinguish the fire pit and go inside.

On my way upstairs, I use the app on my phone to turns off lights, lock doors, arm alarms, and silence notifications.

Besides the sunroom and the summer kitchen, my bedroom is the only other furnished and occupied room in this stupidly large house.

I turn on the shower and strip on autopilot and replay Sin's shock and awe of a visit.

I went from panic, to confusion, to unadulterated lust when she touched her breast. Every drop of blood in my body rushed to my dick, and by the time I was thinking straight again, I'd broken something I hadn't even realized I was holding.

I can't stop thinking about the hurt in her eyes when she left and I'm not sure I'll sleep well until I make things right between us.

I stare at my reflection while I brush my teeth.

How can I tell Sin who I am, what my life is when *I'm* not even sure anymore?

Twenty-One

Sin

Trust the Process

"I appreciate your help so much," I repeat for the tenth time to the young receptionist who was so easy to deceive I feel ashamed of myself.

I assumed this building, one of the most expensive addresses in DC, would have CIA trained front desk staff.

Instead, my prepared and rehearsed sob story fell on the most sympathetic, gullible ears. I didn't even get to the end of my monologue before she was telling me the apartment number and that the person who lived there was away on extended travel.

"Wow, Casey, thank you so much. I don't know what I would have done if you hadn't helped me." I cast my stricken eyes downward and sniffle.

"Tomorrow's my last day at this job, and they've treated me like shit so it's my pleasure." She hands me the key card she scanned for me. "And this might be the first time since I started working here that I *actually* helped someone."

I smile weakly and take the key card back and make a mental note to wait until next week to come back and do the search. She said he's not due back until after Labor Day which is next week. I'll do it the Friday before I head to my parents for the long weekend.

I wonder what Kwame's doing for it.

The thought comes to me unbidden, and I shake my head to clear it and step out into the brisk afternoon foot traffic along New York Ave back toward my car.

After everything that happened with Stephen, it shouldn't have been so easy for Kwame to get under my skin.

Yet here I am, exhausted after a night of lying awake thinking about him.

When I managed to fall asleep, my dreams were plagued with the scenes from that night at his house. Everything was so vivid and visceral that when he groaned my name at the end, it jolted me out of sleep.

I fumbled in my bedside drawer for my magic wand and spent thirty minutes on the edge of release before I gave up.

I woke up before my alarm went off with whatever the woman's version of blue balls is. I've been on the verge of tears all day.

There is only one cure for it.

Him.

But he had his dick in someone else's mouth last night.

The thought makes me want to knock his teeth out.

I've never been in knots like this over a man.

I need someone to talk me off this ledge. I climb into my car and start the ignition. I wait for my phone to connect and then open my messages.

"I need to talk to you." I hit send on the voice note to my best friend, Ediri. She's in London and I can't remember if it's a four- or five-hour difference, but I pray I've caught her during the afternoon slump at her flower shop.

To stop myself from watching the screen of my phone, I rifle in my purse for a piece of gum. I've just popped it into my mouth when my phone rings. I answer it before it rings twice. "Oh, thank God you were free," I say.

"Well, well, well. Now you *need* me, you remember I exist." She shouts the last sentence and I turn the volume down on my phone.

"I'm sorry, Dins." I use the nickname her family uses to remind her that she loves me. "I'm a bum."

She snorts a laugh. "Yeah, you are. But you're my bum, so I forgive you. What's up?"

"I've been in a weird place since this move."

"You can't outrun a problem when the problem is you."

"Kicking your girl when she's down isn't nice, Ediri," I whine.

"I don't want you to get too comfortable being down, Sin. You deserve to feel good about your life."

I groan. "I know. I'm figuring things out and trying to get there again."

"By writing an advice column for *The Spectator*?"

Self-pity momentarily forgotten, I bristle. "Why are you saying it like I work in a crack house?"

She sighs. "I just…I don't understand why you quit your dream job to write…fluff, Sin."

"It wasn't my dream job. And this isn't fluff. It's…" I trail off unsure how to finish my sentence.

She lets out a long sigh, her voice softer when she speaks again. "You have all those awards. You were on one track, then all of a sudden, you made a U-turn. I'm glad Stephen is behind you, and if this is really where you want to be, I just hope you *really* know what you're doing."

"I do." I speak with a confidence that's nowhere near true. Desperate to move away from this topic, I steer us toward the smaller of the icebergs littering the sea of my life.

"I texted because despite everything I said about not wanting anything with anyone, I think I have feelings for Kwame." I'd told her about the reunion with him when it happened.

The silence that follows my confession stretches so long I check the screen to be sure we're still connected. We are. I put the phone back to my ear.

"Hello?"

"Sorry. I have died and am speaking to you from the beyond."

I laugh at her dramatics. "Come on."

"No, you come on. I've been team Sin and Kwame since you told me about him."

"There is no Team Sin and Kwame," I insist and ignore the way regret wraps itself around my heart.

She giggles. "There could be if you'd let it. I think he sounds like everything you deserve."

"Funny how you've never expressed any of this before now."

"Because I know how you are," she retorts.

I snort in affront. "How I am?"

She sighs. "Sin, the *minute* I'd suggested it you would have found a million reasons why it would never work. And honestly, I'm not sure I'm convinced it would either."

My heart kicks against my chest. "What? Why not?"

"Because you seem adrift. Working a dead-end job and keeping secrets from your family."

"I'm allowed to keep things to myself," I snap. But there's a truth in her assessment that stings. "And it's not a dead-end job. It's a *means* to an end."

"So, you feel ready for a relationship?"

"You're getting ahead of yourself. And even if I was, I'm not sure if Kwame is single."

"What makes you think he's not?"

"I went to his house, unannounced and…"

"And? What happened?" she demands in the voice that earned her the nickname Captain when we were in college. "Spit it out, Sin."

I cringe in anticipation of her reaction and just say it. "He was with another woman." My voice loses a decibel with each word until all that's left is a whisper. It doesn't diminish the stab of jealousy that I can't seem to control.

"Who is she?" she asks after nearly a minute.

I let out a harsh sigh and rest my head on the steering wheel. "I don't know. He's never mentioned anyone. He made it seem like he was single."

And I told him I wasn't interested. A pang of longing and sadness twists around the unspoken words I let die on my tongue.

"I'm going to Google him."

"No, Ediri. You know how I feel about that."

"Fine, I won't tell you what I find."

I scoff. "Google search results aren't even reliable," I warn.

"Hmmm" she drawls and then makes a series of tutting sounds.

"What?"

"Did you know—" she starts.

"Stop. I changed my mind," I yell. "I don't want to know."

"Too late," she quips. "Did you know that Kwame Dickson is a pretty common name? But none of the Facebook profiles seem like your guy. Who doesn't have a Facebook account? *That's* shady," she sings and draws the last word out.

I don't like how quickly her imagination is spiraling. "Maybe he doesn't like social media."

She swats my excuse away. "Only people with skeletons don't have social media accounts."

I drop my head into my hands, my remorse growing by the second. "He doesn't suddenly owe me his secrets just because I'm jealous. It's silly to feel that way when we're just friends."

"Maybe you should stop judging your feelings and listen to what they're telling you."

I drop my head into my hand. "I don't want to have feelings for him."

"And yet, here you are."

I snort. "Not unless I choose to be. I just need to remember that."

She's still laughing when we say goodbye.

I pull out into traffic, lighter now that I've gotten all that off my chest.

Maybe too light.

I can't seem to wrap my hands around anything. When I'm unmoored, I've found that the best thing is to surrender and drift.

As usual, my father's voice plays in my head. The line between right and wrong is an ever fixed, binary line. There is no gray area.

It's the moral code, hardwired by my upbringing, that drove my initial response to what I witnessed at Kwame's house. All I could see was everything he hadn't told me.

Now that the shock of it is wearing off, and I've trauma dumped on Ediri, the years of training and working as a journalist kicks in.

Not only do gray areas exist, they are extremely valuable and misunderstand.

It's in the gray where every story finds its roots, its tension, and relatability and it is, ironically, where the truth distinguishes itself from fact.

And the truth is, I spent my morning casing a building I intend to break into and I have zero intention of telling Kwame about it.

I've always believed, despite my curiosity, that everybody is entitled to decide what to share and what to keep to themselves.

It's not fair for me to expect Kwame to have divulged that he's rich or that he's getting his rocks off with someone else. I didn't tell anyone what I was working on. Hell, I didn't tell my parents that I know Kwame, or why I really moved back to DC.

The only deal breaker is if he's involved in any criminality.

I may not know how he makes his money, but I'm a good judge of character, and even if he's hiding things, there's no way Kwame is a criminal.

Just a lying fuck boy who has become my sounding board and friend.

What the hell am I going to do?

The question answers itself as I pull up to the garage of my office building.

"You're going to get to work, Sin. That's what you're going to do."

I finally have a lead that will put me back where I belong and make everyone who's ever doubted me or stabbed in me in the back choke on their words.

I turn my phone off and enter the iconic building that houses the offices of *The Spectator*.

The one-hundred-year-old inaugural front page of the paper is etched into a soaring glass wall that divides the building's elevator banks.

The paper's tag line, 'Your voice in the dark,' emblazoned and back-lit, gives me a rush of pride every time I see it.

When I was a little girl dreaming of being a journalist, this was all I wanted.

I almost have it.

"Trust the process, stay the course," I whisper to myself and walk to the elevator.

Twenty-Two

Sin

Dark Side

After a week of uncertainty, I'm finally ready to execute my plan to retrieve Violet's belongings and get some concrete information on her mystery former employer.

I was almost certain Oz wasn't in town, but I had no idea who else might be in his apartment.

To give myself the best chance of getting in and out without running into an unexpected cleaner, secretary, or girlfriend, I'd gone back to the basics of sleuthing.

I was going to pull the fire alarm.

I waited until late morning so that anyone who wasn't out of town would have left for the office or be on their way out to lunch.

After I'm done here, I'm headed to my parents for the long weekend and want to have plenty of time to beat them home. I want to look through the boxes of research I'm storing there without rousing their interest.

I pause to check my reflection in the mirrored glass that lines the street-level windows of The Wizard's building. I was striving for unremarkable. My hair, which would be a dead giveaway, is stuffed under a beanie. My black turtleneck and loose-fitting dark blue jeans are as nondescript as clothes can be.

I smile at my reflection and savor a thrill of excitement I haven't felt in a long time. This story was supposed to be my career maker.

I thought it was dead. I thought that dream was behind me. Now that I can see again, I'm reminded that when I was a little girl dreaming of being a journalist, this was all I wanted.

This story of stolen art being returned to its rightful owner is a sign of the times. I'm going to fight for it.

I take a deep breath and step through the revolving door into the opulent lobby of his apartment building.

The soaring ceiling is adorned with sleek moldings and dotted by a row of glittering crystal chandeliers that reflect on the black marble floor and gives me the sense of walking on a field of stars as I cross the lobby.

In the center of the space, an atrium serves as sanctuary for a vibrant arrangement of glossy-leafed ficus trees ringed by an explosion of lush seasonal blooms.

The air is infused with a subtle fragrance, perhaps a hint of jasmine or sandalwood, that's meant to enhance the feeling of tranquility. Soft music plays in the background, creating a serene ambiance as a trickle of residents pass through.

Plush seating areas are thoughtfully arranged, featuring sumptuous couches and armchairs upholstered in luxurious fabrics. Low coffee tables are adorned with fresh flowers and aesthetically pleasing stacks of coffee table books with luxury brand names on the spines.

I can imagine this place full of people in the evenings relaxing after work, safely ensconced from the real world and enjoying the fruits of their labor with their fellow uber-rich neighbors.

How the other half live.

I pass the sleek reception desk, manned by a concierge in gold-trimmed black livery. I smile at him like it's something I've done a hundred times. He smiles back and doesn't give me a second glance.

I make my way toward the elevators and duck into the mailroom.

A woman is rooting around in her postbox and wrangling a leash attached to the collar of a hyper little dog that's straining to be free.

"They cram so much crap in here, right? Who's still paying to mail out coupons?" she says over her shoulder at me.

"I know, right?" I smile and nod and pretend to rifle around my purse, my head down until I hear the clink of her mailbox closing.

"Come on, Mr. T." She scoops the dog up. I step out of their way as they pass. She smiles at me. "What perfume are you wearing? You smell divine."

I adjust my sunglasses before I look in her direction with a generic smile plastered on. "I grabbed it off my mother's dresser. I couldn't tell you." I've worn the same perfume for five years, and normally I'm apt to share, but I've already been here longer than I intended and the last thing I need is for someone to remember me well enough to give a description.

"Ah well, that's a pity. Have a nice day." She walks past me and the dog and I make eye contact.

He growls at me like he knows I'm up to no good.

She chuckles. "He's the meanest little dog ever."

She puts him on her shoulder and pats his back like she's burping a baby. "Say bye to the nice-smelling lady."

He bares his teeth at me as they walk away and I flick the judgy canine the bird. I may be up to no good, but I'm on the side of right.

As soon as they're out of sight, and I'm sure no one else is headed this way, I step into the front right-hand corner of the room, keeping my eyes on the door and feel the wall until I find what I'm looking for. I hook two fingers on the red fire alarm's wall switch and pull it down.

I pull my baseball cap down to cover my forehead and then step out into the hallway, positioning myself diagonally from the door to the stairwell.

I've never laid eyes on The Wizard before, but I know it's him as soon as I lay eyes on him. Dark, bald, smooth shaven, taller than average, slim but broad and draped in a black ankle-length tunic and black leather slippers. He looks like a villain.

He's on the phone, head down tilted down, and most interestingly, holding hands with a woman who is so stunning I forget about him for a moment.

Dressed head to toe in expensive but subdued black, she looks like she could be one of the lifestyle influencers I follow on Instagram.

She's not.

I'd remember if I'd seen this face before.

Flawless warm brown skin and high cheekbones that give her otherwise delicate face a feline quality. Her eyes are narrow and thick lashed. Her lips might have filler, but it's so well done, only she and her doctor will know. She's got the bluntest, fullest, most immaculate chin-length bob I've seen in my real life. It's got to be wig or a sew-in because no one can possibly have strands of hair this immaculate and uniform.

Once upon a time, I aspired to this kind of "effortless" perfection.

It's expensive. A man who smuggles priceless artifacts could certainly afford it. If this is his lifestyle, I can understand how he drew a young woman like Violet in.

I watch him now, nuzzling the woman's neck and wonder if she knows how he makes his money.

I take as many pictures of her as I do of him so I can run a reverse image search on her later.

I wait for them to reach the exit before I head into the stairwell.

I run up the four flights of stairs on pure adrenaline.

There's no one in the hallway when I reach his floor, and his is one of only two units on this level.

The key card works without a hitch and I slip inside in seconds.

I found the floor plan for this unit on the property management website and make my way to the small staff suite in the back. I wish I could take my time, because no matter who it belongs to, I love exploring other people's houses. Especially when it's someone like him.

The bedroom that is supposed to be hers appears to be unoccupied. The mattress is bare and there's nothing in the closet or any of the drawers. If Violet's things were here when she left, they're not now.

I walk into the living room and turn in a small circle to see what I can rifle through without leaving any sign I'd been there.

There's a stack of papers and mail strewn haphazardly on the dining table.

It's a stack of pictures printed on legal paper. Stapled together in pairs of two. I pick them up and freeze. The picture on top is of an ivory bangle I would recognize anywhere. It's one of the artifacts that was stolen while I was still in New York. This, along with the photo that matches the one in their files, should be enough.

Behind it is a picture of woman I don't recognize wearing the same bangle. Her arm is held up, her expression blank—it looks like a high-end mug shot.

There's an eight-digit code and date on the back.

I pull out my phone and take pictures of everything in the pile. I browse through the stack of mail on the table.

The name Ozwald Annan is on everything.

Oz.

I laugh at the lack of creativity in choosing his villain name. Maybe he's not as clever as his ability to evade the authorities suggests.

I flip over a heavy card-stock envelope on top. The Museum of African Art's logo is stamped on the back. I open it and pull out the card inside. It's an invitation to an event this week. I can't believe my luck. I take a picture of it and put it back exactly as I found it. Then I get the hell out of there.

On my way down the stairs, I text Leon to tell him I think his hunch was right.

Then, I text Violet to let her know I didn't find anything. I hate that I'm walking away with something for myself and nothing for her but as I review the photos I took, I'm nearly overwhelmed with excitement. I need to verify these pictures are indeed what they appear to be.

The fire department is just starting the building sweep when I come out of the stairwell in the lobby.

I fall into step with the flow of people exiting the building. I blend in seamlessly, moving slowly but purposefully until I'm past the throng of anxious residents clustered near the entrance.

The breath I'm holding bursts out of me in a laugh. I'd forgotten how exhilarating this part of my job was. How much I loved being one step ahead and downwind from the scent of my prey. I've got a lot of work to do but maybe this story has legs again.

I slip my phone into my back pocket and sprint toward the crosswalk to catch the last six seconds on the walk signal.

I'm almost there when I hear it. "Sin?"

Like a deer who hears the click of the rifle's hammer, I freeze.

It sounds like Kwame.

I must be hearing things.

I hear my name again.

This time, the voice is louder, closer, and unmistakably Kwame's.

My stomach lurches and my heart stops, but I keep walking, picking up my pace.

Why, of all people and places, did it have to be here? I race across the street just as the countdown to cross reaches one and the lights turn green.

Only then, with DC's strict jaywalking laws keeping me safe from Kwame's pursuit, do I look behind me. As I anticipated, he's trapped on the other side of the street. His eyes are locked on me and when our gazes meet, he mouths, "Wait."

I shake my head. His gaze darts to the traffic like he's searching for an opening so he can cross before the signal changes. Nothing good would come of letting him catch up with me right now. I don't want to explain what I'm doing there or talk about what happened on Sunday.

When he looks back at me, I wave and shake my head. "Sorry, I'm late for a meeting. I can't stop," I shout across the street. "I'll message you later."

His uncertain smile disappears and his eyes narrow with something that doesn't sit well with me.

I can't do this now.

I don't wait for him to respond before I turn around and speed walk. I can feel his eyes on my back as I approach the corner.

The look on his face flashes in my mind's eye. It was hurt.

He hurt me too, but not intentionally. I showed up at his house without an invitation or warning.

My step falters.

I turn around.

He's still standing there waiting for the walk signal. He's dressed in dark blue. His suit and shirt are the same shade. His shirt is open at the collar and the thin gold chain he always wears is visible.

He's got the sexiest neck.

I shake my head and take a step back.

What am I even going to say? "I wish I'd been the one with your dick in my mouth?"

Why is *that* the first thing on my mind and not questions about the mansion he lives in?

Because it's possible he's your sexual soul mate.

Who has a lover already.

I spin on my heel and continue to my car.

My steps are quick *and* sure now. I can't avoid him forever, but now is not the time.

My goal is close enough to taste.

Kwame, my curiosity, and my coochie will just have to wait.

Twenty-Three

Kwame

The Good Witch, The Bad Wizard, and the Part-Time Bitch

Sin disappears around the corner, and my gut hollows.

My mother always said my pride was my biggest obstacle to having what I truly want. Maybe she was right, but for a long time, it's been my compass and a boundary setter.

I stopped chasing people a long time ago and I'll be damned if I'm going to start now.

Especially when it would mean being late to see the only person who has never let me down and always gives it to me straight.

Alice calling and inviting me to have lunch was a lifeline I didn't realize I needed until I reached out to grab it.

When my mother died, and my father remained as distant as always, she was the person who held me when I thought I'd never stop crying. She's the only person who has no agenda when it comes to me. I don't know why I didn't come see her sooner.

Smile on my face, I knock on the door and get ready for one of her legendary hugs.

When she sees me though, she frowns and then blinks as if she's surprised I'm standing there.

"Are you okay?" I ask.

"Yes. Was just distracted." Her warm brown eyes, untouched by time and strikingly wide set, take on their characteristic twinkle. "Kwame, darling. Come here." She beams a delighted smile and throws her arms around me for a hug.

"Hello, you." I pull her close and inhale the calm clean green-tea scent that is her signature. I press a kiss to each of her soft cheeks and step inside her large entryway. "Did you forget you invited me to lunch?" I slip out of my coat and hang it on a carved mahogany hook beside her door.

She reaches out to grab my hand, her warm eyes full of apology. "Of course not, silly. Food is ready."

I link our fingers and let her lead me through her spacious, sun-drenched sitting room, up a short set of stairs that lead to her massive kitchen and to a table next to a row of windows that makes the most of the building's position next to the gorgeous Kalorama Park. "What a view. I understand why you wanted to live here, now."

I sit and when she doesn't join me, I look up at her and my smile falters. She's watching me with a frown that forces deep furrows between her brows.

My smile falters. "What's wrong?"

"You tell *me*." She turns a pointed glance downward and clears her throat.

I follow her gaze to our still linked hands. "I'm consistent," I say with a self-deprecating smile.

"Yes, you are," she says and sits in the chair next to me. "So, tell me."

"I met a woman. I care about her deeply."

Her eyes light up and she lets go of my hands to clap hers together. "Oh my God. What could be wrong about that?"

"Her family hates Al Palmer. Something about an investment gone bad. But they blame him for ruining their lives. I'm not sure how I'll overcome that once they know I'm his son."

She reaches for my hand again. "Oh, Kwame. I know your father is very polarizing, but surely they won't hold it against you."

I sit back, irked by her excitement in the face of my tale of woe. "I don't know." I rub my temple.

"I'm sorry things aren't going as you hoped, Kwame. But there's a silver lining. You met someone. I was worried you were going to end up with Paloma."

I laugh in surprise. "I thought you liked her."

"I do. But she's not right for you. I want what's best for you."

"I'm not sure Sin is best for me."

"I've found sinning to be very therapeutic, actually," she says with a nostalgic smile and faraway look on her face.

"I didn't say sinning. I said Sin. That's her name. It's short for Arsinoé."

"Oh. I see." She taps her chin and purses her lips. "So you're afraid those obstacles are insurmountable?"

"Yes."

"Fear is just an emotion. You won't know if they are truly insurmountable until you try to surmount them." She grins, and I snort a laugh.

"Is she educated?"

"Very. Smart, too."

"Pretty?"

"That's an understatement." I grin.

"Previously married?" Her gaze sharpens.

I shake my head.

"Children?"

I shake my head again.

"Where is her family from?"

"Ghana."

She raises an eyebrow a pleased smile tugs her mouth. "That's a first. What does she do?"

"She's a journalist."

As expected, she winces. "Oh God, Kwame. Of all things?"

I laugh at her dramatic words. "She's the good kind."

She sighs and shakes her head. "We will see when he comes for the party and you can introduce them."

"We'll see." If she's still talking to me.

"I actually spoke to your father too. Ugh. This thing." She hisses and glares at her smartwatch.

"Excuse me. I have to take it off. It's so distracting." She hurriedly unfastens the watch strap and lays it on the table.

I'm instantly on alert.

I know Alice's tells the way she knows mine. She gets physically uncomfortable when she has to relay news from my father to me.

Resigned, I cut to the chase. "What did he say, Alice?"

The beat of silence that follows makes me wish I hadn't asked. "Just tell me."

"He wants you to consider running for office. He's going to talk to you about it when he gets here. I just…want to give you a heads-up."

I roll my eyes and laugh. "Okay, he can expect whatever he wants, but this isn't the Middle Ages. My mother asked us to try to get to know each other. And all he's done is send me on errands and skip town."

"I know. You don't have to do anything that isn't what you want. I just wanted to tell you what he said so you'd be prepared. I'm Switzerland when it comes to you and your father. I love you both. I'm just the messenger."

I soften my expression and nod. "I know. Thank you."

"What about running for office? Will you consider it?"

"Absolutely not." I'm unequivocally opposed to the idea. "I'm applying for a job. Back with the government."

She purses her lips and nods. "I knew this was coming."

"That's not all."

She hums and raises her eyebrows as if surprised. "What else?"

"I want to sell the house. Or rent it out. But I don't want to live there anymore."

Her brow furrows. "Kwame, your mother wanted you to make it yours."

"It's so big. It's got no personality."

"Have you decorated?"

The empty rooms flash in my head. "No."

She shakes her head. "Your parents were hoping you could make it your home. Raise your family there."

"Isn't that something I should have a say in?"

"Of course." Understanding softens her expression. "If you don't want to live there now, I understand, but selling it or renting it out to someone else would feel wrong. He's done so much so you can have everything he didn't."

"Except be a present father," I mutter.

She slaps my shoulder. "You're an adult now. You don't need him for that anymore. Just…get to know him. Try to understand him. Why he is the way he is."

"I walked away from a career I love and moved here to be close to him. I took this asinine job, I moved into that house, and he took the first chance he had to skip town." I pinch the bridge of my nose and close my eyes to try and ward off the headache blooming behind them.

"Oh, Kwame. You know he would have stayed if he'd been able to." Alice puts a hand on my shoulder.

There isn't a power on Earth that could have made him leave DC if he'd wanted to stay.

I swallow down a flare of irritation. As much as she loves me, Alice is fiercely loyal to my father. When it comes to his character, she may see and hear the evil, but she will never speak of it.

"I know you're angry at your dad for leaving."

"I was. I'm not anymore."

"Then why do you want to move?"

"This has nothing to do with him. I have ambitions beyond his approval you know."

"Kwame," she sighs my name before her lips settle into a deep, contemplative frown.

She opens her mouth to speak when the chime of her front door opening interrupts us.

"That must be Oz." She jumps up from the table and sweeps a critical eye around the room and brushes nonexistent crumbs from the spotless table. "Something was wrong at his apartment so he walked over to use mine. One of the perks of having him next door."

"Oh, I see." I can't hide my lack of enthusiasm. If I'd known there was even a chance I'd see Oz today, I wouldn't have come.

"Ma?"

"Up here," she calls out. Her anxious energy is contagious and I find myself itching to leave.

His heavy footfalls hit the stairs and as if on cue, a cloud moves to cover the sunlight that filled the kitchen seconds ago.

"Is there anything to eat, I'm—" he stops speaking when he steps into the kitchen and sees me. "Oh. I didn't know you'd be here."

Alice stands, straight and at attention by the sink and beams a forced smile at him as he strolls into the kitchen.

"You said something about a fire alarm when you came in. Is everything okay?" she asks and walks over to greet him.

"It was a false alarm. Waste of time. I'll eat and go back to my place." His lip curls in a sneer when he passes me to meet her halfway. He presses a kiss to his mother's cheek.

Loving Alice is the only thing we still agree on these days. I watch as he gathers his things and studiously ignores me.

For the first twenty years of my life, he was the coolest person on the planet. Then I caught him padding his expense account and took it to my father. He's always resented me for it. He's never considered how much it hurt to learn that my idol was a thief who couldn't handle accountability. I told him as much. He exploded.

He told me how much he'd always hated me and told me I'd be nothing if I wasn't Al Palmer's son.

I reminded him that no matter how hard he'd tried that was the one thing he never be. He'd swung; I swung back and broke his nose.

It was the last time we voluntarily shared the same space for longer than a few minutes. Until my mother's funeral, I hadn't seen him in person for at least a decade. We occupy a very different world, and I'd like to keep it that way.

He's still the tallest person in every room. He always dresses to blend in. Today he looks like every other staffer on Capitol Hill—dark suit, blue tie, starched collar, gold signet ring on his pinkie and a Rolex on his left wrist.

 Six foot five, slim as a reed, with the same deep brown skin as his mother, a gleaming bald head and broad shoulders that force crowds to part, he could never blend in.

I glance at my wrist and grimace at the time. "I have a call this afternoon. I should head back and get ready."

She turns to face me, her eyes creased in concern. "Oh stay, please. We weren't done talking."

I glance over to Oz and give my head a short shake. She knows there's no way I'm confiding in her with him here. That conversation is over. "Another time."

"You're coming to the beach still, right? I'm going up today to air out the rooms."

"Yup." I groan internally. This weekend at Highland Beach is another tradition I haven't missed. I only agreed to go this year because I thought my father would be there. Of course, he's since fled the country and won't be back until his bacchanal in April.

"It'll just be us and the Persauds and The Glovers in the Cove. I think Wilde House is also going to be occupied for the weekend, if the butcher's gossip is correct. Not sure by who, though. Maybe Tyson will be there. You two always got along."

I dart a glance at Oz and then back at Alice. "Nice. Anyone else?"

"Don't worry, I won't be there," Oz answers my silent question with a sardonic smile.

I ignore him. "Titus gets in tonight. We'll drive down together," I tell Alice and ignore him.

"See you Saturday." I give her a hug. She wraps an arm around my waist and hugs me back.

"Good luck with your lady," she whispers.

Sin would love her.

An image of Sin, her head thrown back in a laugh, her golden-brown throat smooth and elegant and bared so casually, as if it's not the most beautiful neck ever created. Eleven freckles dot the side of her neck in a curved line that I've traced in my mind a hundred times.

The way things are going, it might be as close as I ever get.

The thought makes my whole body heavy. I give myself a second to enjoy the familiar, comforting warmth of Alice's hug and then I let go.

I don't say anything to Oz as I leave. I'm on the second step down when he calls my name.

"Yeah?" I say, looking over my shoulder.

"Your father expects you to be at Palm Sunday," Oz says from behind his newspaper.

I purse my lips in irritation. "I haven't been to a Palm Sunday in ten years."

"I'm bringing it up now so you have time to wrap your mind around it. It would make him very happy."

My repressed irritation strains against its leash. "You work for him. That doesn't mean you know what makes him happy."

"Are you trying to convince me or yourself?" he drawls and looks over the top of his paper with an amused glint in his eyes.

"*I* don't need convincing and I don't care *what* you think." I add a chuckle to soften the bite in my voice but it's hollow, and there's a beat of silence before he responds.

"Your *father* cares what I think," he says it softly, but it doesn't dull the edge in his voice.

"He values the opinions of *all* his employees."

"Last time I checked, my mother and I were just as much his family as you are."

I scoff. "Sure. You're his nephew. I am his only son." I turn to Alice. "I'm sorry. I shouldn't have said that."

"It's okay." She smiles at me, but it's tinged with regret.

"I'm sorry," she mouths silently. I shake my head. She has nothing to be sorry for.

"I'd better be off, or I'll be late." I flash them both a warm smile but narrow my eyes a fraction when they land on Oz and find him smiling at me like the cat who got the cream.

Twenty-Four

Sin

A Vessel of Dreams

I drove straight from The Wizard's apartment to my parents' house.

On the way here, my convictions ran the gamut.

I should ignore what I saw in his apartment. Pictures of people wearing what looks like contraband don't prove anything.

I'm chasing something dangerous, complicated, and very likely to fail.

Investigative journalism is a shark tank, and I don't want to spend the rest of my career surrounded by people I don't trust.

And yet… every time I think about what I walked away from, what I gave up on, an intense flare of panic comes to life inside of me.

If I don't extinguish it quickly, I'm afraid it could consume me.

I sit on the stairs leading from the garage to the kitchen and open the box full of the non-digital research. "Oh, wow." There's a small gold-colored flash drive on top. I could cry. This is the backup to everything that was on my computer. I thought it was gone. I tuck it back in the box and pull out the first file.

I pull out the document on top and read it.

"Most of us visit museums when we want to see rare, priceless works of art or ancient artifacts. But the .1% of us who can afford it prefer to have a private

audience with the pieces the rest of will only ever see in pictures.

The collection of art and cultural antiquities is worth $50 billion dollars annually. Most of this occurs in reputable auction houses and private estate sales. There is a well-known black market for rare paintings, but when it comes cultural artifacts there is a dark and ugly underbelly to the black market that is an open secret in the art world. The key to stopping it is identifying who is funding it."

I'd forgotten how passionately I believed in this project. Not just because I wanted awards and promotions and recognition. I wanted to have an impact that will outlive me.

The way my life crumbled made me think the universe was trying to tell me something. I was convinced my dreams had been a delusion of the grandest scale. I took this job because I thought I was done.

But now...I know his name. I know where he lives. I have those pictures. I can expose him. If I can find a way to get an invite to one of his auctions I could expose them all.

It's because of people like him that the elephant population is still endangered. He's the reason a whole generation of people is growing up without being able to worship in their sacred temples that were plundered.

I have to stop him.

I need to be less reckless. Even if I hadn't broken in to get it, none of what I got from his apartment could be used in court.

I Google the name Ozwald Annan and don't get a single hit. He's my guy. The only people with no digital footprint are dead or have something to hide.

I'm going to drag him and everyone who's helped him out of the shadows.

On Monday, I'll confirm his attendance before I pitch the story to Kathy and ask for a press pass.

Pleased with my plan, I throw my research file back in the box and drag it out to my car to take home when I leave on Sunday.

I'm covered in dust and decide to take a shower before I settle down to work.

I take my time in the shower and lather on my body oil, Nivea, and spritz myself with the azalea body spray my mother keeps stocked in every bathroom.

Saturated and smelling so good I could kiss myself, I stroll out of the bathroom languid from the hot, high-pressure shower and flop naked and damp onto the bed to air dry.

"I thought I heard the shower running." My mother's voice comes out of nowhere.

"Ma!" I yelp and jump off the bed grab the dark pink cloth from the back of the door and wrap it around myself.

"Oh please, I don't know where you learned this foolish modesty from." She sucks her teeth and steps aside as I come back out of the bathroom.

"It's not foolish. It's normal." I secure the knot in my makeshift halter neck.

She humphs a breath. "Who do you think was changing your nappies and digging compacted feces out with my bare hands when you were constipated?"

I groan. "Ma, please."

"What? If I spare the details, the story isn't as interesting," she shoots back and sits down on my bed.

"We used to wear our cloth like that in boarding school when it was too hot to get dressed. Who taught you to tie yours like that?"

"Ediri. When we were in college."

"How is she and that lovely husband of hers? Did she decide what to wear to her luncheon next week?"

I chuckle. "You'd know that better than me," I remind her.

My mother loves having Ediri to fawn over. In some ways she's closer to my mom than I am. I used to be jealous of it. Now I'm glad she has someone who can give her that. "She's great. She just opened a new branch of her flower shop in Clapham Junction."

"See, she can have it all. So can you."

"So you keep saying," I mutter and pull out my clothes.

"What are you doing on a Friday afternoon? I thought you'd come tomorrow," she says, walking over to my bed.

"I came to look for some files I left in those boxes in the garage and to spend the weekend if you guys are cool with that."

She sits next to my open suitcase and starts rifling through it, her expression creased with puzzlement. "Why didn't you bring any real clothes, Sin? It's Labor Day. We'll have people here."

"Hmmm, funny because I thought those clothes were real. Scary to find out they're just a figment of my imagination that you can see, too."

"You don't take anything seriously."

"Of course I do, but your critique of my clothes wasn't serious to begin with so I was just matching the mood." I stick my tongue out.

"Fine, I'll go look in my closet for something you can wear."

"Don't worry. I brought a dress. It's hanging in my closet."

She purses her lips and closes the case with a resigned sigh. "Instead of playing with my emotions, make yourself useful."

I kiss my afternoon nap goodbye and turn around to face her. "How?" I ask even though I already know what's coming.

"I need to cook a mountain of food and clean the floors in the foyer and sunroom. Now I have help."

I stifle my groan. I haven't been home for an hour. The last thing I want to do is rehash my role as her girl of all work. "Where's Adonis?"

She narrows her eyes at me and sucks her teeth. "Instead of looking for your brother, you should be rolling up your sleeves."

I glance at my laptop and the pile of journals next to it. I was going to spend the day getting ready to make my case to Kathy on Monday. "I have some work to do. I just need an hour."

She pats my cheek and gazes at me with deep affection in her eyes. "You're so determined to do things your way."

I throw an arm around her and bump her with my hip. "Aren't we all?"

She wraps her arm around my waist. "Some of us more than others. I guess I should be grateful that you usually do the right thing." She looks up at me with a rueful smile, "Eventually."

I laugh at her caveat. "I'm glad you can acknowledge that."

She laughs and shakes her head. "What am I going to do with you? My daughter who was born knowing her own mind. I admire you as much as I worry for you."

"Don't worry, Ma. I'm fine. I'm just finding my way."

She gets up and walks the door. "The onions are waiting for you to chop. Fry them until they are golden and *then* salt, Maggi, shrimp powder and the ground pepper and ginger I've left in the fridge. Add the tomatoes and—"

"Stir until my arm falls off," I finish for her.

She ignores me. "Once you're finished, I will come and add the rice. You've got a heavy hand and I want this jollof to be the best I've ever made."

I ignore her slight dig at my first attempt making this staple and beloved dish. "It's a holiday weekend. We should just order a tray from Rainbow and call it a day."

"Aiii. God forbid." She hisses and snaps her fingers over her head three times. "Store-bought jollof at *my* table? No. I'm making it." She points at me. "You're going to help me. We can enjoy each other's company while we cook."

"That's never how it goes," I mutter.

She ignores me but casts one last glance around my bedroom, her eyes lingering on my overflowing suitcase. A small frown furrows her brow and I know what's coming. She closes the space between us and strokes my face with her smooth, elegant fingers. "Why did God make you so beautiful and smart if it wasn't to bring you a *fine* husband?"

"Mama—" I start only to be cut off by the sharp trill of her phone.

"That will be your father. I have to go. Wash the rice for me, please." She disappears from the door as quickly as she appeared.

As much as I hate her continuing to believe that Stephen is a good catch, it's less problematic for me than the can of worms telling her the truth of what happened between us would open.

Twenty-Five

Kwame

Good Advice

"I heard you saw Paloma." Titus sits in the seat across from my desk, eyeing me.

I'm beginning to regret inviting him to drop by my office this evening. "Yeah. I saw her. What about it?"

He raises one eyebrow and smirks. "No need to be defensive. I just thought you guys were done."

"We are. What makes you think otherwise?"

"That you guys hooked up."

My stomach tightens. "God, she talks too much."

"She thought I would know." He gives me a hard, accusing stare.

"There was nothing to tell, Titus. What did *you* tell her?"

"Ouch." He hisses and presses a hand to his chest. "I'll forgive that because you're clearly in a bad mood and not thinking straight. We're friends, but K, you're my brother. That information highway is a one-way street. You know that."

I sigh and shake off some of the tension in my shoulders. It's been a long week. "I know. Anyway, it doesn't matter what she said to who. I ended things for good."

He sits up, leans forward. "I'm not trying to get involved and you don't have to explain."

"I just want you to know I'm not leading her on. We're friends. I was having a shit day. I smoked a joint, we drank some whisky, and I didn't say no when she offered to make me feel better. Then Sin showed up—"

He sits up straight in his chair. "I thought Lo was lying when she told me that part."

"She wasn't. It was a disaster of nuclear proportions."

"What did she say?"

"She hasn't spoken to me. I have to make things right."

"Are you sure about this? I mean, Lo said she's a normie *journalist?* Your family *hates* the press."

I wince at his parroting of phrases I've used in the past. "She's a lifestyle reporter, and a good one."

He snorts. "Damn. If you want to break *that* rule…you must really like her."

Something pleasant bubbles in my chest. "I do."

"So why were you with Lo?"

The question is an indictment and my initial reaction is to defend myself.

"I thought I didn't have a chance. Last time we spoke, I was going to tell her how I felt, remember?"

"Yes, I assume it didn't go well?"

"I didn't get to tell her. I found out her parents hate my dad and chickened out. Now, I'm afraid I've really blown it."

His sigh is weary and long suffering. "It's probably for the best if her parents don't like your dad. I mean, were you really going to bring her into your family fold?" he asks with a chuckle.

"Yes," I snap irritated with myself more than him.

His question gets to the heart of my worry about introducing Sin to the other part of my life. I stand up and walk to the floor-to-ceiling window that overlooks his father's massive back garden. "Why wouldn't I?"

"Same reason you didn't invite her to join us this weekend."

I sigh and roll my neck to ease the tension, resting my forehead on the cool glass window. I watch the stream of cars, pedestrians, and courageous bike riders navigate the roundabout that spills traffic onto Thirteenth Street and wish I was down there, on my way home.

"I could hardly ask her to come all the way to Highland Beach with a bunch of people she doesn't know." I don't add that there's no one there I *want* to introduce her to there. Including Titus.

Not yet.

"Lo said she didn't think she was your type."

Irritation puts a damper on my mood. "Lo doesn't know what my type is."

"Can she handle the spotlight? Is she ready for the scrutiny that will come with being the partner of a billionaire?"

"I'm not a billionaire."

"You will be. Your life is going to change when that happens. You'll pivot easily, but will she?"

Suddenly tired, I sit back down in my chair and close my eyes. "I know it's hard to imagine, but I like my life as it is."

"So you keep saying. I just don't believe anyone would want to live like they're poorer than they are. You've never lost everything. But I have and trust me, you wouldn't want to trade places with me."

Contrite, I let it go. "You're right that I don't know. But I try to do what I can to spread the wealth."

"There aren't many people with money who are as generous as you."

I shrug. "How can I really be rich if the people I love aren't, too?" I don't think I'm as generous as I could be, but the trust has restrictions on how much I can spend at a time.

"Touché. And thank you, Kwame."

"You're welcome."

He glances at his wristwatch and then gets to his feet. "You ready to go? If we hit the road now, we can grab dinner before we catch the charter up."

"We can have dinner, but I have something to do in the morning so I'll stay and make the drive after."

This conversation was the kick in the pants I needed.

I'm over my pride and out of patience.

If the mountain won't come to me, I will go to her.

Twenty-Six

Kwame

Sun Seeking Sky

As I ride over to the Sackey's house, the last conversation I had with mother is at the forefront of my mind.

"Two suns can't share the same sky." It was her constant refrain about my relationship with my father.

Much like TGlo's parting shot on our call the other day, it was her way of telling me I'd too have to choose whether I'd let his light diminish mine or step out on my own.

This job at a US Attorney's office will be my first step in doing that.

I love my father.

I also reject his way of life.

I don't think anyone should have as much money as he does. Not when there is so much need everywhere. Not when that wealth comes at the expense of fairness.

I have tried not to judge him for his choices. He had to flee his home and start his life over with nothing but his wits and cunning. I can't say what I would have done in his shoes.

He is, by every objective measure, a success.

He's also a gregarious host, a brilliant political strategist, and without a doubt one of the wealthiest self-made men of all time. He has the Midas touch, and everyone who wanted to be somebody in Washington,

DC came to kiss his ring. He's respected, revered, and feared by the people who curry his favor.

Yet, at the sunset of his life, no one knows who he really is.

Not even me. The story of his life is the stuff of legends and he's the enigma at the heart of it. And it's not just his story he's rewritten.

His ability to weave a tale is his greatest and most dangerous talent.

He made unimaginable sacrifices for me to have the opportunities and choices I do today. I'm grateful…but sometimes, I'm deeply resentful, too.

Lying to the people you love for the sake of preserving a relationship is, in fact, what creates distance and prevents true closeness.

Years of doing it has made it a hard habit to break.

Whether Sin and I are going to be together romantically or not, I hope we'll always be friends. She has to know the whole truth.

As unsavory as it is.

I have to hope she'll understand that I am not my father.

Or, for that matter, my mother. Despite how much I've behaved like them since I met her.

I grip the steering wheel as doubt, too familiar and white-hot, shoots flares inside of me.

What if I'm wrong?

What if she never talks to me again?

How will I move on if it's not with her?

I drop my head into my hands with a groan.

God, when did I become such a bitch?

Since you met your match.

Bitch.

Twenty-Seven

Sin

Ambush

"This is the last time I'm letting you use my car," I speak into my phone's speaker and then send the voice note to Adonis.

"You better have put a full tank of gas in my car," I add.

My phone rings and his name pops up. I answer with an angry swipe of my finger. "Where are you? I've been waiting forever," I snap at him.

"I'm five minutes late, curb princess."

Confused, I forget I'm annoyed and raise my eyebrow. "What the hell is a curb princess?"

"Someone who acts like having to stand on the curb for a few minutes is the same as being part of a chain gang. AKA, *you.*"

I try to keep my scowl on but it's impossible. "Why is that so accurate, though?" I concede with a laugh. "The eleventh commandment is thou shall not keep Sin Sackey waiting."

"And we love you for it. Don't change."

His words are an affirmation I didn't know I needed. "You people get on my nerves, but you're not all bad. How long until you get here?"

"Less than ten minutes. Go shopping."

I turn and scan the shopping strip and start toward the Nordstrom Rack. "Did you pick up the flowers?" I ask.

"Was I supposed to?"

I stop walking and groan. "Yes. Never mind, we can stop on the way home. Just hurry and get here." I hang up without saying goodbye. That boy is so irritating.

"Sin." The voice comes from beside me, and in my periphery, I see the figure of a man and scream before I realize that it's Kwame.

"You almost gave me a heart attack." I press my palm against my chest and take a deep breath to try and slow my racing heart down. I lean against the storefront window of the Five Below. "What are you doing here?"

He takes a step toward me but doesn't step into my personal space like he did last time I saw him. "I drove to your parents' place and Adonis said you'd be here waiting for him so I drove here instead."

I'm going to *kill* my brother.

"What's up?" Even though there's a flutter of excitement in my chest that he's here, there's more trepidation. I wasn't prepared to talk to him.

"Why are you avoiding me?"

"I'm not. I've been busy." I cross my arms.

"Jesus, Sin," he speaks under his breath through barely moving lips. His eyes narrow and he closes the distance between us. I scurry back and away from him but run into the glass-paned storefront. He places a hand on either side of my head, caging me against the door. I look back and forth between the barrier of his arms and then up at his face. "The other night…at my house." His voice is barely above a whisper but the images his words conjure—of his body, his dick, his face, my name, that *groan*—make an unholy ruckus that starts in the valley of my thighs and spreads.

I shake my head and say, "I don't want to talk about the other night."

"You're acting like you don't want to talk to me at *all*, Arsinoé." The furrow between his thick raven brows is so strong, they nearly touch. My fingertips prickle with the urge to smooth away his frustration the way I have dozens of times before. But with everything so uncertain, I don't dare touch him.

I clasp my hands together in front of me. "That's not true. There just…isn't much to say," I lie through my teeth.

His eyebrows shoot up and he takes a small step back. "Oh, really? You don't have questions?"

Too many to list. "I mean…I guess. But I'm not asking. You have your reasons and they aren't any of my business. I'm sorry I interrupted. We're fine."

"Are you going to pretend you *didn't* run when you saw me on Tuesday?" His lips are only a few inches away and my legs are turning into Jell-O.

I close my eyes and count to five, willing my heart to be still before I open them again and meet his probing gaze straight on. "I wasn't running from you. I was late. Can you please step back?" I ask, my voice clipped.

He rolls his eyes but does what I ask.

Barely.

I can still smell him…subtle, spicy, and safe. Mine.

I wish.

"I came all this way so I could talk to you, Sin."

"What is there to talk about? I'm sorry I interrupted. I'm sorry I watched."

I break eye contact and look straight ahead so my eyes are level with his Adam's apple.

I love his neck. I look down at the ground .

"So you weren't hurt? Jealous?"

"Of course not."

He's silent for a beat, and I look up again to find him watching me with an unreadable expression.

"I swear, it's all good. I don't want to ruin our friendship, Kwame. I really, really don't." I reiterate, this time holding his gaze.

He opens his mouth like he's about to speak and then presses his lips together. "How could getting closer ruin it?" He lets out a long breath and swallows hard. "For me, the closer we get, the better it feels." He steps toward me, and my stomach does a flip.

My phone buzzes with an alert. I glance at my watch and have never been so happy to see my brother's name in my life. "Adonis is almost here. I have to go."

"Sin. Come on." He runs to get in front of me and stops me in my tracks, puts one hand on my shoulder and uses the other to capture my chin and turn my face up to his. His dark brown eyes are so familiar I wish I could stop wondering what's really behind them.

"Who is she?" I ask and get some satisfaction from his wince.

"It was a hook-up between old friends who were blowing off steam."

"Then why not me?" The words are out before I even realize I am thinking them. I clamp hand over my mouth and shake my head. "I didn't mean that." I close my eyes and wish the ground would swallow me whole.

He crosses his arms over his chest and cocks his head to one side. "No take backs," he winks.

To my horror, hot tears fall from the corner of my eyes, and a sob escapes my quivering lips before I manage to press them together.

He brushes them away with the pads of his thumbs. "Are you crying?"

"No." I jerk back from his touch and brush my damp cheeks dry.

His calm demeanor makes me keenly aware of how rattled I am. I feel like I'm standing naked in front of him. Vulnerable and lacking.

"I'm so sorry you saw that."

My eyes snap up to his, blazing with indignation and ready to tell him to take his respect and shove it, but I can see the turmoil in his eyes, and even in the grips of my humiliation, I'm very aware that this entire thing was self-inflicted.

Why didn't you stop when you saw me? I want to ask him so badly.

But that would leave room for him to ask why *I* didn't walk away. I can't answer him…because I honestly don't know. "Why are you here now?"

His expression softens and he takes a step toward me. I should take a step back, but I don't. "The same reason I come to your parents' every Sunday."

"For my mom's jollof?" I peer up at him, perplexed.

"No, you, blind woman." He chuckles and shakes his head. The creases at the corners of his eyes make my stupid heart flutter and I wish we could go back to the space in time where the only thing we did together was laugh. "I'd hoped it was obvious, but now that I've made such a mess of things I realize I should have just said it aloud. I come for you. I'm here now, for you." He's closed the space between us and his breath tickles my eyelashes when he speaks.

I'm not slow, but the implication in his words doesn't compute. "Me?"

"Yes, you."

Butterflies I haven't felt in years burst to life inside me and warmth fills the places that only moments ago felt cold.

"Really?"

He cups my face in his warm, soft hands. "Really."

It feels *so* good I can't stop the moan that spills from deep in my soul.

I have so many questions to ask him, but I can't remember a single one because his skin against mine feels like the answer to everything.

I nuzzle my face into his palm and let my eyes flutter closed. I can smell cognac and woodsmoke, and I lick my lips anticipating the press of his.

His hand slips around my waist and he draws me to him. "No relationship has ever been so easy as the one I have with you," he murmurs and a shiver of anticipation runs through me.

He turns his eyes up and looks at me with an imploring expression. "I just don't want to lose *this* family. Or you."

"That's not how family works, Kwame. You can't lose what's a part of you. Over these last few months, that's what you've become—part of us. None of us know every single thing about each other. So, unless you're going to tell me you're a nazi or serial killer, it's all good." On impulse I lean up and wrap him in a hug.

He hugs me back and rests his cheek on top of my head. "Great. Thank you. I'm so glad you're not mad at me anymore."

I scoff, pull away, and cross my arms over my chest. "Let's not get ahead of ourselves. I'm still reeling from seeing you get your dick sucked."

He groans and looks heavenward. "It was nothing."

My incredulous bark of laughter is humorless. "Imagine you'd walked in on me with a man on his knees between my legs and then tell me again how it's nothing."

His eyes close for a second and his lips press together in a grimace. "Take all the time you need."

I nod, relieved that this conversation is over. "Thank you. You're coming for lunch tomorrow, right?"

"No. That's why I came by today. I have plans. Long-standing commitment."

"Seeing your secret family, are you?" I quip.

He groans. "Sin. It's nothing like that."

He looks so sad that I regret my terrible attempt at levity. "I'm just busting your chops, Kwame. I'm sorry."

He waves away a bee that zips past us. "I deserve it, I guess. As long as *you're* not running from me when you see me, I can handle anything."

I flush at his reference to the morning in Farragut North. "I was really late. Your timing was terrible."

"I'm working on that," he says with a smile that reaches his eyes.

"Thank you," I say.

He tilts his head slightly. "For what?"

"You came all this way to make things right."

He shrugs. "I missed you."

"I missed you, too," I confess and his smile deepens.

His big hand spans the small of my back and he yanks me flush against his hard, warm chest. He cups my cheek and tilts my face up to his.

Be still my heart. I'm obsessed with the way his eyes twinkle when he's happy.

"I'm so glad I found you." He presses a kiss to my cheek.

And then another.

The warmest, sweetest feeling spreads through my center. I can't do anything but soak up his touch.

I wish I'd found him sooner.

I *want* to tell him that.

I *start* to… but he kisses the corner of my mouth and I forget how to speak.

When his impossibly soft lips make contact with mine, I don't want to do anything but feel him and savor every second of this.

His lips, which have always been my favorite part of his face, live up to their promise. They're soft, malleable, tender, greedy.

God, what a *man*.

I sling an arm around his neck, and he cups my ass.

I'm sure I'd float away if he let me go.

He tastes like cognac and smells like the shea butter lotion my mother gifted him.

The squeak of brakes and the crunch of leaves under tires rips a tear into the haze of desire that bewitched me and made me act like a crazy woman. I break our kiss and let go of his neck. But he holds fast. "I could kiss you for hours," he murmurs and presses his mouth to mine again, runs his tongue along my lower lip.

It takes herculean strength to tear my lips away from his. I tug his hands from around me and take a step back.

He grabs me by the waist and drags me back to him.

"Kwame!" I gasp and then laugh, leaning away from his descending mouth, I pull free again.

"We're in public." I admonish but bite my lip to hide my smile.

"I don't care." He shrugs his eyes heavy and focused on my mouth. "Get over here, girl."

Thank God for discipline because it's the only thing stopping me from obeying. "Well, I care. And we shouldn't be kissing."

He raises an eyebrow. "Yes. We absolutely *should*."

"No. We've got unfinished business and we shouldn't let our physical attraction cloud our judgment. You know…walk before we try to run."

He opens his mouth, seems to think better of whatever he's about to say and closes it again. "Okay. Fine. So when can I see you, again?"

"Can I have the week? Just to clear my head and some hurdles at work?"

He sighs in resignation but smiles. "Of course, Sin. Take your time."

"Happy Labor Day, Kwame."

"Yeah, you too." His smile gets an A for effort.

"See you next week." I wave and force myself to walk away.

Thank goodness the days of setting myself on fire to keep everyone else warm are behind me. I'd rather be alone than accept less or settle for less than what I need. But God, I hope Kwame can get his shit together.

Twenty-Eight

Sin

Shot Down

The Monday after a long weekend in DC is usually a slow day. Most people are off on PTO they used to take advantage of the long weekend. But in *The Spectator's* office, we're buzzing with activity.

It's open pitch day and I'm almost ready. I check each stall to make sure the bathroom's empty and send a silent apology to my dad for all the lies I'm about to tell before I press the green phone icon.

The call is answered on the first ring.

"Good morning. Event office. This is Laila. How can I help you?" A chipper woman's voice trills.

I clear my throat and lower my voice an octave. "Good morning. I'm calling from Ozwald Annan's office. I wanted to confirm you received his RSVP for the fundraiser on Saturday. I found the card as I was cleaning and wanted to make sure you had him down." I read the words from a notecard so I don't make a mistake.

"Of course. Let me double-check."

She puts me on hold for forty-eight agonizingly long seconds. "We have your RSVP. It says Zuri walked it in herself. I remember it like yesterday."

"Oh, that's right. She must have forgotten to tell me when we talked this morning." So Zuri is back and working with him. I need to let Leon know.

There's a beat of silence before she answers. "I thought Zuri left. What did you say your name was?" The suspicion in her voice makes me queasy.

"I'm new. Still learning everyone's names. Thanks for your help, bye."

I hang up and glance at my watch.

The open pitch meeting starts in five minutes and today I got confirmation from my task force contact that the man in the picture is the man they'd been looking for. I didn't send the pictures of the items I took. I'm still waiting to confirm their authenticity.

I grab my phone and laptop and head for the conference room.

I take three steps before I remember my suit jacket and dash back to my desk to grab it.

I stuff myself into it while I sprint down the hall.

I pause at the closed doors of the conference room to catch my breath. I open the door to find the room empty. Relieved that I'm the first to arrive, I arrange my notebook, put the coffee service in the center of the table, and snap a selfie so I can remember the moment I took a chance on myself.

Unlike the rest of the spare utilitarian light grays and whites of *The Spectator's* newsroom, The Pearl, as this room is called by us, is luxe. Decorated in a stylish composition of cool purples with accents of creams and golds, it's not like any other conference room I've ever seen.

I choose one of the seats facing the window. The wall of floor-to-ceiling windows opens to a view that never fails to steal my breath.

The emerald-green lawn that starts across the street from our office at Lafayette Square serves as the north and south lawns of The White House. The gently sloping grass lawn runs under the Washington Monument, is broken by the Tidal Basin, but continues past the Jefferson Memorial before it stops on the banks of the Potomac River. Beyond the symbolism of it all, it's fitting that the country's leading news organization occupies this space.

When I look out there, my doubts about taking this job dim. DC may be a town with tunnel vision, but it's the root of all the major stories that have shaped politics and culture for the last decade.

The rest of the writers who plan on shooting their shot file in and soon it's standing room only.

The doors open again and my excitement goes into overdrive

when my editor, Kathy, walks in with Sofia Lallemand, the head of the news division and my idol.

No wonder there are so many people here today. This is my chance. If Kathy had liked my pitch, sending it to Sofia would have been the next step. This is a chance to cut out the middleman.

An awed hush falls over as she takes her place behind the lectern. She's not just my idol—she's an icon in the news business.

Kathy stands next to her smiling like she's displaying a prized and priceless possession. "I know you're all excited that Sofia's here, but we're going to try and have a regular open pitch meeting. This is your chance, so make your case and don't make me look bad." She gives us a warning glare that elicits a round of nervous laughter.

"Thank you for letting me sit in. The paper is very excited about the fresh voices and diversity of opinion you all bring to this newsroom, I look forward to hearing about the stories that are keeping you up at night," Sofia says, her gaze traveling around the table like a ruler taking in her subjects.

The loud trill of a phone ringing cuts through the reverent quiet.

I glance around like everyone else until the weight of several eyes falls on me.

I look down and realize the sound is coming from my pocket and nearly combust from embarrassment. "Oh my God. I'm so sorry." I duck my head and fumble to silence the call and switch off the phone.

I drag my eyes up until they meet Kathy's and swallow hard at the icy annoyance in them. The people gathered around the table keep their eyes glued to the stack of documents, but their pity is palpable.

I clear my throat and force myself to speak but can't look at Sofia. "I'm sorry."

She doesn't reply. "Kathy will introduce you by name and then you may start." She turns to the man on her left. "We'll start with you."

A few minutes into his presentation, I risk a sidelong glance in Sofia's direction and almost faint when our eyes meet. I give a small smile that she doesn't return.

I spend the next hour second guessing myself.

I've made a bad first impression. Maybe this isn't the right time to pitch?

I shake off the negative voice. Stars aligned to make this moment happen. What if it's another six months before I have this chance again? What if the timing isn't right?

This is Sofia's first year in a hyper-visible job. She's not just the first woman to lead the newsroom, she's the first in the organization's one-hundred-and-five-year history who doesn't come from a family whose name is on the side of a museum or stadium.

For those without anything but our grit and talent to recommend us, she's proof that the pinnacle is possible for anyone who works hard enough.

All eyes are on her in this role. The industry has been abuzz about her historic leadership and there are plenty of people waiting for her to fail.

I wonder if that's made her more risk adverse or daring.

"Arsino?"

I've always gritted my teeth and never corrected Kathy on her mispronunciation of my name. Having Sofia here though, I feel like it's important for her to know how to say it.

"Actually," I clear my throat to dislodge the lump of discomfort that's formed there. "It's pronounced R-sin-no-way." I turn my eyes to Sofia. "Most people call me Sin."

"Okay, Sin." She quirks an eyebrow and purses her full, expertly outlined, tinted, and lacquered lips and continues to stare at me for five deeply uncomfortable seconds that inspire a couple of cleared throats and makes mine go dry. Her expression softens and her smile is warm. "Give me the budget line of your pitch."

My pulse kicks up a notch. I wasn't expecting her, but I'm prepared. "Reclamation and Robbery. How the effort to hold on to plundered art is a billion-dollar black market that is fueled by the most powerful philanthropists in the world. Last year I worked on a story that led to the recovery of stolen artifacts and jewelry, all of which have significant cultural significance to the countries they—"

"Wait." Sofia holds up a hand and looks down at her laptop.

Startled by the interruption, I press my lips together and stifle the nearly feral urge to ask her what's wrong while she scans her screen for nearly a full minute. The rush of blood in my ears grows louder by the second and I wish I could read people's minds. My mind's latest party trick is its ability to create narratives based on a single glance. My therapist said it's a defense mechanism. But right now, it only makes the waiting harder. Does that raised eyebrow mean she's about to tell me I'm brilliant?

Or is she about to laugh in my face? I'm prepared for anything.

"Hmmm," she begins finally. "It says here that you're the advice columnist. What has art got to do with that?"

I was ready for this question too. "Nothing. But I could write this as well. I've done all the research. I know a politician's wife is wearing a piece of jewelry that I recognize as one of the items stolen from a transport truck earlier this year."

She lifts her brows. "How would *you* know that?"

My face hurts from the effort it takes to smile and pretend her condescending smile doesn't infuriate me. "As I was saying, I worked on a story earlier this year that led to the recovery of over one hundred items. I ate, breathed, and lived that story for two years, and I am familiar with every single piece. They were stolen while in transport the MAAHC."

A smirk pulls up one side of her mouth and she huffs in dismissive amusement. "You think an politician's wife is wearing a piece of stolen jewelry?" Her words are dripped in skepticism that sends chuckles rippling around the room.

I sit up straighter and let their humor at my expense roll off my back. I'm used to being dismissed and have learned to appreciate the power in being underestimated. They won't be laughing when this story gets A1 placement.

"I *know* she is. I spoke to one of the people who used to make deliveries for the individual *I* believe is behind the thefts and the sale of the items."

She leans back in her seat. "You *believe?* Oh good, let's just chase tips based on vibes and gossip."

I'm too insulted and surprised to respond.

She looks at Kathy. "I thought you said she was sharp."

Kathy glances at me with something like panic her eyes. "She's still learning how our desks work."

"I see." Sofia wrinkles her nose.

"Well, your belief isn't going to save us in a defamation suit." Disappointment slices through me like a knife to the gut and the backs of my eyes burn.

Asshole editors in chief aren't anything new. But the dressing down in front of the entire newsroom is.

Heat creeps up my neck, and I don't shift my weight, but I don't want her to see me sweat. I push my emotion aside and put on my combat gear—my unshakeable faith in myself. "No, but my extensive research will." I flip open the file in front of me. "I only knew this person by the moniker they use to sign off on the communications I was able to access from several well-placed sources in law enforcement.

Now I know their real name, *and* that they will be in DC for an event on Saturday. It's VIP, by invite only. Except of course the press pass."

"How do you know he'll be there?" Sofia interrupts my breathless monologue with an unreadable expression on her face.

"I have a source who has direct knowledge of their attendance." I dodge the trap set by her use of a male pronoun, and her snide smile compresses into a pinched, tight-jawed sneer.

My training has taught me to keep thinking even when my body's instinctive response to perceived danger turns me into a bundle of quivering nerves and roiling insides. Her raptor-like focus and over-the-top interrogation is a tell. I'm sure of it, but of what, I don't know. I catch myself chewing my lip and force my jaw to relax.

She leans forward, her eyes keen on me. "Is your source from the venue or from this person's organization?"

"Why is that relevant?"

Something flickers across her face before an angry frown wipes it away. "It speaks to the reliability of your tip. But you're right. It is irrelevant." She folds her hands in front of her and the cold satisfaction I detect in her eyes tells me everything before she turns her attention back to my editor.

"Kathy, you'll need more before you can justify issuing a press pass for an event like this. If he's invited, I assume he's someone with power and connections. We can't afford to piss anyone like that off right now for a story that's not important."

My stomach falls. "I can show you my research, the articles about the pieces that were missing from the batch that made its way from New York. I've seen the ring, and I know he's the person who sold it."

Sofia holds up a hand to silence me.

"I'll remind you that you are a lifestyle reporter."

"Yes, but—"

"Stay in your lane."

I'm still seething when the meeting is adjourned. I gather my things and focus on getting out of this room.

"Arsinoé, I'd like you to stay." This comes not from my boss but Sofia herself.

I freeze half over my seat, my hands bracing the arms of the chair, and my mind goes blank.

"Okay," I say and lower myself back down.

I glance at Kathy, my eyes wide with alarm.

She grimaces, gives her shoulders a tiny shrug, and she mouths "sorry" before she hurries out of the room.

I take a deep breath and remind myself that Sofia is one of the reasons I wanted to work at this paper.

This is an opportunity to fix the terrible first impression I've made.

She's sitting in her chair, arms crossed, watching me. I plaster a contrite, warm smile on my face and when she doesn't say anything decide to show some initiative and break the ice.

"I'm so sorry about my outburst, Sofia. I've been so eager to meet you—"

"Oh, I'm sure you have. I can smell your ambition." She speaks in a neutral voice, but there's no mistaking her comment for a compliment.

I clear my throat, desperate to break the ice. "Umm. Well, it's because my family is from Ghana, too."

She sharpens her gaze and gives me an assessing once-over. "I was sure you'd married into that last name."

I resist the urge to roll my eyes and nod. "I know I don't really look it, and my name is Egyptian, and my last name is European. But yes, both of my parents are from Kumasi."

She scoffs and tilts her head, a frown creating brackets around her mouth. "And? Do you think that means something *here*? The news doesn't care if we're friends. It cares if we write stories that make people want to pay us to read them. I don't know how Kathy runs this team, but in *my* organization, a cute and clever routine doesn't mean shit."

I can't stop my incredulous laugh before it escapes me.

Her eyes narrow. "Something funny?"

I sober instantly. "Not, not at all."

"You want to make a name for yourself, try walking humbly before you try to run."

I wish the floor would swallow me whole, and I can't find a single word to say that wouldn't get me fired on the spot. I keep my simmering anger below the surface and force myself to look diminished. That is clearly her goal, and I'm fine to let her think she's accomplished it. "Understood."

"You came in here loud and overly confident because you wanted my attention. Well, you got it, and I am not impressed."

Me neither, bitch. "I'm sorry to hear that."

She nods and the animosity on her face morphs to indifference.

"Leave." She waves her fingers in the direction of the door. Dismissed as suddenly as she summoned me, I'm dazed and disillusioned. What the hell just happened?

Kathy is waiting in the small reception area outside of her office and hops out of her chair as soon as I step into the hallway. She falls into step with me, brimming with barely bridled curiosity.

As soon as we're out of earshot of her secretary, she pounces. "What did she say?" She grabs my arm and forces me to stop and face her. Her eyes are wide with anticipation.

"She hates me." The words come out before I realize the thought has formed and I shake my head, disbelieving at how badly things spiraled just now.

She gasps. "No. She's a hard-ass, that's all." She pats my arm. "You'll win her over."

"Maybe," I hedge. "I'm not sure that's possible. We got off to a bad start. First impressions are hard to overcome."

"Oh, it was the same for me. I spilled my Hibiscus cooler all over her desk. Ruined her beautiful journal."

I gasp. "Wow."

"Yeah, well, I apologized, replaced the journal and got a gift certificate to the spa at the Four Seasons."

I give her a bombastic side-eye. "That's a lot."

"It was. I needed her to like me. So do you. There's no getting ahead here if she's not in your corner. I did whatever it took to win her over because I love this brand."

When she talked like this during our interview, she made me forget there's no such thing as a "dream job" in corporate America.

It didn't take me long to remember though. A job is a means to an end. *The Spectator* on my resume will open the doors to everything I want—long-form features and my own column. A book deal borne of a story I breathed life into.

If the only way to get ahead here is to be on Sofia's good side, then this may not be the place for me.

If the bottom line is *her* red line, I'm not sure I want to be on her good side.

"Let's grab lunch later. I'll order something, and we can eat in my office. Have a good catch-up," she says with a glimmer in her eye, and I know right away she's got an update in the never-ending saga of her and the man she's been seeing. I want to scream.

I'd rather get to know the other staff writers, for a competitive profession, journalism is also incredibly collaborative. But I need Kathy on my side if I have any hope of getting into that event.

"Okay, sounds great." I smile as we reach my desk. I crane my neck to see if anyone's sitting behind the dividing wall and then speak in a hushed voice. "I actually want to talk to you about the story I pitched in there."

"What about it? Sofia shut it down." She leans against the frame of my cubicle, arms crossed over her chest, lips pursed.

My throat tightens at her dismissal, but I press. "I know. But she'll be going back to her end of Pennsylvania Ave. She'll never know you ordered the press pass. And when I get the story, she'll take credit for it herself."

She cocks her head slightly and looks at me closely. "Sneaky aren't you?" Her smile is more calculating than sincere.

"If I have to be. This is a rare opportunity" I bite my lip. "It's a solid lead. If I'm right, it'll be a huge story. Corruption all the way to the top. I just need a chance. Please." I press my hands together not too proud to beg.

She sighs heavily and straightens. "Art theft and priceless contraband would be entertaining, I guess." She tugs the lapels of her sharp black blazer and takes a step back and out of my space. The temperature between us falls.

"It's more than entertain—"

"Be that at as it may, I fail to see the value in diverting you from our editorial plans. You're not an investigative journalist anymore, remember? Stay in your lane, Sin." She puts a hand on my arm and smiles at me like she feels sorry for me.

After how thoroughly she abandoned me in that meeting, it takes every single inch of my willpower not to yank my arm away. "I can do both. I don't need more resources. Just access."

My heart plummets to my toes when she shakes her head. "Even if I *wanted* to, it would be career suicide if she found out. She's powerful and has a very long memory."

"I promise she'll never know. Kathy, please."

She squeezes my arm and lets go. "Don't worry, kiddo. You've got time to make a name for yourself. Do the work, *then* go for the glory."

"You're right," I say so she'll stop talking.

We say our goodbyes, and as I watch her walk away, I begin formulating my story for canceling lunch.

Kathy is a conundrum. She was so excited about hiring me but all she's approved for me to write is fluff. I started to suspect she was sabotaging me but dismissed the thought because we're friends. I'm not sure that's true. The last thing I want to do is alienate her any more than I already have. I have two days to figure out how to get her to change her mind.

I can't let this go. I need to think and strategize.

I grab my coat and head for the one place I know I'll find an open ear.

Twenty-Nine

Kwame

Opportunity Knocks

I'd resigned myself to not seeing her until Sunday, so Sin is the last person I expect to find at my doorstep on a dreary Monday night. "I know it's late. I just took a chance you'd be here and free," she says when I open the door.

"Uh…hi." I stare dumbly at her, my vision clouded by surprise that doesn't know which way to assert itself. I've never been so happy to see anyone as I am to see her now. But I also know that if she's here something is wrong. "Are you okay?"

"Can I come in, or… do you have company?" She looks up at the sky and it's only then that I notice the drizzle of rain visible in the beams projected by my security lights.

"I'm alone, and of course you can come in." I open the door to make room for her to step through it.

She exhales as if she was holding her breath. "Thank you. I'm sorry to drop by like this." She slips past me and takes her black, pointed toe flats off and lines them up neatly next to the pair of basketball sneakers I left there a few hours ago.

I gaze down at them side by side and like the way it looks. She clears her throat, and I look up to find her watching me. I even pretend that I'm sorry she caught me and my smile deepens.

Her eyes narrow "What are you smiling at?"

I shrug. "Just…you're here."

She quirks her pursed lips and shrugs. "I know I asked for space but I really needed to talk to someone, and it's you."

Flattered and happy doesn't begin to describe how it makes me feel to hear those words. "I'm glad you came. I'm just cleaning up after dinner. Do you mind hanging out in the kitchen?"

"Sure." She looks down, and I follow her gaze to her bare feet. She wiggles her cute pink-tipped toes, and I have to rip my eyes away and swallow the saliva pooling in my mouth.

She clears her throat, and I drag my eyes back to her face. Her brown skin is glowing despite the cold and her dark brown eyes are limpid in this light. I wonder if she's remembering the same thing I am, but know better than to ask. "Do you have an extra pair of *chale wotes*? I hate being barefoot."

I nod and smile at her use of the Ghanaian colloquialism for flip-flops. "Then you've come to right place. I do, too. Excuse me." I point to the wall panel behind her. "I need to get in there."

"Sure." She ducks her head and steps aside. I press the wall with the flat of my hand. The top panel springs open to reveal a cabinet full of house slippers in every color and size. "Take your pick. I ordered a dozen pairs in every size when I was in Ghana last."

She stares at the wall long enough for me to wonder if she heard me. I'm about to repeat myself when she takes a step toward it.

"Wow, a secret panel full of shoes…I thought I'd have to die and go to heaven to see something like this," she says and pulls out a black pair covered in a gold and white pattern made up of the Adinkra symbol my parents used to create our family crest, and that adorns everything with his name on it.

She murmurs something under her breath as she inspects them.

"Will those work?" I ask.

"Yeah, this is Bese Saka."

"My mother had it embossed on her stationary. It stands for affluence, abundance, and unity." I smile despite the wistful pang in my chest.

"Talk about manifesting your life." She waves her hand around the grand room.

"Except she never really got to enjoy it. This was her dream house…and she never lived in it." I laugh like I've made a joke and turn away from her before I say more. The slap of the rubber shoes hitting the floor is followed by the shuffling of her soles.

I make my way without waiting for her, but she catches up with me in a matter of steps. "So, she left it to you?"

"Yes. She wanted me to make it a home. She loved it."

"I see why. It's beautiful," she says, her head swiveling to take in the cavernous, furniture-free living room and dining room. "Why don't you have any furniture?"

"I have everything I need. Just…haven't gotten round to decorating."

"If I lived here, I'd never leave. It's gorgeous."

It's funny how differently we see this space. I realize that I haven't actually looked at the parts of the house I don't live in. She's right. The rooms have two-story-high windows that overlook different ends of the massive back lawn.

"I work a lot. But maybe I should—"

"Oh my God," she gasps as we step into the kitchen.

"What?" I ask, looking around for what could have elicited the sound.

"This kitchen, it's beautiful. It's a dream." She walks over to the first island and runs the flat of her hand over the white, grey and gold counter tops and shakes her head in awe. "Wow, I've never seen stone like this."

"It was made especially for the house in Ghana. Much like everything else they purchased for the renovations." That pang of wistful regret is back. I hate that my mother never got to live in this house that she built with so much care.

The walls are paneled with white wallpaper embossed with the Adinkra symbol. The only things that aren't are the appliances.

"I could live in here," she says as she strolls through the space, touching every surface with a reverence I wish I could inspire. She opens the fridge. "SubZero, commercial size and empty," she mutters.

"I hate cooking for one, so I eat out."

"Or at my mom's," she quips and throws me a teasing smile over her shoulder before she walks over to the butler's pantry.

"Holy shit. You've got more dishes than a restaurant."

"Yeah, my mom loved crockery. I inherited her collection and even though I'll probably never use them, brought it here with me."

"I'd eat on these every day." She sighs and gazes at the cabinets while I gaze at *her*.

Her profile is sharp and striking. Only the outrageously full swell of her lips hints at the lushness of her whole face.

A dainty jawline, straight broad-bridged nose, and high cheekbones form the perfect pedestal for her upward sloping almond- shaped eyes. Her lashes are dark, thick, and nearly straight.

On a heavy sigh, she lets her head loll back and closes her eyes.

I stop staring and am instantly alert. "What's wrong, Sin?"

"I wish I'd been born wealthy instead of good looking and smart." She casts me a baleful look.

"What?" I bark a surprised laugh then quell it when she scowls and walks out of the pantry.

"Wait, are you serious, Sin?"

"Yes, money is freedom and choice."

I shake my head. "No it's not."

She shuffles over to the bar and hoists her lush ass onto the buttery yellow leather chair that cradles it so perfectly I'm jealous of it. It's closer than I've been in a long time.

She props her elbow onto the counter and rests her chin on a closed fist.

"So, if you didn't have bills, you wouldn't work?"

"Of course I would work. But not like this. For people who lie, backstab and care more about cozying up to sources instead of reporting on them."

I slide into the stool next to hers. "What happened?"

She and slumps in her seat. "I hate my job."

I nod in understanding even though I'm surprised. She's always talked about work as a calling. But as I think about it, she doesn't talk about it much at all. If I didn't bring up her column every Sunday, she might not talk about it at all.

"I'm not sure I even want to be a journalist if this is all it's going to be." She looks despondent.

"You love your job."

"I love the idea of it. The possibilities it holds." She lets out a sigh and stares straight ahead unblinking.

"But the reality?" I prompt when she doesn't continue after a few seconds.

She shakes her head slowly and blinks as if to clear her vision. "The *reality* is I'm stuck with an editor with an aversion to thinking outside the box and I pissed off the one person I needed to impress. And you know what? I don't care. She's an asshole and if she liked me, it would mean I was, too."

"Not necessarily, but I get your point."

She purses her lips. "I took this job because I wanted to be back in DC, but also because I wanted to do something that didn't consume me the way investigative work used to. I thought this was what I wanted."

"And it's not?"

"No, it is. I mean, I don't want to end up where I was a few months ago."

"Where was that?"

"With my work stolen, and nothing to show for it."

"Damn that's grim."

"That's what's happened before. But it doesn't matter. I've learned my lesson and the story…it doesn't want to let me go. I want to see it through and let it go."

I understand the feeling. "Are you sure that's what you want?"

She bites her lip and shakes her head. "Yes. I'm so close to nailing this person down."

"So, what's stopping you?"

"My target is someone who is normally impossible to pin down and I found out he'll be at an event in DC in two days. I need is a press pass."

"And your boss said no."

"Yes."

"Well fuck her. Go anyway."

"I can't sneak my way into that kind of event." She looks down at her hands and frowns. "He's going to slip through my fingers again."

"Who is he?"

"I can't tell you. Not yet. Not until I've got him." She curls her hands into fists at the same time a smile curls the corners of her mouth.

I let out a low whistle of appreciation. "I'd hate to be the person you're thinking about with that blood-thirsty glint in your eye."

She scoffs and curls her lip. "He's everything I hate. A criminal with power and money who plays the good citizen by day but is nothing close to it. I want to expose and stop him."

"Then you will."

She growls low in her throat and slaps the counter. "It's the perfect story for the paper. *I'm* the perfect person to write it. She shot it down like I'd suggested writing about an alien invasion."

"Did she say why?"

She rolls her eyes and sucks her teeth, the universal West African sign of disgust that makes me miss my mother. "Her reasons were bullshit. And she did it in front of the entire department."

I wince in empathy. Seeing her so defeated makes my chest ache. I run a hand up her back and massage the base of her neck. She's so tense. "I'm sorry."

She presses her lips together and her eyes narrow. "I swear, today, it felt like she was *trying* to sabotage me. And I don't know why." Her face is taut and emotionless for a couple of seconds before her lower lip trembles. "Do you think I'm crazy? I mean, this career I've been dreaming of…all these near misses. Close enough to smell something great but never close enough to touch. Maybe, I'm not cut out for it."

Sin is a lot of things but defeated has *never* been one of them. "Her not understanding your ideas doesn't make them less valid, Sin. If you weren't cut out for it, you would have taken her no on the chin and gone home to write whatever it is you're supposed to be writing."

Her composed expression crumbles and she presses her trembling lips together. "Kwame. Don't be nice to me. You're going to make me cry and I really don't want to cry tonight."

"Okay, no crying. Maybe I know someone who knows someone. Where's the event?"

"At the Museum of African Art. It's a fundraiser, invite only. Only VIPs, dignitaries and press will be there."

Awareness makes me sit up straight. "On Saturday?"

"Yup. I confirmed he'll be there, ripe for the picking. I'll be home praying for lightning to strike the same place twice." She groans and stares straight ahead.

I'm only torn about what to do next for half a minute.

I pick up my phone, open my email, and scan until I find what I'm looking for.

The email's subject line is *Project Return*. My stomach twists into a knot. This is the last thing I want to do, but something kept me from RSVP'ing with my regrets. My finger hovers over the link to reply.

Do I really want to mingle with a crowd of people I was desperate to get away from?

No.

But I want to help Sin more than I to want keep my father's world hermetically sealed away from this part of my life.

I throw caution into the wind and hope for the best. "I have two tickets to that fundraiser on Saturday."

"Huh?" The look of genuine confusion on her face is so damn cute I almost smile. But the pit of dread in my gut won't let me.

I clear my throat and attempt to relax my shoulders. I put my phone down and tilt it so she can read the screen. "Here. See?"

Her eyes bug out and her lips pucker and twist as if she's confused.

"Is this not the same event?"

She raises her eyebrows. "I am not—I'm not pocket watching okay? It's obvious you have money, but wealthy people are a dime a dozen in DC. But *this* event is for dignitaries, people with security clearances. The VP, the mayor of DC, the governor of Maryland will be there. How did *you* get tickets?"

Her incredulity is so naked and loud it makes me laugh. "My father was a big donor in his heyday."

"He must have been a whale," she says.

I nod, my collar suddenly tight. "Something like that."

I've seen the glimmer of greed often enough to spot it in even the most practiced parasite in waiting. There's only dubious hesitation in her expression.

She crosses her arms over her chest and eyes me with undisguised skepticism. "So *you* have tickets to this event tomorrow? Or your father does?"

I force a smile. "Me. I'm his social proxy when he's not in town. I have a plus one, and you're it if that's what you want."

She throws her arms around me and presses her face into my neck. "Oh my God, thank you."

"You're welcome." I hug her back and savor the warm softness of her body and the sweet smell of jasmine in her hair.

She pulls away too soon. "I need to get ready. I don't have anything to wear. I came over here planning to have a pity party, and you turned it all around."

"It was timing and luck. I'm tempted to ask what are the odds, but when it comes to us, that question is starting to sound silly."

"Right?" She smiles but it's strained.

"What's wrong?"

She shakes her head. "I'm grateful. I am. It's just." She lets out a heavy sigh. "I work *hard*. I have vision. I'm dedicated to my craft, I take risks and somehow, I find myself relying on luck to get ahead." She looks away and down and bites the corner of her mouth. "Or maybe I'm just kidding myself that my efforts alone should be enough. My editor thinks I'm trying to walk before I can crawl."

I wish I could throttle this editor person. "Don't listen to her. You're talented and you've got good instincts. And luck would never find you if you weren't ready for it."

She presses a hand to the base of her throat and turns to look at me with a smile on her face. "Thank you for saying that."

Our eyes meet and my heart skips a beat at the vulnerability in hers. "It's just the truth, Sin."

The smile she gives me is sweet, but her eyes are full of something that makes me want to lean in and bite that full lower lip of hers.

The air between us crackles and her gaze drifts to my mouth. I'm so tempted to lean in and kiss her.

Patience.

I clear my throat and slide off my stool. "So, Saturday. Do you want to be my plus one or…nah?." I pick up my phone and walk over to the other side of the island so we're face to face.

"If you're sure it's okay." The skepticism in her voice is absent from her expression. She's grinning from ear to ear.

"More than." This is the first time I've ever been glad about my dad's position in life.

She hops down from her the barstool and presses her hands together. "Then yes. I'll owe you.

"No. Just pay it forward."

Her grin melts into a close-lipped smile that manages, somehow, to be dazzling. "Thank you, Kwame. I'd *love* to be your plus one."

I hold my phone out to her. "It starts at seven o'clock. What time shall I pick you up?"

She clears her throat and tucks a lock of hair behind her ear. "Um… No offense, but how?"

"I have a driver with access to something nicer than my ten speed."

She wrinkles her nose. "That's not very encouraging Kwame."

"Trust me. And if you don't like it, I'll drive us over in your car, okay?"

"Okay. Done."

"And they'll need to clear you through security so I'll need your full name and how you'd like to be addressed on the place card for dinner."

She cringes. "I mean, okay, but I'll be there to work. Will you be okay by yourself or are you clingy?" Her cheeky smile creates a dimple I've never noticed high on her left cheek.

"Clingy? In your dreams." I smirk. "I'm perfectly capable of entertaining myself."

"I'm just making sure we're on the same page, and if you want to text me we should probably finally exchange phone numbers. I'll put mine in." She nods at my phone. I open contacts and create a new entry before I hand it to her.

She bursts into laughter when she sees the name I used for her. "Good Sin?"

She rolls her eyes, but her smile deepens. "It's an oxymoron."

"It's aspirational," I quip. "Only time will tell."

She laughs and swats my chest playfully. I grab her wrist before she can pull it away and tug her closer to me.

Her laughter dies abruptly and her eyes meet mine and hold. "What are you doing?"

"I don't know," I answer honestly.

The tension, the attraction, the longing that has been between us since the night we met is stronger than it's ever been.

I stroke the index of her wrist with my thumb. "Your skin is so soft."

She looks down where I'm touching her on a sharp inhale of breath. "Kwame," she breathes, and it sounds so conflicted that I feel like a creep and instantly let go.

"I wasn't thinking. Won't happen again."

She steps back and rubs her wrist. "I hope that's not true. But we need to talk first, and I have to go. I still have a deadline for this week's column and I need to figure out what I'm wearing." She smiles but she fumbles with the zipper of her purse until I nudge her hands away and open it myself.

"It's always getting stuck." She gives me a wan smile.

"Here you go." I hold it out to her.

"Thanks." She avoids touching me the way Superman might avoid touching kryptonite.

The thought lifts my mood. At least I'm not alone.

"No problem," I say and return her smile.

She tucks a lock of hair behind her ear and clears her throat. "So, tomorrow? Pick me up at six thirty?"

"Yes. It's a date."

She holds up a finger. "It's *not* a date."

I nod, my eyes on her mouth. "Figure of speech."

"And I meant it. No kissing," she says with an arched eyebrow and a stern set to her mouth.

She's killing my pride. I scoff. "Honestly? It's the last thing on my mind."

Her expression puckers at the taste of her own medicine. I have to bite my cheek to keep from laughing.

"Well, that's a relief." She gives me a stiff smile and slings her bag over her shoulder. She's been gone for five whole minutes before I realize what I forgot.

I text her. "I need your full legal name to put you on the guest list."

She writes back. "Arsinoé Ama Sackey. And thank you again."

"The pleasure is all mine."

It is the truest thing I've said all day.

Thirty

Sin

Paranoid

"Why haven't you replied to my text?" I demand when my brother finally answers his phone. "I sent it half an hour ago."

"Because I haven't seen it. I've been peeling onions for this nonsensical lunch Ma is throwing."

I snicker at his characterization. "What's the occasion?" I turn around in front of my floor-length mirror and run a critical eye down the line of my back and my ass.

"She wants to show off the new deck and hot tub." He does a perfect imitation of the aggressively British accent my mother puts on in front of company.

I cackle. If keeping up appearances was an Olympic sport, our dear mother would be a gold medalist.

"It's not funny," he says through his own laughter. "I can't wait to leave, too."

I hear myself in his pity-pocked griping, and I say what I wish someone had said to me back then. "I feel your pain. It sucks not being able to prioritize yourself. Your time is coming. But right now…" I let out a deep breath and turn back to the mirror. "Mine is running out. I need your help. Please, Don?"

"Begging doesn't suit you. Hold on."

"Thank you. But can you hurry? I've been trying to reach you for an hour."

"Damn. Can a man wash his hands first? I swear, the three of you act like I'm your house boy."

"Adonis, stop complaining," I snap. "I have an important event for work and you're the only person I trust to tell me the truth."

"You don't act like it, but I'm glad you appreciate my gifts. Let me see what you sent."

I bite my lip to hold back my growl of impatience and wait for him to finish.

"Ohhh. I see. This is…different for you," he finally says.

"Different good or different bad?" I ask, fretting now.

"Very good. Are you going on a date? I've never seen you wear anything like *this* to work."

"I'm going to a private fundraiser and I want to make a certain man swallow his tongue when he sees me."

"In that dress, he'll probably swallow yours, too. Ten out of ten."

I shake my hips in triumph. "Oh thank fuck. I don't have time to change." I run to the closet to grab my shoes.

"What about the rest of you?"

"I got my makeup done and I'm wearing a pair of black sling back Aquazzura's."

"Can't wait to find out who was worth this effort."

"I'm worth the effort. He's just collateral damage," I quip.

The crunch of wheels in my driveway makes my heart skip a beat "Oh shit, hold on. I think the car is here."

"You hired a car?"

"Something like that."

I pull back the long white curtain covering my living room window and peer outside and gawk at the black Rolls Royce pulling to a stop in my driveway.

"Never mind. Just someone turning around."

I walk back to the mirror, grab my lip gloss out of my purse to touch it up. God, my makeup looks amazing. Kwame may not be thinking about kissing me tonight, but I'll make sure he thinks about it so much he chokes.

Just a little.

The slam of a car door wipes the self-satisfied smile of my face. I drop the lip gloss and hustle back to the window.

"Woah." I gawk at the tall man in a dark suit with a monochromatic black shirt, tie and gloves. From here he could be *the man who held a gun in my face*. My blood runs cold, and the phone slips out of my hand.

The clatter shakes me out of my fear frozen state and I pick up my phone. "Hey, I have to go."

"What happened?"

"I dropped the phone." I hit the wall safe with my palm and it springs open. I pull out the heavy black pistol I've only taken out for a couple of trips to the practice range. I check the clip but keep the safety on.

"I've really got go, Adonis. I'll call you back."

"You better or I'll be on my way over there to find you."

"Love you, bye," I add speaking over his protest.

I disconnect the call and with trembling hands open my phone's keypad and key in 9-1-1. I crouch under my window, my heart and mind racing.

What are the chances that I'd be burgled at home twice in one year in two different cities.

The short, sharp knock on my front door almost makes me pee myself. The are lights on everywhere, but if I'm quiet maybe he'll think I'm not here and leave.

My phone buzzes in my hand and I look down, ready to decline the call.

It's Kwame. I decline the call and send him a text.

"Sorry I can't talk. Are you on your way?"

"My driver just arrived."

My heart sinks. "Tell him to circle the block. I'm not ready."

The man knocks again and irritation and fear spike at the same time. "There's someone at my door. A strange car parked in my driveway. I think I need to call the police."

"He's at the door knocking. Tall, light-skinned guy with short dark hair. I'll let him know you need more time."

My body sags in relief. Tears sting my eyes and then I realize. "You're not in the car?" I text him back.

My phone rings again and I answer on the first ring. "Hey sorry about that. Where are you?"

"Sin, hi. I got pulled into a meeting unexpectedly. I'm going to be late so I sent the car ahead. Is everything okay?" His voice is hushed.

"Of course. I just… wasn't expecting such a fancy ride," I quip.

"Would you like to arrive in something else? I can arrange it."

"No, it's great. Better than. Thank you. I'll be right out. Sorry to keep him waiting."

"No need to apologize. He's at your disposal. His name is Ian and you're in good hands. I'll be there as soon as I can."

He hangs up, and I peer outside at the half-a-million-dollar car in my driveway.

Wow.

What did Mrs. Dixon do for a living?

I put my pistol back in the safe and arm it with my thumb print.

I hate the way it feels in my hand. I hate that I felt like I needed it.

I haven't been to the practice range since my first round of lessons. My instructor said I've got good aim.

I hope I never have to find out if that holds up under pressure.

I smooth a hand down my dress, take one last glimpse in the mirror and grimace at the thin sheen of sweat on my forehead. I grab the handheld fan from my everyday purse and drop it into my clutch. I lift my armpit take a sniff and hurry to answer my door.

"Miss Sackey, good evening," the driver greets me with a friendly expression on his face that softens his hired hitman look.

"Sorry to have kept you waiting."

"Not at all. I am on your time tonight. The car is ready whenever you are."

"Thank you. Let's go."

I follow him down the crumbling walkway that leads from my house to the driveway and remind myself that this is just a temporary stop and that it's better than moving in with my parents. I text Adonis that it's all good and climb inside the cool, sleek interior of the car.

I spend the short ride down Sixteenth Street reading through all the notes I've made about Ozwald and decide that it's a good thing Kwame's not here. DC is a small town. With this new era of leadership in the executive branch, the nation's capital has become the place to be for the entire global arts community. Tonight, African Diaspora—from the United States, almost all of the ECOWAS countries, the Caribbean and South American nations—is out in full force. I'm convinced that diaspora wars are something that only exist online because I've never experienced it in person.

I force my focus back to the reason I'm there.

I see The Wizard for the first time while I'm waiting in line to go through security. I turn my face away when he strides past me. He doesn't stop to speak with the press gaggle who shout his name, and he sails past the step-and-repeat without being photographed.

I ignore the huffs of indignation as I skip to the front of the line and hand my purse to the security man with a smile and a fifty-dollar bill that I'll miss very much.

I get in just as he and another man break off from his larger entourage to head away from the event hall and up the escalator.

I fish my compact out of my purse and use the mirror to watch. I wait for them to step off before I follow.

It's impossible not to be in awe of the stunning design of the newest of the Smithsonian museums.

The lights from outside sift through the tiny holes casting patterned, shadows over the entryway. It's a magical display that's enough to make me forget why I'm here.

I'm jolted back to reality by the rough grasp of a leathered clad hand around my wrist.

"What do you want?" The man who had been with Annan glares down at me.

Panic blinds me for me a moment before my training kicks in. I glare up at him.

"I'm looking for the bathroom." I yank my wrist away out of his grasp.

"You passed it." He points in the direction we've just come from.

I look in the direction he's pointing and turn back with a sheepish grimace on my face. "Oh, I didn't see it."

His expression doesn't soften. "Now you do. Be on your way."

"Fine. No need to be rude."

I turn slowly, craning my neck over his shoulder as I do and spot Ozwald stopped a few feet away.

He's talking to a woman whose face is obscured by decorative topiary. I don't need a full visual or more than the momentary glimpse my slow rotation affords to know who it is.

That collarbone-skimming perfectly blunt bob is a dead giveaway.

They appear to be having an unremarkable exchange. Until she leans forward to press an air kiss to his cheek and he lowers his head to press his nose to her throat for the briefest second.

"What are you waiting for?" the man asks me, and this time, he pulls his jacket back to reveal a shoulder holster.

My heart leaps in my throat.

"Nothing. I'm just admiring the art. Are you museum security or something?"

"It doesn't matter who I am. You're not allowed to be here. Leave. Now," he says through barely moving lips.

"Copy that," I say with a mock salute before I turn on my heel and get the hell out of there.

Thirty-One

Kwame

Late

I'm finally on my way into the museum when I spot Lo coming out.

"I didn't know you'd be here."

She reaches up to press a kiss to my cheek. "I didn't know you'd be here either. I just came to show my face."

I nod and try to inconspicuously wipe my face where her lips touched. "Right, nice to see you, but I gotta run. See you soon?"

"Wait." She grabs my arm to stop me from moving on. "Why are *you* here?"

"I had tickets."

"You have tickets to everything. You never attend. Why this event?"

"My father asked me to be here, show my face and get to know the people."

"So it's not because the woman you chased the other night is here?"

Trepidation flares in my stomach. I was hoping their paths would never cross again. "Is she?"

She rolls her eyes. "As if you didn't know."

I scan the crowd for her before looking back at Lo's pleased smile. I ignore it. "Did you meet?" I ask, my heart speeding up with each beat.

"No. Not yet, anyway."

Relief makes my knees weak, but I only smile vaguely. "Maybe next time. Good to see you."

She places a hand on my chest to halt my exit. The familiar touch feels out of place somehow. I glance around for Sin again.

"Kwame, look at me."

I force my eyes from their hunt and look down at her. "Yes?"

Her smile is tight. "We've been friends nearly our whole lives. She's a new kid on this block. Until you know her…"

I cover her hand with mine. "Her family has known mine for decades." It's an embellishment but I need her to understand the hierarchy right now. "I like her very much, and she's not going anywhere." I lift her hand off and let it fall by her side.

She blinks in surprise. "You were serious that night? Like, as in for real?"

"Yes. For real."

She frowns but it curves up in a smile. "Okay, then, I like her, too. I can't wait to meet her."

The thought makes me intensely uncomfortable but it's inevitable. Lo and Titus are like family. "We'll make it happen. Now, if you'll excuse me."

"Of course. Have a good night. Oh. Heads up, Oz is in there too."

Jesus, of all people. I hope Sin can get what she needs and we can get out of here before our paths cross. I head inside to find her and get this evening over with.

Thirty-Two

Sin

Blindsided

I melt into the crowd and grab a drink from a passing waiter, and smile politely at people who smile at me, but I don't stop moving until I reach the cordoned off space where tables are set up for dinner.

I grab my glass of wine and scan the room for a glimpse of Paloma Persaud. She's on my research list for this week. My Google reverse search told me that she's the daughter of the newest governor of Virginia.

A man who's seen as the future of American politics. He's a first generation American whose parents came here from Guyana and founded Blue Cab of DC. Wikipedia has a lot to say about the man's career and background but only mentions his children's first names and his wife is his high school sweetheart. Further research revealed that her mother is a member of one of the original Black families of Baltimore.

Paloma Persaud herself has zero online presence except for a TikTok where she posts pictures of pretty plates of food with no caption or context. I need to figure out how they're connected and if she's involved in the cultural theft ring.

A friend of mine from *The Post* is seated at the press table, and I walk over to say hello. He raises his eyebrows when he sees me. "Look at you. Eating with the grown-ups, I see."

I brush off his teasing. I thought I'd be uncomfortable on this side of the rope line, but I like being inconspicuous. It makes me harder to avoid.

I wrinkle my nose. "I couldn't get a press pass for *The Spectator*, so I called in a favor."

His brows knit. "What do you mean? *The Spectator* is here."

I'm shocked. I scan the table. "Who?"

"Sofia the Great. She's over there." He points to the front of the room. Sure enough, Sofia is seated at a table. And next to her is The Wizard, Ozwald Annan. Their heads are bent together and his lips are moving. She throws her head back and laughs at whatever he said.

I feel like I've been dunked in cold water.

What the hell is going on?

She jumped in and shut my request for a pass down so forcefully.

I didn't say his name but maybe she knew who I was talking about because she knows he's the person behind the ring I was trying to expose.

That conniving bitch.

I see red.

I should wait until we're in the office to ask her about this. But I can't stop myself from marching across the room and putting my hand on her shoulder.

She jumps and whips around, the smile on her face disappearing when she sees me. Her eyes narrow and she shoots to her feet, blocking my view of Annan. "What are you doing here?" she asks me like I'm the one who's been caught in a lie.

I cross my arms over my chest. "I'm with a friend. Not working. Did you shoot me down because you wanted this story?" I ask before I think of a diplomatic way to phrase the question burning a hole in my head.

Her brows snap together in surprise before she catches herself and puts that battle-ax scowl on. "Don't be absurd," she hisses.

"How else do you explain it? Being here? With the press pass I requested?"

Her eyes narrow. "You need to remember who you're talking to. And you need to leave." She puts a hand on my shoulder and tries to steer me away.

Like hell. I squirm out of her grasp and place myself in The Wizard's line of sight.

"Sofia, are you not going to introduce me?" I say loudly.

"I was just about to ask her the same thing." Annan rises to his feet behind her, towering over us both. His bald head gleams like a high-tech helmet under the yellow, green, and red lighting.

He even looks like a villain. His gaze is piercing and perceptive, and I take an instinctive step back, my heart racing as if I'm in danger.

Sofia's smile looks carved out of granite as she pivots so she's able to see us both. "If I must. This is Arsino Sackey."

"Arsinoé," I correct her with a quick glance so she knows I know she did that on purpose. I extend my hand to shake his. "Nice to meet you."

He steps forward and closes the distance between us in two strides and grasps my hand. "Pleasure is all mine." He lifts my hand to his lips and kisses the tips of my fingers instead of the back of my hand.

I gasp and pull my hand away. "I actually came tonight hoping to meet you." I shoot my shot and ignore Sofia's laser gaze at the side of my face.

His smile falls. His eyes slide to Sofia for a moment. "Is this the person you mentioned?"

I whip my head to look at Sofia, too shocked to hide it. "You were talking about me?"

"She was doing you a favor. I don't take kindly to people talking about me. Especially when they have no idea what they're doing. You're out of your depth," he says in a voice that reminds me of a snake's hiss.

Sofia comes to stand beside him and looks down her nose at me. "You'll thank me in the long run."

I shake my head in disbelief and my stomach drops to my toes. She must have known who I was talking about at the pitch meeting. She sabotaged me.

"Sofia, you're a journalist. How could you do this?"

"You are on thin ice, Sackey."

Oz puts a hand on Sofia's arm, and she clamps her mouth shut.

"She's done you a great service, Ms. Sackey. I don't take kindly to people defaming my character. It never ends well for them." His smile widens but his expression is nothing but ice-cold malice.

Sofia turns and puts a hand on his shoulder. "Ozwald, Ambassador Makumbi just arrived. We should go speak with him now."

"No rest for the wicked, it seems. Till we meet again." There's a smile on his face as he puts a hand on my elbow, but there's something in his eyes that makes me hope I never see him again.

Sofia turns to me and leans in so her mouth is by my ear. "If you want to have a career in news or journalism at all, you aren't going to bring this night up to anyone, ever. And if you want to have a job at *The Spectator* or any news organization again, you and I will never talk about it either. Now, leave before I have you thrown out."

My heart kicks against my chest and I want to scream loud enough to shatter the windows.

I get on the escalator and pull my phone out to text Kwame to let him know not to bother coming after all. I'm about to hit send when I catch a glimpse of him walking up the path that leads to the front door.

We meet just as he's coming through the entrance. He cuts a striking figure in a steel-grey tuxedo paired with a monochromatic teal shirt and tie.

Seeing him makes me reconsider leaving. He looks too good not to be seen tonight. I wear a lot of black but there's nothing I love more than a well-dressed man who's not afraid of color.

His suit looks like it's custom tailored and it makes the most of the fit body genetics, running, and regular weightlifting have given him. Several heads turn as he strides through the clustered crowd of attendees. He stops to shake a few hands. But once he spots me coming down, he slips his hand in one pocket and navigates the crowd like he's making his way to the end zone, his eyes intent on his path. And on me.

I can't believe this dashing, immaculately groomed, custom couture wearing gentleman is the same casual, bike-riding hottie with a patient smile and beat-up sneakers who I've been sitting across my mother's dining room table from for months. He looks like a totally different person.

"Hey, Superman," I quip when we meet in the middle of the large reception area.

He wrinkles his nose. "Superman?"

"I'll explain later. You ready to go?"

I hook an arm through his and turn us around toward the exit.

He digs his heels in and stops us mid motion. "The party's that way." He points over his shoulder.

"The person I came to see isn't here, and there's nothing interesting happening. But, if you want to go in and check it out, we can stay."

That last part was my guilt for wasting his time and lying about it talking.

I cross my fingers he doesn't take me up on it.

He looks over his shoulder, expression contemplative before he shakes his head. "Nah, I'm only here because you are. If you're ready to go, so am I." He reaches up and unclips his bow tie. "I can't stand most of these pretentious assholes."

I laugh, and just like that, the knot in my gut is gone. "Thank you for being so cool about everything."

"Of course. I sent my driver home so it's just us."

Just us. The words make something in my chest flutter. We step out in the unseasonably cold evening and the noise of people and cars moving up and down Fourteenth Street. Before I can express my regret over not bringing a coat, he drapes his tuxedo jacket over my shoulders.

"Thank you." I snuggle into the warm silk-lined garment and allow myself a long inhale. He smells so good. I look at the sky and say a silent thank you to whatever star he fell from.

Thirty-Three

Kwame

Double Life

I'd been annoyed that I'd had to send Sin ahead just to have the wind taken out of her sails. But now that we're driving away from DC, tie loose, heels in the back seat, I'm glad I got to skip to the good part of the evening.

We haven't spoken since we agreed to get food from Ben's Chili Bowl on our way to my car.

I put on the heated seats, cracked open the moon roof, and turned on the radio. The quiet rush of wind and WHUR's Quiet Storm show serves up the perfect soundtrack for a night that feels, suddenly, full of possibility.

"I love this song," Sin says quietly, just loud enough to be heard over New Edition's "Can You Stand the Rain?" She leans forward and turns the small volume knob on the console.

I can't remember a time that we've been together this long without her talking. Titus' comment about me not being open comes to me as the silence stretches. I'm not used to having to ask what's on her mind, but maybe I should do more of that. "What's on your mind, Sin?"

"What?" She turns the music down. "Sorry, I was a million miles away. What'd did you say?"

"I asked what was on your mind."

"Hmmmm," she says on a long, heavy sigh. "We're both living double lives."

It's not what I was expecting to hear and even though she's not wrong, my first reaction is to reject it. I feel exposed and judged. "I see…" I force my hands to relax their grip on the steering wheel.

"I mean, I don't want to speak for you, but from what I can tell, you've got a rich family or a trust fund and friends and interests that you've been very deliberate to keep hidden from me."

"It wasn't—"

She puts a hand on my wrist and strokes the back of my hand with her thumb. "It's okay. You're allowed to have your secrets. Lord knows I have my own."

I slide my eyes to her. "You do?"

"Doesn't everyone? Like, I can't tell you what I'm really working on. Or how old I was when I lost my virginity. It's okay, and I don't want you to tell me things you're not ready to share. I know what that feels like."

I let out a deep sigh. "Thank you for understanding. I'm not keeping secrets…per se. Just not sharing things that don't seem relevant."

"That's why I called you Superman. Tonight, you look like a different man. More like the man you were the night we met. You've been showing up to my parents' looking like Clark Kent and tonight, I saw you and realized I wasn't sure which one is the disguise and which one is skin you're most comfortable in."

She's not asking me for an answer and I couldn't give one if she was. I don't know.

"I don't think of it as double life. I wasn't hiding. I just wasn't talking." I glance over and see she's staring out of the window again.

"Where are we?" she asks as we pull into the parking lot of the small park.

"Theodore Roosevelt Island. This is the best view in DC. At least *I* think so."

"Are we allowed to be here this time of night?"

"I hope so." I put the seats down in the back of the SUV and open the tailgate so we can sit facing the river. We spread out a blanket and sit down and grab our hotdogs.

"I can't believe I lived here all these years and never realized it was open to the public."

"We used to drive up here when I was a teenager," I tell her.

"You went to high school near here?"

"No, I went to a boarding school in New York, but I spent some of my summers here."

"Wow." Her mouth is full of food, and she holds up a hand while she chews and swallows. "So, you've been rich your *whole* life?"

I stiffen, still not sure what to say and how. "Yeah. Sin, I'm sorry I didn't tell you."

"No, I already told you. You don't have to tell me anything until you want to. I just don't want to be lied to. No matter what kind of relationship we have. If you tell me something, tell the truth. Okay?"

My heart is beating a hundred miles an hour. "That sounds extremely fair."

She nods. "I'm very good at brokering solutions. At least for other people." She laughs and steals my breath. Jesus, I don't know if it's pheromones or what but everything about her excites me. She intrigues me and makes me think. And lets me be myself.

She balls up the napkin she spread on her dress to catch crumbs and tosses it over her shoulder. "Okay, so how about this? We introduce the Kwame and Sin that we'd like each other to know. No questions. We do this for as long as it feels good. No expectations. Just friends who also have sex."

Her expression is so earnest, and the tension I've been holding since the Sunday everything started to unravel finally starts to ease.

"I'd like that."

"Let's lie down," she says.

I grab a blanket from the backseat and use my coat as pillow and arrange myself with one arm bent so I can cradle my neck. She lays on her side next to me and puts her head on my shoulder and presses herself into my side.

It feels good.

Safe.

I close my eyes. "I'm Kwame. Born in the UK to Aloyisuis and Constance. My dad is from Ghana. My mom's parents were American. When I was three, my mom was accepted to a masters' program in diplomacy at Georgetown, so they decided to settle in Virginia."

"Wow, I didn't know that about her."

"She never worked in her field. She just supported my dad's career."

She strokes my chest, and I cover her hand with mine and keep it there while I talk.

"I was taught at home by a tutor until I was twelve and then I went to boarding school. I left for college when I was eighteen."

"Where'd you go?"

"London School of Economics for undergrad."

She sits up. "You did? No way. I did my junior year abroad at the School of African and Oriental Studies. I lived in that library on The Aldwych." She does the math and shakes her head. "That would have been your final year, right?"

I nod. "I wonder how many times our paths crossed before we actually met." My heart thunders in my chest.

"Timing is everything. So what did you after LSE?"

"I came back to the US and went to law school at UCLA. Went straight from there to the California DOJ."

"That's where you were when we met."

"Yup. I'm spending the year as Of Counsel at a law firm in DC."

"What's that?"

"It's like being a partner without an equity stake in the practice. It's only a temporary position and I mainly do civil litigation work. I'm trying to get back to criminal prosecution because it's what I love and what I'm good at."

"So why'd you leave that?"

I take a deep breath. "When my mother died, she left me a letter with a list of requests. One of them was to move back to DC and try to live the life they'd hoped I would. To give my dad a chance to be the father she thought he could be."

"Wow. That's a lot."

"Yeah, but I'm glad she used her last words to steer me. She also left me the bulk of her estate which was worth over a billion dollars."

She's silent, and I look down to find her mouth open. "Wow. A billion?"

"Yup, that house was part of the bequest. She wanted me to make it a home. But…I wasn't sure I wanted to stay in DC at first. Being close to my dad wasn't an exciting prospect."

"Why not?"

"He wasn't happy with my decision to go to LSE or law school. He didn't like that I didn't want to use their money and status or step into his shoes. He basically exiled me when I refused to do what he wanted. I saw my parents once a year at Christmas in Ghana, and my mother when she came to the US every spring and summer. They're kind of public figures but intensely private at the same time and I've never publicly associated with them. We only reconciled right before my mother died."

"That recently?" she asks.

"Yeah. My mother and I weren't ever at odds really. He wanted a very specific thing for my life, thought he knew best, and I wanted to find out for myself what I was good at. You would have thought I'd spit in his face. After she died, we agreed to try to get to know each other. He lined up this job for me and started introducing me as his son everywhere we went. Three weeks in he said he had to deal with a crisis on one of his new projects and left."

"But you're on better terms?" she asks with what sounds like hope in her voice.

I shrug. "I don't know. Kind of. We're speaking." I let out a weary sigh. "I guess the fact that this is the first time I'm mentioning him is a clue."

"Oh, Kwame. I'm sorry."

"No, it's okay. He tried, but he's not made for sitting still and I'm not interested in playing golf and constantly working to amass money I don't need."

"Wow, is that really how he is?" She sounds horrified, and I feel guilty for speaking so harshly about him.

"Look, he's not a monster. But he's not a good man either. He just…only does what is best for him. He invests in causes he abhors and people he wouldn't share a meal with if the return is good. Sadly, for the world, he's very good at it. He's bankrolled some of the biggest brands and products of the century, it's made him very rich. But the only time he actually spends with people is when he's doing business with them. He doesn't know what a personal conversation is. He's eccentrically private and notorious all at once."

This is so hard to talk about, and I feel breathless after that monologue. My heart thuds as I wait for her to respond. I can't take it back and whatever happens next will be fine. I hope.

She strokes my chest as if she knows my heart needs soothing. "I bet you wish he was just your dad, right?"

"Yeah, I wish that would have been enough for him."

"You don't need to be enough for him. You're enough for *yourself*. I'm sorry you didn't have a dad who made you feel like you were important. I'm glad you figured it out for yourself and built your own life. You should be proud of yourself."

The boulder of anxiety I've had over sharing this with her lifts. "Thank you. I have to add, because no matter how big of an asshole he is, he's still my father. He can be funny, supportive, generous. I think of his greed like a disease or an addiction. He's insatiable. Everything else will always come second."

"Yeah, it's good to accept it so you can stop chasing something that you could never catch," she says in a distant voice.

"Sounds like you're speaking from experience."

"I have Ghanaian parents too, remember?" she says.

"Your parents aren't like that. Come on."

She shrugs. "Not to the same degree, but I do feel like we were vessels for all their unrealized hopes. Our achievements are a testament to them and our failures were an indictment of some sort."

I laugh at a memory. "Oh yeah, bragging rights. My dad used to put my academic awards on our family Christmas card each year."

She sits up, and gazes down at me. Her eyes are kind, her lips soft and smiling. "You're not your parents. Their choices don't have to be your burden."

"Easier said than done."

"What isn't? But it's possible. Maybe that's the new American dream—having the ability to make your own choices. Remember what you said that first night about their sacrifices not being our burden? I heard that in my soul. We're *not* our parents. Even if they can't see that."

I rub a hand down her back. "I know, Sin. I didn't mean to diminish that."

Her shoulders relax and she takes a deep breath. "It's okay." She stays sitting up and tucks her legs underneath her. "It's taken a lot of therapy to figure it out and stop internalizing it. I have the right to live my life how I see fit. You owe it to yourself to do the same. The people who love you will be beside you. And if there's no one beside you, fuck it. You've still got you."

I grin up at her. "You give great advice. Has anyone ever told you that?"

She rolls her eyes. "I'm serious."

I grab her hand and sit up, too. "I know. It's one of the many things I like so much about you."

"So…you like me?"

"Very much." I cup her face and look into her eyes so she can see how much.

She nuzzles my palm and the silky softness of her cheek makes me want to see her as God made her. But first things first. "I want to kiss you."

A smug grin parts her full lips. "I thought you weren't thinking about kissing me anymore."

"And you knew I was lying." I trail my finger down her throat and cup the back of her neck. My fingers slip into the soft hair at her nape and I flex my hand to stroke her neck.

"I did. Yes." She whimpers like she's in pain. "It's *all* you think about."

"Yes. Well, that and eating your pussy, fucking your mouth, being inside of you, falling asleep with your nipple in my mouth." I lean in close enough that our lips barely brush, and my breathing goes ragged from the effort it's taking to restrain myself.

She sucks in a breath and holds it. "Really?"

"Yes."

"Well, what's stopping you?" She sticks out her tongue and licks my lower lip.

I groan and then pull my head back.

"Right now, those raw onions you put on your hotdog," I deadpan.

She throws her head back and laughs.

She's exquisite. Her dress fits her like she was sewn into it. Her long legs are bent at the knee and tucked under her. The black silk of the skirt splits to reveal her luscious thighs. The bodice wraps her torso and tiny breasts so tight I'm jealous that it gets to be so close to her skin. Her shoulders and neck and arms are bare and glow.

She smells like fresh flowers. I bet she smells good everywhere.

"Full tint," I speak to the car's AI assistant.

The windows of the car tint. "You have one hundred percent privacy, Kwame."

She gasps. "That is *so* cool."

I kneel in front of her and place a hand on each of her thighs.

She trembles at my touch but untucks her legs and puts one on either side of me.

My breathing is ragged. My mouth is watering. "I should have asked before I touched you."

"You have my permission."

Her husky voice makes my dick so hard. I press her thighs apart, and she offers no resistance.

"You're so soft." I slide my palm down her stomach and cup her pussy. The lace of her panties is warm and damp. I pull my hand away and lift it to my nose. "What are you doing?"

"I want to smell you." I look up at her and slide my hands up and then in between her thighs. My fingers brush against soft skin, hot and damp, and she whimpers. "Get a preview of what's to come."

She closes her eyes and slumps in her seat. "Definitely that," she pants.

"I want to kiss you but…"

"But the onions."

I shake my head. "I was kidding about those. That couldn't stop me."

"Then what?"

I drop my head and press her thighs as far apart as the seat will allow. I kiss the soft inner skin on each of them and slide the scrap of silk down her hips and all the way off. "I like the way you keep your pussy trimmed." I run my fingers along the light dusting of hair on her mound.

She rolls her hips. "Don't tease me."

"It's not a tease. It's an appetizer. Public fornication is a crime."

"Being good is no fun."

"Spoken like someone who's never been caught."

She taps my chest with the tip of her finger and smiles up at me. "*You*'ve caught me. Now, make me pay for my crimes."

"Careful what you—"

"Stop talking," she growls, and I obey.

She clutches the lapels of my jacket and presses her mouth to mine.

It's hard to catch me by surprise but she does, and by the time I'm aware of what's happening, she's on top of me, my hand is cupped on her neck, and I've taken control of the kiss.

Her lips are so soft and warm and full. I suck on them until she pulls away abruptly and scoots further down my thighs. "What are you doing, Sin?"

"Taking what I want." She pants against my mouth and whips my belt loose in one masterful stroke.

"You're crazy." I chuckle and lift my hips, brush her hand aside and unfasten my pants myself.

She grins. "You have no idea." Her hands clasp around the back of my neck. Her lips brush my ear, and she whispers to me. "I wanna show you something."

"Now?" I ask.

"Yes, right now because I've been wet for you since Easter, and I can't wait a second longer to have you inside me."

My breath leaves me in a rush, and my dick turns rock hard.

How long have I imagined what it would be like to take all of her clothes off and feast on her body?

She is intoxicating and right now, I am entranced.

"You don't have to wait, Sin. I'm ready whenever you are."

"Do you have condoms?" she whispers.

"Yes. I carry them around like I carried that earring," I say and reach past her to feel for my wallet.

"Lift up," I say and when she does, I take my throbbing dick out and make quick work of the latex.

Her small, warm hand wraps around the base of me and my head falls back to rest on the seat at the full body rush of pleasure.

She's going to kill me.

I grab her ass and squeeze the soft abundance of it as she lowers herself onto me. She takes me in slowly. Her eyes are closed, her lips are parted and I'm fighting to keep myself from plunging up and into her.

I let her take the lead, set the pace, find our rhythm because I already know that this is going to be good for me.

I grab the strap of her dress and tug it down to reveal her bare breast, her fat nipple hard and calling my name. I lift my head and suck it into my mouth and am rewarded with a tightening of her core muscles around me.

She increases the pace and my head falls back. A bead of sweat falls onto my cheek from her chin and she leans down to lick it off. I cup the back of her neck and pull her lips to mine and kiss her hot mouth. I don't understand how a kiss can feel so good. The minute my tongue slides past her I forget my restraint and move us until we're lying flat, hip to hip, and I fuck her like I've wanted to since that night in April.

She wraps an arm around my neck and whimpers into my mouth. I slide a hand between us, find her clit. She circles my wrist to slow me down. "Like this," she breathes against my lips.

I take us up as high as I can and when I finally come inside of Sin, it like I'm free-falling and I'm not sure I'll survive.

I'm not sure I want to.

Thirty-Four

Sin

Secret Lovers

I didn't realize I was nervous about seeing Kwame until I pulled up at my parents' house and saw that rickety old bike sitting in their driveway. I pull down the mirror in my car visor and frown at how much make-up I'm wearing. This man has me dressing up for Sunday lunch.

"Wow, look at you," my father remarks as soon as I walk through the front door and all eyes turn to me. My brother and sister-in-law turn away from the football game with polite smiles of benign agreement and distracted hellos.

"Hi, Daddy," I kiss him on the cheek and sit next to him before I finally let myself look at Kwame.

He's dressed the way he always is on Sundays. Gray sweatpants and a black T-shirt and a pair of white socks on his shoeless feet. He's sitting where he always does, on the floor with his back against the couch. Legs stretched out, crossed at the ankles, a bowl of Doritos and a huge bottle of water on either side of his thighs. While everyone else turns their attention back to the main event, his eyes stay on me.

I woke up to find him gone this morning and was annoyed he hadn't said goodbye.

Until I found a bag of my favorite coffee beans, a bag of bagels, and a big tub of cream cheese from the bakery at the corner sitting on my counter with a note that simply said, "Eat this."

After living with a man who had a comment about everything I put in my mouth, I was tickled that Kwame is so intent on feeding me.

It's also nice that even though he's a gym devotee he's not waking me up to go with him.

I stick to the rivers and lakes I'm used to with Pilates and twenty thousand steps a day.

"Hey Sin," he drawls, a smile spreading slowly across his face as he watches me watch him. He's got a twinkle in his eye and is wearing the grin of a boy who's got a secret that he wants to tell the whole world.

I shake my head at him and give him a quirked eyebrow that says, "Really?"

He stops smiling and cock his head to the side.

I roll my eyes and walk into the kitchen and he follows me. "I can't say hi to you?"

"Of course you can. Just not like that. And not in front of my family."

"Are they not supposed to know about us? "

The cluelessness of his question is alarming. "Of course not. You *know* how they are. If they get a whiff of something between us, my mother will start talking about knockings, traditional engagements, and dowries. There's no such thing as casual dating in this house. Stephen is the only man I've ever brought home and it took me a year to do that."

He grits his teeth. I can't tell what irritates him, whether it's my mention of Stephen or that I'm telling him no.

"My answer won't change because you don't like it. You know that about me. I know my family and I don't want any confusion or issues because we blurred lines. We're having sex. We're friends. Those two things are mutually exclusive."

"How?"

"Because, even though we may always be friends, one day we'll stop having sex."

"Why would we do that?" He wrinkles his brow.

I can't tell if he's being facetious or not. But it feels important to reiterate the situation.

"Listen, if you think that is going to be a problem—"

"It's not. I'm playing. You think I want to give your parents the wrong impression and then have them mad at me when we move on to other people? I'm trying to *keep* my invite to Sundays, 'cause this is the best meal I eat all week."

My relief is dulled by a strange pang of sadness that I dismiss. I smile up at him. "I knew you were using us for food."

"I'm earning my keep. Your mom had me outside frying fish a few minutes ago."

"You're officially a member of the family then."

He grins. "Come on, bestie. Someone dropped off an order of fresh Ga kenkey and fried croaker."

"Anyway, come and help me pour this pepper into bowls."

"Of course."

A text from Leon pops up. I've been waiting to hear from him. I messaged to ask where Violet was days ago. His reply is brief. "Don't know. She's gone."

Perplexed by his curt reply, I scroll to see if I still have her number. I do, but when I call there's a message that says her number is no longer in service.

"Arsinoé, why are you still standing there?"

I jump and put my phone into my back pocket. I'm being silly. The woman probably uses burner phones given her proclivity for living on the wrong side of the law.

So why can't I shake the feeling that something isn't right?

Thirty-Five

Kwame

Boundaries

"Oh, before I forget, I hear you were at the NMAAHC last week. I didn't realize you were still involved with that project." The Governor and I had just said our goodbyes, and I catch his question right before I hang up.

"My mother's donations are ongoing. I wasn't there for her. The tickets were my father's. I wasn't going but a friend wanted to."

"Would this be the friend that my daughter says displaced her for your affection?"

"I'm not sure how to respond to that," I say after an awkward pause where I listened for sounds of humor in his voice and heard none.

"Honestly would be good. You know that I would've liked for the two of you to come together. You seemed to be rekindling things."

"No, we weren't. We're just friends."

"I see. Well, given your lack of political ambition for public service, maybe it's best that you go your separate ways."

The way he characterized it rubs me wrong. "I'm interested in public service. I'm not interested in politics."

"Running for office to represent your fellow citizens is the highest form of public service. Trying to climb the DOJ ladder is all good but feels like you're making the safe choice."

"In what way?"

"You're more interested in winning than being great."

"What makes you say that?"

"You're letting fear keep you in your comfort zone."

"I'm not." I know he's goading me, but it still gets under my skin. His opinion matters to me maybe more than anyone else's. He is everything that I thought my father should be. And yet here he is on the same page as my father. Neighbors they may have been, brought together by their wives' friendship more than their own mutual interest in each other.

They play golf together, but I get the sense it's only because they are members at the same clubs.

They couldn't be more different. Governor Persaud has been married for almost forty years to the same woman. He's got children who respect and trust him. And he got something that's rare for politicians, a sterling reputation and being known for his integrity.

If he has skeletons in his closet, they are there so well buried that they may as well not exist because as many times as he's run for office, his opposition has tried, and the worst they could come up with was a credit card he defaulted on when he was in college. And all that did was make him more relatable to the voters.

"It's not that I win more in court. It's that I am getting results for the people who need them. All politics looks like is people getting results for the people who paid to send them there."

"That's what you think of me?"

"Of course not, but you're not running for Congress are you? You're the governor of the commonwealth. You have one term to serve. You'll do good and go back to private practice."

"I'm not going back to private practice. I like politics."

"Oh, so the Senate, then?"

"I'm not interested in lawmaking. Executive office seems better suited to my talents."

"I see. But you only get one term as governor. Where do you go after that but the oval office?" I laugh.

He doesn't. "Between you and me, Kwame. I'm beginning to explore the possibility of running for president."

My eyes bug out of my head. "Wow. I didn't know you had that ambition."

"I didn't know it either. It's been floated by the party. Donors like your father are ready to open their checkbooks."

I bet he is.

"Well, you'd have my support. It would be historic—the Guyanese American President."

"Why not? America seems to be in a history making mood."

I ponder it. He's right. Two years ago, the voters chose a radical path forward and now, a woman whose grandparents were enslaved and toiled to build the White House sits behind the Resolute Desk. The country could be ready for a man whose parents came here with empty pockets and built a dynasty in a single generation-.

"I know how to make something out of nothing and I love this country. We have our first woman behind the Resolute Desk. It's past time we have a first gen member of the global majority representing the most prosperous country in the world." His voice is like steel and yet full of passion. It's not surprising he won his election by a landslide. "It would be greatest honor of my life to lead a country that gave my parents refuge and opportunity."

Not for the first time in my life, I wish he'd been my dad. "I don't understand my father's loathing of the only place on earth where this story is even possible."

"He doesn't loathe America. He just wants it to bend to his will and hates that it won't."

"That's even worse," I say dryly.

He chuckles. "Listen, your father is who he is. He's not going to change. You should stop expecting things you know he's not capable of and you'll see him more clearly."

"I see him just fine. I just wish he'd see me too, and that me making this choice won't lead to World War III and another decade of estrange-ment."

"You know that the sky can only support one sun, right?"

Gooseflesh blooms on my scalp and runs down my back. "My mom used to say that all the time. Did she say it to you, too?"

"She must have. And she's right. I admire your father and think he's a very smart man, but he doesn't know what's best for you. And don't let your desire to march to your own drum keep you from pursuing something that could be good for you."

"What do you mean?"

"There's going to be a vacant Senate seat that I'll have the power to fill. You've got a lot of options, and a lot of talents. But I think you'd be the perfect appointment. Seriously."

The thought excites and repulses me all at once. "Thank you for your faith in me, but it's just not for me."

"You've got six months to decide. Never say never. Anything can happen."

I glance around my office with a view that stretches all the way to the Jefferson Memorial.

It's gorgeous, but I'd rather be in a windowless office doing work that's important to me and makes me want to get out of bed in the morning instead of dreading work like I do now.

I start work on my application for the State's Attorney. These are highly sought after and coveted jobs. I'm in for a rigorous months-long interview process. As stressful and competitive as that will be, it'll make telling my father what I've decided look like a cake walk.

Thirty-Six

Sin

Rematch

A few months ago, Sofia was still someone I was excited to know. This all-hands meeting would have been the highlight of my year. Instead, I'm watching the clock with bated breath and have only spoken to her in greeting.

My phone buzzes and I glance around the room at my colleagues who are sitting around the same conference table.

It buzzes again and I know it's Kwame. I shouldn't, but I need something sweet to help me survive the rest of this daylong seminar.

I make sure everyone else's eyes are where they should be, while I choose myself.

My phone is out of my pocket and placed in my lap, I lean back slightly from the table so that I can read it as inconspicuously as possible.

"I'd like to have you for lunch. Meet at my place?"

I bite my lip to hide the smile that wants to split my face in half. I love how much he wants to see me, but I think I love that he calls his house home more.

I write back. "Yes. Will need a pick-me-up after this snooze fest."

"Keeping you from something important, am I?" The voice comes from right, over my shoulder and snaps my spine straight. I jump in my seat and drop my phone.

I scramble to pick it up but she gets to it first. She holds it in her palm and looks down her stupidly small nose at me. "We have a no phone policy during these seminars for a reason." She points to the basket by the door with the sign over it that says "Phones Here."

"Is that a new thing?" I ask. I look around the room to see if anyone else is disturbed. "Confiscating phones?"

"Yes, it is. If you read the company wide bulletins we sent, you'd know."

"I do read them. I must have missed it. I'm sorry."

She glances down at my phone. "Kwame says he's hard for you already."

There's a collective gasp and then the room is silent. Mortification makes my stomach drop to my toes.

My elation from a moment ago is gone so completely, I'm not sure I didn't imagine it. I see red. "That was private," I say through clenched jaws.

She scoffs and strides over to the basket and tosses my phone in. "This is a company issued phone. Nothing on it is private."

"You had no right to read that, you—" I say, my throat burns from the effort it takes not to finish my sentence.

Her eyes narrow. "Everyone out," she barks. There's only a second hesitation before everyone gets up and files out. No one looks at me, but their pity is palpable.

My heart races and I brace for whatever's coming next now that we are alone.

"Do you know how lucky you are to have this job? Do you know how many journalists would kill to have *The Spectator* be their soft place to land and start over?"

I bristle at her framing. "I'm not starting over. I'm pivoting. I'm still an experienced writer and reporter and even if you don't find value in the story, I'm compelled to pursue it. If I'm using my free time—"

"You're not allowed to do that," she hisses.

I blanche. "Of course I am."

She purses her lips. "Your contract explicitly forbids you to do any freelance work while you are a full-time salaried member of *The Spectator's* editorial staff." She narrows her eyes. "I heard you were difficult," she murmurs.

I rear back like she slapped me. My jaw drops.

"You think you're being sabotaged. You're not that special, Ms.

Sackey. You're new and there's a pecking order. Know your fucking place."

My skin feels too small for my frame. My heart and lungs are working overtime. I blink back angry tears because there'll be a cold day in hell before I cry in front of this bitch. I leave and need restraint not to slam the door behind me.

Two decades of working in this industry has turned my feelings to Teflon. But no one has ever spoken to me like that.

This is where my choices have brought me. I can't afford to burn this bridge. If I don't have a paper behind me, it won't matter how explosive this story is.

I sit at my desk and get to work on my reply to a letter from a man confessing to lying about how much money he spends on his Candy Crush habit.

It sucks, but least now I've got a nice dick to ride away my frustrations at the end of a hard day.

Thirty-Seven

Sin

Spin the Block

"Heads up, Stephen is here."

"Why?" I turn to face the open doorway where my sister is standing. I stab myself in the eye with the mascara wand, but the pain barely registers over the wild flare of panic in my chest. "Stephen? As in my ex-boyfriend?"

"Is there another one?"

My heart skips a beat and then starts hammering. "He's in *this* house?"

She nods slowly. "He's running his mouth downstairs as we speak."

"Why?" I cry and throw my makeup back into the bag hastily.

"He came to drop off some mail for you. Mom invited him to stay."

"Why would she do that? How could *you* let her?" I point an accusing finger at her.

My sister crosses her arms and glares at me. "How could I stop her? You won't tell anyone what really went down. You made it seem amicable and all she can see is that Kwame is *right* there, making lovesick eyes at you, obviously infatuated with you, fine as hell, and you're still just friends." She puts air quotes around the word friends.

"Oh stop it." I roll my eyes and wave it off. But inside I'm see-sawing between hope and fear that she's right. Infatuation was two exits ago for me and I'm not sure he's going to catch up. Or if he's even trying to. "Do you *really* think Kwame is infatuated with me, Mae?"

"Yes, I think you feel the same way. But something is holding you back."

Butterflies shake their wings in my chest at the mention of Kwame's name, but I feel guilty that I've burdened her with this secret. *One crisis at a time, Sin.*

I force my focus back to the matter at hand. "I don't understand why he accepted her invitation. He's got to know I wouldn't be happy to see him."

"Well judging from the flowers he brought you, the case of spirits he brought Dad, and the shit-eating grin he's wearing, I would say he doesn't know that at *all*. Kinda wish I didn't have Shelly's shower today."

"He brought what?" I shoot to my feet, makeup forgotten and grab the chocolate brown pleather skirt off the hanger on the back of my door, tug it over my hips and zip it up. "How dare he?" I start for the door and Mae grabs my arm.

"I know you're surprised, but please don't make a scene. You know how his mother likes to gossip, and Ma still has to see her every week at The Ghana Association meetings."

"God, I hate this. I'm so sick of censoring myself for the sake of a bunch of people who only know the highlight reel version of my life."

"I know. You don't have to make nice, but be civil. Mom went to a lot of trouble today."

"And then ruined all her hard work by inviting that goat to stink up the place."

"Sin," Mae chides.

My blood is rushing in my ears. I close my eyes and count to ten. "I will be civil."

"Arsinoé!" My mother's voice carries up the stairs and reverberates against my bedroom door. My sister and I look at each other in alarm. The last thing I need is her to come upstairs and start fussing about my hair and clothes.

"Coming!" I call out, slip my feet into my pink furry house slippers, check myself in the mirror and say a prayer for my sanity.

"How do I look?"

"Like a smoke show. Are *you* sure you don't want him back?"

I chose this outfit because I knew Kwame would like it. I wish I'd saved it. I curl my lip in disgust. "I want that man less than I want to get my period next week. Have fun at Shelly's." I hug her and watch her rush down the stairs and call her goodbyes without stopping on her way to the front door.

I check the mirror one more time and then get downstairs as fast as my formfitting skirt will take me without breaking my neck.

"Hi, sorry to keep you—" I skid to a stop when I see the stuff of nightmares in front of me.

Stephen and Kwame. My parents are sitting next to each other on the couch with Kwame in between them, holding a phone I don't recognize, their heads bent over a piece of paper.

"What's going on?"

They all look up when I walk into the room, and I know right away this is even worse than I thought it would be and a weight settles on my chest. "Arsinoé, why?" My mother's eyes are full of disappointment and horror. My father doesn't look up, and I can't bring myself to even look at Kwame.

"Why what?"

"Why do you have a gun?" She holds up the certificate of ownership.

I frown, alarmed, caught off guard, and irritated all at once "Did you open my mail?"

"No, I did." Stephen gets to his feet, his expression full of worry. "And I was so shocked I felt like your parents needed to see it."

I glare at him. "Why? Did you hit your head and forget that I'm an adult?"

"Between this, the way you left your job, left me. I felt like I had to say something." He has concern etched all over his traitorous face.

"Sin, why did you buy a gun? You know how we feel about weapons." My mother sounds hurt and disappointed.

I wish I could beat Stephen over the head with my shoes.

I turn to face her and my stomach sinks. She looks horrified. "Yes, I know, but I feel safe with it."

"Safe from what? You've lived your whole life without one."

"If you still lived with me you wouldn't need that," Stephen says.

I sputter a laugh, mind boggled that he said it with a straight face.

I didn't want my family to know what kind of man he really was. But, the truth is, I didn't want them to know what a fool I'd been.

I turn to my parents and the alarm on their faces makes me my stomach hurt. My eyes fill with tears. Everything I've been carrying suddenly feels like too much and I wish I'd told them to begin with. "The week before I came home, I walked in on someone robbing our apartment."

I close my eyes so I can tell the rest without crying. "In hindsight, it was silly of me not to realize something was wrong when the door wasn't locked." I clasp my hands together and twirl the ring on my finger as the terror and pain of what followed finds me. "I came face to face with a man running out of my office. He was holding my external hard drive and my laptop." I shudder the memory.

"I always thought I'd fight back in a situation like that. But when he put a gun in face and told me he was going to kill me all I could do was pray."

"My God, Arsinoé." My mother's hands fly to her face and she looks at my father with stricken eyes. "George, our baby." She turns back to me, her eyes wide, and my heart constricts at the hurt in them. "Why didn't you tell us?" My mother gets up and walks over to me. "You have a family. That is what we are for."

"I didn't know how. I didn't want it to become a defining story of this part of my life. And I didn't want you to know what kind of man I'd foolishly stayed involved with."

"You were happy, Sin." Stephen protests.

"I wasn't happy in New York. I wanted to come home, so I did. It was six months ago. It's all water under the bridge."

"That's not that long, and you've kept it all to yourself."

"Ma, I'm fine," I reassure her when her arms clasp me so tight it hurts.

"Where was Stephen?" My mother's question draws me back to the story. "Where were you?" she asks a suddenly mute Stephen.

I sigh deeply and continue. "When he finally called me back, he was at the airport about to catch a flight to Vegas for a fight."

All eyes turn to him, and he takes a step back, his mouth opening and closing repeatedly. Then he points at me. "You cheated on me," Stephen blurts.

I ignore the collective gasp that ripples through the room and turn on him. Speechless that he laid my shit out like that.

Every eye in the room is on me, but I don't mind. I'm not ashamed of anything I just shared, but I wouldn't have done it this way. Now that the truth is out, I wish I'd said something months ago. The burden of this secret was heavy and isolating.

"You asshole. Yes, I was unfaithful. But only once and only after you cheated on me." I glare at him. "Yes, I know. I saw you with her. You made me feel like I was lucky to be with you. My family acted like it was crazy of me to leave you. And I let them to stop them from knowing that you're a low-down lying dog who slept with the woman who sabotaged me and had just been given the promotion I worked my ass for. On my desk," I shout.

The room was quiet before, but now it's as still as a tomb. I can't bring myself to look up and wait to see if anyone will say anything. Kwame has moved and is hovering near the entryway behind Stephen.

He has one hand in his pocket, a shoulder resting on the wall, legs crossed at the ankle, looking for the all the world like he's a neutral observer. Except his eyes are darker and more intent than I've ever seen them.

My eyebrows knit together. Seeing him and Stephen side by side makes their generally similar appearance hard to deny but I can't believe I ever thought they looked alike. I may have a type, but I've also learned how to take the true measure of a man.

As I look at Stephen now, I can't remember what I found attractive about my ex in the first place.

"Sin, I'm so sorry," my mother breaks the silence.

I turn to her and shake my head. "I'm not."

"Don't say that," Stephen says, his face in his hands. "It was a mistake, Sin."

"No, it wasn't. It's who you are. The mistake was trying to see something that wasn't there."

I use the last thread of my strength to stand. "Now, if you'll please excuse me, I'm going to clean up, come back, and enjoy lunch."

Thirty-Eight

Kwame

Wants and Needs

Chaos erupts right when Sin leaves the room.

Then everyone is talking at once. Fingers are pointing in every direction and I'm reminding myself that it's a crime to hit someone. That Stephen isn't worth the trouble that an assault charge will create. But God, I want to knock his teeth out for making Sin bare her soul and relive the hardest days of her life before she was ready to.

I couldn't look at her as she spoke. The hurt in her voice was unbearable.

I'm not sure what to do next, but I am certain that this is a turning point.

Sin may not *want* a partner, but she needs one.

She's taking so much on by herself and I'm not built to stand by and watch someone struggle when I know I can help.

I can't force it on her, but I will be there the minute she recognizes it for herself.

We promised to keep things casual and to keep this to ourselves. But I haven't been able to bind the emotions that have grown inside of me since we started sleeping together.

But my inability to open up has played a role in hers.

If I want her to trust me, I've got to show her that I trust her.

I love her.

I don't want this to be casual. I don't think she does either.

Sin comes back in and the chatter of conversation stops. I get to my feet and walk over to her, and she smiles at me but gives a barely perceptible shake of her head. I stop a few feet away. "Are you feeling better?"

"Yeah." Her tight smile and the noticeable bob of her throat say otherwise.

She looks so alone and brave and it's hard to stand here and not pull her into my arms.

In fact, it's utterly unbearable.

I ignore the weight of watchful eyes and ignore Sin's stiffening posture and yelp of protest when I pull her into a hug. "I'm sorry you had to say all of that before you were ready."

Her breath hitches on a barely audible whimper and she relaxes against me with a soft sigh. "Thank you." She rests her forehead on my shoulder for the space of a few heartbeats and then pulls out of my arms to face everyone else.

"Oh my God, you're still here?" she says when she sees Stephen.

"I know I did wrong, and I've apologized more times than I can count. I know you're not ready to forgive me yet. But I want us to try," he adds with a broad smile.

She makes a sound in the back of her throat that sounds like a laugh, but I know is muffled scream.

I scowl at him. "What a fucking stupid thing to say."

"Kwame!" Mrs. Sackey chides.

Stephen stands up and looks at me like he's only now realizing that I'm there.

"Sorry, who are you?" He takes a step toward me.

"None of your business, chief." I square my shoulders.

Sin rushes to stand between us. "This is Kwame. He's a family friend."

"He doesn't look friendly," the idiot chirps.

"I'm not. Especially not to assholes."

"I know you. Don't I?" Stephen stares at me, narrowing his eyes. "What's your last name?"

Dread coils around my gut like a constricting snake. My throat goes dry.

Sin leans out of my arms and bares her teeth at the man. "It's none of your fucking business."

"Sin!" her parents shout at the same time.

"Sin, you're my business."

"Not anymore," I snap. "This is all me, now. Friend," I snarl.

There's an awkward silence and Mrs. Sackey turns to look at me. "What is all you?"

I turn to Sin and her eyes meet mine, full of a silent but undeniable plea. I want to tell the truth. But she just had her other secrets laid bare and her trust violated. The last thing I'm going to do right now is break my word to her.

I immediately deflect. "It means, she's my best friend. No one can talk to her like that if I'm here," I say. But this game of pretend isn't going to work anymore. We'll have to talk it out, but I can't wait to tell her parents that she's not just my best friend and is the most beautiful woman I've ever met, and I've been falling in love with her since I laid eyes on her.

"Oh, that's so nice," her mother says but her smile doesn't reach her eyes.

"I'm tired," Sin says. "Mama and Daddy, I'm sorry for everything. I didn't want to disappoint you."

"Sin, we love you. We want the best for you. I'm sorry we haven't made that clear."

They hug each other, and I'm so grateful to be able to witness this kind of love between parents and their child.

"Kwame?" Sin's voice is tired and I get up and go to where she's sitting.

"Could you take me home, please?"

"Absolutely."

Thirty-Nine

Kwame

Home

We agree to drive Sin's car back to her place. We ride in silence, a comfortable but poignant absence of conversation. When I park around the corner from Shake Shack in Logan Circle, she doesn't ask where we're going. I walk around to open her door and offer my hand as she climbs out. She takes it and links her fingers with mine as we walk to the restaurant. It's colder than normal, and she wraps her wool coat tightly around her even once we're inside.

She orders for both of us without asking what I want and remembers exactly how I take my burger. We sit across from each other, holding hands, not speaking until our food is delivered to our table.

She wolfs down her food and finishes before me. I can barely eat. I'm dreading this conversation, but it can't be put off any longer.

She wipes her mouth and puts her napkin down.

"Why did you look so scared when he asked what your name was?"

"My father's name is Al Palmer." The words spill out like air from a shaken-up soda can.

She furrows her brow in confusion and then her eyes widen and she covers her mouth. "Oh my God, Al Palmer, the owner of The Golden Palms, is your *dad?*"

I grimace at the nickname. I nod. "Yes. I didn't know the connection to your parents until the day I came over and he was on TV."

She groans and her eyes slide shut. "No *wonder* you left so fast that night and didn't come back."

I flush hot under my collar at the memory. "I mean… I'm used to getting a reaction when I say his name. People have questions, opinions, and a great investment he needs to get in on. I knew he was polarizing in the Ghanaian community, but I didn't know why until that night."

"Oh my God. I'm sorry about the things I said about him," she says, her eyes full of angst.

"Hey, no. It's okay. You were saying how you feel."

"*That's* your dad? Holy Shit. You grew up at The Palms?"

I snort a derisive laugh. "I know."

"How come no one knows you're his son?"

"Oh, plenty of people know. Everyone who knows him personally, anyway. But he's never advertised having a son. It's not that uncommon. Do you know Steve Jobs' kid's name? Or how many kids he has?"

"No, I guess not."

"It was more about safety than anything else at first. People with that kind of money are always targets for kidnappers. He didn't have me until he was in his forties because he was worried about having that liability."

"Liability?" She sounds horrified.

"Essentially. Yes. They may have been public figures, but they only showed what they wanted to. Even before he had money, he was superstitious and secretive. It was a way of life. All I knew."

"Wow. He was in the papers all the time when I was growing up. Both here and abroad. You must have had more moments like the one at my parents."

"Oh yeah, anytime I'm in DC or in Ghana. I can't describe how intensely uncomfortable it is to have conversations with strangers who feel like they know my father and not be able to say anything."

"I can only imagine." I can feel her biting her tongue, trying to respect my privacy, and I fall all the way in love with her.

She's a reporter and naturally curious. For all his notoriety, my father never gave a single interview and never allowed any press onto the estate where he threw the parties he's now most known for.

She blows out a breath. "I don't blame you but honestly, I know so little about him. He was a legend that everyone talked about at Outdoorings and Independence Day parties.

But in our house he was a third rail we didn't touch. I couldn't help being fascinated by the idea of him—especially because he was so private. Taking an active interest in him felt like a betrayal. And honestly, I don't find billionaires particularly compelling unless they're changing the world with their money, and as far as I could see, he was just throwing parties."

I don't correct her assumption about how he spends his money and loosen my grip on the fear that kept me from sharing this with her. "So…you're not going to ask me for a tour of The Palms or an invite to Palm Sunday?"

She blows a raspberry with her lips. "Listen, I'm a journalist in Washington, DC. I write for the Lifestyle section. The Palms is one of the most iconic properties in the country and no photographs of the inside have been seen since your dad bought it. Of *course* I would love a tour and love to be the reporter that gets the first interview with Al Palmer. But no, I'm not going to ask."

I let out a breath I've been holding since I met her. "I promise the myth is bigger than the man, anyway."

"I guess I'll find out the day I meet him."

The thought makes my stomach flip. My smile slips before I can catch it and she frowns. "Do you not want that?" she asks.

I don't, but if she's going to be part of my life, it's inevitable. I have to choose my words carefully to answer her honestly. "I do, of course. Sure. Next time he's in town, we'll make it happen… Just remember, he's a showman. He's obsessed with *The Great Gatsby* and thinks he's the modern-day reincarnation of Mansa Musa."

"It's amazing how far the apple fell from the tree."

"I'm glad you think so, but what are we going to do about the fact that your parents hate my father?"

"Oh yeah.. that." She chuckles until she sees the unease drawing my mouth into a straight, grim line. "What do you think will happen once they know?" she asks.

I laugh without any humor. "Oh, I don't know. I imagine they might not be thrilled to know the son of the man who ruined their lives has been eating at their table and sleeping next to their daughter."

She tuts in disapproval but reaches across the table and takes my hands into hers. The contact grounds me and reminds me what I have to lose all at once.

I link our fingers and press our palms together. "Do we have to tell them?" I ask with a chuckle to hide my deep unease.

"Kwame, they don't really hate him. I think, deep down they know it was a bad investment but—"

"But he was such an asshole about it, he made himself the villain of the story," I finish the sentence for her.

"*But,*" she squeezes my hand for emphasis, "their pride has made him a convenient boogie man. *And* your mom more than made up for it. They should know that's what inspired her gift. And *you* should trust that they care about you. Even if they're upset at first, they'll be fine. I'll come with you. We'll do it together."

I let go of a breath that feels like I've been holding for months and it carries words I've been holding back out of my mouth with it. "I love you, Sin." The silence that follows my declaration isn't awkward and I'm not sorry I said it even as I watch her struggle to receive it. "You don't have to say—"

"I love you, too Kwame. So much." She leans back in her seat, her eyes grow heavy lidded, and her smile makes me sorry we're not alone.

"Oh, I almost forgot. I got you a present."

"Did you?"

She stands and nods. "It's something you can eat."

I rub my stomach. "You know us *Fantsefo* are always ready for a good meal."

She leans over so her blouse falls forward to reveal a bright yellow lacy bra. "Let's go home, so I can feed you."

Forty

Kwame

Official

"I should tell you," Sin whispers in the dark. We're in bed, wrapped in each other, naked, clean, slathered in that body lotion of hers, and exhausted from a vigorous session of fucking and a nice long shower. "I'm not sure how to do this part."

"What part?" I trace circles on her arm.

"Relationships. I'm so used to doing everything myself. I'm not great at asking for help."

"Good thing I'm pretty good at offering it before you have to. I can't read minds so you're going to have to get better at that part."

I stroke a hand down her arm and she snuggles close. She runs her toes up my leg. "I love how hairy you are."

"Hmmm." I pretend to contemplate what she said. "I think that counts as you expressing yourself." I pull her closer.

"So we're doing this?"

"Yes. No more 'just' anything when it comes us. From now on it's all, everything, completely, and ten toes down."

"Okay," she whispers and nestles into my side. "All, everything, completely, and ten toes down, I love you."

I fall asleep with a smile on my face.

Forty-One

Kwame

Ready or Not

"You're acting like you're meeting them for the first time," Sin says when I ask her for the tenth time if she's sure I shouldn't wear a tie.

I scowl at her. "In a way, I am. I want to spend my first Christmas with them without anything but love and honesty between us. I just hope they understand."

"It'll be fine," she says and wraps her arms around me from behind, pressing her face against my back.

"I know." When she's holding me like this, it feels that way.

"If it makes you feel any better, I'm uber nervous about meeting your dad, too. I almost wish I could do it at one of his parties where he'd be too busy to ask me any questions."

"Trust me, you wouldn't like that at all. Those parties are the worst."

"I'll take your word for it, although I can't pretend I don't want to be a fly on that wall. Is it really like a real live *Fight Club*?"

I shrug. "It's just a bunch of rich people getting drunk on champagne, full on caviar, dancing badly, making deals, and being seen."

"Sounds dreadful," she says with a mock shudder.

"It is," I say before I catch the sarcasm in her voice. "No, for real."

She blows out a breath. "Okay, I can't wait to meet him."

"Really? After everything you've heard?"

She nods. "Yes, he's not just some abstract personality now. He's the father of the man I love."

The way the words flow off her tongue so easily makes my whole body light up. Maybe I was wrong. Maybe this won't change anything. "So if your parents can't get past it, could you be with the son of a morally gray man your parents hate?"

She presses her lips together and is silent for long seconds. "Can *you* be with a morally gray woman?"

I burst into laughter until I realize she's not joining me in it.

"What do you mean? You're morally gray? How?"

She shrugs and looks away. "I impersonate people, pick locks, and ignore rules all the time to get what I need for my stories."

"You do?" My laughter ends on a choke when she nods.

I peer at her. "What happens when you get caught?"

"I'm careful and shockingly good at it."

"At breaking the law?"

"Oh my God, you should see your face." She throws her head back and laughs. I'm obsessed with the sound of her joy and the way she looks when she laughs. I'm tempted to lean back and allow myself to be captivated by the way her teeth gleam in the moonlight and think of ways to keep her just like this. But all of that is outweighed by my concern.

"You're very cavalier about breaking the law, Sin."

She stops laughing but her eyes stay soft. "I'm sorry." She cups my face and leans over to kiss me softly. "I take it very seriously and only do it when I have to."

"Do what?" I've forgotten what we're talking about. I lean up and brush a kiss along the base of her throat.

She giggles but pushes me away and seeks my eyes. "About breaking the law. I want you to know that I am very careful, and I only do it in pursuit of the truth and justice. I accept the risks that come with doing my job well. I'd do almost anything to give a voice to people and shed light on issues that matter and deserve attention."

I know she means that with the purest intentions, but the law is blind and there are a lot of people in jail who were trying to do good but ended up ruining lives.

"I'm an officer of the court. I'm not your lawyer or your husband so there's zero privilege in these conversations. It's best you don't tell me anything incriminating."

Her brows shoot up. "Would you turn me in?" She looks scandalized.

I nod. "Not happily, but if you tell me you've committed a harmful criminal act, I'd have to. Or risk being your accomplice."

She stares at me for a long time and I wonder if this will be the hill we die on. It's not negotiable for me. I don't want to stop her from her mission. I believe that she's on the right side of history. And if she ends up on the wrong side of the law, at least she's got someone who can help her navigate it successfully.

"I wouldn't do anything that might have a negative impact on my family or friends. I'm not *totally* reckless."

There's an edge of defensiveness in her voice that makes me instantly contrite.

"I'm sorry, Sin. I know that. I'm nervous about this conversation. You don't have to explain yourself to me."

She moves to stand in front of me and presses her palms to my chest. "You don't have to be sorry. I know it's because you care. I promise that I only bend rules when there's no other way to get at the truth. And I'd never like…kill someone."

I snort a laugh. "That's good to know. Now, let's go get this over with."

Forty-Two

Sin

Forgiveness

I hadn't been sure it was a good idea for me to accompany Kwame to see my parents. Now, I'm glad I'm here. Watching him be so sincere and seeing my parents give him so much grace made me love all of them more than I ever have.

"Thank you for giving me a chance to explain. Thank you for understanding."

"Of course we do. That is what family is for," my mother says and pats Kwame's knee.

His relief is palpable and brings a tear to my eye. I'm so glad he found us. My parents' love for him has moved beyond him being the son of their benevolent benefactor. Kwame covers my mother's hand with his. "I don't have a model for this, Auntie Adele. I've never had a real family. One that expected me to hold them accountable. One that held me accountable, too. Even when I didn't know what it was, I yearned for it. I'm sorry I didn't tell you the truth sooner."

My mom speaks first. "Oh, Kwame. We knew."

I am shocked. "You did?"

"What?" Kwame says at the same time, shooting to his feet.

My mother wrings her hands and glances at my father. "When we went to file the deed, we saw your mother's full name and made the connection."

"Why didn't you say something?" I ask with exasperation. We've been agonizing over it for no reason.

"It was clear he didn't want us to," my father says.

"Since when has what anyone wanted stopped you from anything?"

My mother sucks her teeth. "We wanted you to fall in love with him. The minute I think something is a good idea you run in the opposite direction."

"No I don't," I protest.

"Yes, you do," Kwame, my father, and my mother answer in unison.

"No one asked you." I scowl but I can't stop the smile forming on my mouth.

"Fine."

My mother reaches across the side table between them. "You're not your father. And none of us is as bad as the worst thing we've done. If you love someone, accepting them with thorns and all doesn't feel like a chore."

"I love Sin," he says it like he's answering a question.

My heart smiles and I wish we were alone. "And I love him," I add.

My mother nods, her smile as wide as mine. "Yes. That is obvious."

My dad clears his throat. "Okay. Well now that's settled. Can we have dessert?"

Forty-Three

Sin

Beware of the Thorns

"Someone's New Year is off to a good start," the lady delivering my flowers remarks.

"Yeah, it is." I smile and sign for the massive bouquet of roses.

I take them into the kitchen and open the card.

I knew they would be from him but seeing his name on the card still makes everything flutter.

Kwame.

He's so romantic and sweet. He brings flowers home randomly, makes my coffee perfectly every morning, and lets me be when I need it.

I couldn't ask for more.

I've never been so well fed, rested, and doted on.

I find myself smiling at nothing a lot.

Just…smiling.

My heart skips a beat as I remember falling asleep with his arm for a pillow last night and how hard it's getting to leave his house every night to go back to my place to get ready for work.

I open the card stuck to the arrangement. A picture falls out and flutters to the ground. It's a four-digit code and a note. "It's been nine months since the night we met. When you get here tonight, let yourself in with that code. Come ready to celebrate."

I've never celebrated a milestone like this. It's so sappy and sweet. I can't believe it's' happening to me.

I'm so in over my head. But… Flowers like this, and the way I catch him watching me tells me that he might be in over his head, too.

My phone rings and I see Leon's name. I haven't heard from him since that day at the museum. "Hello stranger, Happy New Year!"

"Hey Sin. Did you get my message on your website?" He sounds out of breath.

"No. I haven't checked that mailbox since it got hacked. What's up?"

"There's been another robbery."

"Where?"

"Here at the museum. Someone broke into our storeroom. We only realized when we came in to gather items for a new display. I don't know how this happened." His voice breaks.

My stomach dips. "How can I help?"

"I remember you took pictures when the lot was still in New York. I sent over a list of the missing items. Can you see if you have pictures that match the descriptions?"

"I'll have to see. A lot of them were on my laptop when it was stolen. I had it backed up on a flash drive. It's in a box I haven't unpacked. I'll check as soon as I can."

"I hate to rush you, but can you do it tonight? I want to file the report myself. Even if I get fired, I can't do nothing about these thefts." He sounds distraught.

"What do the police say?" I ask without much hope.

His laugh is bitter. "They say there are no signs of a break-in. Referred us to the same task force that hasn't done shit to help."

"You should check your CCTV footage from the nights you have private events," I suggest. Ozwald Annan was walking around the museum like he owned it the evening of the gala.

"Thanks, Sin. I have to go. I'm sorry. Send over whatever you have as soon as you can. Thank you."

He hangs up. I stare at my screen helplessly.

More thefts, no one reporting on it, law enforcement is apathetic, the thieves are only going to be emboldened.

I need to look for that drive, but I have no idea where to start and an appointment with my lash lady I can't be late for.

I'm running late when I get back. I still need to shower and change for whatever Kwame's got planned for me tonight.

I fumble for my keys and lean against my front door only to have it give way. I stumble inside.

My place looks like it's been torn apart. My blood runs cold.

I stumble back outside and it's only then that I notice the picture taped to my front door. I grab it and run back to my car.

My heart feels like it's trying to break free of my ribcage by the time I'm at my car. I get in and lock the door before I pull out the picture again. It's me walking up the small path between my driveway and the rear entrance to my house. I'm not sure when it was taken, but I bought the coat I'm wearing at a Black Friday sale.

Someone is watching me.

And they want me to know.

Panic makes me lightheaded. I'm flung back to a time when I was afraid of everything.

Terror builds inside me until I can barely breathe.

I can't go through this again.

I lean over and fumble to open my glove compartment.

The second my hand brushes the moleskin journal, I'm one step closer to calm and my pulse slows, I breathe in deep and then push all the air out again.

Calmer, I open it and uncap the fountain pen I keep clipped inside. I write my feelings down until they're not choking me anymore. I use my breath to slow my heart down and by the time I've released the fifth one, I can think clearly.

I haven't worked on this story since Sofia made it clear it would cost me my job.

Why am I getting this now? The day Leon called me, hours after I said I had a flash drive in my house.

My heart trips. Does this mean someone is monitoring my calls?

I text Leon and tell him I don't have the pictures and can't help.

For good measure I add that while the robbery is unfortunate, I think he should focus on showcasing the pieces they have. I know he'll be confused but I don't dare put anything in writing. I'll go by there this week.

Right now, I need my anchor. With trembling hands, I call Kwame.

Forty-Four

Kwame

All that Glitters

"Will there be anything else?" The woman I hired to decorate for to-night sticks her head into my office.

"Oh, are you done. That was quick."

"I've been here for almost four hours."

"Already?" I glance at my wrist and grimace. "The day has flown by."

"Do you want to check it out before I leave?" She jerks her thumb over her shoulder.

I get to my feet. "Yes. I'm sure you did a great job."

"It looks just like what you showed me. You moving all the furniture out gave me a perfect canvas."

"Great." She doesn't need to know that there was no furniture to move out.

We walk through my house and I'm acutely aware of how bare it still is. I should take Sin up on her offer to help me decorate.

"Here we are."

I asked her to help me recreate the aesthetic of the dining room at Dogon where we first met.

I didn't expect her to capture the ambiance so perfectly without it looking like a replica.

The whole thing looks like a tribute to the night sky. Navy blue mirrored glass lines the wall parallel to the door and seems to dissolve into the wall of windows that it intersects with.

The canopy is made of a wispy fabric in bold shades of blue shot with white and gold. It's moody, mysterious, and inviting. Just like my girl.

The table at the center is low to the ground and surrounded by cushions the size of love seats.

Perfect for what I've got planned for her after dinner.

"Oh, wow. Sonja, you outdid yourself."

"I think she's going to love it." She beams with pride as I walk her to the door.

I pull my vibrating phone out of my pocket and smile when Sin's smiling face is on the screen.

"Hey sexy. Excited about tonight?"

"Uh, yeah. I am. I just…I came home early to change." My mood shifts at the slight tremor in her voice.

She makes a sound that sounds like a muffled sob. "Sin? What's wrong?"

"I think someone's been here," she says in a thin, watery voice.

I grab my keys. "Been where?"

"My house."

My stomach drops. I get to my feet. "I'm on my way."

"No," she shouts, and I stop.

"Why not?"

"Can I just come to yours?" She swallows audibly.

"Did you call the police?" I ask in as measured a voice as I can manage. I don't want to upset her more than she is already.

She scoffs. "That's the last thing I'm going to do."

"What? Why not?"

"Uh, I'm alone, I'm a woman, I'm Black, and I have no proof that anyone broke in. The best-case scenario is that they'll take a report. That's not worth the risk of the worst-case scenario."

I stop myself from arguing with her. She's right, especially the fact that she's alone. "Okay. Fine. When you get here, we'll go to down to the precinct together and file a report."

She groans. "Kwame, come on. Can we do that tomorrow, please? We were supposed to be celebrating tonight, right? I want to enjoy that if possible."

I relent against my better judgment. Only because she sounds okay.

And I want her to enjoy tonight, too. "Okay, but I don't think you should stay there until we're sure it's safe."

There's a stretch of silence, and I look at my screen to check if the call is still connected.

"Sin?"

"Yeah." She clears her throat. "I'm sorry it's just that I was about to say the same thing, and actually, that's why I called instead of just heading over. Can I crash at yours? I promise I won't disturb your solitude. And just until l can get my locks replaced and finally get an alarm system?" She's so hesitant and halting that it makes me feel like an asshole.

"I mean, I like my solitude, but I like you even more. Of course you can stay. As long as you like," I add without hesitation. I mean it. This woman is more than my lover. She's my best friend.

"Oh my God, Thank you. It's a lot to ask. I know you don't like sharing a bed. So, I'll sleep on the couch—"

"Unless you don't want to, we can share my bed," I cut off that whole line of conversation. No way is that woman sleeping anywhere but where she'll be most comfortable. "If you prefer, I'll sleep on the couch," I offer.

"You can't sleep on the couch in your own house."

"Emphasis on *my* house. No arguments, Sin."

"I'd love to share the bed, then," she says with a sheepish smile.

"We'll look at furniture for one of the rooms so you can have your own space, too."

"Thank you so much, Kwame. It won't be forever, I promise."

It actually sounds more like a threat. "You can stay as long as you need."

She lets out a shuddering breath. "God, I *hate* feeling like this. I hate that I need a fucking gun. Thank you for not making me feel paranoid."

"That's not paranoia. It's trauma. You were attacked in your home by someone who broke in. That's not something you just get over. And your body remembers and reacts when it perceives something that's hurt it before. Please don't beat yourself up and second guess your intuition. Trust yourself."

"Baby," she says on a soft sigh that I feel all the way in the center of my soul. "You always know what to say. I'm sorry if I've ruined our anniversary plans."

At the reminder of what the rest of the night has in store and reassured that she's okay, I switch roles with her and bring the light back to our conversation. "You couldn't ruin anything if you tried, Sin. In fact, now that I know you're not doing your Cinderella at midnight routine and sleeping over, I predict it's going to be even better than I imagined."

She giggles at my melodramatic voice. "Oh my God, Kwame, you're so crazy. And wonderful. I can't believe you actually made me laugh."

My chest swells with satisfaction. "I've dedicated a lot of time to honing that craft, baby. I'm very happy to hear it works."

"I like it when you call me baby," she says in a voice that makes blood rush to my dick.

"Do you? Well, baby, get over here so I can feed you, feast on you, and fuck you to sleep."

"Oh Kwame, why are you so amazing?" she says in a soft voice, free of the anxiety she started this conversation with.

"You bring it out in me." I mean it. She does.

"Say less. I'm gonna pack a few things, and I'll see you soon."

I hang up, torn between my excitement and my concern.

I'm sorry someone scared her tonight but I'm glad she's coming to stay.

Forty-Five

Sin

Claimed

"I love the way you look against my sheets."

I close my book and roll onto my side to gaze up at Kwame. I run my hand over the soft, cool bedding beneath me and smile. "I like the way your sheets feel against me," I admit with a slow smile at the gloriously naked wall of a man who, by some miracle, I have all to myself.

"Did you bring your book to bed in case you got bored?"

I cock an eyebrow. "No, I take a book to bed every night, and thank goodness I had it because you kept me waiting."

"I'll make up it to you." He reaches down and grabs me by the hips and flips me onto my back. "You are so damn sexy, Sin. This body is my favorite place to play." His eyes devour my naked breasts and my nipples pucker and tighten under the heat of his regard.

"I've seen you this way so many times, and God, it gets better every time."

He climbs onto the bed and presses my thighs apart to make room for his hips.

"Hello," he whispers, bracing his upper body braced on his arms but letting the weight of his legs rest fully on mine.

I gasp at the hard weight of his fully at attention dick against my thigh.

"Am I too heavy?" he asks, leaning down to brush a kiss on my cheeks, and grinds his hips into me, wetting his groin with my arousal.

"No. Perfect. I love it," I pant and stop myself from saying what's on my tongue. This whole evening has been incredible.

"How is this?" he whispers and lowers his torso to give me more of his weight.

"Not enough." I grunt. I can't move but I like the feeling of being at his mercy.

"Kwame," I breathe his name.

"Yes, my good, good Sin."

"I love you," I say it because I can't not.

"You fucking better," he growls. "Because I love you too, and I'm never letting you go, Sin. Guarding what's mind like the jealous simp I am for you."

I laugh despite the air it costs me. I reach up and grab his neck and pull his mouth down to mine and bite his lip.

He hisses and covers my mouth with his hot open one and licks my upper lip. "You're so sweet, Sin. Everywhere. Your mouth, your skin, your pussy, your ass, behind your knees, in the crook of you neck—there's nowhere I don't want to lay claim on and make sure that no one else will ever do for you again."

I've always thought this kind of possessiveness would turn me off but instead, I melt and burn and squirm to coax him closer.

"Would you like that?" he speaks into my ear, his breath tickles the side of my face. "To be mine and no one else's?"

"Yes. I already am," I confess and he grunts in approval and bites my lip and then sucks the sting away.

"Good," he says before he kisses me again. "We're finally on the same page."

I taste his need and feel his pent-up passion that I didn't even realize he'd been holding in until I feel the searing heat of it in the grip of his hands and the tickle of his chest hairs against my nipples. I tighten my grip on his nape and hold him as tightly as he's holding me.

"I need you," he says and reaches into the drawer at his bedside for a condom.

"Let me," I say and he lifts off me and onto his knees and hands me the silver packet.

I tear it open, roll it on him slowly, and enjoy the way his muscles tense from my touch.

He moves fast, pushing me onto my back and lifting one leg to wrap around his waist.

"My love," he murmurs in my ear and drags his length through the soaked, sensitive skin between my hips. The head of his dick presses into my clit and the burst of sensation is outrageously good, and I whimper and lever my hips up to seek more of it.

"You like that?" he asks and drags himself over the same spot, slowly enough to allow the good to turn into great and spread up and out so that my body pulses with it.

He lowers his head and touches his tongue up the center of my chest and across my breast and by the time his mouth closes over my pulsing nipple, I'm completely overrun with sensations I've never felt before. I close my eyes and see stars.

"Oh, God." I clutch the sheets in my fist, and he grabs my wrist and tugs the sheet loose and drapes my arm around his neck.

"Don't hold on to anything but me," he growls in my ear and bites my earlobe.

"Okay," I pant and nip his chin with my teeth.

I arch my back excited and impatient for him to deliver me from my needs. He starts slowly, prodding, testing the ease of ingress until I whimper a curse and rock my hips up to take more of him.

"I'm going to fuck you so good, baby. Because that's what you deserve." He fills me in one hard thrust that moves my body up the bed and brings his hips flush with mine.

I groan at the exquisite stretch and the overwhelming fullness of him.

I roll my hips and moan at the sparks of pleasures that fly at the friction we create.

His groan is guttural and his eyes are narrowed to slits as he gazes down at me. "You're always so wet for me, Sin. Always so fucking open." He drops his face into my neck, presses kisses to my throat and moves his hips in shallow, but forceful thrusts and out in one languid glide. "Do you love it?" His breath is hot in my ear. "Can you trust me to take care of you? Not just your body, but to be your partner?"

My eyes snap open and my heart drums against my ribcage. Below him like this, connected in the most intimate way I have never felt so vulnerable. "I trust you. But, I can take care of myself."

He rolls his hips, brings a hand up to cup my cheek and looks down at me with blazingly bright eyes. "I know you can. I can take care of myself, too. I think you make me better. I think I make you better. I want you to trust me with things that matter."

My heart bursts into a thousand butterflies and they flutter around chasing away the cobwebs of doubt I'd left up as a reminder of things that don't serve me anymore.

Every crevice in me is filled with love for this man and I let him see it as I let down my wall completely. "You better not break my heart, Kwame Palmer," I warn.

"As if I could," he chuckles and pulls back so the broad head of him stretches my entrance and then he drives back into me and then wraps one big arm around me, cups my breast with his free hand and brings his mouth down over my nipple and sucks it while he starts fucking me in earnest.

He licks and sucks and bites my breast and makes me feel like I'm being revived inside and out.

"My *good* Sin," he breathes against my neck and drags his lips up my throat. "You're everything I thought I'd never find."

Tears sting the back of my eyes and one escapes the corner of my eye. *God, please let this be real. If I'm dreaming let me sleep forever.*

He doesn't rush, he's fucks me until I'm slick with our mingled sweat and I'm sure the building tension is too much and I can't feel anything but his hardness inside of me laying waste to my resistance and taking me higher than we've ever gone.

My body breaks in half with my climax and becomes a trembling mass of flesh and bone and the whole world seems within my grasp, everything I've ever wanted is already mine.

He hisses sharply and jerks out of me, his muscled torso sweaty and heaving. He bites his lip as he rolls the condom off and wraps his fist around his dick and kneels between my splayed legs and strokes himself until his sperm shoots out onto my stomach.

"I want to taste it," I say and flush when his eyes grow wide.

"Fuck yeah," he says and then straddles me and moves forward on his knees until he's at my shoulders. His balls touch my chin as I lean forward and take his cum covered head into my mouth.

"Oh damn," he groans and leans forward to rest a hand on the headboard, and I suck and lick until he pulls away and drops to the bed beside me, panting like he's just run a marathon.

We lay there in silence staring at the ceiling for a minute. I turn my head to look at him. He's got a hand pressed to his chest and his eyes are closed. "Are you okay?"

A smile cracks his face, and he opens his eyes halfway and turns to look at me.

"Better than."

"You?" he asks and I roll to my side to face him.

"Luck is finally on my side."

I look down at my stomach and know I should wipe it off, but I don't want to.

I meet his eyes and my breath catches at the tenderness there and at the thought that fills my head. "I found my person."

"It's always been on your side. You just needed to shift a little so you could see it."

"Well, thank you for helping me make that shift. Thank you for not judging me and for not holding me back."

"Never. We're a world of our own, and here, anything is possible." He drops a kiss on my lips and rolls away and off the bed.

"Where are you going?"

"I'll be back in a minute." He walks to the bathroom and less than a minute later walks back with a towel rolled up in his hands.

He drops it on my bare stomach and I gasp at the heat. He picks it up and wipes me clean.

"That's nice," I say.

"Thank you."

"I told you I'm nice," he says and tosses the towel away.

He runs his hands down my hip bones and cups my pussy and smiles.

"I like that you don't shave," he murmurs, stroking my hair.

"I do. Just not everything," I say with a giggle and then a moan when his finger finds my clit and rubs small circles.

He moves and scoops me up with him.

"What are you doing?"

"Getting comfortable."

He drops me into the chair beside his bed and kneels in front of me.

He cups each of my thighs and drapes my legs over the arms of the chair so I'm wide open in front of him. Making me like an offering to him.

"Hello, my pet," he speaks directly to my pussy like it's going to talk back.

"Your pet?" I giggle.

"Yes. Mine." He rests his chin on my thigh and gazes up at me. "I love you, I know you. You are my best friend. My secret garden. The master of my universe. The ruler of me. I'm not saying we're immortal, but I think this could last forever."

My heart is flying a thousand miles an hour, screaming at the top of its lungs when he lowers his head, almost like he's bowing to it to pray, and then his tongue is on me, moving up, licking and setting the world on fire.

He parts my lips with his thumbs and runs his tongue along the inner seams. I arch my back and whimper his name.

His tongue prods my entrance, and I buck up against him and groan loud and long when his mouth descends on me. The flat of his tongue applies pressure as his lips suck and nip and his fingers find my nipples and tug and pinch and I am undone.

His mouth is inhaling and my heartbeat is so loud I'm not sure I'll survive but when he takes me over the edge, I do so much more than survive.

I fly so high I swear when we kissed, I tasted the sun.

Forty-Six

Sin

Choice

I don't know how it happened, but I've been at Kwame's house for almost a month straight. It's been interesting. Mostly in good ways. Waking up next to him is a top tier dopamine hit that starts my day off right.

We don't share a bathroom or a closet and he's outfitted one of the other rooms into an office for me.

I wasn't sure how I'd feel living with anyone again, but I love it.

And him.

The aroma of fresh coffee and toasted bread wakes me up this morning. As nice as that is, I run a wistful hand over the pillow where his head would normally be.

I glance at the clock, and my rose-colored point of view clarifies. It's already after seven, I have a meeting with Kathy at eight thirty. I should hurry.

In the weeks since my run-in with Sofia, every story I've submitted has been cut from the digital version of *The Spectator*. It happens to the best and most seasoned staff writers but not every single week. I'm salaried so my income isn't affected. But I didn't become a journalist to collect a paycheck. It's killing my soul, but Sofia's words echo in my mind. Is that my reputation? Difficult?

I drag myself out of bed and trudge to the bathroom.

"I thought you'd be done with the shower by now." Kwame comes in just as I've turned the shower on.

He's wearing my pink and white batik patterned house robe. I gape at him and shout over the roar of water hitting the tiled shower floor. "Oh my God, why are you wearing that?"

He frowns and looks at himself in the mirror. It's a one size fits all and the sleeves are voluminous on me. It hits me at the knee. On him, it's barely long enough to cover his thighs. And the tip of his dick peeks out below the hem. "I like it. And all my clothes are in the laundry."

"Maybe if you owned more than seven pairs of underwear or let me send your laundry out with mine, you wouldn't have this problem." I stick my hand under the rain shower head to test the temperature. It's perfect, as always.

"Why do you send your laundry out? We have a washer and dryer."

"Because it saves me time or lets me spend the evening reading instead of folding and sorting and ironing. And I always have clean clothes."

"But then I wouldn't have an excuse to wear your robe. It smells like you. Well, when you're clean." He winks, taps my ass, and leaves before I can think of anything clever to say.

When I get out of the shower he's sitting on the bed, reading something on his phone.

"Hey, I've been meaning to ask. I haven't seen your column in the digital version in weeks."

I roll my eyes. "Yeah, that's because it's been cut."

I open his closet and pull out one of the garment bags I brought over and unzip it.

"What do you mean?"

I look at him puzzled and then remember that I never told him what happened with Sofia. "Ugh, sorry I was so upset when it happened that I didn't want to talk about it and then…I guess I just moved on."

He tosses his phone onto the bed and gives me his full attention. "Tell me."

I fill him in on my conversation with Sofia from last August and when I'm done, he's staring at me in disbelief. "She said that to you?"

"Yup."

I slip my skirt on, and he stands to zip it for me. "Thank you." I caress his shoulder and slip my blouse on.

I give myself a critical once over and frown. "I'm not sure I should wear white. I'm notorious for spilling things." I walk back to both closets and eye the meager selection I have here.

"You look like you're trying to decide whether to take the blue or red pill," Kwame jokes from behind me. "Why are you going to work in a place that treats you like that?"

"I can't have her as an enemy and succeed at *The Spectator*."

"Does this feel like succeeding?" He asks and comes to stand beside me, eyeing me as critically as I was eyeing my blouses.

"I don't know." I bite my lip and try not to let my self-pity get the best of me this morning. "I'm not sure I can do better than this right now."

"If you think like *that* you certainly can't."

"I'm being realistic. I haven't been there a year. I don't want to look like I can't keep a job. This woman has a direct hand in my future."

He takes my hands in his. "*You* have a direct hand in your future. What are you afraid of, Sin?"

I close my eyes and want to cry. "That I'm not cut out for this and everyone can see it but me. That's why I keep getting passed over."

He lets go of my hand and picks up his phone. "Can I read you something?"

I eye him warily. "Sure."

He nods and clears his throat.

"She has worked extensively as a journalist covering the stories of people who are often forgotten in the headlines. Her work has followed the rules of climate injustice in migration patterns, the exploitation of refugees, the immigration detention center systems and in 2021 she managed to find her way into a federal prison to record footage of neglect and abuse.

She's testified for Congress about the repatriation of stolen artifacts. She has been honored with the Sarah Coleman award in 2019. She's also the 2015 winner of the Peabody future of media award."

He looks up at me. "Does that sound like someone who's not cut out for her career?"

"Oh my God, where did you get that?"

"You have a whole Wikipedia page, Sin. People know who you are. *You* know who you are. And I remember someone telling me that even if I didn't have anyone, I had myself."

"Oh my God, thank you. You always know what to say."

"I'm glad. Because if you're unhappy, my only concern is fixing it."

Joy bubbles up inside of me and pushes a laugh up and out of me. I'm overwhelmed by everything I'm feeling and bury my face in my hands.

"Hey, hey," Kwame is back by my side and he puts an arm around my shoulder and pulls me into his side.

I wrap my arms around him and hug him tight.

"What's wrong, baby?" He lowers us to sitting on the bed and I crawl into his lap and cup his face again and rest my forehead on his.

"Nothing is wrong. I'm so happy." I bury my face in his warm neck and pepper it with kisses. "You really mean that, don't you?"

He circles me in my arms. "Of course," he leans away. "Are you surprised?"

I swipe at my cheeks with the backs of my hands and give him my brightest smile. "No. I guess I'm still getting used to it."

"Get used to it. I'll always bet on you, Sin. But it doesn't matter if you won't bet on yourself." He kisses me swiftly and heads to the bathroom.

I didn't get where I am by playing small or being a doormat. Nor have I ever hid my ambition. Where would I be if I'd waited for someone to give me a chance? I've always made my own luck.

He's right. It's time to bet on myself.

Forty-Seven

Kwame

Sins of the Father

"Mr. Palmer, I know you asked not to be disturbed." My secretary's voice startles me out of my deep focus.

I've told her not to use the intercom like that unless it's an absolute emergency. I hit the flashing red button on my desktop phone. "Then why are you disturbing me?" I snap.

Q4 reporting is in full swing and I'm busier than I've been since I started work here.

"You've got a visitor. I explained that you weren't available. He said if you didn't speak to him now, he'd send a subpoena."

That makes me sit up straight. "Where did you say he's from?"

"He didn't say."

"Ask him again." I'm stalling because it doesn't really matter. Subpoena power trumps my deadline for this brief. I close my laptop and begin putting sensitive documents into their files.

"He won't say, sir," she says in a low voice.

Shit. "Alright. Give me two minutes and then escort him in."

I straighten my tie and use my phone to check for crumbs or food in my teeth and then shake myself out of it. I've been away from criminal practice too long. I'd forgotten how intimidating we could be. Showing up unannounced and threatening subpoenas is how we establish our dominance. Not even the most powerful people in this country are above the law.

Precisely two minutes later there's a brief knock on my door before it opens. I stay seated when the man who made my battle-ax of a secretary stutter enters.

His eyes go to my closed laptop and he frowns. "Are you on your way out?"

"No. How can I help you?"

"I'm from the Department of Homeland Security. I'd like to discuss your application to the US Attorney's Office for the District of Columbia."

The hairs on the back of neck stand up. "I see." He could have knocked me over with a feather. My stomach drops. "This seems… irregular," I say.

"Highly. But, so are the circumstances that bring me here."

"Okay."

"Aren't you going to ask what those circumstances are? Or do you already know?"

"I'm waiting for you to tell me. I'm not the one who showed up at your office."

He strolls the perimeter of my office, peering at my diplomas and artwork. I watch him and don't react. He wants me to know he's going to control the pace of this conversation. But I know he's here because he needs something from me, and I've got a hot date and a brief to finish before then, so I cut to the chase.

"If you don't start talking in the next minute, I'm going to take you up on that subpoena you threatened. I'll come to you. And when I find out who you're trying to keep this visit a secret from, I'll make sure they know of it."

He chuckles. "I heard you were an asshole."

"Only when necessary. You've got twenty-one seconds."

He expels a harsh breath. "I guess I should get straight to it."

"Please." I wave at the chair and try to ignore the thundering in my chest and wait for him to drop the hammer.

He sits and looks down at the ground for a beat before he meets my gaze. "I have a friend at Secret Service and he does me a solid by giving me a heads-up when I need it. And today, he called about you. Your background check came back."

"Okay?"

"How come you didn't disclose your nine-figure net worth and the billions you'll inherit?"

The hairs on the back of my neck stand up again and unease tickles my gut.

"Because that money is in an irrevocable trust that I don't control. I get an income from it, and I disclosed that."

"No one who worked with you at the LA prosecutor's office knew either."

"I didn't know how much money my coworkers had either."

His pale cheeks flush at my even reply. "Well, I can assure you that none of them are billionaires."

I expel an aggravated breath. "I'll have to take your word for that."

"You can take it to the bank, Mr. Palmer. Just like we'll need to be able to take yours if you're lucky enough to join our ranks. And we don't keep secrets from each other."

"I'm not keeping secrets. It's none of anyone's business how much money I'm going to inherit, and it has nothing do with how well I do my job."

"I'm the judge of that, and I don't agree."

I've had enough of his cryptic smugness, and I bite back the urge to ask him to get the fuck out. He's a federal agent and right now, he appears to be standing between me and this job that I've made my light at the end of the tunnel.

I keep my expression neutral. "Are you going to enlighten me, then?"

He uncrosses his legs. "What's your relationship with Oz Annan?"

It's the last thing I expect him to ask and my irritation morphs into unease. "Uh…he's a cousin but we're not close. Why?"

He arches an eyebrow. "Are you sure about that?"

"If you already know then why are you asking?" I ask, irritation clipping my words.

"Because I want to know the whole story."

I sigh wearily. "Ozwald Annan's mother is my father's sister. She's also worked for my parents since I was a child. She lived in a cottage on the property and naturally her son lived with her."

"So, you grew up together." His nose twitches like a bloodhound catching a scent.

"Hardly." I scoff and brush off his attempt to frame our relationship. "He's ten years older than me, and by the time I was old enough to make formative memories, he'd moved out."

The man nods. "File says he went to college at Oxford. He must be a very smart guy. I don't blame your father for keeping him close."

"Yes. My father gave Oz a job at Prosperity Partners after he graduated from business school. He worked there for five years in the real estate group. He wasn't a vital employee and he works for himself now."

He blows out a breath and hangs his head, shaking it like he's disappointed. "Do you know what he does for a living now?"

"He's a lobbyist and represents governments seeking to do business with the United States government. I think. Again, we're not close."

"And did you know that your father, in his personal capacity, is his largest client?"

"What personal capacity? And what has Oz got to do with me and this job?"

He sighs and leans back in his chair, his expression grows grave. "I'm going to share something with you. You signed several nondisclosures when you applied for this position and they apply to this conversation, too."

I have to stop myself from shifting in my seat. "Understood," I say through tense lips. "Go ahead."

"Ozwald Annan has been the subject of a multi-year investigation into a criminal syndicate that runs a black market in priceless artifacts and contraband like ivory fueled by a sophisticated burglary ring. We suspect he's the person known by members of the syndicate as The Wizard."

"Based on what?"

He cocks his head. "You don't seem surprised."

I laugh humorlessly "That you suspect a wealthy Black foreigner doing business with countries you don't like of being a criminal? I'd be surprised if you didn't. But those things in themselves aren't crimes."

"He does fit a profile, but so do you. So do a lot of men in the country. They're not all suspects. He is because we have credible evidence. We just need an airtight case. We'll only get one shot at him. He's slippery as fuck."

"I can't help you. Like I said, we didn't grow up together. We haven't had any reason to be in each other's lives. We're practically strangers."

He purses his lips and looks up at the ceiling like he's thinking. "Hmmmm. And your father? When will you see him next?"

I sit up straight, sensing danger I hadn't before. "What has my father got to do with Oz's potential criminality?"

"That's what we'd like to know. Given his support of that last re-gime, we can't ignore his penchant for cozying up to bad actors. Even if he himself isn't bad, it's a question of judgement."

"My father has excellent judgment."

"I hope so, because if even half of what we suspect Annan is in-volved in turns out to be true, then your father is doing business with a dangerous, ruthless man who will do anything for money and who has no loyalty to any country or person."

I mean, I knew he was an asshole with no integrity. But my head spins to hear Oz described that way. "Is my father in danger?" I ask.

"No." He shakes his head. "But your job prospects could be."

Resignation and resentment form a weight in my stomach. "Unless what?"

"All you'd have to do is put this little device I'll give you within ten feet of his phone for at least ninety seconds, and we'll do the rest."

Time seems to slow, my pulse thrum in my ears. I shake my head, incredulous. "You want me to collect intel on my *own* father?"

His expression grows cold and he slaps a hand on the desk. "If he's collaborating with an enemy of this country, I *expect* you to."

"He's not. If he was, I'd be the first person to turn him in. Your intel is bad. He's not doing business with him."

He looks at me with eyes narrowed, shakes his head like I've got to be an idiot. "They're in it together, and you know it."

I balk at his characterization. "Saying that won't make it true. You're wrong."

"If I am, what have you to got to lose by helping me confirm it?"

Everything. My only living parent, practically the only family I've got.

"They were together in London last summer. A transport on its way to Dover was robbed and a cache of ivory that had just been confiscated was stolen two days after Annan arrived and less than forty-eight hours before he hopped back on a plane to DC. A plane, I might add, that belongs to your father." He leans back in his chair and folds his hands behind his head.

He's making leaps in logic based on intel that's not complete but he's not going to take my word for it.

"Kwame, help us with the investigation. Prove your loyalty and trustworthiness and patriotism. And once Oz is out of the picture, your dad won't be important enough to merit a mention in the report I'll sub-mit to the hiring committee. And if you don't help us, we'll find another way to get what we need."

Dread courses through me at the unmistakable threat in his voice.

He gets to his feet. "You have until the end of April."

"So, if I don't rat my father out, I don't get the job?"

"If you won't cooperate with the government, then you become an enemy of it. And we will treat you like one."

An icy pool of dread and impotent rage forms in my gut as he leaves my office.

I wait until security downstairs confirms he's left the building before I text the Governor.

"I think I'm in trouble."

Forty-Eight

Sin

Done

"You can go on in, Sin," Kathy's assistant smiles up at me from her desk, where she's been doing her best to pretend she isn't dying to know what's going on. I leave the box I carried up with me on the floor by my chair.

There have been no more invites to gossip in her office since the whole press pass battle. We're back to her staff meetings are the only meetings scheduled. I was surprised when she put me on her calendar so quickly.

"Have a seat." She gestures to the seat on the other side of her desk and avoids my eyes as she waits with undisguised impatience for me to cross her ridiculously large office.

I sit down. I've been so afraid of this for months but now that it's here, I'm strangely calm.

I'm not going to wait for them to decide my fate.

"What can I do for you, Sin?" She keeps scribbling in her notebook.

"Why did you hire me?"

Her head pops up. "Sin, you've got to grow up." She takes her glasses off and rubs her eyes. "You think I'm trying to hold you back. I'm just trying to save you from destroying your career. We are here to speak truth to power, but we also have to be rational. This newspaper has an owner, a board, and shareholders. I am accountable to them."

"I understand how corporate media works. But shouldn't we still try to tell stories for the people who are counting on us to inform them of what's happening in the world? None of the things we write about happen in a vacuum. We owe our reading public the truth."

She scoffs and rolls her eyes. "You can't be this naive. Newspapers only exist because businesses needed a way to advertise. If we piss them off, it's lights out."

She sighs. "You've always thought you were better than everyone else. You ran off to New York with stars in your eyes and got your ass handed to you. I gave you a job when you needed one. You should be thanking me. Pretty privilege may have been enough in New York. Here you've got to have more to offer than charm and a nice ass. I'm honestly disappointed. I expected better."

I'm not bothered when people imply I used my looks to get to where I am. What kind of fool would I be if I didn't use every talent and gift I have to make my way in a world that was designed without me in mind?

But I won't let anyone tell me I haven't worked my ass off for every single thing I've attained. I'm a Black woman in an industry where only three percent of the other journalists look like me. I've had to be exceptional to get opportunities that people with half my credentials get handed just for showing up.

I put a palm down on her desk. "If I'd known I was coming to work for cowards and liars, I wouldn't have taken your call that day and said yes to a job I was overqualified for with a boss who doesn't have half the accolades I do."

Her eyes go wide and her back arches as if she's been struck by an arrow. "Are you *trying* to get fired?"

Her question makes me feel like a deer in the headlights.

I didn't see it coming but I'm not scared of this fork in my road.

My indecision resolves itself, and I make my choice.

"As if I'd let *you* fire *me*." I move my finger in the space between us and suck my teeth so loud I know my grandmother in heaven is proud as hell. "I quit."

Forty-Nine

Kwame

For Her

It's mild for February and I'm back to riding my bike to my office in Gallery Place. The DC metro area has got some of the worst traffic and drivers in the country but the views more than make up for it.

This corner of Georgetown is starting to grow on me now that Sin greets me at the front door every evening.

Tonight, though, as I approach my house, I don't slow down to enjoy the charming canopy of trees I pass under.

I've wanted to work in federal prosecutions all my career.

To have come this close only to be in an impossible position because of my father is infuriating.

I didn't know he was using Oz's firm to do business here but that isn't a crime. And my father is a lot of things, but he's never been a criminal.

He's terrified of going to jail.

I won't help anyone trying to make that possible.

So, unless a miracle happens and Oz's investigation is wrapped up or my father cuts ties with him, this job I've wanted my whole career is out of my reach.

When I get home from work the house is dark, but something smells good.

She's made herself at home in my kitchen, and the house has more furniture than I even knew it needed now that she's here.

She changes the sheets every three days and every time she takes a shower, it smells like a bakery and florist had a baby. I've even adopted her ethos that laundry is best done by someone else.

Thank God life here is good because everywhere else it's shit.

It's not my pride. I don't need the money.

I stopped by the store to grab a bottle of champagne but tuck it into the coat closet when I realize Sin is crying.

"Hey, what's wrong?" I walk over and join her on the window seat.

"I made a huge mistake coming back here," she says, her voice watery.

"What happened?"

"I quit my job today."

It's the last thing I expected her to say but I hide my surprise. I put a hand on the middle of her back and stroke a small circle. "Okay. Start from the beginning."

"I didn't tell you sooner because I wasn't sure what was really going on."

"Okay, I'm listening."

"On the same day I came home to find my door open, I'd received an email on my website asking for my help with the investigation into a crime related to my story."

The cryptic, vague answer irritates me but not as much as the new details she's adding to the night she called me in distress. "Why didn't you mention that before?" I lean back in my chair, stunned. "Why didn't you tell me about that? Are you kidding?"

"I couldn't tell you that without telling you about my story and—"

"You can't talk about that," I finish for her unable to hide my exasperation.

I understand her needing to keep her sources private, but I'm starting to resent how little she's willing to share with me.

"I'm sorry, Kwame. I wasn't trying to resurrect it at that point. After the event at the museum, I just…wanted to move on and feel safe."

She looks so tired and as much as I want to press her for more details, it can wait until she's had some rest.

I put an arm around her, inviting her to lean on me. Instead, she leans away.

"I had so much riding on that story and it fell apart and now I'm writing an advice column that is being shadow banned by my own paper.

But that's what I get because dropping it the way I did was such a bitch move. I'm a journalist. I shouldn't have been run off a story I cared about so easily. But I felt threatened by him. He knows who I am, where I work. And if he's still trying to stop me from writing this story all that tells me is that I'm on to something."

"Are you sure you can't tell me anything? Maybe I know him," I press, desperate to help.

"That's what I'm afraid of. I don't want you to feel conflicted, and I don't want to feel like I can't be honest. It's not just this story or you," she adds when my expression doesn't soften.

"Okay," I say slowly and put myself in her shoes. "I understand. But you can trust me and when you're as sure of that as I am, I hope you'll let me help you. Until then, you have a place to live, and I have enough money to take care of whatever bills you've got."

She puts a hand on my chest. "Thank you. Let's see how I feel two months from now." She laughs dryly and then bites her lip. "I just… need a job or a story that I can use to get an editor to take a chance on me."

Fifty

Kwame

Yellow Brick Road

It's taken me three weeks to make this call but as soon as my father answers the phone, my doubts about what I'm doing disappear.

"Son. To what do I owe this surprise?"

"I'll come to Palm Sunday."

"Heh!" he shouts and then switches the call to video. He's standing in the bathroom with a towel around his waist. His face is half covered with shaving cream. "Do you mean it?"

I laugh at the astounded grin on his face. "Yes. I mean it."

He claps his hands together and peers at the phone. "That's my boy. I knew you'd see sense."

"I'm glad you're happy because I need something from you first."

He laughs out loud. "Finally, you're learning. What do you want?"

I sigh and look toward the bedroom where Sin is getting dressed and singing along to "If I Ruled the World" at the top of her lungs.

My heart skips a beat. I'd do anything to keep her singing, hopeful, happy.

"I'll come to the party as long as you let go of your grudge against The Sackeys."

"Why would I do that?"

"Because you want me to come to Palm Sunday," I answer simply.

He scoffs. "Don't play prosecutor with me, Kwame. You know what I'm asking. Why would *you* want me to do that?"

"Because I'm in love with their daughter."

He sputters. "How?"

"Mom introduced us," I say, and my smile is irrepressible.

"How?"

"Dad, I know you. I've got about three minutes before another call cuts in and interrupts us. I'll tell you the how when I see you, but I just need you to understand that I love her. She's a journalist."

He makes a choking sound. "Why?" he huffs.

I cough to cover my laugh at his reaction. "You can ask her that. She'll be with me at the party and before that, I want you to grant her an interview. About the house and you. Let her take pictures of the house, tell her your story, and let her write an article about it."

"Fine. But there will be conditions and she will have to sign several nondisclosures," he says with a grim face.

I lean in and eye him. I'd come prepared to fight for this. "So… you'll do it?" I ask stunned at how easy that was.

"Yes. I'm getting a call. Put her people in touch with mine. See you in two months."

"See you."

"Oh, and Happy Birthday."

I blink. "You remembered."

"Of course. Did you think it was your mother who sent you a card every year?"

"Frankly, yes."

He rolls his eyes. "Typical. Speak soon." And then he's gone.

"I think I like being a kept woman," Sin declares when I walk into the kitchen. We had a quiet dinner at home and she's loading the dishwasher.

"Is the kept woman in the room with us now?" I ask and look pointedly at the stack of tile samples in front of her. "You've been working harder on this house than I have since I've lived here."

"It's beautiful. Thank you for letting me have free rein over it."

"I have another present for you."

She leans back and her eyes light up. "Kwame, you're spoiling me. You've already given me so many gifts today. I only got you one thing."

"It's something money can't buy," I say as casually as I can.

"We're going on a double date with Jay-Z and Beyoncé." Her eyes light up.

"No. I think this might be better."

"Well shit! Tell me, then!" She nudges my shin with her toe.

"I'm glad you like it here, and I'm glad you've enjoyed being a domestic goddess but are you ready to get back to work?"

She puckers her lips and leans a hip on the counter. "Do you have a job for me?"

"No, but I have something that could help you get one." I stroll to the fridge so my back is to her and let my smile free.

"I didn't want to tell you until I had an answer but, my father, he's agreed to sit down for an interview with you the Friday before Palm Sunday. It could be a bargaining chip to land your next gig. So even if your lead is a bust, you'll have that. If you're interested—"

She screams and presses her palms to her cheeks. "Oh my God. Yes, of course. It may not be my heart song, but an interview with Al Palmer about anything would be one hell of a pitch."

"You'll have to sign an NDA. He insisted."

"Done," she says and takes a shuddering breath. "I can't believe this. You don't know what this means to me, Kwame. I would never have asked. But honestly, it's exactly the kind of break I need." She swallows hard and her eyes fill with tears. "Thank you so much."

She throws herself into my arms and hugs me so tight it makes taking a deep breath hard. I love it.

"I'm sorry I didn't offer sooner." I hug her back and ignore the twinge of guilt that I didn't consider it until her back was against a wall. "We'll leave the Thursday before so we can have a couple of days to ourselves before everyone else arrives. You'll love The Palms."

"Kwame. Are you sure?" She peers at me like she's trying to see inside my skull.

I chuckle and lean away. "For you, yes."

She frowns. "You said you hate Palm Sunday and The Palms. You don't have to do this for me. I mean, I'd love to talk to your dad and write about the property. I would never have asked."

I can tell she means it, and it makes me even more sure I'm doing the right thing. I can trust her with this.

"I want to do this for you. And I need to stop thinking the property has some sort of power over me. It'll be great. You can explore, take pictures and when my dad arrives you will get your face-to-face. His team will reach out, set parameters, conditions. I'll look at the disclosure agreements before you sign. Is that okay?"

She nods and then she covers her mouth with her hands to muffle an excited scream.

"I'll take that as a yes."

"Yes," she shouts and then throws herself into my arms. "Thank you, Kwame. This is literally the best gift you could have gotten me. I promise you won't regret it."

"I know I won't." I wrap my arms around her and press my lips against her neck. I breathe in her familiar sweet scent and pray I'm not wrong.

Fifty-One

Kwame

Prosperity

"When's the last time you were home?" Sin asks as we approach the gates of the house.

I punch in the code. I don't think of this place as home, but I don't know what else to call it. My father bought it from the family that had owned it for nearly a hundred years.

The previous occupants include a vice president, an ambassador and several US senators. When my father bought it, it was called Meridian Ridge.

He changed the name to The Palms. He plucked out all the fir trees and planted palm trees. He demolished as much of the original colonial building as he could without violating the heritage protection laws and extended it with this modern behemoth of a house that he uses to cosplay his "to the manor born" fantasy.

He picked the perfect spot. The house sits on a rock cliff on the banks of the Potomac River.

Owning it is something he is deeply proud of. It's a harbinger of the shift in what it means to be American that he owns this property that was stolen, worked by enslaved people at a time when a man like him wasn't even a figment of the original settlers' wildest imaginations.

"Finally! You're here," Alice calls from behind me, and I'm relieved she's the first member of my family Sin will meet.

"Alice, I'd like to introduce you to someone very special."

Alice opens her arms and her smile lights up her pretty face. She says, "Come here. I've heard so much about you. It's been long over-due."

Sin gives me a wide-eyed, thrilled grin over her shoulder as she embraces Alice with the same gusto that Alice has hugged her with. They pull apart and lean back and just smile at each other.

"He said you were pretty, but my goodness, I don't think he said enough." Her eyes dance as she takes Sin in from head to toe.

"I don't know what to say 'cause I'm terrible at receiving compli-ments but thank you so much, and I'm glad that you approve," Sin says with a smile that's as demure as I've ever seen her.

Alice beams at her. "Of course I approve. I trust Kwame's judg-ment implicitly, and he has never introduced anyone to me before and so the fact that he's brought you tells me everything I need to know. Hope you'll enjoy yourself here."

Fifty-Two

Sin

Heaven

The view of the Potomac River from our bedroom is like an emerald-tinted dream. The hills seem to go on forever and the sky and the earth meet in the most glorious kiss with the sun trying it's best to come between them only to add to the glory of it all.

The Palms is the most beautiful place I've ever had the pleasure of waking up in. The house itself is grand, immaculate and staffed so that not a speck of dust has the chance to land on the gleaming mahogany floors.

Every meal is served on dishes edged in gold and red and green and black. There are cooks, a butler, an army of cleaners, and groundskeepers. I glance to my right at Kwame and smile at the way he's positioned himself so he's bathed in the rays of mid-morning sun that spills into our room. His chin is propped up on his bent wrist, and I'm mesmerized by the swell of his bicep and how soft that skin feels when I touch him.

How is this my life?

I never imagined I'd have so much. I didn't even know so much existed.

I didn't even know a life so beautiful existed.

I've always felt that Kwame and I align on the belief that hoarding more money than you can spend in three lifetimes isn't something to be proud of.

After the last few days, I'm not sure that, in my case, it's less of a value and more the acceptance of my reality.

I'm not sure I could walk away from all of this.

It's not just the money. Although, I can't pretend not to understand its appeal now that I've seen how the other half lives.

It's about convenience, choice, safety, freedom, and comfort.

Things all humans are wired to crave. Sadly, most of us will never experience all five.

Much less at the very same time.

It's instantly addictive.

I'll go into withdrawal the first time I have to think about whether or not I have enough eggs to make the breakfast I'm craving.

The first time I miss one of my walks because it's raining and I don't have a treadmill—or space for one—I'll probably cry.

I'll never forget our time here. Being on the grounds, even without access to the entire property, while researching its history has been a magical experience.

I've gone to bed exhausted in the most delicious ways. Full of good food, and Kwame's thick dick.

I let out a sigh of satisfaction and stretch my arms, fingertips straining for the ceiling. "Do you believe in heaven?" I ask Kwame. It's the first time I've spoken today, and my voice is rough with sleep.

I love that he doesn't mind that I like to wake up and not talk until I'm ready. It's one of the luxuries I discovered from living alone. The ability to have quiet whenever I need it.

I also love that he doesn't mind if we skip good morning and get straight into whatever is on our minds.

"Is that a rhetorical question?" He doesn't look up from the tome on Byzantium history he's been reading all morning.

He brings one of his long fingers to his mouth, licks the tip of it and turns the page leisurely.

"No." I turn onto my side, propping my chin "I'm asking because I want to know what you think."

"About heaven?" He closes his book and places it on the table next to his side of the bed and stretches his muscular arms and turns his face toward the sun.

"Yes. Or have you never heard of it?"

"Ha! You're the sinner in this duet, baby. Literally and figuratively." He grins and dodges the swipe of my pillow.

"Are you going to answer the question or just make fun of me?" I prod his calf with my foot.

He rolls his eyes upward as he ponders my question. "I *hope* there's a heaven. For the sake of everyone who believes in it."

"But not you?"

"It feels hypocritical when I absolutely don't believe in hell. What about you?"

"I believe in heaven. But I live like this world might be all there is and try to make it as close to what *feels* like heaven to me."

"And what's that?"

"Waking up knowing what my purpose is. To not owe anyone anything. To be proud of my work. To have the security of a roof over my head, fair pay for the work I do, people I can close both eyes around."

"Sounds like you've got heaven."

"It's felt like that all week. There's something so tranquil about this place."

"I think you could make anywhere feel like that." He sighs and gazes out of the window that lines the wall our bed is facing. "It is so beautiful to look at though," he says with a wistful twist to his mouth.

I scoot close to him and drape an arm over his waist and lay my head on his shoulder. "It is. You have a stretch of the Potomac riverfront all to yourselves."

He nods. "I was obsessed with this river when I was growing up. It's the oldest thing in this landscape. Ancient. It's a different river depending when you encounter it. But here, after it goes over the great falls, it shallows out. And you see that stone island?" He points out into the distance, and I sit up straight and follow his finger to a pile of rocks that splits the current.

"That's the primordial bedrock that was here before the first humans arrived here a thousand years ago."

"Wow, is it *that* old?"

"Older. But also brand new. The riverbed is constantly eroded by water that has never stopped running. It's never the same river twice. And every time I stepped into it, I was a different person, too."

I nod in agreement. "Yes, every day is an opportunity to do something different."

"Spoken like a true romantic and optimist."

I search his face. "Are you making fun of me?"

He frowns and the humor melts into affection. "Never. From head to toe, inside out, there's nothing about you I don't take seriously. Not one part of you I don't appreciate. Not a single thing I'd change. Good

Sin, Bad Sin, I don't care. As long as you're *my* Sin."

I'll never get over the way it feels when he speaks life into me like that. After a lifetime of being critiqued, always thinking about leveling up, never feeling like I'm quite where I want to be, he's more than watered a desert in my soul, he's helped new life bloom there.

"Thank you, Kwame. For everything. This has been one of the happiest times of my life."

"Mine, too." He kisses me softly and tucks an errant heatless curler back under my bonnet. "And your optimism is one of my favorite things about you, for the record."

"I'm not an optimist by choice. It's the only way I have been able to keep moving forward."

"That's something my father says, too. But his optimism is motivated by vengeance. Besting his doubters and enemies is what gets him out of bed in the morning."

Kwame has barely spoken about his father while we've been here, and I'd almost forgotten that he's the reason I'm here. My stomach dips "I'm so nervous about meeting him. I'm so glad you'll be there for lunch."

His brow furrows. "Uh…" he presses his lips together.

"What?"

His phone buzzes on the bedside table, rattling against the glass and stealing his attention. "One second."

He answers the call. "Morning." He listens and nods. "Yup, I'll be there by eleven, but I've got all day."

Just like that, our tranquil love fest comes to a screeching halt. He glances at his watch and groans and sits up.

"Where are you going to be at eleven?"

"I've got to get to DC for a meeting. I wasn't planning on joining you for lunch."

I shoot up to a sitting position, clutching the sheet over my bare chest. "You're not joining us?" I ask, incredulous. "What do you mean?"

He sits down. "I didn't know you expected me to. I thought you were going to be interviewing him during lunch, and I have a meeting with my mentor."

I toy with my hands in my lap, unsure what to say. "It's cool. I just…I thought you'd be there."

He squeezes my thigh. "I'll be back for dinner. I promise."

He glances at his watch and groans. "I have to get in the shower." He pecks my lips, distractedly "Sorry Sin, really."

I watch him, and all I can think is *Me, too.*

Fifty-Three

Kwame

Where the Apple Falls

I feel like shit that I'm not joining Sin for lunch. I didn't think she'd want me there, and I wanted to put off seeing my dad until I had things squared away on this role at the DOJ. Now that it's completely dead in the water, I'm not sure what I'm going to do next.

I run around to open Sin's door and help her down from the car. She's dressed in a suit for the first time since I've known her and looks like she belongs behind an anchor's desk.

"Do you think I'm ready?" she asks as we walk up the short stone path to the door.

"You were born ready, Sin. But if you hadn't been, the work you've put into research would have made up the difference."

She flashes me one of her iconic megawatt smiles and my nerves settle just a little bit. She smooths a hand over her skirt. "I hope he likes me."

"Of course he will," I say with full confidence. She's exactly the kind of person he likes.

In truth. I'm worried that she won't like him.

"How do I look?" Sin's voice is a welcome reprieve from the swirl of negative thoughts in my head.

I turn around, smile, all ready to face her, and my heart stops when our eyes meet. "In another time, nations would have launched a thousand ships just to see you smile."

"Sweet talker," she waves away my praise.

"I'm proud of you," I say in earnest and hand her the tote bag I've been carrying for her.

"Save that for when I'm done. I'm so nervous." She blows out a breath.

I take her hand in mine. "You shouldn't be nervous at all. You're the asset here. I'm just praying you'll still want me when I get back from DC." I laugh but the worry is real.

She steps into me so that her chest is pressing into my abdomen and she looks up at me, her eyes shining with that affection I'll never ever get used to. "As long as the stars shine, as long as the sun rises, and even after that, I'll want you," she says.

I kiss her goodbye and for the first time in months, feel hopeful. I hope the Governor has some solutions for me today.

Three hours later, I've got the Governor of Virginia on the line confirming my worst fears. "The best thing you can hope is for the investigation into Oz's activities to be concluded. Otherwise, this will hang over your head. It won't just be the DOJ. It'll be any federal agency you apply to. Even if I could help in my capacity as governor, I wouldn't want to risk the appearance of putting my thumb on the scales of justice for my biggest donor."

"It's not about him," I remind him. "And I wouldn't ask you to do anything improper. I just wanted your insight." I keep my frustration with the implication out of my voice. I'd only told him the bare bones of my meeting with the agent. It was enough for him to understand my predicament. Without the details of what they suspect Oz of doing, it does sound like they think my father is involved.

"You're a prosecutor. You know how this goes Kwame."

I nod in silent agreement and pull into my driveway. "Either they get a lead that gives them the ability to indict or evidence that clears him of suspicion."

"Exactly. You've got to decide where your loyalties lie."

I already know. I email the agent to say I'm on my way and put the address for the Hoover building into my GPS.

Fifty-Four

Sin

The Emperor is Fully Dressed

When you're a little girl with a loud voice in a world that values your compliance over your conviction, muffling yourself is often an act of survival.

The examples of what happens to women who dare to make enough noise to be heard over the maddening crowd is a catalog of tragedy and unsettled grievances.

Careers derailed, reputations ruined, their names become synonymous with words like difficult, polarizing, angry.

So, when I had something to say that could *only* be said in a loud voice, I wrote it down.

First in my journal.

Then in my school newspaper under the plum de nom that would become my byline. A. Sackey, for its simplicity and androgyny. Even before I was a working journalist, I understood that in such a male dominated field, the barriers to entry for women start at the top of your resume. The lens with which your work is viewed becomes clouded by ingrained misogyny.

I graduated from college in the age when social media was still about connecting with people you knew rather than building a platform. No one cared about the person behind the writing and so I didn't correct people's assumption that I was a man.

My nom de plume helped me punch through the glass ceiling with the kind of ease that can only be created by the universe's lubricant made of impeccable timing.

Those high rates of acceptance of my submissions allowed me to build a career and a body of work that was undeniably impressive and always got my foot in the door.

And that is all the chance I've ever needed.

I wasn't very interested in telling his story, if I'm honest. I was genuinely excited to get this scoop. But writing about a billionaire known for doing business with anyone for the right price and throwing excessive parties isn't exactly what I'd call compelling.

I wasn't worried though. Making the rest of the world understand why the people I choose to write about are extraordinary has become my specialty.

I spent weeks learning everything I could about him. Kwame's stories of his father have one note—mistrust. They didn't spend much time under the same roof, and when they were together, it was heavily orchestrated and full of ceremony. He couldn't even confirm that the birthday on Wikipedia is correct.

Given that he's never done an interview, everything that's been written about him is pure speculation. So I've decided to begin our conversation by getting his biographical information down.

I was prepared for Mr. Palmer to be skittish and to need his ego stroked before he'd open up.

I couldn't have been more wrong. As soon as he walked into the room, it was clear that Al Palmer doesn't need anyone to remind him that he's extraordinary.

He was born knowing that he was special and has made it his life's mission to ensure that the rest of the world knows it, too.

All while not saying a single word publicly.

He's rarely photographed and some of the attendees at his infamous party leave uncertain whether they actually met him.

So face-to-face time with Al Palmer is rare.

I note that for someone who doesn't like the spotlight, he's dressed like a modern-day Mansa Musa. He's wearing a vibrant purple silk suit that's lined with gold satin fabric. There's a gold ring on every finger, and he carries himself with a gold-handled walking stick dangling from his hand that he clearly doesn't need at all.

It's ostentatious but tracks with everything else in his house. Larger than life, unmistakable symbols of wealth that run so deep, it's endless. He's got the kind of power that's rooted in myth but is real enough to move markets, influence lawmakers, and demonstrates its dominance without regard for authority.

At its most potent, it moves in silence.

You never see it coming but you always know when you're in its presence.

When we're done eating, and I've gotten his background information squared away, his fashion choice is the first thing I ask him about.

"When you're bigger on the inside than the outside you have to distract people from that fact or you'll never get anywhere."

His small stature is somewhat of a surprise but only because his son is so tall and broad. He's petite, for lack of a better word. But it only takes a few moments in his presence to forget all about it. "Do you really think your height has something to do with your success?"

His gaze narrows. "I wasn't talking about my physical size."

Heat steals up my neck. "Oh. I'm sorry. I just assumed—"

"It's fine." He waves my tongue-tied excuse away with the flick of his elegant wrist. "I learned at an early age that if you can't convince the world that the deficits they see when they look at you are immaterial, then you'll find yourself famished for things like acceptance, compassion, tolerance…approval and praise," he adds with the lift of one of his heavy gray brows. A knowing smile tilts up the corners of his severe mouth as if he knows how viscerally affected I am by what he's saying. It's like he's reading straight out of sixteen-year-old-me's diary.

I swallow hard. "Right."

"So, you either live with less than you need or you figure out how to make the world give it to you."

"Is that what you did?"

"I couldn't live with less. Not when I knew what I was capable of. So I chose to distract them by being confident before I had any right to be. By taking risks no one else would and being a very gracious winner when they paid off. I did that until my name became synonymous with power and prosperity. Until they needed me more than I needed them."

I nod, understanding the notion of proving everyone wrong. I refer to my notes and grimace at the next question. I act like the writer I want to be and ask the question. "How do you deal with failures? Like the chain of hotels you financed that went bankrupt last year."

He quirks an eyebrow. "You've done some digging." He's smiling but his voice is hard.

I nod, unabashed. "I call it research."

"You say potato," he says, his voice losing some of its edge.

"I wanted to be prepared."

He smiles. "Of course. I don't call anything a failure, and I don't air my woes."

"So, for you, the perception was more important than actual success?" I ask for clarity.

His nostrils flare. "For me, the perception that my stamp of approval is akin to a Midas touch that makes heads of state who used to tip me without looking me in the eye want to rub shoulders with me *is* winning. I know who I am. I also know what I look like. I'm not going to let people's biases and shortsightedness define and limit me. Tell me how you plan to portray me."

"You're a modern-day Jay Gatsby but with the confidence of the *Asantehene* himself, Mr. Palmer."

He snorts but nods in approval "I like that. Very iconic imagery that almost everyone will understand. You'll make it clear that my backstory isn't fabricated. I know they like to speculate that I started with a leg up in life," he says with a twinkle in his remarkably clear eyes.

"I will. But only if I can confirm that," I advise him. "There's very little public information about you before Jubilee Field was discovered. Is that also deliberate?"

"Yes. Who I was before I was rich is the least interesting part of my life. The man you see before you wasn't created out of thin air, but that's what I've worked very hard to make people believe. I've thrived in anonymity and plan to continue doing so even after you publish your story on me."

He gives me a warning glance.

I nod. "As you know, for now, this story doesn't have a home. I will pitch it but the conditions we agreed to will apply when I find a publisher for it. No pictures of you shall appear in any publication. No references to your height. No references to your age, your business dealings, or the composition of your family. This conversation is limited to your acquisition and ownership of the property and its history," I recite the list of restrictions in the NDA I signed.

"Very good. Kwame was very protective of you in his negotiation with my team over the documents I asked you to sign as a condition of this meeting," he says with a dry, humorless chuckle.

I flush. "I signed them all the time and didn't have any issues."

He shrugs. "I don't really care how you feel about it as long as you abide by it. If you don't, I'll sue you for so much money that your grandchildren will be sending mine checks." He delivers this threat with such alacrity that the menace in them takes a few seconds to resonate. And somewhere in the back of my head, I wonder if he'd feel that way if those grandchildren were his. I push that thought aside. No need to get ahead of myself.

"You don't need to worry. I won't print anything you're not happy with. Even if it's not explicitly listed in the NDA," I add solemnly.

He purses his lips and folds his hands on his lap. "Said every journalist who was given an inch and used it to create a mile of lies. I'll be convinced when I see the article that goes to print."

I shift in my seat and have my first niggle of doubt about the wisdom of this. It's not unheard for people to sit down willingly and then have "source remorse" that derails the whole story.

I don't want to risk walking away with nothing after spending time here and pitching the story to prospective publications. "Mr. Palmer, if you're so unhappy about this conversation, why are we having it? You certainly don't need the publicity."

"My son asked me to," he says with a simple smile.

The simplicity of his answer warms me to him. I know he and Kwame have a complicated relationship but it's clear he loves him.

He's been my family's boogeyman for too long and Kwame has told me too much about him for his subtle but potent charm offensive to make me forget that he's a greedy, self-centered strategist.

"Is that truly the only reason?" I press.

"He hasn't asked me for anything in twenty years." He smiles wistfully. "Can you imagine how I feel? Being so rich and the son I did it all for doesn't want anything to do with it. I'm sure you wouldn't have turned your nose up at your parents wanting to pay to for college." He looks at me expectantly and I realize it wasn't a rhetorical question.

"No, I wouldn't have. I mean, I didn't. My parents paid for all of us to complete our bachelor's. The rest was on us. I write Nelnet a check every month and I would be very happy to be putting that money into my savings."

"See? Do you know Kwame had student loans until his mother passed away?"

I do know that, but something stops me from telling him so. The way our conversation landed on Kwame makes me distinctly uncomfortable. "I was very sorry to hear about the passing of your wife. I understand that The Palms was her pet project. The only article I could find on her was from right after your purchase. She said it was love at first sight. Was it the same for you?"

He stares at me so intently for a full minute that I'm certain he's not going to allow me to pivot.

"I don't believe in things like that. I bought this property because it was the most expensive piece of real estate ever listed in the state of Virginia."

"Yet the first thing you did was tear it down."

"As it should have been centuries ago. This land was stolen from the people who first inhabited it. The first European colonists brought disease that wiped out the indigenous people and then used enslaved people to build grand homes with walls painted white to try and hide what they'd been and what they stood for. I tore down those ugly, tainted buildings and built on the only part of the property that hadn't been inhabited."

"Was this stretch of Great Falls Road appealing because of its moniker as the Gold Coast?"

He sneers. "No. Can you imagine calling this rocky stretch of wilderness the Gold Coast? Colonizers always have delusions of grandeur." He smiles more to himself than me. "But it does add a sense of poetic justice that I own the largest house in a state where, if I'd been here at its establishment, I would have been chattel."

"So was that why you tore down the original residence?"

"I tore it down because I could. My direct ancestors may not have toiled here. But their oppressors came to Ghana, tried to steal our land, and make second class citizens of us."

"So this house symbolizes a reclamation?"

"No, it is the embodiment of the siren song America uses to lure people."

"But you called it a siren song. Which is used to lure people to their deaths. You're very much alive."

"Not everything is literal. I am alive. It is a death of something that most immigrants experience once we realize the America dream is just that...a dream. What's real is that if you're willing to work harder than everyone else and if you are willing to bet on yourself, and nowhere else on earth that a man like me can buy his way into the history books."

"So for you, this is about legacy?"

"Yes. And about enjoying my money and building something that, just like the houses that were here when I bought it, will tell the story of *this* time and reflect the way the world has changed. The way power has shifted."

"So then why have you hidden it away from the public? Limited access not just physically, but with the restriction on pictures?"

"Because I didn't want the Daughters of the American Revolution at my front gates raising hell about me tearing down the things that they saw as their ancestral connection to the land. My wife saved most of the trees, but the palm trees that line the drive used to be hickory and pine."

We spend the next hour walking through the thirty thousand square feet of living space. It's a beautiful property with priceless artwork from all over the world and finishings that scream of no expense being spared.

By the end I'm in awe of what he's built.

He's got a fascinating story.

If only he'd let me tell it.

This is a beautiful home. It's new construction mortared with history. Everything it's made of may be brand new, but it melds with the past in a way that makes you think about the future.

It's a monumental achievement that seems to be a testament to the power of opportunity. He wasn't born with anything but his own talent and determination. He's made his money honestly. Thirty years ago, he had more of it than he could spend in two lifetimes and somehow, that wasn't enough.

It sounds like he sacrificed his relationship with his only child in pursuit of more.

I'm grateful that Kwame somehow found something else to motivate him because as nice as it's been, this kind of wealth is impossible to enjoy if you have even a little bit of a conscience and don't live in a bubble.

At the end of my eight hours there, I'm still in awe of the fact that this mansion is one person's home and that I'm a guest here.

It's heady to walk through a house that smells like a resort and is the kind of luxury I've only seen in Bond films and my favorite rich family television drama *Billions*. I understand why the house was set so far off the road. People would slow down to gawk, take pictures, want to know who lived there. Some would be awed, but plenty more would be shocked to see the size of a home that housed three people at the height of his family's tenure.

It's the ultimate symbol of his overwhelming success and the perfect place to hold court and hide your treasure. And your sins.

This man is a legend in the true sense of the word. Everything about him is larger than life. Except for his authenticity. He seems so calculated. Every word is measured, rehearsed, stale.

As wonderful as it's been, this isn't the kind of story that excites me.

It's moving, but besides the public fascination with seeing what's behind those white gates, I can't see a lot of interest being garnered by that alone.

I pivot to the only fact about him that I find somewhat compelling. "Kwame said you have some artifacts, bronzes and stone carvings from Mali that used to be on loan to the Museum of African Art, but are now back in your private collection. Is that housed in this property or elsewhere?"

All of the art on display is contemporary.

"Oh." He raises on eyebrow, his eyes twinkle with interest. "Do you have interest in ancient art?"

"I do, yes," I reply eagerly, smiling genuinely. "I was actually instrumental in the return of the pieces to the Government of Benin and the Brong-Hafo people last year."

He straightens his spine. "I funded that exhibit, I believe. Instrumental in what way?"

"Oh, I see." I blink, surprised by that information. I hadn't known that. "I wrote the story that put pressure on the Metropolitan Museum in New York and the Prussian Cultural Heritage Museum to return the Benin Bronzes. I'm quite proud of that work. Besides seeing things returned to their rightful ancestral owners. I get to see and feel the weight and history of things most people will only ever see in a book. They are thousands of years old, but the blood of the people they belonged to runs in my veins today. It…" I sigh and search for words. "Makes me feel connected to the past at the same time it grounds me firmly in the present."

"Well, you're passionate. That's good." He claps his hands together and leans forward. His eyes narrow and watch me intently for a moment before he speaks. "Can I show you something very rare?"

"Is the world still turning?" I ask in response.

"I'll take that as a yes." He smiles at me genuinely for the first time and I smile back.

"It was an absolutely yes."

"This is not for public consumption and any mention of it in your article will lead to consequences you won't like."

I have to stop myself from stamping feet to hurry him along. "I understand. Can we see it now? I'm starting to feel desperate."

He laughs. "I like you."

He abandons his desk and walks slowly to the wall of curtains and draws it back. I watch in astonishment as the wall swivels a full one-hundred-and-eighty degrees and then wish to God I could go back in time and said absolutely not.

"That's the Prestige Stool," I gasp, my eyes wide in shock and horror.

"You've heard of it?"

"Yes, of course. How do you have it?" I turn to face him unable to keep the accusation from my voice.

"It's a replica," he snaps and walks over to the panel next to the glass case and presses a button. The door revolves and closes.

I sag in relief. Of course it is. It couldn't be anything else. "Did you know that the original was stolen?" I ask.

He nods. "Yes, I heard. I don't know why it wasn't better protected. The first time it was taken, the thieves had guns, and the Ashanti's weren't able to fight back. They get it back after two hundred years and the first thing they do is lose it again." He curls his lip in disgust.

"They didn't lose it. It was stolen."

"Do you know what the stool means to the Ashanti?" His tone is clipped, his question posed more like a challenge.

"My parents are Ashanti."

"Your parents," he says it with disgust. "Shame they didn't teach you to see yourself that way too."

"I was born here. I'm American."

"Only on paper. I'm not surprised your parents haven't instilled this in you."

My back stiffens. "My parents did everything they could to keep us connected, but this is where I was born and where I grew up."

He shrugs. "If you say so." He opens the panel again. "Did you know that each stool is carved out of a single piece of wood?" he asks.

I nod before I realize he's not looking in my direction. "Yes, I knew that."

"They are more than just part of ancient lore." He points at it. "This one is unusual. The unusual five-legged form is referred to as *kontonkrowie*, or 'the circular rainbow.' It evokes the Akan proverb 'the rainbow is around the neck of every nation,' and reminding us of the chief's role in uniting and controlling the kingdom."

I nod with an unfeigned reverence. Replica or not, to be in the presence of one always fills me with awe. It's closely followed by indignation that it's not in its rightful place.

"A leader's stool is so integrally linked to his identity that his death is described by the phrase 'a stool has fallen,'" Mr. Palmer continues his recitation. I know all of this, but I don't say so.

"Which is why it's so heartbreaking for it to be lost. For a chief to be separated from his stool isn't just his loss. Every guardian of it is warned that if it is ever destroyed or lost the entire kingdom would fall."

"And yet, they let it go. If this was the real one, I'd never return it to the very people who lost it in the first place."

"That's the same argument western museums made against returning them. But shouldn't the people who heaven entrusted as stewards of it be in charge of its fate? It's not as if they didn't fight to keep it. And to get it back. It being stolen is such a tragedy."

He doesn't respond and when I turn to face him, he's watching me with an expression I can't decipher but that makes me sorry I said anything. Something less than disdain but…

"Most people have never laid eyes on that stool. How did you recognize it?"

My stomach flips at the question and for a moment I'm not sure I should tell him. But that's silly. The theft is public knowledge.

"I worked on a story about the artifacts before they were moved from New York to DC. I'd seen a picture of it. I never thought I'd see it in person, so I was shocked when you pulled back the curtain. That's an amazing replica. Kwame said you're quite the art collector. Besides the modern art on the walls, he said you've got sculptures from all over. I'd love to see that," I add with a smile.

He doesn't return it. "What a pity. Everything has been moved to the lodge because we have so many contractors here setting up for the party."

I don't know him well enough to be certain, but he seems rattled. I pretend not to notice and close my notebook with a smile. "Could I walk over to the lodge?"

"No, we're having some work done near it and it's not safe to access."

"Ah, maybe next time Kwame and I—"

His smile is tight. "Don't hold your breath. He avoids this house like the plague." He glances at his watch. "I hope you got everything you needed."

I'm dismissed and he's clearly done with playing Lord of the manor.

"Thank you for the everything. I did. My photographer will be here tomorrow morning."

"As long as they're gone by one o'clock."

He'd said they could have the whole day when we arranged this. I don't know what changed but I don't miss a beat in agreeing. "We've scheduled for them to be finished by eleven-thirty."

"Fine. I have to run," he says and turns toward the door.

"See you at dinner," I call after him.

He stops short and turn to face me. "I've had a last-minute invitation that I'm going to accept. I will see you on Sunday. I look forward to reading your draft. Enjoy your stay at The Palms."

Just like that, it's over, and he's gone. It felt like a hard goodbye. Like he didn't intend to see me Sunday or ever again.

Oh Sin, stop. Why would that be true?

Because he has the stolen stool.

But how? I know Oz worked for him but is it possible that he's one of The Wizard's buyers?

It's not out of the realm of possibility.

They're related.

"Are you ready?" A woman's voice from behind me startles a scream out of me and I whirl around to find Alice standing.

I glance at the closed door. "I didn't hear you come in."

"I came through the wall panel. It's an access hallway only used by staff." I scan the wall and can't see any indication of a hidden door.

I turn back to Alice with a forced but friendly smile. "Wow. I thought I'd seen every corner of this house. It's endless."

"It's not but I know what you mean. Let's be on our way."

She cups my elbow and steers me back in the direction we've just come from.

I wiggle free of her hold as casually as I can. She's not nearly as friendly as she'd been the first time we met.

"Is Kwame back?" I ask as we start up the grand staircase and take the left side wing.

"Not yet." She stops at the first door along a corridor with black walls and gold sconces lighting the artwork that lines it.

I smile in thanks and then step into the room. It's bigger than my entire apartment was in NY. It's the same black and gold motif of colors but white walls make the space bright and welcoming. The views of the river are astounding. I've never seen anything like it.

"If you're hungry use the call button to let the kitchen staff know."

"Can I just go downstairs and get something if I need it?"

"No. That would be disruptive and the lower level is for staff only." She chides me like a naughty toddler, and I have to remind myself that she's Kwame's favorite person.

"Okay. Anywhere else off limits?"

"I think you'll find your rooms to be equipped with anything you might need. And if it's not, we're just a buzz away."

When she leaves, I'm still trying to decide whether she meant that to sound like a warning. I look out at the river that, just this morning, made me think of heaven.

Now I see a chasm keeping me from the world I belong to. I feel an unsettling urge to leave. What would happen if I said fuck this party?

Fuck the glory of this byline.

Fuck the thrill of the chase.

I shake my head rapidly to stop my thoughts from spiraling. I'm safe. I'm just unsettled by the questions my conversation with Mr. Palmer stirred up.

I need this story. I've bet my future on it.

And all of those stolen items deserve to be back where they belong.

I'm just tired.

I lay down, eyes wide and wonder why I can't sleep.

Fifty-Five

Kwame

Home

"Where have you been?" she grumbles as soon as I walk into the house. She's sitting at the bottom of the bifurcated staircase in the same dress she'd been wearing when I left her here nearly twelve hours ago.

"The interview went long and threw my whole day off."

She stands on the second step from the bottom and cups either side of my neck.

I glance around the foyer for signs of life. I'm not sure I'm ready for PDA in front of my dad. "Where is he?" I whisper.

"Out," she says with a wide-eyed smile. "He has more energy than I do."

"He's always worked hard and played even harder."

"Have you been waiting long? I thought you would have gone to bed."

She yawns and lets her head fall forward to rest on my chest. "I didn't want to go upstairs without you. This house is huge and after the stories he told me today, it's got to be haunted."

I roll my eyes and use my arm to turn her so we're both facing forward. "I need a shower, food, and sleep."

"Hard day?" She hooks her arms around my waist and we start up the stairs together.

"Long. I had a meeting with the Governor."

Her step falters. "Of Virginia?"

"Yes."

"Why?" she asks with naked incredulity.

"He used to be our neighbor. Technically, he still is. He's my mentor, sounding board."

"That feels like a pretty major detail to not tell me." She lets go of me and continues up the stairs ahead of me.

I could kick myself. I'm tired, hungry, and not thrilled to be spending the night here again. I take the stairs two at a time to catch up with her. "Sorry, Sin. I talk to him infrequently these days and see him even less. But he asked to meet with me today. I promise I'm not keeping it from you. I'm just exhausted and have so much on my mind."

I open the door to our room and walk in ahead of her. She sits on the bed and drops her head into her hands. "I know you're not. I shouldn't have said it like that. We've still got a lot to learn about each other. I forget we've only met a year ago."

I shake my head in amazement. "It feels so much longer." I walk over, massage her shoulders and breathe a sigh a of relief that we didn't escalate that landmine. "I'm sorry I didn't mention it. You're going to meet everyone who is important to me this Sunday. But this world isn't where I feel at home and I kind of…don't want it to intrude on what we have."

"I understand that. Let's cross that bridge when we get there, okay? Or at least when I'm not exhausted and hungry."

"Shit, of course. How was your interview? I hope my dad wasn't too much of a jerk."

She yawns so big her jaw pops. I wonder if that's why she's so drained.

"Sorry. Gosh," she smiles. "I had a great conversation with your dad. Better than I expected. He's fascinating. So much of what he said really resonated with me."

I don't know why that makes something in me recoil, tighten. "That's amazing. I'm glad you're not running for the hills."

"Hardly. He's charming and elusive at the same time. I've never met anyone with so much self-assurance."

"And you likely never will." I'm glad she liked him. I wanted her to.

So why does my skin feel tight?

"Tomorrow, we'll get photos, and then I can start putting the package together. I think it's going to be an easy pitch." She looks like a kid who's getting ready to meet Santa. I don't want to be her Grinch.

"I'm glad you're happy." I tug my tie off and sit on the bench in front of the bed to pull off my socks.

"Now that you're back I am. It's nice here but I miss home." She sits on the bed behind me and rubs my head.

Her calling our lives outside of here home is music to my ear. "Two more days," I murmur then groan when she digs her fingers into my neck and rubs the tension resting there. "I love that."

"I know. Even though you kept me waiting and hungry, I can tell you needed it." She leans over to press a kiss to the spot behind my ear.

"How long did I keep you waiting?"

She cocks her head to the side, her smile fading and eyes darkening. "My whole life, it feels like."

I climb up onto the bed and lay next to her. The minute our eyes meet and I see my whole heart in hers, I forget my hunger, forget the disastrous meeting I had today and just breathe. I slip my arm around her waist, savoring the way she curves into me and fits like she was made to. I press my forehead to hers. I take her hand in mine and hold it between us so that we're chest to chest, thigh to thigh, heart to heart, and right now I would risk it all for her.

"Well, isn't this nice?"

At the sound of Alice's voice, we jump apart and off the bed.

She stands, her hands clasped in front of her smiling. "I knocked but you didn't hear me."

"Oh, no worries." I tuck my shirt back in and walk over to her and turn her around so she's not looking at Sin anymore. "How are you?"

"Fine. Sorry about the intrusion. I'm not used to you being here with someone. I just wanted to tell you that there's dinner in the kitchen if you're hungry."

I look at Sin.

She sitting on the bed watching us with an expression I can't read. "'Did you still want to eat?"

"She wanted to wait for you," Alice replies before Sin can. I turn back to her. "There's plenty for both of you. Feel free to help yourselves. The staff has gone to bed and I'm right behind them. Good night." Alice presses a kiss to my cheek and then shuffles down the hall.

"I'm starting to think Alice doesn't like me," Sin says when we get inside our room.

I chuckle. "Alice likes everyone. She even likes my dad."

"I don't know. She never meets my eye." She pouts and opens her wide-set dark brown eyes to stare at the ceiling. I cup her chin and turn her face toward me.

Her shoulders sag and she sighs. "So, tell me about the Governor. What did he say?"

"There's about to be a vacant seat in the US Senate. The Senator from Virginia is resigning ahead of a scandal."

She grins, eyes wide. "What? Are you giving me a scoop?"

I shake my head. "No, just talking to my girlfriend. Or should I have asked you to sign an NDA first?"

I sound more irritated than I should; but not as irritated as I feel.

She blanches. "I'm just kidding," she mumbles. "I wouldn't do that."

"I know. Sorry. I'm tired too. Anyway, that's not even the news. He wants to appoint me to the seat."

"Wow, that's wild." She flops down on the bed and her eyes flutter closed. "As if you'd turn down the AUSA for that."

"I didn't get the job," I say. My tongue feels as heavy as lead.

She opens one eye and then the other. Her mouth forms a perfect "O."

"It's okay."

"You wanted it so much. I'm sorry. You found out today?"

"Yeah. I'm not sure what to do. I'm not staying on at the firm."

"Won't there be other roles at the DOJ?"

"Yeah, but…I don't know, Sin. I don't want to talk about it. At least not until I eat. I'm starving."

"Me too. Let's go eat."

I grab her wrist to stop her from getting up.

"Or, I could just skip dinner and have you for dessert."

"Anything you want, K."

Her words illicit a flash of trepidation at how insatiable I am for her. She says anything I want but all I want is her. And the more I have, the hungrier I become.

Being here has made me anxious about us in a way I can't explain.

Maybe it's that I can't stop thinking about my mother while I'm here. I wish we'd been closer. I wish I'd had the chance to get to know her.

I don't want to make the same mistake with my dad.

I withdrew myself from consideration for the AUSA job after my meeting with the Governor. There is no way to take that job without selling my family out and inviting trouble to my own doorstep.

Fifty-Six

Sin

Game Day

"I have a surprise for you," Kwame says as we make our way up the granite-paved path from a private pool that's only accessible through this wing of the house.

"I don't like surprises," I admonish, but I can't help but give a smile.

"I think you'll like this one. It's set up in the east wing of the house and I can't wait to see what you think."

We walk arm in arm through the long window-lined hallway. I glance out to the tree-dotted lawn, the tickle of irritation and worry at his declaration forgotten as I take in the views. The white corrugated roof of a building at the south end of the estate catches my eye.

I've been waiting for a moment to drop the request casually. "When we're done, can you show me the lodge?" I ask Kwame.

"The storage shed? Why?" he asks.

"The art is stored away in there. Your dad said it's inaccessible, but I don't even know where it is."

He frowns but shrugs. "It's down the back terrace. All the way at the bottom on the way to that labyrinth. I'll show you before we leave."

"Great, thank you." That went so much better than I'd hyped up in my head.

We walk into the lush room with its oversized, comfortable-looking chairs and vantage point that means during the day it gets the best light. I see a woman standing in front of a clothes rack and what from here looks like half a dozen people standing behind it, waiting for us.

My steps falter, and I grab Kwame's hand and squeeze it to me and stop. "What is that? Who are those people?"

"Wardrobe, make-up, your glam squad. And a stylist from the salon you mentioned."

I chuckle and glance up at him. He remembers everything.

The first night we spent together he listened to me grumble as I put my hair in pin curls, whining about wishing I'd gone to Cole Stevens for my blowout before we left. A young woman approaches us. "Ms. Sackey. We are at your service. We've set up the in-home spa. We will get started, have a small break for lunch, and then finish just in time for the people who will be dressing you to arrive."

My eyes widen and I look back at Kwame, who is watching me with a smile on his face. "Is this for real?"

"One hundred percent," he says and grins, and then he walks over and drops a sweet kiss on my mouth and against my lips. "You deserve it, have fun. I'll see you in a bit."

Fifty-Seven

Kwame

Full Picture

Growing up in Washington, DC, I hear people described as game changers all the time. Hell, I've been called one myself. But I didn't truly understand what the phrase meant until the day she walked into my life, pulled me in, shook me up, and rearranged my world view irrevocably.

And tonight, she's stunning.

Sin likes to be the observer and almost exclusively wears all black to blend in. Tonight she is dressed like she wants to make sure she'll never be forgotten.

Her traditional two-piece shirt and top is made of the purple Kente cloth specially woven for this year's Palm Sunday.

The skirt is the traditional floor-length mermaid silhouette. The top is a strapless white bodice that clings to her torso and has a dramatic lift on one side that looks like a wave breaking on a shore.

Her neck is bare but for a gold necklace string of Adinkra symbols that collar her throat like a string of golden runes. Her hair is in a sleek bun that shows off her elegant bone structure.

Every head turns as she passes them on her way to me.

She puts her hand into mine and expels a breath as if she's relieved when our fingers link.

"You're late," she grumbles, and I want to lean forward and pull that pouty lip between my teeth and then lick it.

"How long have you been waiting for me?"

"My whole life it feels like," she purrs and steps into my side.

I slip my arm around her waist, savoring the way it seems to curve perfectly into her side, and how she moves into me without any hesitation at all.

"Are you okay? Being here, I mean?" She searches my face and the worry in her eyes kill me. I thought I was hiding my discomfort with being here better.

"I'm fine. I had a great afternoon, and we're leaving tomorrow."

I stroke my thumb down her cheek and her eyes flutter closed, her face leans toward my hand like a flower reaching up to the sun to get more of it.

I want to give her all of it. But what is going to cost me?

Being in cahoots with my father again.

I worked so hard to get away from this life.

How did I end up back here?

You chose this.

"You look good as fuck by the way." She kisses my bare arm.

"You wear your Kente well. I hate that everyone's getting a look at my man's back though. I hope I don't have to cuss anybody out tonight."

I laugh at her baring her teeth and adjust the cloth draped over my shoulder. "They're going to be too busy making deals and trying to get pictures with each other to notice me."

"Let's find a quiet corner and watch," she says.

l lean down to kiss her temple. "You've got sense."

She laughs, links fingers with me and smiles. "And I've got you."

"I love you," I whisper.

"More," she mouths and my anxiety about tonight goes away. We're the same Sin and Kwame and our life outside of these gates won't be changed by the occasional visit to The Palms or spending time with my father. I just hope I can keep Oz away from her. I don't even want them to meet.

"Come, let's go have a good time."

Fingers linked, we walk into the grand ballroom and Sin stops short. "Holy shit," she says and I can't pretend I'm not impressed.

My father has put Ghana on display tonight.

Golden stools, Kente cloth linens, Adinkra symbols adorn everything. The bird of paradise and other tropical flowers that explode from the floral arrangements are the only real color in the room and call to mind sultry Accra nights that my mother loved so much.

For all the nods to home, it's also a nod to the American Gilded Age that has always been such a source of fascination for him.

The air is thick with an intoxicating blend of music, laughter, and conversation. The energy is vibrant, almost carnival-like and the room pulses with it.

Sin squeals and shouts in my ear every time she spots someone famous. It's different seeing it through her eyes. I found these parties to be such a drag when I was a young man, but I can see why everyone looked forward to it.

Glistening chandeliers hang from the ornate ceiling, casting a warm, golden light over the scene. The walls are draped in rich fabrics—plush velvets and shimmering silks—interspersed with the Adinkra motifs that are a fusion of the event's theme. My mother wouldn't have liked this one bit.

At least that's what I tell myself, but she was right beside him for these parties, year after year.

"Let's get a drink." I lead Sin to one of six lavish bars set up all over the room.

We make our way over and despite my wariness about being here, the excitement in the room is infectious.

The dance floor is packed, where couples twirl effortlessly and nearby, a card table is bustling as guests lean in to test their luck.

The gold gilt feathers, streamers, and confetti add a sense of whimsy to the atmosphere. Sin is grinning from ear to ear when I look down at her.

Maybe tonight won't be so bad after all.

Fifty-Eight

Sin

Face to Face

It's almost midnight. The party is packed, in full swing with no signs of slowing down.

It's been an incredible night doing my favorite thing—watching people who think they aren't being watched.

A lot of these people I've only ever seen in films and on TV. So many of them are smaller, more ordinary in person than I could've imagined. There's a part of me that wishes I'd never seen them.

I enjoy my imagination much more than I do the reality of anything. If writing has taught me anything it's that no human being belongs on a pedestal.

Kwame has barely left my side tonight. He's introduced me to countless people.

My head was spinning with the effort of keeping them all straight. And then he whispered, "Don't worry. No one remembers anyone's names here and most of them like it that way."

The dress code is strictly traditional. Kwame's purple Kente is draped over his shirtless torso and chest. Matching linen trousers skim long muscular legs and his feet are adorned in traditional leather and gold sandals.

He looks like the man of my dreams.

His arm is draped lazily around my shoulder. He's gazing out on the dance floor with an apathetic expression that makes him look like a casual observer.

He's been looking for his father all night.

"Kwame, you old devil." A lithe, dark-skinned Black woman saunters up to him and leans in for a kiss.

"Mrs. Wilde."

"Call me Tina," she coos and turns her dark eyes to me.

"I'm Sin."

"I bet," she quips.

"Sin, this is Tina Wilde, head of one of the largest conglomerates in the world. Tina, this is my girlfriend, Sin. She's a journalist." He introduces me with such pride in his eyes.

She nods. "I have a daughter-in-law who's a journalist. I bet you keep him on his toes." She winks. "Lovely to see you. Glad Palm Sunday is back. It's one of my favorite places to do business."

"I can see why," I say only because it sounds like the right thing to say.

"As much as I love talking to you, Kwame, I must make hay."

She gives up both air kisses before she glides away.

"Wow, I've never heard of her, but I feel like I should have."

"She's based in Houston and Paris. And her real estate development company is building a community in Maryland so you'll be hearing more of her. What did you call it? Baader-Meinhof."

"That's not real." I roll my eyes and glance around the room.

My stomach drops.

Ozwald Annan and Paloma Persaud are walking together seemingly deep in conversation. Like he feels my eyes on him, Oz looks my way and when our eyes connect, recognition seems to flare in his.

I swallow down the knot of dread that builds when he leans down to say something in Paloma's ear. They both look in our direction and Paloma smiles at me and flutters her fingers in a wave.

I turn back to Kwame but he's in the middle of a conversation with someone who looks familiar, but I can't place. I'm itching to interrupt him and tell him that Oz is here.

I look around the room again and freeze when I lock eyes with the man himself. My pulse is racing and I reach out to put a hand on Kwame's arm and squeeze. He looks over his shoulder at me, "You okay?"

I nod but his smile fades at whatever he sees on my face. He turns to face me fully. "What's wrong?"

"He's here," I mouth tipping my head as discreetly as possible in Oz's direction.

"Who's here?" His eyes move in that direction and his expression hardens. "Fuck." He mutters and gets to his feet. I turn to look for Oz and gasp. He's ten feet away from our table.

I move to stand but Kwame puts a firm hand on my shoulder. "No, Sin. Wait."

"Why, what's going on?"

He bends so we're eye level. "Trust me." His smile rings false but before I can say anything, he straightens and moves to stand in front of me just as Oz reaches our table.

Kwame's body blocks my view as he and The Wizard start speaking in hushed tones. I can't hear a word over the din of the party.

My mind is reeling. I thought I'd be observing Ozwald from afar.

It never occurred to me that I'd have the chance to talk to him face to face.

I wait for Kwame to turn around and introduce me. When he doesn't, I get to my feet and step around so I'm beside him.

They stop speaking and in unison turn their heads to look at me.

I focus on Kwame, not hiding my bafflement. "Aren't you going to introduce me?"

His back goes rigid and his hands curl into fists briefly at his side. "I told you to wait."

Shocked at his tone, I take a step back.

"We've already met, haven't we?" Oz says his icy gaze on me. "Why are you here?"

Goosebumps run up my arms, and I wish I'd kept my ass in my seat.

"She's my guest," Kwame answers for me and steps between us again.

"Your father wants to see you. Now," Ozwald says and the hairs on the back of my neck stand up. Why is he running errands for Mr. Palmer? What the hell is going on?

Kwame turns to face me. He cups my shoulders and looks me in the eye. His expression is impossible to read. "I'll be right back."

"How do you know him?" I mouth my eyes gesturing to the man behind him.

He looks down at me, his eyes sad and my blood runs cold. "I'll be right back and I'll explain."

His voice was low and grave in my ear and his eyes are pleading. But for what?

I'm keenly aware that we have an audience, so I repress the urge to demand he explain what the hell is happening.

I smile, grab his hand and gave it a quick squeeze. "I'll be here when you get back."

He turns to walk away but Oz lingers a moment. His eyes sweep over me and linger on my face longer than is comfortable before he turns to walk with Kwame.

Menacing, ice cold, ruthless, and dangerous.

That's all I see when I look at him.

Should Kwame be going off with him alone?

I'm half out of my seat when my path is blocked. This time by a lithe body clad in white silk.

Paloma Persaud. She flashes a million-watt smile. "Finally, we meet."

Fifty-Nine

Kwame

Loyalty

When I look back at Sin, Paloma is sitting in the seat I just vacated. My stomach drops. I never want Sin to know it was Paloma she saw that night.

Paloma's got a streak of mischief in her that makes her hard to predict. But she knows better than to say anything.

I hope.

"How well do you know the woman you were with?" Oz 's question draws my attention back to him and raises my hackles.

"She's a family friend."

"Really? That's news to me."

"On my *mother's* side of the family. You wouldn't have met her." I mean it as a simple statement of fact but then his jaw tightens and his shoulders tense. I forget that my mother is a sore spot for him.

She was a stickler for propriety when it came to staff. She wasn't unkind to Alice, but she treated her like the help all the time.

I hated it. Oz may not have been a doting son but I can imagine he didn't enjoy watching his mother use the service entrance to come into the house every morning.

It's not lost on me that after being treated like a poor relation, he's the one leading *me* through the halls of the house now.

I take him in. I guess the pipeline from falsifying company card expenses to selling stolen goods on the black market is slippery as hell. It sounds far-fetched but Oz's need for more than his portion is insatiable.

To know that he's robbing countries of their identity and facilitating a marketplace built on the exploitation of endangered animals, cultural theft, and blackmail. All so he can come to parties like this and live a life of luxury.

It tracks. He's always been so shallow. My dad wanted a protége so badly. The pit in my gut is heavy with guilt and regret. If I had come back sooner, maybe he wouldn't have turned to Oz. Maybe if I hadn't been so determined to keep him at arm's length, we could have found some common ground.

He's not the kind of man I want to be. But he's the reason I've been able to spend so long at a job that paid me shit. I supported myself but I also never worried about being short at the end of the month.

He's my father. I love him. As much as he's disappointed me, I keep hoping we can have the kind of relationship my mother wanted us to.

We reach my dad's office and he presses a button that's built into the wall. A small square panel opens, and he places his palm on it. It flashes green, beeps, and the door opens.

This is my father's most private space. The biometric entry was supposed to only allow me, my mother and Alice entrance. Why would Oz have it?

"Kwame, come in so we can close the door," my father calls out. I grit my teeth and fight back a growl of irritation when I realize Oz is not leaving.

I sit in the chair across from my father's desk. "Why haven't you come out to the party? Sin is waiting to see you."

He looks up at me and smiles. "Oz doesn't trust her." He quirks his eyebrow.

I whip my head around to look at Oz, incredulous. "What the hell does that mean?"

"She's been investigating me for more than a year now. I don't know how she ended up getting close to you, but I'm sure she's using you to get to me," Oz says.

I burst into laughter. "You think she got close to me so she could get close to you? She's never even mentioned you."

"Well maybe she doesn't tell you everything. I know for a fact she was working on a story until her editor killed it before she could do much damage, but now she's here. Does she know you're related to me?"

I feign calm but a five-alarm fire is burning suddenly. "Not yet."

"So you lied to her?"

"You're not part of my life. I don't consider us family."

If my words sting, he doesn't show it. "Is that what you tell yourself? I swear, you could teach the CIA a thing or two about living a double life."

"I'm not living a double life. She knows everything about me that matters. And if I'd known it was *you* she was looking for, I would have brought her here sooner."

A loud splintering crash startles us both and we look in the direction of the noise. The white brick fireplace is dripping with red wine and glass lays in shards on the floor.

"What the hell was that?" I ask when I realize my father threw his glass across the room.

"You wouldn't stop talking and I needed you to." He looks between us. "Oz, I want to enjoy my son attending his first Palm Sunday in a decade. Kwame, Oz is here to do what he does best, network."

I sneer at Oz. "That's right, go do your job so I can talk to my father alone."

His expression doesn't change but the corner of his left eye twitches from the effort it's taking for him not to let his anger get the best of him. "I don't take orders from you."

I turn to my father. "Will you ask your dog to heel?"

"Shut up Kwame," Oz snarls. "Or I'll shut you up." He takes a step toward me, and I get a tingle of excitement at the dangerous glint in his eyes.

I get to my feet, an amused smirk on my face. "Last time you tried *that*, I broke your nose. Nice reconstruction by the way."

His nostrils flare. "I let you land some licks that day because I didn't want to hurt you." He looks me up and down and grins. "Today, it'd be a fairer fight. Let's see who's got the Palmer blood in him and who's just an accident of birth."

I scoff. "Nothing you do will make you more than what you are. I really hope one day, that will feel like enough."

"For fuck's sake," my father roars. "Why are you two still having this argument?"

Oz and I stare at each other, eyes burning with mutual disdain, lips clamped together in a show of mutual restraint.

Like a pair of clocks that broke at the same time, we agree one thing—this feud of ours isn't for public consumption.

A pulsing beep from my father's computer draws Oz's eyes away from mine and his expression goes from furious to focused. My father moves aside for him as he rounds the desk to study my father's computer monitor.

"What's going on?" I ask.

"Something tripped an alarm at the lodge," my father says absently.

He and Oz exchange a meaningful glance. "I'll go check on it." Oz straightens and heads to the door. He stops next to me and leans in long enough to whisper, "You'll never win."

Sixty

Sin

Curiosity Kills

"Alone at last." Paloma sits down next to me. One of her expertly arched eyebrows lifted in question, her smile warm and interested.

"At last?" I parrot.

"I think Kwame's been hiding you from us."

"Has he?" I ask, still bewildered.

She laughs and leans forward. I'm not sure what to make of her. "Or maybe it's us he's hiding."

I tilt my head, incredulous and skeptical. "You and Kwame are friends?"

She smiles. "We're more like family, actually. You're the first woman he's ever brought here. You must be special."

She's smiling so warmly but I get the feeling she's trying to remind me that I'm an outsider. I smile like I'm not bothered. "I hope so. He's the love of my life," I say it before I can catch myself.

It's true. He is. I just wish I'd said it to him before I blurted it to his friend.

Her eyes widen. "Love? Already?"

I nod and regret speaking so freely. If they were really that close she'd already know. "We met a year ago. Been together almost nine months. How do you know Kwame?" I turn the tables on her.

She nods. "We grew up together. My parents owned the house next door. We went to undergrad together. Separate law schools but graduated the same year."

I can't hide my surprise. "Oh wow. What a history."

She sips from the champagne flute I hadn't noticed in her hand. "Yeah, he went on to practice, and I'm still a student. I'm working on my PhD at Georgetown."

"In Law?" I ask.

"Yup. And Politics."

"Wow, that's pretty amazing. I barely survived my Master's program."

"It was that or practice and *I hated* practicing law so back to school I went while I figured out what was next."

"Still, a PhD at Georgetown isn't exactly a gap year."

"No and I busted my ass to get in there. Being called a nepo baby for most of my life gave my pride such a battering that part of me just wanted to prove I could do hard things on my own. Being under-estimated can be a blessing but I get so fucking sick of having to prove myself. Do you know what I mean?"

It's such a vulnerable answer and so relatable that my wariness of her wanes. I lean in a bit, nodding. "It's exhausting. That's why I'm not doing it anymore."

Her delicate brow furrows. "What do you mean?"

"I quit my job. Trying to see what life as a freelancer is like."

Her mouth drops open and she keeps at me like I just told her that I went to the moon. "Wow. Now that's what I call having the courage of your convictions."

"Thank you," I say, realizing how badly I needed to hear someone say that.

"What did your parents say?"

I'm surprised by her question and it must show. "I'm the oldest daughter of immigrants, too," she says.

I nod in understanding. "So, you get it."

"Too well." She grins and we share a commiserating laugh.

I take a long sip of water and use the opportunity to dart a glance in the direction Kwame went. How long has he been gone and why does it feel like hours?

"So, is Sin short for something?" Paloma asks as soon as I put my glass down.

I nod and remind myself that it's normal for your partners friends to want to get to know you. "It's short for Arsinoé."

Her smile widens. "That's so pretty. What does it mean?"

"It's Egyptian but derived from ancient Greek words that mean a woman with an uplifted mind."

"That's cool." She leans back in her chair, still eying me. "So, you don't have a day name like Kwame?"

I check my impulse to bristle at the question. "Every Akan has a day name, whether we use it or not." I explain then frown. "How did you know I was from Ghana?"

"Kwame told me, silly. He's told me all about you."

That makes one of us.

I flash a smile in acknowledgement and take another long sip of my drink.

She's been nice but something in her demeanor is tap dancing on my nerves. Maybe it's because I know she's involved with Oz.

"So nice to talk, Sin." She looks at something behind me and waves at someone.

"You too," I return. "I am glad to finally meet you."

She meets my eye again. "I'm glad this wasn't weird."

I blink in surprise. "Why would you think that?" I ask, unpacking her sentence.

She grimaces. "Well… given what happened the first time we met I wasn't sure you wouldn't want to scratch my eyes when I came over."

"We've never met before."

She giggles and covers her mouth with her hand. "Maybe *meet* is the wrong word. We didn't actually speak."

"Okay, you still haven't told me where and when this happened." The way her smile sharpens makes my throat go dry and sip my water.

"It was at Kwame's. I was on my knees with his dick my mouth. And you watched."

"What?" I blurt and choke mid swallow. I'm consumed by a fit of coughing.

"Oh my goodness," she exclaims loud enough for the occupants of our table to hear her before she moves to stand over me, whacking my back harder than necessary in her pretense of helping me.

She leans down, presses her lips to my ear. "The second time was when you broke into Oz's apartment." Her voice is a whisper, but it booms in my ear.

If I hadn't been sitting down my knees would have failed me. I look up at her sharply and meet her square in the eye and cut straight to the chase. "What do you want?"

Her beautiful mouth curves into a smile. "I don't know what you're *really* after, and I don't care. Just don't cross me, and I'll let you keep your secrets…and Kwame."

She presses a kiss to my cheek and straightens. It takes all my self-control not to grab her by the hair and drag her back.

She's not the person I'm really angry at, anyway.

I get up and go in search of Kwame.

I'm reeling as I walk out of the ballroom.

Paloma Persaud is some sort of secret villain?

And she's been watching me. I can't even imagine how she and Kwame are friends. How close can they be if he's never mentioned her?

Does he know about her and Oz?

Did he bring me here to help me or distract me?

The thought makes me want to curl up in a ball and cry.

I've trusted him with everything. Why couldn't he trust me?

Distraught, I abandon my original mission and go in search of fresh air.

I need to think.

I open one of the sliding doors that line the back of the house and step out onto the stone terrace.

I walk to the ledge and lean into the slight breeze.

The dark hides the ever-present Potomac River but the loud rush of it reminds me that no matter what's happening inside that weird party, I'm still standing on solid earth.

One week of living in Kwame's world has been enough to last me a lifetime. No wonder he left.

Restless and desperate to put distance between myself and this house, I take the short flight of steps and follow the labyrinth-like walk-way that leads around the pool area and ends where it meets seemingly endless lawn.

In the distance, I see the windowless white clapboard building they call the lodge. It doesn't look like it's under construction.

I look around to make sure I'm alone, slip off my heels, and head for the structure I was told is off limits.

Closer inspection reveals it to be repurposed shipping containers stacked two high. I approach the door and press my ear to it. I don't hear a thing.

I try the handle and almost squeal when it disengages. I open it and wince at the white light that pours out. I step inside and pull the door closed behind me and turn in a circle to take in the space.

White paneled walls are lined with tribal masks, iron tipped spears, gold adorned carvings of gleaming mahogany, and large ivory tusks. I recognize several pieces from the stolen artifacts database. The length of the room is columned by enormous floor-to-ceiling shelving.

Before I can process that fully, a young dark-skinned woman with waist-length goddess braids dressed in a black jeans and white tank top steps out from behind a row of shelves.

"What are you doing here?"

I stop dead. Shocked to see Violet staring at me, her eyes are wide with terror. She looks to the door and then back at me. "Are you alone?"

"Yes." I put my hands up. "What are you doing here?" My heart is beating so fast, I'm lightheaded. "Are you with Oz again?"

"You can't be in here. You're going to get in trouble. You should leave."

"Come with me."

She shakes her head violently. "You need to leave." She points at the door. "And then forget you ever came here. Go. Before someone realizes you're here." Her eyes are stark and wild.

"If you're in trouble, I can help."

The question seems to propel her backward and something that looks like panic is building in her eyes. "What?" She takes another step back. "No. I'm not in trouble. But if you don't leave, I will be."

I want to press her on it but can see that it would be futile. And it's not important.

"Let me call for help." I look at my screen and curse under my breath. "There's no reception down here. We should go outside."

"No. I can't. Why are you even here?" she wails and waves a hand up and down her body.

"These things are stolen. Are you helping him?"

"No, I'm just trying to get what I'm owed. Get out of here."

"Fine, I'll go and call 9-1-1. They should know—"

Her eyes go wide. "Don't call the police. They work for him."

"Who is him? Ozwald or Al Palmer?"

She shakes her head, her eyes shuttering. "You should just leave."

My heart skips a beat. I nod. "I'll be right back. Wait here for me, please," I say and step outside into the dark copse of trees surrounding the lodge. I fumble with my phone and text Kwame to tell him where I am. I hit send and then wonder if I should have. I hit unsend and put my phone's flashlight on and head back to the main house.

I haven't taken two steps when a man's shadow crosses in front of me and then suddenly he's standing there. Oz, staring down at me looking every bit the villain that I now know he is. "What are you doing here?"

Sixty-One

Kwame

Come Clean

As soon as the door closes behind him, I turn to my father. "What is going on with you and Oz?"

He gives me a quizzical but amused look. "Nothing. My security people are a client of his, and he has the same system." He plucks a cigar from the lacquered humidor on his desk, snips the end and sits back in his chair to light it.

"Do you really trust him, Dad?" I ask and take a seat across from him.

"He's family, Kwame. He's loyal, and he makes the most of every opportunity I give him." He takes a draw from his cigar and blows out the acrid smoke, and eyes me through the haze. "Which is more than I can say for you."

"What does that mean?" I bristle.

"I've heard that you're applying for a job at the US Attorney's office."

My stomach drops. "Who told you that?"

He shakes his head, his eyes steady on mine. "It doesn't matter. I should have heard it from you."

"I was going to tell you when I had something to tell you."

"Where are you in the process?"

I contemplate how much to tell him. I wonder how much he already knows. "I'm waiting for my background check to clear."

He snorts a laugh. "There's something holding it up?"

I look up sharply. "Why?"

"Is it me?" He continues drawing on his cigar, calm as the sea on a moonless night.

"How can you know that?"

"Because I know *them*. They have a problem with the fact that I've flourished in places they've failed to find a foothold."

"Who is they?"

"The government of *your* country."

I like how it's my country when he's the one who chose it. "Dad, you're building luxury real estate in a country they've got sanctions against."

"People live in those countries, and they deserve to have a nice place to live. I'm not doing anything wrong. I do business with anyone it makes sense to do business with. It's not illegal. They do it, too. So why should I not be allowed the same?"

It's the same argument I made that day. I wrestle with what to share for a minute before I finally do. "I want to tell you something, but you've got to keep it between us."

He nods. "Of course."

I eye him and hope he keeps his word. "You're not the real problem in my background check. It's Oz. The feds are investigating him."

He sits up, sputtering, his face contorted. "And you brought her *here*? Are you crazy? You asked me to let her interview me?"

"Yes. What has that got to do with Oz?"

His eyes narrow. "That girl is trying to poke your eyes out, and you handed her a sharp stick."

Perplexed, I lean away. "Dad, this isn't about her. This is—"

"What the *fuck* is wrong with you?" he roars and gets to his feet so he's towering over me. The change in his demeanor is so dramatic it gives me whiplash.

"She's not going to make a bit of difference for whatever bleeding-heart crusade she's on." He slaps the table with an open palm and the back of his rings crack against the wood. "But she could uncover things she won't understand and will misconstrue in a way that could destroy everything I've worked so hard to build."

I lean back in my chair, the weight of his words hitting me like a burst of open flame to my face. "*Destroy* you? Things like what?"

His expression goes grim. As grim as it had been the morning my mother took her last breath. "I told your mother this wasn't a good idea."

The anguish in his eyes makes my stomach swoop. "Dad, what do—"

A simultaneous thundering boom of sound and the percussive vibrating of the trembling ground beneath our feet.

Sixty-Two

Sin

Landmine

Ozwald Annan stands in front of me like my worst nightmare.

"What are you doing here?" he repeats.

"I was looking for the bathroom," I lie.

"In the woods?" He looks past me to the door that I just came out of and then turns narrowed eyes on me. "Were you in the lodge?"

"No." I press my back against the door. "I mean yes. But only long enough to know it wasn't the bathroom."

"Get out of my way." He grabs my arm and yanks me forward so hard I stumble.

He steps around me and my heartbeat sounds like the thunder of horse hooves. It takes all my strength not to scream for him to stop when he grabs the door handle and yanks it open.

I hold my breath as he steps through the door and brace for him to see this girl who is clearly not supposed to be in here.

He doesn't say a word, so I follow him in. I scan the room twice before I believe my eyes. She's not here. She couldn't have vanished into thin air.

What the hell is going on?

I make my expression as remorseful as possible. "I didn't mean to cause any problem. I'll just be on my way back to Kwame."

"I'll walk you back. Give me a minute to lock up." He gives me a cold smile.

I nod my agreement and try to breathe normally while every cell is screaming for me to run.

I *should* run. But then he'll know I know something. And he won't let me get away without a fight. I'm lightheaded with fear when the door closes behind me. I lift my phone up to the sky and watch for my signal to return.

Who am I even calling? I don't know if I can trust Kwame.

The thought makes my heart ache, but I can't deny what I've seen and heard this week and tonight.

These are his people.

This is happening in his father's house.

Behind me a loud crack scares a scream from me. It's coming from inside the lodge. Alarmed, I run back, but before I can take two steps the night explodes.

My body jerks forward and then I slam into something jagged and hard, I open my mouth to scream and inhale a thick, acrid, gritty smoke before the world goes dark.

I open my eyes and groan at the throb of pain in my head. I hear screams from somewhere nearby. It's only when I put my hand to my throat that I realize the sounds are coming from my mouth. A man's shape looms over me, and I'm seized by panic like I've never known and then there's nothing.

Sixty-Three

Kwame

Aftermath

"What the hell was that?" I ask turning to my father.

He's sitting stock-still, gripping the arms of his chair, his face frozen in an unblinking, wide-eyed, open-mouthed stare. "Dad?"

He doesn't appear to hear me. Alarmed, I walk around to his side of the desk and snap a finger in his face. He blinks rapidly but his eyes remain unfocused. He's aged twenty years in the last minute.

"Dad, do I need to call your doctor?"

His eyes come to mine. "It just…reminded me of the night they came for my father."

I want to go and see what's going on out there but I'm not sure my father is okay. His father died when he was a baby. What is he talking about.

The same sound that had drawn Oz out of the room is back. It flips a switch and whatever was gripping him lets go. His eyes clear and he swivels to look at his computer screen and curses. "Something is wrong at the lodge."

"What do you mean? Didn't Oz just go there?"

"It's offline. Why hasn't my security arrived?"

A text from Sin pops up on my phone. *At the lodge, where are you?*

A surge of panic cures my indecision, I turn for the exit. "I'll be back. Stay here."

"No. Wait until someone comes. Anything could be happening."

"I'll be fine."

He shakes his head, his eyes glassy. "Kwame, wait. Please." He looks down at his lap. "I can't lose you," he says quietly.

"I'll be careful," I reply even though I get the feeling he's not talking to me.

I yank the door open and sound comes rushing in. The soundproof room muted the complete pandemonium from the center wing of the house.

"Stay here," I call to my father before I close the door and start running.

From the wall of glass sliding doors that lead to the terrace I see the cause of the disturbance.

The blaze of fire and plumes of smoke from the bottom of the back lawn looks like something from a horror movie.

I run against the flow of people moving toward the front of the house scanning the crowd for Sin's face. I reach the doors that open to the back without finding her.

I run to the ballroom and find it completely empty.

A roar fills my ears as I sprint toward the fire praying like hell that I'm not too late.

Acknowledgments

This book has been a true labor of love—one I could not have seen through on my own.

First, I have to thank Liz Berry and Jillian Stein at Blue Box Press for believing in this story and me. No one would be holding this book in their hands if it wasn't for you, and I will never stop pinching myself that I get to work with you.

To the editing team at Blue Box Press—Chelle, Stacey, and Liz—thank you for helping me find the heart of the story through the half dozen drafts we worked on together. Thank you for not blocking me. I owe you all a massage.

A very special thank you to the amazing cover artist Alan who created a true work of art that is more beautiful than I could have asked for. You did your big one!

Thank you so much to my beta readers—Alise, AJ, Christy, Ann—you helped me believe this story was special, and I am so grateful for your early feedback. I will never take it for granted and can't wait for you to see how wonderfully the story came together.

This story wouldn't have taken shape without Lauren Clarke—editor and writer extraordinaire. Thank you for your patience and wisdom. I wouldn't be the writer and storyteller I am today without you.

To my Dreamers—those of you who have known and loved me as Dylan and unquestioningly supported me as Lucy—you are the wind beneath my wings and the reason I fought so hard to come back after so many years away. Thank you isn't enough, but please know I love you endlessly.

To my family—my parents, my sisters, the brothers in love and the nieces and nephews they have given me—you are the stars in my sky, and I hope we get to be together in every lifetime. Thank you for believing in me and loving me so thoroughly.

Last but not least, I want to acknowledge my husband and my two sons. You are my greatest blessings, my greatest loves, and my best everythings. May the bashment never end. I love you deep and true. To the edge of the universe and back forever. And ever.

About the Author

Lucy Wilson-Tagoe is a Ghanaian American writer and lawyer. She writes suspenseful women's fiction and romantic thrillers that center around characters from all over the African Diaspora and other parts of the Global South.

She's an avid cook, a serial hobbyist, and a voracious reader.

She also writes contemporary romance under the pen name Dylan Allen and is a *USA Today* bestselling author.

Lucy studied history at Tufts University and law at Howard University and The London School of Economics. A child immigrant and the child of immigrants—she calls the world home. She's a self-described nomad and currently lives in Maryland with her husband and their two children.

I love to hear from readers! Stay in touch with me at:
Dylan@dylanallenbooks.com.

Discover More Blue Box Press Authors

Go to www.TheBlueBoxPress.com for more information.

Dylan Allen
Jennifer L. Armentrout
Kristen Ashley
Xio Axelrod
Steve Berry
Lexi Blake
Audrey Carlan
Marie Force
C. W. Gortner
Heather Graham
Donna Grant
Larissa Ione
Suzanne M. Johnson
J. Kenner
Randy Susan Meyers
Jennifer Probst
Christopher Rice
M.J. Rose
Kennedy Ryan
J.R. Ward

On Behalf of Blue Box Press
Liz Berry and Jillian Stein would like to thank ~

Steve Berry
Benjamin Stein
Kim Guidroz
Chelle Olson
Alan Dingman
Chris Graham
Tanaka Kangara
Jessica Saunders
Stacey Tardif
Suzy Baldwin
Grace Wenk
Dylan Stockton
Peggy Boulos Smith
Richard Blake
and Simon Lipskar